Books by Fern Michaels

ABOUT FACE
ANNIE'S RAINBOW
CELEBRATION
CHARMING LILY
DEAR EMILY
FINDERS KEEPERS
THE FUTURE SCROLLS
THE GUEST LIST
KENTUCKY HEAT
KENTUCKY RICH
KENTUCKY SUNRISE
LISTEN TO YOUR HEART
PLAIN JANE
SARA'S SONG
VEGAS HEAT
VEGAS RICH
VEGAS SUNRISE
WHAT YOU WISH FOR
WHITEFIRE
WISH LIST
YESTERDAY

Books by Holly Chamberlin

LIVING SINGLE
THE SUMMER OF US
(coming in May 2004)

Books by Marcia Evanick

CATCH OF THE DAY
CHRISTMAS ON CONRAD STREET
BLUEBERRY HILL

Published by Kensington Publishing Corporation

LET IT SNOW

Fern Michaels

Virginia Henley

Holly Chamberlin

Marcia Evanick

ZEBRA BOOKS
Kensington Publishing Corp.
http://www.kensingtonbooks.com

ZEBRA BOOKS are published by
Kensington Publishing Corp.
850 Third Avenue
New York, NY 10022

All Kensington titles, imprints and distributed lines are available at special quantity discounts for bulk purchases for sales promotion, premiums, fund-raising, educational or institutional use.

Special book excerpts or customized printings can also be created to fit specific needs. For details, write or phone the office of the Kensington Special Sales Manager: Kensington Publishing Corp., 850 Third Avenue, New York, NY 10022. Attn. Special Sales Department. Phone: 1-800-221-2647.

Zebra and the Z logo Reg. U.S. Pat. & TM Off.

First Printing: November 2003
10 9 8 7 6 5 4 3 2 1

Printed in the United States of America

Contents

A Misty Harbor Christmas

Marcia Evanick

One

Olivia Hamilton took the kettle off the stove as soon as it started to whistle, and poured the boiling water into the waiting teacup. Her grandmother always told her that there was no problem in the world that a good cup of tea couldn't solve. Her grandmother had been wrong.

There was no way a cup of herbal tea would bring her grandmother back to life. This particular cup of tea wouldn't even stop the tears she could feel once again pooling within her eyes. For the past week, all she had been doing was crying. It had to stop. Her grandmother would have never approved.

Olivia blinked back the tears and carefully carried her cup over to the solid oak table and the windows that overlooked the backyard. The same table Olivia had sat at as a little girl helping her grandmom roll out pie dough or dropping heaping teaspoons of cookie dough onto baking sheets. Every summer since she had turned two, she had visited her grandmother in the small Maine town of Misty Harbor for months on end. The visits had stopped about the time Olivia had turned sixteen and her summers back in California became busy with working, boys, and school activities. Between high school, college, and then a career, Olivia hadn't stepped foot in Misty Harbor in ten years. Over those years, her grandmother had been the one to fly out to California, at least twice a year, to stay with her son and daughter-in-law. Olivia, being her only grandchild, had seen her at her parents' home, but those visits had never been the same as the ones from her youth.

She had always meant to come back to Misty Harbor for a nice long stay with her grandmother. She just never had the time. Now it was too late. She was once again in her grandmother's house, but it wasn't the same.

Olivia's fingers trembled as they traced a bright red poinsettia on the tablecloth her grandmother must have put on the table before coming to California for her semiannual family visit. There were a few other touches of the holiday spirit throughout the house. A wreath hung on the front door, two baskets overflowed with silk poinsettias in the front parlor, and a beautiful red and green centerpiece graced the formal dining room table. It was as if her grandmother would be walking in the front door at any moment.

Maybe that was the reason her grandmother's death hit her so hard. It had been so sudden. So unexpected. Her grandmother, Amelia Hamilton, had never been sick a day in her life. At seventy-five years old, she had been the picture of both mental and physical health. One day she had flown out to California for a four-week visit, and the next she had suffered a massive heart attack while shopping for Christmas presents at Macy's.

Olivia had never even gotten to say goodbye. The trip to bring her grandmother home to Misty Harbor had been an emotional drain on both her and her parents. The services, which were held yesterday morning at the local Methodist church and then again at the cemetery, had gone by in a blur. People, names, and faces had all tangled together as she had stared, huddled in her winter coat for warmth, at the bronze-colored casket under the weak December sun. Winter on the coast of Maine wasn't conducive to outdoor activities.

The only one who had stood out in her memory was her grandmother's best friend, Millicent Wyndham. Olivia hadn't seen Millicent in ten years, but the town's matriarch hadn't seemed to age one bit. Millicent and the Women's Guild from the church had organized what they called a "small luncheon" for after the funeral. The "small" get-together had well over a hundred people in attendance. Her grandmother had been loved and admired both in town and the surrounding community. Amelia's son, her father, had been greatly comforted by the support, but she had been in such a daze that nothing really registered but the simple fact her grandmother was gone.

After the luncheon, she and her parents had driven to Sullivan, a nearby town. They had an appointment with Amelia's lawyer, a Mr. Francis Haskel. Mr. Haskel turned out to be eighty-five years old, if a day, and tended to fall asleep during the lulls in the conversation. Amelia's will had been simple, and surprising.

Her grandmother had left her church a very generous gift. To her only son she had left all of her stocks and investments. The surprise had been that her grandmother had left the balance of her estate, including the house and all its furnishings, to her only grandchild, Olivia.

Olivia slowly sipped the hot tea as she glanced around the large kitchen. Her large kitchen. What in the world was she going to do with a large house on the coast of Maine, when she lived in sunny southern California? As a weekend retreat it was a bust.

The chiming of the doorbell interrupted her thoughts. Hopefully it wasn't another neighbor with more food. Thanks to Millicent and the Women's Guild, the refrigerator and freezer were already jam-packed with more food than she could eat in a month. She made her way to the front door, turning on some lights as she went. The dreary and wet afternoon had made the rooms look gloomy and depressing. The only good news was, it wasn't snowing. Yet. They were predicting snow by tomorrow night.

Olivia opened the front door without checking to see who

it was first. She was in Misty Harbor now, not southern California. A bone-chilling wind whipped across the porch as she stared at the man before her. She didn't feel the wind or the chill. What she felt was a heated vibration in the pit of her stomach.

Her gaze traveled up from expensive loafers, over perfectly creased brown pants, to a buttery soft golden sweater. A well-worn brown leather Bomber jacket completed the relaxed yet stylish look. It was the man's face that captured and held her attention. A face she hadn't seen in ten years.

A stubborn chin, with just a hint of a five o'clock shadow, was exactly as she remembered it. He had worn his golden brown hair longer back then, but his nose still had the same cute little bump at the bridge of it from when he had fallen off his bicycle. His mouth looked as tempting as it had been all those summers ago. At sixteen, she had no idea what had been so tempting about it. Now, at twenty-six, she knew. His light brown eyes were different. Older, wiser, and they didn't hold the amusement or the annoyance they had had back then. Now they held a spark of interest. Male interest.

She softly smiled at the distant childhood memories of summers past. The gorgeous college boy had turned into one very sexy-looking man. "Ethan Wycliffe."

It might have been her imagination, but Ethan's gaze seemed to linger on her mouth a moment before he slowly smiled. "Ah, Summer Breeze, you remembered me."

She chuckled in delight when Ethan used the nickname he had given her when she had been about twelve. For the first time in days she felt like laughing. Her heart felt lighter. "Who would ever forget you, Ethan?" She refused to think about the fool she had made of herself all those years ago when she had ceaselessly followed him around town. Ethan had the distinct honor of being her first adolescent crush. "Come on in out of the cold." She moved aside and opened the door wider.

The enticing scent of his aftershave teased her senses as he walked past her and entered the house. She closed the door against the elements and asked, "Would you care for a cup of tea? The water's already hot."

"No, thank you. I don't want to impose." Ethan glanced around the house. "Where are your parents?"

She glanced at the grandfather's clock softly ticking away in the hallway. "I'd say somewhere over Utah about now. I drove them to the airport this morning."

"They left you alone here?" Ethan kept glancing down the hallway toward the kitchen as if he expected someone to join them any moment.

"I'm all grown up, in case you haven't noticed." Ethan sounded like he wanted to call child welfare and report her parents for abandoning a child to the wilds of Maine. "I've been living on my own for four years now. Ever since I graduated from college."

She tried not to laugh at the flush sweeping up his cheeks, but she knew her voice held amusement. Ten years was a long time to finally turn the tables on someone. "Heck, out there in California they even let me drive, drink beer if I want to, and vote."

Ethan's gaze drifted to the front of her old UCLA sweatshirt. "I noticed."

"Noticed what?" There were a lot of things she wouldn't mind Ethan noticing. Her baggy sweatshirt and ratty jeans weren't two of them. Leave it to her to change into her oldest clothes right before the sexist boy, *no, make that the sexist man,* in Misty Harbor paid her a visit. So much for first impressions.

"That you went to UCLA." Ethan leaned against the newel post of the formal staircase leading to the second floor. "Amelia told me you got your degree in 'those darn fancy machines.' I figure you know something about computers, or you're a Maytag repairman."

"My grandmom hated computers." She rapidly blinked away a fresh wave of tears. "She was missing some pieces to her good china set that she had gotten for a wedding present. While she was out in California, I was going to show her how to go on eBay and see if we could find her pattern and then bid on some of those missing pieces."

Ethan took a step closer. "I'm sorry, Olivia." His fingers grabbed ahold of her hand and gave it a gentle squeeze. "I came over to offer my condolences and to see if there was anything I could do. I didn't mean to make you cry."

"I'm not crying." She wiped the sleeve of her sweatshirt across her eyes. "My grandmother thought tears were a waste of precious time, and didn't solve a thing. A cup of tea was her remedy for whatever ailed you."

"If that offer for a cup of tea is still open, I think I would like one." Ethan looked at her with concern in his eyes.

"Of course you can have one." She led the way back toward the kitchen. "Take your coat off and stay awhile." She could use the company. The house was beginning to feel too big and lonely for one person. How did her grandmother stand it for all those years?

Ethan hung his jacket on the back of one of the chairs. "Do I get a splash of Amelia's secret ingredient?"

"What secret ingredient?" She had no idea what Ethan was talking about. As far as she knew, a cup of tea was a cup of tea.

"Sit." Ethan flashed her a smile and waved his hand at the chair she had been sitting in earlier. "I'll make you a fresh cup using Amelia's secret recipe."

Olivia sat and watched as Ethan bustled around the kitchen. He seemed quite at home in her grandmother's kitchen. "I take it you've done this before?"

"I've watched Amelia make tea countless times over the years, but she never let me help." Ethan flashed her a sexy grin. "My specialty was lemonade." The grin slowly faded. "Amelia loved my lemonade."

Her grandmother used to mention Ethan once in a while over the years, but she had never known they were that close. "I take it you saw my grandmother a lot?"

"Nearly every day during the summer. Amelia was always puttering around in her garden." Ethan leaned against the counter. "Not as much in the colder months."

She knew Ethan's parents owned the house directly behind her grandmother's. There was even a wide wooden gate between the two properties. A gate that was never locked, and hardly ever closed. "You still live with your parents?" Ethan was thirty years old, and didn't seem the type to be living with Mom and Pop.

Ethan gave her an indignant glare before reaching for the whistling tea kettle. "My parents live in Naples, Florida. They retired and moved there about six years ago. I bought their house."

"Now that you mention it, my grandmother did say something about your parents living in Florida." She had completely forgotten that piece of news. She watched as Ethan reached up into the cabinet above the refrigerator and pulled down a bottle of blackberry brandy. A half-filled bottle at that. "My grandmother drank?"

Ethan chuckled as he splashed a drop or two into the two cups of tea he had steeping. "Of course not. Amelia only touched the stuff during the winter months. She claimed it warmed her old bones."

"Hmmm, my father claims it puts hair on your chest."

Ethan glanced between the cups and her baggy sweatshirt. "Lord, I hope not."

She chuckled and relaxed into the chair. "So how are your parents? Your father still like to play golf?" From what she could remember, all Stan Wycliffe had ever talked about was playing golf. The Wycliffes even had a miniature putting green in their backyard which no one was allowed to walk on.

"He finally dragged my mother into the insanity." Ethan placed both cups of tea on the table and sat down. "They play golf nearly every day. My mom's parents are still living down there, so they are close by to keep an eye on them." Ethan took a sip of his tea. "I was just down there visiting for a few days. Got home too late last night to stop over, and this morning I had to check in at the gallery to make sure I still had a business. I'm sorry I missed the services yesterday."

That was why she didn't see Ethan at the church service or at the cemetery. Daze or no daze, she would have remembered seeing him there. "That explains it."

"Explains what?" Ethan's golden brown gaze never left her face.

"Your tan." She flashed him a big smile. "I've been trying to figure out how you got one, because I can't picture you lying in some tanning booth toasting your buns." Lying on some sandy beach with a bikini-clad woman, definitely. Artificial lighting, never. She glanced at his strong, neatly manicured fingers holding his cup of tea. Not a ring in sight. Which didn't mean a thing nowadays.

She was pretty sure her grandmother would have mentioned it if Ethan had gotten married.

Ethan flashed her a sexy grin that looked incredibly white in his deeply tanned face. "I can't recall ever toasting my buns, in or out of a tanning booth." He took another sip of tea. "My parents' condo not only has its own golf course, it has a dozen tennis courts, an indoor gym, and the biggest pool I have ever seen. The seniors have activities scheduled from early morning to late at night. Visiting them is like a trip to a spa." His grin grew wider and just a tad wicked. "My buns never saw the light of day at their poolside."

"That's a shame."

Ethan raised a brow at her comment.

"From what I remember of your buns, the sight of them would have given more than one senior citizen the thrill of her lifetime." She could still remember the sight of Ethan and about three of his friends skinny-dipping down at Sunset Cove one hot summer day. She had to have been around ten at the time and hadn't seen anything more than a quick flash of pale skin. The boys hadn't known that. All they had known was that they had been spied on by a bunch of giggling girls hiding in the bushes. Ethan hadn't looked her in the eye for the rest of that summer. He also had barred her from using his tree house.

"I was only fourteen at the time." A brilliant flush swept up Ethan's cheeks, turning his tan darker. "I was doubled-dared by Paul Burton. What was I suppose to do? Go through life being called a yellow-bellied sissy?"

"Absolutely not." Her smile was so wide her cheeks actually ached. "You did the right thing, and I thank you for the experience."

Ethan slowly lowered his cup. "I don't remember you being such a smart-ass."

Olivia's only response was a wide smile.

What he did remember of Olivia Hamilton hadn't been anything to write home about. Olivia had been all skinny arms and legs, a mouth full of metal braces, and a tangled mess of black curls she had called hair. Oh, and at sixteen, she had been totally flat-chested.

Ten years had turned the summer pest into one gorgeous woman. As much as the baggy sweatshirt tried to hide the fact, it couldn't conceal generously rounded breasts and a trim waist. Faded denim caressed every inch of her long shapely legs and hugged her curved bottom like a pair of desperate hands. Olivia was all grown up and he had nearly tripped over his own tongue when she had answered her grandmother's door moments before.

The college graduation picture, which Amelia had framed and was sitting on the mantel in the front parlor, didn't do

Olivia justice. The black robe and black cap, with Olivia's black hair and pale face, all just washed one another out.

He hadn't even realized Olivia's eyes were blue. Let alone the same exact shade of the pale, light blue of the morning sky in July. The tangled mass of black knots that Amelia, on more than one occasion, had sworn bats had nested in, were now soft shoulder-length silken curls that made his fingers itch to touch one.

Ten years ago Olivia had followed him around town as if she were some loyal puppy and he had been the master. It had been embarrassing and he had suffered more than one teasing about his shadow. Truth be told, he hadn't minded too much. In a way he'd felt sorry for Olivia. He couldn't imagine what it must be like to travel halfway across the country to stay with one's grandmother every summer. Away from your parents. Away from all your friends.

Every summer Olivia blew into town with her California tan, the latest fashions, and the strangest vocabulary. Half the kids in town picked on her. The other half were envious. He hadn't been either. What he had been was protective of the young girl who had seemed to shadow his every move. Everyone in town knew whoever messed with Olivia would answer to him. Thankfully, he hadn't had to step in and act the "older brother" too often. There had been only one incident that he could remember with certainty. It had taken place out at Sunset Cove about a week before Olivia had returned to California the last summer she had visited.

He watched Olivia sip her tea and stare out the window. In the fading light of a weak December sun, Amelia's gardens looked depressing. He couldn't remember if Olivia had ever visited her grandmother during the winter. If she hadn't, the sight of the now-dormant gardens must be unsettling. During the summer months, Amelia's gardens were a riot of color and a thing of beauty.

"How come your parents went back to California, and you didn't?" He was curious as to why she had stayed.

"Dad and Mom both had to get back to work, and there really wasn't anything for them to do here." Olivia lowered her empty cup back to the saucer.

"You don't have to get back to work?"

Olivia gave a weak laugh. "I'm currently in between jobs. The computer industry has been hit hard, first by the bottom dropping out of the dot com business, and now with the recession. California in particular was hit hard."

"I heard." He had never been laid off himself, but he understood about struggling in a business. It had taken him two years before his art gallery could support him. Now, after five years, good years, he was ready to expand. "Anything look promising out there?"

"I was at an interview the morning my grandmother had her heart attack." Olivia shrugged and blinked back a fresh wave of tears. "They told me I was overqualified for the job, so they weren't even going to offer it to me."

"Why not? You would think they'd snap you up in a hurry."

"They were smarter than that." Olivia gave him a crooked smile. "They knew that as soon as a better-paying job came along, one that I was qualified to do, I'd take it."

"So in the meanwhile you are unemployed?"

"True."

"So how long are you planning on staying in Maine?"

"I have no idea." Olivia glanced around the kitchen as if the answer would be written on the wall. "I guess as long as it takes."

He didn't like the sadness that was in Olivia's eyes or the fact that she was alone in this great big house. "How about I take you out to dinner? There's a great restaurant in town, Catch of the Day." He didn't add that it had been one of Amelia's favorite places to eat. He had been back in Misty Harbor only a day, and already he was missing the old gal.

"Thanks, but I have a better idea." Olivia stood up and walked over to the refrigerator. She swung open the door and said, "How about you stay here for dinner and help me eat some of this food?"

He stared in awe at the jam-packed shelves. He had never seen so much Tupperware, casserole dishes, and plastic wrap-covered bowls in his life. The Women's Guild had struck again.

TWO

Olivia tugged her new hat down lower over her ears, and then grinned at her reflection in the plate-glass window of Krup's General Store. She looked twelve years old in her new fluffy purple knitted hat and the matching mittens. Krup's selection of outer wear had been dismal and uninspiring, so she had gone with warmth. The short stroll from her grandmother's house to the Main Street shopping district had all but frozen her ears off.

The cup of hot chocolate she had had at Krup's soda fountain counter had warmed her insides and brought back some wonderful memories. Many a summer afternoon she had sat at that same counter with her friend Carol Ann drinking cherry Cokes and discussing boys, fashion, makeup, and gorgeous movie stars.

Carol Ann Black had been one of those girls who at sixteen had more than filled out the bikini top her parents hadn't known she owned. Carol Ann had also smoked cigarettes, knew how to drive her boyfriend's stick-shift pickup truck, and had known all about French kissing and what everyone did up at "Lookout Point." If there was something going on in town, Carol Ann knew the who, what, and where of things.

Carol Ann had been a whole eleven months older than Olivia, and her idol, ten years ago. Next time she saw Ethan, she was going to ask if he knew whatever became of Carol Ann. If her friend was still in the area, she would like to get together to relive some old times and hear any current gossip going around. Especially if it concerned a certain art gallery owner.

Olivia swung her bag holding more recent purchases from Krup's General Store as she window-shopped her way down Main Street. There wasn't much to see. The one thing that caught her eye was the mannequin in the window of Claire's Boutique. The plastic woman with the mop of blond curls was wearing the most wonderful black evening dress and shawl. It was the beaded and fringed black shawl that caught and held her attention. It would make a wonderful birthday gift for her mother, whose birthday was next week.

Twenty minutes later the brightly wrapped present was added to her bag as she left the shop. It had been a little more than what she had been planning on spending, considering her unemployed state. But once she was in the boutique, she couldn't pass it up. It was perfect for her mother.

Directly across the street was the store she had been looking for and the main reason she had braved the cold walk from her grandmother's house up on White Pine Street to Main Street. Ethan's Wycliffe Gallery looked just like she had pictured it last night when he had told her about it. She still couldn't get over the fact that Ethan owned his own gallery. An art gallery at that.

Ethan's gallery was one half of the single-story building. Bailey's Ice Cream Parlor and Emporium had the other half. Bailey's was closed for the season. Its pink and white striped awning, which shaded the couple of tables and chairs placed out on the sidewalk during the height of the tourist season, was neatly rolled away. The plate-glass window, with its fancy white-painted border and neatly printed words proclaiming for all the world to see that this was Bailey's, was dark and deserted looking. The bubble gum-pink front door with it oval glass was closed tightly against the winter wind and could definitely use a fresh coat of paint come spring.

Bailey's looked sad and neglected, while Ethan's gallery looked expensive and exclusive. She couldn't remember seeing such a mismatched pair of shops side by side.

She looked in both directions before crossing the street and headed for the gallery. She told herself that the slight hitch in her heart rate was due to the excitement of exploring the shop, not because she was going to see Ethan again. What woman didn't like to shop.

Ethan's half of the building was painted a brilliant white with deep burgundy trim. Glittering brass on the doorknob, the kick plate, and a reproduction of an antique lantern hanging by the door reflected the afternoon light. An iron bench, painted the same shade of burgundy, sat beneath the display window, encouraging tourists to sit a spell.

Olivia wasn't interested in sitting outside on a day like today, but she did stand in front of the window to check out what kind of merchandise Ethan sold. The gallery's window was smaller than Bailey's and bordered in elegant gold swirls. Dark green velvet material covered the display area, but there were only a few pieces of jewelry and some carelessly tossed gold ribbon lying on the velvet. It looked like Ethan was in the middle of rearranging the items and adding some holiday trimmings.

All of the stores on Main Street were already decked out for Christmas. Even the antique lantern-style streetlights had garlands wrapped around the posts and huge red and gold bows atop each light. Ethan was behind schedule, yet he had made time in his busy day yesterday to stop by and pay his respects. Ethan had also stayed for dinner and had helped dry the dishes. He had even insisted on walking through the house to make sure everything looked all right before leaving her alone in the big house.

Ethan was not only gorgeous, he was sweet and nice. Thirty years old, single and never married, owned his own home and business, and wasn't in a steady relationship. The way he had been checking out her body last night, there was no way he was gay. So what was Ethan's flaw? The man had to have one, and it must be a humdinger. Why else wasn't he married with at least a baby or two drooling on his broad shoulders and a minivan in the driveway?

She entered the shop and slowly looked around the gallery and then at the chaos surrounding Ethan. By the frazzled and dazed look upon his face, she was afraid she knew his flaw. Ethan Wycliffe was either a perfectionist, and the mess in the shop was getting to him, or he was one of the most disorganized persons she'd ever met.

Her money was on him being a perfectionist.

"Hi," she said as she made sure the door was securely closed against the blustering December wind. "Did I catch you at a bad time?"

"No, but you did catch me in a UPS nightmare." Ethan stood with his hands on his hips glaring at about three dozen boxes. The cartons were blocking just about everything in the store. "I can't believe that orders from six different suppliers arrived on the same day."

"When it rains, it pours." She stepped around a few boxes to study a stunning watercolor hanging on the far wall. The artist had done a wonderful job depicting Misty Harbor in full summer glory. The discrete price tag made her flinch. She could pay two months' rent on her apartment back in California for the asking price. "I see you are in the middle of decorating for Christmas."

An eight-foot tree took up a good portion of space toward the back of the front room. Through a wide opening she caught glimpses of a second display room. The pine tree was bare except for a halfway-strung string of white lights.

"Trying to decorate would be more accurate." Ethan piled two boxes on top of each other. "By the time I'm ready for Christmas, it will be January."

"I thought you said you had an assistant." She didn't see

anyone else in the shop, and there weren't that many places a person could hide. The shop had two other doors. One, she could see, led out back. The other was behind the cash register area and was closed. It probably led to an office, a storage area, and a small powder room. The shop wasn't big enough for anything else. Ethan had been right last night. He definitely needed more room.

"I gave Karen a couple days off, so she can get her own home ready for the holidays. She did an outstanding job filling in for me while I was in Florida visiting my parents and grandparents. She has three school-age children, and hasn't even started her own Christmas shopping yet."

Ethan piled more boxes on top of each other so there was more room to walk around. "Who would have thought everything would come in on the same day?"

She lowered her bag to the floor and helped Ethan stack the boxes and move them off to the side. "How about if I help you unpack these or at least decorate your tree for you?"

"I can't ask you to do that."

"I'm not asking for a job or a paycheck, Ethan." She gently placed two smaller boxes, marked FRAGILE, on the counter so that they wouldn't get stepped on. "Since I'm not putting up a tree at my grandmother's place, I would like to help you with yours here. It will help me take my mind off of cleaning out my grandmother's things." Which was the main reason for the walk into town. She couldn't face packing up all of her grandmother's clothes for charity just yet. Heck, she couldn't even bring herself to borrow a pair of gloves or a scarf from the hall closet. Her fingers had lovingly smoothed out a wrinkle in the bright red scarf hanging on the back of her grandmother's closet door. But she couldn't bring herself to put it on.

Packing up her grandmother's belongings was going to be the hardest thing she had ever done. What was one more day? There wasn't any hurry.

Olivia dropped her newly purchased mittens and hat into her shopping bag and started to unbutton her coat. "Since you already have up half the lights, and they are the hardest part of decorating a tree, the rest should be easy. You just tell me what you want on it, and I'll try to do it."

"Are you sure?" Ethan glanced between her and the bare tree. "Karen usually does all the fancy decorating. She has a more 'feminine touch' than me. But Kevin didn't drop the tree off until yesterday afternoon. I set it up before coming over to Amelia's yesterday so the branches had a chance to fall."

"I'm not Martha Stewart, but I can hang a few balls and bows." She draped her coat over the doorknob to the office and rubbed her hands together in glee. "Just show me what goes on it, and what kind of look you are going for here."

Ethan reached over the cash register, and grabbed a torn-out page of a magazine. "I can do better than that. I'll show you." Ethan handed her the picture. "This is the look we are going for this year."

She glanced down at the picture and nearly choked. The twenty-five-foot full and bushy Scottish pine looked like it belonged in the White House. The gold room of the White House. There was no way that a normal dad, mom, and little Tiny Tim had decorated that tree. It would take a team of professional decorators a month, working seven days a week, twenty-hour days, to complete such a masterpiece. Ethan wanted her to do this to the Charlie Brown–looking twig in the corner?

She handed him back the picture. "No way could I do that, Ethan. The most I could guarantee you is that I would try not to put two of the same-colored balls next to each other."

Ethan chuckled and pushed the page back into her hand. "You already offered, and I accepted." He headed for the tree. "Come on, it won't be that hard. Karen has already purchased everything we need, and she made the bows. The rest of the stuff that goes on the tree is merchandise. Karen has already priced it. All you have to do is hang the stuff to its best advantage, and to make sure people can see the price tags without knocking anything off the branches."

She noticed boxes filled with hand-blown glass ornaments, hand-painted balls depicting everything from the harbor to Santa Claus, and intricate white lacy angels trimmed in what looked like real pearls. Another box held gold ribbon, gold beads, and several dozen gold bows. A gold satin tree skirt and a stack of brightly wrapped presents were nearby. Everything one would possibly need to do up a Christmas tree right.

"Okay, I'll try this, but I'm not promising anything spectacular." She picked up the string of lights and waved Ethan away. "Go do whatever you have to do with all those boxes. If I need your help, I'll holler."

An hour later Ethan had all of the boxes either stacked in the office, or in the tiny space behind the register. Four boxes had been unpacked and their contents inventoried, priced, and now displayed throughout the shop. He should have had twice as much done, but he had been too busy watching Olivia.

He enjoyed watching Olivia.

The woman was never still or quiet. Olivia sang off-key to the soft Christmas carols he had playing on the gallery's stereo system. She talked, whispered, and sometimes argued with the decorations and the tree. She bounced up and down the step ladder like the Energizer Bunny. He had even learned a new creative use for a common verb when it came slipping out of Olivia's mouth while she was untangling a massive knot in the string of gold beads.

All in all, it was one of the most pleasant afternoons he had ever spent in the shop. The tree wasn't looking too bad either.

He placed a green pottery bowl, with hand-painted holly leaves and berries, on the display shelf between two carved reindeer. There were another dozen or so pieces of the same design throughout the shop. Last year he had sold every piece of it and customers were already looking for it again this season. If he had a bigger place, he could keep it in stock throughout the year. As it was, the summer design of blue pottery with hand-painted blueberries on it had been taken off the shelves to make room for the winter holly design.

It had been after the Christmas season last year that he had decided he needed a bigger place. Finding just the right place was the problem. Marv Bailey wasn't interested in getting out of the ice cream business, so he couldn't expand the gallery. He needed a place either on Main Street or close enough that the tourists would find the gallery during the peak selling season. So far nothing suitable had come onto the market.

He stepped behind Olivia and smiled at the way she worried her lower lip with her teeth every time she placed a ball onto the tree. "Relax, Summer Breeze, it looks great. You're doing a fantastic job."

Olivia worried her lip more. "You think so? I only put up half the balls and glass ornaments and six angels. I didn't want to crowd the tree, or people won't be able to see the details. Plus I figured you need the spares to replace what people bought. Right?"

"Right." He pulled his gaze away from Olivia's tempting mouth. If anybody was going to be nibbling on that luscious lower lip, he wanted to be the one. "I've got some fancy boxes in the stockroom. We can fill them with colorful tissue paper and place some of the ornaments in there to display them." He headed for the office.

Two minutes later he stood in the middle of his shop and watched the enticing sway of Olivia's jean-clad bottom as she shimmied her way under the tree and tried to straighten out the satin tree skirt around the stand. He finally figured out what he wanted for Christmas. He wanted Olivia under his tree, and in roughly the same position. Now that was one present he would love to unwrap come Christmas morning.

"Ethan?"

"Yeah?" He wondered if she was stuck. He hoped so.

"Do you remember Carol Ann Black? She was about three years younger than you." Olivia wormed her way out from under the tree and started to arrange the brightly wrapped presents on the skirt.

"Sure I know Carol Ann. What about her?" Ethan handed her two more presents. Both boxes were empty, but Karen had done a superb job of wrapping them to make them look like a million bucks.

"Is she still in the area? I haven't seen her in ten years and I thought it would be nice to get together with her since I'm in town."

"She married Tom Burton right out of high school if I remember right."

"She's married?"

"And a mother."

"Carol Ann has a baby?"

"Last I saw her, she had three kids. The oldest boy must be around six. There's a girl a little younger than that, and a baby around a year or so." He remembered seeing Carol Ann pushing a stroller with a screaming baby inside down Main Street with a kid on either side of her. The little girl had her fingers jammed in her ears. He also remembered praying they wouldn't be coming into his shop. He liked children. Just not in his gallery.

Olivia sat on the floor and stared up at him. "She has three kids?"

"At least." By the look on Olivia's face, one might think he'd just told her that Carol Ann had delivered humpback whales instead of babies.

"I told her that French kissing would get her in trouble."

Olivia chuckled as she shook her head, placed the last present just so, and stood up.

He tried to hide his smile. "I don't think it was the kissing, French or otherwise, that got her pregnant."

"No, but that's how it starts." Olivia shook her head. "Who did you say she married?"

"Tom Burton, Paul's younger brother."

"The skinny-dipping double-daring Paul Burton?"

He refused to blush again at something that had happened half a lifetime ago. So what if Olivia had seen him in the buff. A lady wouldn't have looked. "One and the same."

The sound of the front door opening interrupted whatever Olivia was about to say. By the sparkling gleam in her eye, he had a feeling it would have been some smart-ass comment.

"Go see to the customer, while I straighten up some more." Olivia carefully folded the stepladder and carried it back to the office.

He went to handle the customer.

By closing time he had unpacked another dozen or so boxes, and sold a painting, two pieces of pottery, and an amber and silver necklace. Olivia had finished the tree, placed all the spare ornaments out in the fancy boxes, and arranged the display window with mostly Christmas merchandise. He might have chosen to place one or two of the more expensive items in the window, but he would never have thought to hang a few of the ornaments from gold ribbon in the window.

Ethan made sure that the office light was off and that the back door was locked before joining Olivia near the front door. "I think I owe you dinner tonight for a job well done."

Olivia tugged on her new hat and mittens and picked up her shopping bag. "Nonsense, I enjoyed myself too much. I owe *you* dinner, and I still have a full refrigerator. Want to come over for more leftovers?"

If this were a normal night, he would go home, eat a solitary meal, and then come back to the shop to finish unpacking the shipment that had arrived today. Tonight wasn't normal, and he had just been invited to dinner by a very beautiful woman. He wasn't stupid. "I would love to join you for dinner." He ushered Olivia out front and locked the door. "Did you drive?"

"No, did you?" Olivia tugged her hat lower over her ears against the cold.

"Afraid not." He took the bag from Olivia, tucked her arm under his own, and hurried down the street. "I think we'll need a cup of tea with Amelia's secret recipe once we make it home."

Olivia used his body to block the wind. "Heck with the tea, just pour me a shot or two of the brandy."

He tried to pick up his pace, but he didn't want to leave Olivia behind. He shook her bag. "What did you buy today?"

"I found my mom a birthday present at Claire's." Olivia's breath was clouds of white fluff. "I also picked up this hat and mittens from Krup's, along with warmer pajamas and some socks."

"I like the hat and mittens." He thought she looked adorable in them. "What kind of pajamas?" They turned off Main Street and onto White Pine. He was trying to keep Olivia talking and her mind off the fact that her teeth were chattering so badly he was afraid she was going to damage the enamel. Thinking about Olivia's pajamas kept him warm.

"Warm ones." Olivia was taking two steps to his every one. "Long-sleeve, thick flannel ones."

He tripped over his own feet. "You sleep in flannel pajamas?" So much for his fantasies. He was picturing flowing gowns of gossamer silk or at least a very enticing oversized T-shirt and panties.

"I do when in Maine." Olivia moved closer to him as a snowflake landed on her nose. "In case you haven't realized it, it's darn cold up here."

He chuckled as he hurried her up her grandmother's walk and onto the porch. "This is nothing, Summer Breeze. You should be here during a nor'easter." He took her keys out of her mitten-covered hand, found the right one, and got her into the house before she hopped the next plane back to sunny southern California. "Maybe you don't have the heater set high enough."

"The radiators banged and clanged all night long. At one time I thought it was the ghost of Jacob Marley coming to visit." Olivia flipped on some lights.

He closed the door and peeked into the shopping bag. Amused, he pulled out a plastic-wrapped pair of red flannel pajamas with white polar bears and igloos printed all over them. A six-pack of men's thick over-the-calf white cotton socks was still in the bag. Eskimos slept in less. "You couldn't have been that cold."

"Make a bet?" Olivia glanced out the front parlor window to the streetlight beyond. "It's starting to snow. Maybe I should have bought two pairs of jammies and that thick robe. The navy blue one that was down to my ankles, made out of some bedspread, and zipped up the front."

He glanced at the flakes and chuckled. "Those are only flurries. We aren't expecting more than an inch or two."

"Two inches of snow in southern Cal would cause major accidents and the freeways would be backed up for miles."

"This isn't southern Cal, Olivia. You're in Maine now. We don't even break out the snow shovels until at least half a foot has fallen."

"Oh, great," groaned Olivia. "I knew I should have bought that electric blanket back at Krup's. I'll never be warm again."

Three

"I think I see the problem already," said Ethan as he stepped into her bedroom. "Your bed is right up against the window. These old windows are pretty drafty and totally energy inefficient."

Olivia glanced at the twin bed with its pink billowy bedspread and half a dozen pillows. All the furniture in the room was white French provincial and a good twenty years old. Her grandmother had bought her the entire set when she was about five years old. At five, Olivia had felt like a princess anytime she came to visit. By sixteen she had hated it, but didn't have the heart to tell her grandmother.

Amelia had kept the room dusted and clean, but hadn't changed a thing in it for the past ten years. When she had first opened the door, it had been like entering a time warp to her past.

The pink rosebud wallpaper and pink lace curtains didn't help the decor. The room reminded Olivia of the time she gorged herself on sugary sweet pink cotton candy at a local fair, and the Pepto-Bismol she had consumed afterward. Not the best memories to be sleeping with every night.

"I guess I can move the bed to another wall." She glanced at the writing desk and chair. Her laptop and a stack of papers were spread out across the desk.

"Grab one end of the desk, and we'll do it now." Ethan

moved the chair out of the way and picked up his end of the desk.

She unplugged the laptop and helped maneuver the desk away from the wall to make room for the bed. The bed was harder to move. The frilly bedspread kept getting caught in the wheels, and while the headboard was bolted to the frame, it was anything but sturdy. Ethan's chin got wacked twice in the process.

After the desk was in position under the window, Ethan rubbed his chin and asked, "Explain to me again why you are sleeping in this Disney nightmare instead of some other room. I happen to know there are three other perfectly good bedrooms in this house, and that doesn't include the attic."

She frowned at a few dust bunnies that skidded along the edges of the wooden floors. "I always slept in this room. This is my room. When I was five, my grandmom asked me what my favorite color was." She tossed one of the pillows, which had fallen during the move, back onto the bed. "I told her pink."

"Amelia probably did some psychological damage to you by making you sleep in this mess. It reminds me of Bailey's Ice Cream Parlor." Ethan pushed aside the curtain and glanced out into the night. "Didn't you have nightmares sleeping in that bed?"

"Nope. In the summer I used to open the curtains and the window wide and stare up at the stars. The Big Dipper was always above your house." Her bedroom window was directly across from Ethan's. The last couple of summers she had spent more time staring at his window than at the stars.

Ethan allowed the curtain to fall back into place. "Nice view."

"I liked it." She grinned. She knew Ethan had noticed the youthful crush she had had on him way back then. Only a complete idiot wouldn't have noticed the totally flat-chested girl with the mouth full of metal following him wherever he went.

She'd be heading back to California as soon as she figured out what to do with the house and her grandmother's things. A real estate agent was stopping by tomorrow morning to work up an appraisal. It seemed contemptible to sell her grandmother's house, but what else was she supposed to do with it? Her father didn't want it, and legally it was now hers to do with as she pleased.

What would really please her was to move the whole house to some southern California harbor town overlooking the Pacific Ocean instead of the Atlantic. But that wasn't going to happen. Three thousand miles was one hell of a commute.

The cash inheritance that came along with the house would be enough to pay for upkeep for a couple of years at the most. Then what? The simple truth was, she couldn't afford to keep it.

The house had to go.

But in the meanwhile, Ethan was still her neighbor, and while she couldn't say she still had a crush on him, she did think he was incredibly sexy. How many women got a chance to relive a ten-year-old crush?

"Olivia? Are you listening?" Ethan was kneeling next to the radiator on the far wall and looking at her strangely.

"What? I'm sorry, my mind must have been drifting. What did you say?" She had a sick feeling her cheeks matched the decor perfectly.

"I asked if your father turned the radiators up in all the rooms? Amelia probably didn't keep them all operating at full steam when there was no one staying here but her." Ethan felt the nickel-plated radiator with the palm of his hand. "It's warm, but not as hot as it should be."

"It's working." She touched the metal and was surprised it wasn't nearly as hot as the ones downstairs. "I heard it banging and clanging all night long."

Ethan turned the nozzle at the base of the radiator. "The valve was only opened a little bit. Enough for some warmth to come through, but not enough for actual heat." Ethan gave the nozzle another turn before standing up. "That should do it. You might want to think twice before wearing your hat and mittens to bed tonight."

She felt the radiator, and the warmth from only moments before was now decidedly more intense. "You did it." She gave Ethan what she hoped was a sexy grin. "How can I ever thank you?" It was a loaded question to ask a man whom you were alone with in a house, and in your bedroom. She knew what most men would say, but she was curious as to how Ethan would respond.

"You already fed me tonight, so that's thanks enough." Ethan headed for the doorway as if suddenly realizing how alone they were. "Plus you spent hours at the gallery helping me this afternoon. How would I ever sleep tonight knowing you were freezing in your bed and shaking the poor polar bears right off your pajamas?" Ethan stepped out into the hallway and headed for the stairs. "Did you want me to check the radiators in the other bedrooms?"

"No thanks. I'll turn them up when I start going through them to pack away my grandmother's stuff." She didn't even want to think about how long that was going to take, or what she was going to do with it all. Every room in the house was filled with antiques and sentimental items. She followed Ethan down the stairs and into the living room. The front parlor was for entertaining guests and more formal occasions. The living room was for relaxing, watching television, and enjoying a blazing fire on a cold winter's night.

Tonight it was cold, and Ethan had started a fire while she had warmed up dinner.

"Do you know what your father is planning to do with the house?" Ethan added another log to the burning pile. "Are he and your mother going to keep it as a vacation home? Maybe they will retire here."

"My grandmother didn't leave my father the house." Olivia curled up at one end of the sofa and watched the muscles bunch and release in Ethan's thigh as he stood. Tonight Ethan wore another pair of Dockers. This pair was charcoal gray, and the burgundy sweater he wore contrasted perfectly with them. She wondered if Ethan knew that he matched his gallery.

"She didn't?" Ethan seemed surprised. "I thought your father was an only child."

"He is." She hugged a needlepoint pillow against her chest. In a small town news would travel fast, and it wasn't as if it was some secret. Amelia Hamilton's last wishes would be known all over town in a matter of days anyway. "My grandmother left him all her stocks and investments. She left me the house and all its contents."

Ethan stared at her for a long moment before softly asking, "What are you planning on doing with it?" Ethan's gaze caressed her face. "Any chance that you'll be moving to Maine and keeping Krup's profit margin up by buying every pair of flannel pajamas in stock?"

For one insane minute she wanted to tell him yes, she would be staying and was thinking about a career change. How does lobster fisherman sound? Sanity prevailed as she remembered the résumé upstairs she had been trying to enhance and improve upon last night after Ethan had left. She was a California girl, born and bred. Her family was out there, and so was her career, once she found it again. Misty Harbor, Maine, needed a computer systems specialist like Palm Springs needed a lobster fisherman.

She gave Ethan a small forced smile as she shook her head. "I've got a real estate agent coming tomorrow morning to appraise the house and get it on the market."

"You're selling the house?"

"I can't take it back to California with me, Ethan." She could feel the tears once again pool in her eyes as she glared across the room at him. Didn't he realize how hard this was on her? "What do you want me to do with it? Let it sit here empty and abandoned?"

"I'm sorry, Olivia." Ethan sat on the other end of the couch and gave her a small smile. "It's your right to sell it. What else can you do?"

"Nothing." She turned her head and stared into the fireplace at the dancing orange and yellow flames. "Absolutely nothing."

Ethan stood in what was his old boyhood bedroom, but now was his office, and stared out into the night. Two inches of freshly fallen snow blanketed the ground and tree branches. Next door, Selma Moore had left her back porch light on again, and she was lighting the neighborhood. He had a perfect view of Olivia's dark bedroom window.

She had gone to bed about an hour ago.

He tried to ignore the heat and desire pumping through his veins. It was impossible. Even when he pictured Olivia in those oversized flannel pajamas with goofy-looking polar bears all over them, thick white socks, and an afghan wrapped around her shoulders, she was still the most desirable woman he had ever seen. How could ten years change a person so much?

A sixteen-year-old Olivia had been a royal pain in the ass.

Every summer, since he turned sixteen, he had taken a job down at the docks or worked for one of the local fishermen. He knew by the time he was seventeen that making his living on the sea wasn't the life for him. Today, the smell of ripe bait could still make him gag. His father had called it character building. He had called it torture. Looking back on those summers, he really hadn't had it that bad. Most of the fishermen worked hard, but they also knew how to play hard.

For his twenty-first birthday, a group of the older fisherman had taken him out to The One-Eyed Squid and had gotten him stinking drunk. His mother still hadn't forgiven Abraham Martin or his croonies for, as she liked to put it, corrupting her boy. His father hadn't said too much about it, but he had been the one to wake his son's sorry butt up at the crack of dawn the next morning, and send him off to work. He could still remember the gleam of laughter in his father's eyes that morning.

Nearly every day Olivia, usually with Carol Ann in tow, had shown up at the docks. Carol Ann had been one of those girls who just naturally flirted with every boy. Olivia had been shy and barely said a word to anyone. He had known why Olivia had been there. Anyone with eyes in their head could see the girl had a severe case of puppy love. It had been painful to watch, but he hadn't once encouraged her.

Ten years later, and he was afraid he'd be the one who started following her all around town.

For all the good it would do him. Olivia was going back to California just as soon as she handled her grandmother's estate. She had been very clear about that fact. There could be no future between them. She was bikinis and palm trees, and he was blazing fires and thick cable-knit sweaters.

He studied the shadowy outline of what was now Olivia's house. In the light of day he knew the large, spacious house had clapboard siding that was painted yellow with white trim. The shutters, the front door, and the decking of the porch were all painted a soft green. From the second-floor balcony, off the master bedroom, there was an unobstructed view of the harbor. A white picket fence and large gardens surrounded the entire property.

It was a wonderful house, and if his memory served him right, it had been built by one of Olivia's distant ancestors. It

was a real shame that it was now going to be sold out of the
family. But Olivia was right. What else could she do? Seeing
the graceful old lady fall into disrepair as it sat neglected year
after year with only the occasional visit would be heart-
breaking.

Who would tend Amelia's wonderful gardens? Who would
give Ethan beautiful bouquets of freshly cut flowers in exchange for tall glasses of his famous lemonade? Whom was
he going to sip tea laced with blackberry brandy with on
those long cold winter nights? Amelia was gone, and soon
Olivia would head back to sunny California.

But the house would remain. Amelia's wonderful house
that was only a short distance away from Main Street and
what constituted Misty Harbor's shopping district. Tourists
would surely find it easily. It was as close to perfect as he was
likely to find.

Amelia's house was bigger than what he had been looking
for, but with all the woodwork and character of the home he
wouldn't want to overcrowd the rooms. He could even carry
a few antique pieces of furniture and still have plenty of room
left over for his usual stock. Karl James, a local artist who
worked mainly in wood, wanted him to carry some of his
larger pieces. At the current gallery it would be impossible.
Some of Karl's work was massive. Amelia's yard and wide
porches would make perfect display areas for work not only
by Karl but by other artists as well.

It would be the perfect solution to his gallery problem.
Now if only he could figure out what do about Olivia and the
attraction he felt growing between them.

"So, how was your day?" Ethan asked as he set a match to
the kindling in Olivia's fireplace. He had been held up at the
gallery for longer than he had expected. Twice during the day
he had tried to reach Olivia by phone. She hadn't answered

either time. Now, it was way past the dinner hour and he wasn't even sure if she had eaten yet. He had stopped by her house on his way home from work just to check on her. Olivia looked depressed as all hell.

"Horrible." Olivia cradled a cup of steaming coffee in her hands as she sat curled up on the couch.

"Didn't the real estate agent show up?"

"He was here about ten o'clock." Olivia took a sip of the coffee. "He practically drooled all over everything in the house and handed me two different business cards of antique dealers. He also told me the house wouldn't be on the market long, considering its location and condition."

"That's good news, right? So what's the problem?" He brushed off his hands and joined her on the sofa. "I thought that would make you happy."

"After he left, I took a drive into Bangor." Olivia set the cup on the table next to her. "I figured if I could commute to Bangor, where I just might be able to get a job in my field, I could stay here and keep the house."

Last night he had lain in his lonely bed and thought of ways to turn the house into a gallery and what was the top amount he could afford to spend on the transformation. He also had spent a ridiculous amount of time thinking about Olivia and the attraction he felt for her. Right at this moment he would give up the possibility of buying the house if Olivia would stay in Misty Harbor. He wanted to spend time getting to know her better. There was something there between them, he just knew it. Every time he looked into Olivia's eyes, he saw his future. Strange, he had never once believed in love at first sight or any such nonsense. Besides, he had known Olivia since she was two and his parents made him share his sand-box with Amelia's granddaughter.

"What happened?" Downtown Bangor was over an hour away on clear roads, sunny days, and with perfect traffic conditions. He would hate to know how long it had taken Olivia to drive into the city on a miserable day like today.

"I can't drive in snow." Olivia's sky blue eyes filled with tears. "It's not in my genes or something." With a couple of rapid blinks, the tears were gone. "I did pretty well until around Ellsworth. They got a lot more snow than we did, and it got worse the closer I got to Bangor. I slipped and slid all over the place. The front end of the car went one way, the back another, and the steering wheel another. The slower I went, the more people blew their horns." Olivia gave him a watery smile. "Some old man, who had to be around ninety, yelled at me and asked me if I got my license in a Cracker Jack box."

He tried not to laugh. He really did. It was impossible. "You never drove in snow before?" Instead of questioning Olivia, he should be counting his blessings that she hadn't been in an accident.

"Never even tried until today. The few times I've been ski-ing, either my father or friends had been behind the wheel." Olivia rubbed her hands together as if remembering how hard she had gripped the steering wheel. "An hour commute out in California isn't unreasonable. Out there you have to put up with rain, smog, and twenty miles of bumper to bumper traf-fic. Today I had drifting snow, ice patches the size of Iowa, and fifty-mile-an-hour wind gusts blowing me all over the road. I didn't need my grandmother's Chrysler, I needed a Hummer or a tank."

"Commuting to Bangor every day isn't for the faint of heart, Olivia. I wouldn't even do it."

"Because from November to April the weather sucks, and blizzards have been known to swallow whole anything smaller than a Mack truck?"

"It's not quite that bad, but the winter months are hard. The summer months, with the rubber-necking tourists clogging every coast road, aren't much better."

"Forget it. It was just some lamebrain idea I had." Olivia pressed her cheek against the back of the couch and stared at him.

She looked so sad that he wanted to pull her into his arms and give her a big hug. "Did the real estate guy give you a fair market value?"

Olivia gave him the price.

He ran some quick calculations through his mind. If he nixed any major improvements for a year or so, it was doable. The decision had been made late last night so it was senseless to run any more figures. "I'll take it."

"Take what?"

"The house." He glanced around the living room and grinned at the confused look upon her face. "I'll buy Amelia's house for the fair market value."

"You want to live in my grandmother's house?"

"No, but this house would make a perfect gallery." Ethan stood up and paced around the couch. He could see into the foyer, the front parlor, and the formal dining room. "I told you I've been looking for a bigger place. This is as close to perfect as I can get." He glanced up the stairs and visualized framed artwork going the whole way up. "What do you say?"

"You'll pay the asking price? No haggling?"

"I wouldn't dream of haggling." He hadn't been expecting any discounts for being Amelia's neighbor.

Olivia shrugged her shoulders. "Okay, it's yours."

"Really?"

"Really." Olivia gave him a small smile. "It saves me the aggravation of cleaning it and showing it constantly until it does sell."

"Good." He stopped in front of her and pulled her up into his arms. "Now that that is settled, I can do what I've been dying to do for the past two days." He lowered his mouth and kissed her.

Olivia melted into the warmth of Ethan's arms and the tenderness of his kiss. Her arms encircled his neck and she pressed herself closer. Ethan kissed like she always knew he would. Ethan kissed like a dream. A hot erotic dream.

One of them moaned. She was pretty sure it had been Ethan, but it could have been her. Ethan's hands pulled her closer as he deepened the kiss. Her teeth nibbled on his lower lip. His tongue outlined her upper lip before slipping past it to explore her mouth.

For the first time in hours she wasn't cold. The harrowing drive home from Bangor was forgotten. She felt safe, warm, and incredibly sexy. She was coming apart in Ethan Wycliffe's arms. The sixteen-year-old girl inside her cheered. The woman she was today wanted more.

More than she had the right to want. She didn't make love with a man just because he was handsome and willing. The bulge in Ethan's pants pressing against her hip told her how willing he was. There had to be more, way more.

It didn't matter how much she wanted to take their relationship to the next step, it wasn't going to happen. She'd be heading back to California soon enough. With Ethan buying the house, it would be sooner, rather than later.

With a slow lingering caress of her mouth, she broke the kiss. She couldn't tell which one of them was breathing the hardest. Ethan's golden eyes were dark and hungry as they searched her face. She was afraid if she looked into a mirror, the same desire would be reflected back at her.

She stepped out of his arms and tried to appear confident and sophisticated. It was impossible to achieve, considering Ethan had just rocked her world. "I don't do casual sex, Ethan." Her fingers trembled as they brushed a wayward curl out of her eye. "I'll be leaving Misty Harbor soon. Maybe it would be a good idea if you went home now." It wasn't that she didn't trust Ethan. She didn't trust herself.

The pad of Ethan's thumb traced her lower lip. "I'll leave now, because you asked." He brushed a quick kiss across her mouth. "Lock up tight after I'm gone." Ethan picked up his jacket, which he'd tossed over the newel post half an hour ago. "And, Olivia?"

"Yes?"

"When we make love, there will be nothing casual about it."

She listened to the front door softly close behind Ethan. Heat still pooled low in her gut and her breasts still ached for his touch. Ethan hadn't said "if we make love"; he had said "when." The man had seemed quite confident and sure of himself and of her.

Considering the way she had kissed him, she didn't blame him one bit.

There had been nothing casual in their first kiss.

Four

"Tell me again why I'm doing this." Olivia looked at Ethan, who was busy setting the table in the large kitchen. Ethan was setting places for seven.

"Because you wanted to see Carol Ann again, and were curious about her husband and kids." Ethan aligned the forks perfectly with the knives. "When she invited you to dinner, you decided it would be easier if you, not Carol Ann, cooked for everyone."

Olivia glanced in the oven at the meat loaf baking away. The potatoes were ready for mashing, two different vegetables were in the microwave, and the rolls were ready to slip into the oven. Carol Ann and her family were due to arrive at any minute. "You didn't hear the baby screaming in the background. There was no way I could have let her cook me dinner." She still shuddered remembering that constant screaming and yelling. Carol Ann probably hadn't had a good home-cooked meal in months. She frowned at the bowl of freshly made salad. Ethan had been the one to cut up the tomatoes and cucumbers. "Do you think they will like meat loaf?"

"What did Carol Ann say about it?"

She chuckled. "She said the 'monsters' would eat anything, and that Tom would probably bow down and kiss my feet if I served him a meal that hadn't come from a box."

"I think meat loaf will be fine, Olivia. Stop worrying. I don't think Carol Ann has changed that much over the years."

"She's married with three kids! How could she not change?" She had been so worried that when Carol Ann and her family showed up tonight, she would have nothing in common with them. Or that she and Carol Ann would pick up just were they had left off ten years ago, and then Tom would be left out of the conversation. She had gone grocery shopping, and then stopped at Ethan's gallery to invite him to her first, and probably her last, dinner party in Misty Harbor. "Tell me again about Tom Burton. Which one was he?" She remembered different boys from back then, but she couldn't place Tom.

"Tom's a diesel mechanic, and a darn good one from what I hear." Ethan leaned his hip against the counter and smiled. "He was always down at the docks, usually showing off for Carol Ann. He was the one with dark brown hair and he never had his shirt on."

"What's with those Burton boys? Paul couldn't keep his pants on, and Tom had problems with his shirts." She picked up the masher and started to pound on the potatoes. "I remember him now. He always had a tan and real white teeth. His shorts hung so low on his hips that Carol Ann and I used to bet cherry Cokes about when they would fall down." She laughed at the memory. "Carol Ann bought me a lot of cherry Cokes that summer."

"Which way were you betting?" Ethan didn't look amused by the story.

She was saved from answering as the doorbell rang. All of a sudden she was nervous. "They're here." She looked down at the half-mashed potatoes. "I'm not ready yet."

Ethan gently took the masher out of her hands. "Go answer the door, while I finish pulverizing these."

"Really?"

Ethan's mouth tenderly brushed her lips in a kiss so soft and quick that she might have imagined it if she hadn't felt the heat.

"Go." Ethan gently pushed her toward the hall. "Let the party begin."

Two and a half hours later Olivia glanced over at Carol Ann and cracked up laughing. She couldn't tell if the laughter was because she was so darn happy to see Carol Ann again, or because she had drunk a little more wine than she was used to. It didn't matter—she was sitting in the living room with her best friend from her childhood, reliving the past.

A good past, filled with marvelous memories of great people and a wonderful town. Memories filled with her grandmother's love. She hadn't realized how much she had missed Maine until now.

"What's so funny?" Carol Ann sipped her wine and sank deeper into the couch.

"You. I can't believe you have gotten married, have three adorable children, and you are still the same Carol Ann I remember." She took another sip of wine and put her feet up on the coffee table. She wasn't driving anywhere. Neither was Carol Ann. Tom had taken the kids home about half an hour ago, giving his wife time to catch up with her friend. Ethan had left shortly thereafter. "What I want to know is how Tom puts up with you."

"Tom puts up with me? Shouldn't that be the other way around? The man is constantly in a great mood. The blasted man wakes up happy, even when I make him get up with Devin in the middle of the night. Nothing fazes Tom. You should have seen his face when I told him I was pregnant with Elizabeth. Samuel wasn't even a year old and we had decided to wait a few years before having our second child. I was ready to slice my throat because Samuel was a colicky baby, and there's Tom grinning like a fool and calling everyone he knew."

Olivia smiled at the thought of having a husband one day

that would be that devoted. "Tom's so sweet." She raised her glass and toasted Carol Ann. "You caught a good one there." She took another sip and mentally reminded herself to congratulate Ethan on choosing such a great wine. "Most men would never have taken the kids home to get them ready for bed, and left you here."

"Most of the time I swear Tom handles the kids better than I do." Carol Ann finished off her glass of wine. "With Sam in school all day and Elizabeth Claire in kindergarten, I have to admit, life is getting more manageable. But Devin is a handful. He's what his doctor calls a 'verbal' baby. Devin loves to hear himself talk, scream, babble, and sometimes just cry. When he was first born, I was in the doctor's office every week swearing there must be something wrong with him. Turns out he's physically fine. Tom says he'll probably end up being the lead singer in some heavy metal band."

"And this doesn't bother you?" She silently laughed at the image of Carol Ann and Tom in some mosh pit at age fifty cheering on their son.

"As long as he doesn't practice in our garage, I wouldn't care." Carol Ann gave her a look that said she was about to get serious. "I might have stayed the same, but you've changed." Carol Ann's mouth turned up into a teasing smile. "For the better."

"Hey, what was wrong with the way I was?" There had been a lot wrong with her ten years ago, but she didn't think Carol Ann had cared if her friend had been flat-chested and had more metal in her mouth than most refrigerators.

"Nothing was wrong, you're just different now." Carol Ann picked up the wine bottle they had brought into the living room with them, and divided the rest of the wine between their two glasses.

"How?" Olivia wasn't sure, but she thought that might have been the third bottle of wine they had polished off. Of course, the guys had helped during dinner.

"You're not as shy as you were." Carol Ann toyed with her glass. "You're more self-confident. You grew into your beauty."

"You mean I finally grew boobs." She glanced down at the sweater she was wearing and grinned at her chest.

"Oh, Ethan definitely noticed them, and Tom noticed too. Of course, he would never admit it, because he knows I would have to hurt him then." Carol Ann's stockinged feet were resting on the coffee table, and she was staring into the dying fire. "Ethan's fire is going down."

Olivia gave a misty smile at the slowly dying embers. "He always makes one for me. Isn't that sweet?"

"Yeah, sweet." Carol Ann glanced at the glass in Olivia's hand. "So, what's the story with you and our local art gallery owner?"

"No story."

"You still got a crush on him, or are you just toying with his affections?"

"I'm not toying with his anything." She waved her hand in the air and chuckled when she realized how wrong that had sounded. "He's buying the house from me."

"So I heard over dinner. Something about turning it into a gallery and enlarging his business." Carol Ann gave her an amused look. "I couldn't help but notice the lip lock he put on you before he headed home for the night." The wine in her glass sloshed around as she set the glass back on the table. "It's awfully convenient him living directly behind you. He could come and go at all hours of the night, and no one in town would even know it."

Olivia snorted. "Selma Moore would. That woman is up all hours of the night. Her back porch light is always lit, but I never see her dog."

"Selma doesn't have a dog, Olivia. The woman is eighty-seven and goes to bed by eight every night." Carol Ann shook her head. "She probably just forgets to turn the light off, that's all."

"Her electric bill must be outrageous." She shook her head and wondered how the dear sweet woman could afford it. "Someone should tell her."

"Tom's mother knows her daughter. I'll tell her tomorrow, and maybe they can either take the lightbulb out of the porch light, or put the switch on a timer." Carol Ann brushed her hair away from her face. "So you still haven't told me what's going on between you and Ethan."

"Nothing, nada, zip."

"Why not?"

"I live in California, and will be heading there as soon as the lawyers and the real estate people get their heads out of their butts and figure out how and when Ethan can close on this place."

"So there is a boyfriend back in sunny California waiting for you."

"No boyfriend, no fiancé, no husband." She stared at her glass and wondered if perhaps she hadn't had enough. She was starting to depress herself. "There's no one there but my parents and some real good friends."

"You've got friends here." Carol Ann opened her arms and said, "What am I, chopped liver?"

She laughed at the absurdity of it. Carol Ann was chopped liver the day Olivia Hamilton became a glamour queen. "Lord, I have missed you."

"Ditto. We should have stayed in touch. Once in a while when I ran into your grandmother, I asked about you and what you were up to."

"You did?" She remembered Ethan saying about the same thing. "Ethan asked too."

"So what are you going to do about Mister Gorgeous Gallery Owner?" Carol Ann stood up and stretched. "I might be an old married woman, but I know there was more than just meat loaf cooking in that kitchen, Olivia."

"I'm not into casual sex." She stood up and swayed for a moment before catching her balance. "Ethan says there will be nothing casual about it."

Carol Ann started to choke or laugh; it was hard to tell which. "And you let him walk out of this house after a comment like that?"

"What was I supposed to do? Invite him upstairs?"

"Hell yes." Carol Ann shook her head. "Aren't you curious to see where all those sparks you two shot off each other can lead to? You're a grown woman. He's a grown man. There's no one back in California waiting for you. And I'm pretty sure he's not seeing anyone from around here. So what's stopping you?"

At one time Carol Ann had known all of her secrets. They had shared everything, from their fears to their desires. Even though they were as different as night and day in some ways, deep down inside they had been the same. There had been nothing but truth between them. In a rush of fear, Olivia blurted out the truth. "I don't want to be hurt."

Carol Ann gave her a big hug. "You can do nothing, go back to California and not be hurt, but you would never know the 'might-have-beens.' Or you could take what time you have left here and explore a couple of those possibilities. I'm not saying to jump his bones the next time he comes over"—Carol Ann wiggled her eyebrows—"even though I can think of worse ways to spend an evening together."

Olivia walked Carol Ann out into the foyer. "They are such nice bones too."

Carol Ann chuckled as she stepped into her shoes and pulled on her coat. "I'm not blind. I noticed."

Olivia stepped into her shoes and started to lace them up. "I'll tell Tom on you."

"He won't believe you because I'll be too busy jumping his

bones." Carol Ann frowned at her. "Where do you think you're going?" She pulled on her hat and gloves.

Olivia pulled on her own coat, buttoned it way up, and then tugged on her purple knit hat and mittens. "I'm not letting you walk home alone."

"It's only two streets over. I think I can find my own house."

"Never doubted that you couldn't." She picked up the key to the front door and stepped out on the porch. "We always walked each other halfway home. Why stop now?"

"Because you're half drunk." Carol Ann chuckled as she stepped off the porch.

"Fresh air will cure that, and I'm not that drunk that I wouldn't be able to find my way home again." They started to walk down the middle of the street. For only being nine-thirty at night, the streets were empty of traffic. The residents of Misty Harbor were all tucked in their warm little houses. The cold night air felt crisp and fresh. "There's no smog in Maine."

"Can't say that there is." Carol Ann turned right onto Main Street. "Did I thank you for a wonderful dinner? You didn't have to go through all that trouble of baking cupcakes for the kids. But they were so cute, with those snowmen faces on them."

"It was only meat loaf, and I enjoyed decorating the cupcakes." She had packed up the remaining treats and sent them home with Tom and the kids earlier. The alcohol haze in her brain was starting to clear. "And your kids aren't monsters. They were adorable and polite."

"I know, but in our house 'monster' is a term of endearment." Carol Ann stopped and glanced down Main Street. All the antique lantern lamp posts were lit and decorated for Christmas. The display windows in all the shops were lit and cast a warm golden glow over the sidewalks. Snow blanketed roofs, lawns, and the occasional spot where the snowplows or shovels hadn't reached. "It's beautiful, isn't it?"

"I used to think it was as near to perfect during the summer months. Now, I'm not too sure. Winter here has its own charm."

Carol Ann turned up Ethan's street. "Come on, I know a shortcut."

Olivia followed her up the street and smiled at the houses all decorated for Christmas. Multicolored lights were strung everywhere. Lit icicles hung from eves of houses. Plastic Santas, complete with sleigh and reindeer, were perched on rooftops. She loved the decorations, but she hadn't bothered to put any up at her grandmother's. The wreath her grandmother had hung on the front door before coming to California was the only exterior ornament. She wanted to cry at the thought of that lonely wreath.

"This is where I leave you, Liv." Carol Ann gave her another hug. "We need to get together again before you leave. Maybe do some Christmas shopping or stop in at Krup's for a cherry Coke or two."

"Definitely." It had been great seeing Carol Ann and her family. Her friend had made her laugh and cry and brought back all those wonderful memories.

Carol Ann pointed to Ethan's house, up the street. "Ethan won't mind if you cut through his yard. Then you'll be home safe and sound."

"Where are you going?"

"Through old man Thompkins's yard. I live right behind him, and he never minds when the kids use his yard as a soccer field. I just have to outrun his stupid dog, Salisbury, and I'll be home free."

"His dog?" She didn't like the sound of that. "What kind of dog?"

"A little one, don't worry." Carol Ann gave her another

hug, hurried across old man Thompkins's front yard, and then disappeared around the side of the big dark house.

Olivia stood there in the middle of the street wondering what she should do now. Should she go check on Carol Ann or just head home? A vicious high-pitched barking emerged from the back of the house Carol Ann had just disappeared around. She heard her friend yell something that suspiciously sounded like, "Oh shit," and the barking grew more frenzied.

The little dog sounded like it was going to have a heart attack or at least bite Carol Ann's leg off. Lights in a few of the surrounding houses went on, and she could tell that a couple of back patio lights were flipped on as well. She hurried across the front yard and moved closer to the side yard that Carol Ann had disappeared around.

A moment later, while she was looking for a big stick, she heard Tom's voice yelling at Salisbury to be quiet before he woke the kids. Then Tom was yelling at a giggling Carol Ann. She could tell that Tom wasn't angry at his wife, and in the middle of his tirade his words stopped suddenly. A moment later she heard Tom curse and say, "Let's go inside before someone sees you and we'll get arrested for indecent exposure."

Carol Ann's laughter was probably waking up the kids and half the neighborhood. A moment later a door slammed somewhere and the barking stopped. Quiet filled the neighborhood once again.

Amused, yet encouraged that her friend had found what she had been looking for right in her own hometown, Olivia wondered if she should just head home the way they had come, or should she cut through Ethan's yard. Ethan didn't have a dog, but he had something much more dangerous.

She was afraid that Ethan had the power not only to turn her world upside down. Ethan held the power to hurt her like she had never been hurt before.

Five

Ethan jotted down another idea on the yellow legal pad in his lap. The ten o'clock evening news had just started, but he wasn't paying it any attention. He had more important things to concentrate on, like the expansion of his gallery. Watching Carol Ann's kids enjoy their snowmen cupcakes earlier tonight in Olivia's kitchen had given him another idea.

He could open up a tearoom in the large kitchen. The kitchen was big enough to hold a couple of small tables and chairs. Amelia's slate patio had room for quite a few more tables, possibly with umbrellas for shade. Customers could enjoy a tall glass of something cold to drink and fancy little cookies, or some other delicacy, while enjoying the gardens and some discretely tagged exterior merchandise. Winter months there would be plenty of coffee, hot chocolate, and cinnamon tea served in the toasty warm kitchen.

The more he thought about it, the more he liked the idea. Of course, that meant hiring some additional help, but he would be needing to do that anyway if he increased the size of the gallery. It would give potential customers another reason to step into his shop.

The ringing of the doorbell pulled him away from his latest brainstorming. Who could that be at this time of night? He wasn't expecting anyone. He put the pad and pen down and went to answer the door.

He opened the door and felt his heart rate kick up a beat or two. Olivia, bundled up against the cold, stood on his doorstep. "Hi, is something wrong?" He stepped back and allowed her to enter his home. "Where's Carol Ann?"

"I just walked her halfway home." Olivia glanced around the foyer with interest. "I was going to cut through your yard, but I decided to stop in and say hello first." Olivia stepped into the living room. "Am I disturbing you?"

Under his breath he answered, "More than you would ever guess."

"What was that?" Olivia tugged off her hat and mittens and started to unbutton her coat.

He noticed that Olivia wasn't quite walking right. She was listing to the side. Olivia and Carol Ann had obviously celebrated their reunion in style. Adorably cute Summer Breeze was drunk. "I said no, you didn't disturb me. I was just writing down some ideas, that's all."

"And watching the news." Olivia frowned at the television screen, which was showing some perky weather girl pointing out the smiling-faced clouds blowing wind across the entire state of Maine. A few fancy snowflakes dotted the shoreline. She pointed at the screen and demanded, "Does that mean *more* snow?"

Considering that the grass was still peeking up through the snow on his front lawn, he didn't want to see how Olivia would act when a full-blown nor'easter hit. "That means flurries. Probably won't amount to much."

"What's your not much?"

"An inch or two." He wondered if she realized how cute she looked with her black curls all over the place and the flush of cold brightening her cheeks. Or the way her blue eyes sparkled like precious gems. Olivia was pure temptation. "Did you and Carol Ann open that last bottle of wine?" Maybe buying three bottles of wine hadn't been that good of an idea. The second bottle of wine had been half empty when he had left.

Olivia gave him a lopsided smile as she tossed her coat onto the recliner he had been sitting in earlier. "Did you know that you have excellent taste in wine?" Olivia sat down on the couch and flashed him a come-hither look that heated his blood.

"You finished that third bottle, didn't you." He couldn't tell how tipsy she was. Olivia wasn't falling-down drunk, but that didn't mean she was in her right mind.

"Carol Ann poured it about the same time she was advising me to explore the possibilities." Olivia glanced around the large living room and smiled. "I like your house. You changed it from when I was here last."

"My parents liked everything dark. Dark paneling, dark carpet, dark furniture. I prefer something lighter." During the six years he had owned the house, every room had gone through a total transformation, except for the guest bedroom. He kept that the way his parents liked it, because they were the ones who used it the most. He knew he shouldn't ask, but he was curious. "What possibilities were you and Carol Ann talking about?" *Was there a chance that Olivia was thinking about staying in Misty Harbor?*

"About all the possibilities life throws at us, and then how we choose which one to go for." Olivia nodded toward the fireplace, where a low-burning fire was glowing. "You have a thing for fires, don't you? Every time you come over to my place, you light one."

"I'm a winter-type guy. I like to relax in the evening in front of a fire, especially if snow is falling."

"I'm a summer person. I love lazy days swimming, sunning, and eating ice cream. I even like to putter around in a garden." Olivia gave him a strange sad look. "We're total opposites, aren't we?"

"That's one way to look at it." He had to wonder if it was true that opposites did attract. "Or we could have complementary personalities. You know, like on a color wheel, the complete opposite is a complementary color." He liked that theory better.

"I never thought of it that way." Olivia grinned. "It must be the artist in you."

"I'm no artist." He chuckled at the memory of all the art courses he had taken over the years. He had passed every one of them, but not because he had any talent. His grades had reflected his effort. He had tried like hell to be something he wasn't. He had tried his hand at painting, sculpturing, pottery, animation, and even a course in stained glass. He had been mediocre at best. The only hobby he enjoyed and still did was photography. He didn't possess the talent to make it in the art world, but he could take a decent picture. "You know the old saying, those who can't, teach? Well, in the art world there's a saying, those who have no talent, sell it."

"That's a little harsh."

"But true." He liked the fact that Olivia was trying to stick up for him. "I might not be able to draw or paint, but I know a great painting when I see one. I can spot talent a mile away. Most artists prefer to be left alone to do their craft. They know virtually nothing on how to sell it, price it, or even where to find the customers. Their only concern is to make enough money to barely get by and to buy more supplies so they can go on to their next project."

"That's where you come in, right?"

"Right." Olivia didn't seem so tipsy now, but there still was no way tonight would be ending the way he wanted it to end. With Olivia in his bed. He had never taken advantage of a woman in his life, and he wasn't about to start with Summer Breeze. "Come on, I'll walk you home."

"Now? Don't I get a tour of your home?"

"Yes, now." Olivia's soft fluffy sweater clung to her breasts, and considering how wonderfully tight her jeans were, they would be outlawed in three different states that he knew of. Just having her in his living room, all soft and inviting, was enough to test his resolve. There was no way he was getting Olivia within twenty feet of his bedroom. "You can have a tour tomorrow night if you still want one."

Olivia stood up and her slight wobble confirmed his resolve to take her home. He got on his shoes and coat and watched as she tugged on her winter gear. He checked his fireplace, to make sure it would be fine for the next couple of minutes, and then headed for the back door. "We'll go through the backyards. It's shorter than walking around the block." He opened the door and followed her out into the night. Selma had left her back porch light on again, and while the yards were cast in shadows, there was still plenty of light by which to see.

Olivia stopped under an old oak tree and looked up. "You got rid of the tree fort."

"About eight years ago. I was too old to play in it, and the lumber was starting to rot." He had many fine memories of his old tree house. If memory served him right, Olivia had been in the fort only twice. Both times had been at his parents' urging.

"That's a shame." Olivia shook her head and walked through the gate separating her backyard from his. "My grandmother never closed this gate, did she?"

"Not that I can remember. Once in a while I did, but never Amelia."

"To keep me out of your hair, right?" Olivia laughed. "I was a royal pain, wasn't I?"

"That's a double-edged question if I ever heard one. If I say yes, you'll be mad. If I say no, you'll know I'm lying."

Olivia laughed as she stepped onto the slate patio and nearly slid. He wrapped his arms around her before she went down. "Watch your step, it's icy." Her purple mittens clung to his arms. A fat black curl had escaped her hat and was tickling his nose. He could smell the fruity scent of her shampoo. Olivia smelled like apples and pears.

What was it with women and their fruity temptation? Wasn't it Eve who offered Adam a bit of the forbidden fruit?

He slowly released her and gently held her elbow as they walked the rest of the way across the slick patio to the kitchen door. "Got your key?"

"It's unlocked."

He turned the knob, and sure enough, it was unlocked. He shook his head, waited for her to enter the warmth of the kitchen, and then followed her in. "I know this is Misty Harbor, and a far cry from southern California, but you have to at least lock the doors, Liv."

Olivia liked the way he shortened her name. He made it sound all intimate and breathless. She also had liked the way she had felt in his arms moments before. She held up the keys she had put in her pocket when she had headed out the front door with Carol Ann earlier. "I locked the front door, does that count?"

"Only if you want to be half robbed." Ethan unzipped his coat, but didn't take it off. "Let me go check out the place to make sure no one got in while you and Carol Ann were out staggering in the streets."

"We weren't staggering." She stuck her tongue out at his back. She might be in a wine-induced good mood, but she wasn't drunk. She would know the difference. Since Ethan obviously wasn't planning on staying, she stood in the middle of the kitchen and waited for his return. She heard him go upstairs and then there was the occasional squeak above her head marking his progress through the rooms. She tossed her coat and hat onto a chair. A moment later she could hear him coming back down the steps.

She didn't understand why he had been in such a rush to get her out of his house. She had been rude enough to ask for a tour, and he had been impolite enough to refuse. Strange, she had thought Ethan would be more than glad to experience some possibilities with her.

His comment the other day that sex with him wouldn't be casual had been her first clue. The second had been the knee-melting, toe-curling kiss they had shared earlier this evening when he had left her and Carol Ann alone to reminisce. She and Ethan had been alone in the foyer, and Carol Ann, the sneak, was supposed to be in the kitchen drying the last of the dessert plates. When he had pulled her into his arms, there hadn't been a moment's hesitation on her part. She had wanted that kiss as much as Ethan.

So why the sudden change of direction? Ethan didn't strike her as the kind of guy who got cold feet. Ethan didn't strike her as the kind of guy who got cold *anything*.

"You're all locked up," said Ethan as he entered the kitchen. "I turned off your front porch lights and checked on the fire." Ethan headed for the door.

She stepped in front of him and pressed her palms against his chest. "What, no kiss goodbye?"

"I don't think that's such a good idea right now."

"Why not?"

"Because there are three empty wine bottles sitting on the counter behind you." Ethan brushed his lips against her forehead. "I'll kiss you goodbye twice tomorrow night, okay?"

"No." She leaned forward and teased the corner of his mouth with her lips. "I'm not drunk, Ethan."

Ethan groaned as her lips slowly moved to the other corner of mouth. "What do you think you're doing, Liv? I'm only human."

She could feel the rapid beat of his heart under her palm. "I know, I can feel your heartbeat." She trailed her mouth back over his lips. "The beat matches mine."

"Liv?" Ethan's arms wrapped around her waist and pulled her closer.

"Shhh. . . ." Her tongue outlined his lower lip, and her arms encircled his neck. The leather of his jacket felt cool beneath her fingers, but everything else was warm. "I'm experiencing some possibilities." She smiled as Ethan deepened the kiss and crushed her breasts against his chest.

Ethan released her mouth and trailed a moist path down the side of her neck to the valley below her throat. "I have no idea what you are talking about."

Olivia tilted her head back, to grant him further access. "I'm tasting possibilities." The back door pressed against her shoulders as Ethan continued his downward path with his mouth. Ethan's large warm hands cupped her bottom and tilted her hips forward. She gasped as his mouth brushed the front of her sweater, directly over an overly sensitive nipple. She had never felt this way with another man before. What was so special about Ethan that he could make her want so much with a simple kiss? On a sigh, she whispered, "Wonderful possibilities."

Ethan's hands caressed her hips and the indentation of her waist on their course upward. He raised his head and gazed into her face. "Tell me again you're not drunk."

"I'm not drunk." She caressed his rough jaw and read the heat and desire in his eyes. She also could see the doubt. Ethan didn't believe her.

She groaned out loud when Ethan released her and took a step back while shaking his head. Her empty arms fell to her sides. "You're leaving, aren't you?" She knew the answer, but wanted to hear him say it.

"Have dinner with me Saturday." Ethan's thumb caressed her lower lip. "We'll go someplace nice and have a real date."

"What? My cooking isn't nice enough?" she teased. "I'm all out of leftovers, so I won't be forcing you to eat everything in my refrigerator anymore." She was happy that he wanted to take her out, but it wasn't necessary. She'd much prefer the privacy of her own home when she was with Ethan. Just in case the temptation to explore a couple more of those possibilities arose.

"After dinner we'll go back to my place and you can help

me decorate my tree." Ethan's fingers wove their way into her hair. "You did such a fine job decorating the one at the gallery, that I really could use your help at my house."

"You'll give me a tour of the house?"

"If you want." Ethan's gaze caressed her face. "I'll give you anything you want, Summer Breeze."

Olivia felt the softness of the Persian rug beneath her stocking-clad feet as she stretched to reach a higher branch to hang an ornament on Ethan's tree. Saturday night had finally come, and with it a wonderfully romantic dinner out with Ethan.

The past three nights she had seen Ethan, discussed the future sale of her house, and even watched some television with him. They had shared popcorn, opinions, and the most fabulous kisses in the world. Ethan was always the one to call a halt when things got too heated on the couch, on the porch, or in the kitchen. It didn't matter where they were—they always seemed to be kissing.

She liked that about Ethan. The man loved to kiss, and he was a world-class kisser.

Tonight there was something special in the air between them. Something hot and primitive. It had nothing to do with the seven-foot tree in Ethan's living room, and everything to do with the way he had looked at her over a candlelit dinner. Ethan had looked at her as if she were the only woman in the world for him.

Considering the heat that had been in her stomach and the rapid pounding of her heart, she was afraid she had been looking back with the same emotion burning in her eyes. She was pretty sure the dinner had been first class all the way, but she wouldn't swear to it. The only thing on her mind all night long had been the fact that they would be coming back to his place, and he had promised that he would give her anything she wanted tonight.

Tonight she wanted it all.

She had been thinking of nothing else since that first afternoon Ethan had showed up on the front porch ringing her grandmother's doorbell. She didn't think it was possible to maintain a crush for ten years, without seeing the object of that infatuation. What she'd felt for Ethan ten years ago had been nothing compared to what she was feeling tonight.

She was still heading back to California at the beginning of January, as soon as a settlement took place. But she'd be going back with the precious memory of making love with Ethan. She wanted that memory.

Ten years ago out at Sunset Cove, one hot summer night, one of the local boys had tried to get a little fresh with her. At first she had thought she was handling the jerk pretty well. Then the jerk decided he didn't like no for an answer. The jerk wanted first base and beyond, and it didn't matter if she was letting him up to bat or not. It had been Ethan who had heard her protests and come to her aid.

Ethan had taken one look at her tear-streaked face, glanced down to make sure she was physically okay, and probably to check to see how far the boy had pushed it, and yelled at the top of his lungs for Carol Ann. Her best friend had ditched her boyfriend for the rest of the night and offered comfort, anger, and plans for retaliations. Payback hadn't been necessary. Ethan had handled it. Rumor had it that Ethan had dragged the boy home to his father and explained the situation, leaving her name out of the conversation. The father had taken care of the rest.

She had come away from that experience a little bit wiser about whom to kiss, and with a whole lot of embarrassment when it came to facing Ethan again. Carol Ann had been her rock, and with her sense of the absurd, the incident had been put into proper perspective and never had the chance to fester into some life-altering psychosis. She never saw Ethan as a hero. Her rescuer, her protector, yes. Hero, no. To her, a hero put his life in danger to perform a service to someone else. Ethan's life was never in jeopardy. He had outweighed the jerk by a good fifty pounds and was four years older. She might have had a crush on Ethan ten years ago, but she never hero-worshiped him.

Looking back on that night, she had been the young and foolish one to get into that situation in the first place.

"What's on your mind?" Ethan was standing next to her holding out another glittering Christmas ball.

She brought the tree back into focus and realized they were almost done decorating it. They probably hadn't said more than a few sentences to each other since Ethan had opened up the first box of decorations. "Sorry, I was just remembering something."

"Care to share?" Ethan handed her the ornament and reached into the box for the next one.

"I was thinking about a certain night, the last summer I was here. Out at the cove." She wondered if Ethan ever thought about it again.

Ethan appeared to be concentrating extra hard on hanging one simple ball. "What night was that? I was there a lot back then."

"You remember which night." She stepped away from the tree and looked at him. "I never got to personally thank you for coming to my rescue."

Ethan frowned. "You baked me a chocolate cake and left it with my parents the next day without an explanation. My mom thought it was cute, while Dad gave me a lecture on stringing along a young girl."

"Ouch." She tried not to smile as she took the last ornament from the box. "Sorry about that." She reached up and placed the ball in the only empty spot on the tree. She turned to Ethan and placed a kiss on his cheek. "Thank you."

Ethan looked surprised. "That's it?"

"What were you expecting? A parade?" She liked the way Ethan flushed. "That night was beginning to feel like an elephant around my neck. We both knew it was there, but neither one of us was willing to bring it out in the open."

"You're okay with it?"

"Okay, no. But it did propel me into taking some self-defense classes in college. It didn't leave any scars, if that's what you're asking. I'm not afraid of men, or forming a personal relationship, and I'm not frigid."

Ethan seemed to relax. "I'm glad I could help."

"You did, but Carol Ann helped more." She chuckled at the memory. "Do you know how many ways there are to castrate a sixteen-year-old male?"

Ethan cringed. "That sounds like the Carol Ann we all know and love." He reached out and captured her cheek with the palm of his hand. "Why are you telling me all of this now?"

"Because once we are in bed together, I don't want you thinking I'm doing it out of gratitude." She slowly smiled. "And just for the record, I no longer have a crush on you. You were replaced by Robby Koznecki at my seventeenth birthday party. He had long hair and a motorcycle. My parents forbade me to see him. It ended tragically when he knocked up one of the cheerleaders at school."

His fingers trembled against her jaw. "I see." His gaze locked with hers. "When exactly is this event going to take place?"

"Tonight." She reached out and wrapped her arms around his neck. Once they had started to decorate the tree, Ethan had taken off his suit jacket and tie. His white shirt was crisp and bright against the strong column of his throat.

"Tonight?" Ethan's fingers skimmed her throat and teased the pounding pulse he found there. "Why tonight?"

"Because time is growing short. I've got to leave in a couple of weeks." She gently nipped at his lower lip. "I want to spend every moment I can with you, Ethan."

A rumble worked its way up Ethan's throat as he tugged on her lower lip and sighed, "Thank God," into her mouth. The kiss started hot, and built toward desperation.

She broke the kiss and tried to catch her breath. "Ethan, I want that tour now." She playfully bit his chin. "Start with your bedroom."

Six

Ethan slowly lowered Olivia to her feet. His heart was ready to pound out of his chest. He wasn't sure if it was from anticipation or from carrying Olivia up the flight of stairs. Olivia had come right out and said she wanted to make love with him. What man's heart wouldn't have been thundering?

He brushed a kiss across her forehead and whispered, "This is my room."

Olivia's gaze never left his face. "Nice room."

He chuckled. The little minx hadn't even glanced around. "Did I tell you how beautiful you look tonight?" His fingers skimmed her arms and caressed the satiny smoothness of her long-sleeved dress. Olivia's demure black dress was seductive in its innocence. It concealed more than it showed, and that was probably the enticement. All through dinner she had been driving him out of his mind with her hungry glances and knowing smiles.

"Twice, but the third time might be the charm." Olivia's fingers toyed with the buttons on his shirt. "You look handsome, as always. But I already told you that." The first button slipped through the buttonhole.

His fingers trailed up Olivia's backbone, feeling the zipper as he went. He felt the second button on his shirt come undone, and slowly started to pull the tab of the zipper downward. Olivia smiled slowly and a third button was released. The zipper stopped its descent below her waist. He stroked his fingers back up her backbone. This time he felt nothing but warm silky skin and a very thin bra strap.

Olivia tugged his shirt from his pants, quickly unbuttoned the rest of the buttons, and then slowly pushed it off his shoulders. With hurried fingers, she quickly pulled his white T-shirt up and over his head. It landed without a sound somewhere over his right shoulder. He shuddered as Olivia's palms caressed his bare chest.

He closed his eyes and savored the feel of Olivia's hands rubbing his skin and her delicate fingers weaving their way through the dark curls splattered across his chest. How many nights had he been dreaming of this moment? Praying for this moment? Too many to stand there with his eyes closed, that was for sure.

With a gentle touch, he brushed her dress over her shoulders and down her arms. The black dress, which had driven him to distraction all night, pooled at Olivia's feet.

He hadn't bothered to turn on any of the bedroom lights. The hall light was lit, and there was plenty of light pouring in through the open doorway. Olivia stood before him, standing in a pool of golden light, looking like every one of his fantasies blended into one. A cloud of black hair framed her beautiful face, and a mouth begging for more than just kisses gazed back at him.

Olivia's skin was pale as moonlight and crying out for his touch. A lacy black bra cupped her generous breasts. A tiny waist and the gentle flare of female hips caused his breath to hitch. What caused his mouth to go dry as the Mojave Desert was the tiny black triangle she was wearing as underwear, and the lacy garter belt holding up sheer black stockings.

It was a darn good thing he hadn't known during dinner what she had been wearing under that dress, or he would never have been able to swallow. As it was, he was having a difficult time breathing. Maybe the flight of stairs had done him in after all. At the ripe old age of thirty he was going to suffer a heart attack.

"Ethan?" Olivia's voice sounded worried, and shy.

He forced himself to glance up from those incredibly long legs. Seeing the confusion in her eyes brought him back to the living. "You're beautiful." He stepped closer and tenderly took her mouth with his own.

Olivia melted against him as he swung her back up into his arms and then gently laid her on his bed. He smiled at the picture she made lying across his bed. Her pale skin contrasted with the dark comforter. Olivia looked like she belonged there.

He felt like a little boy on Christmas morning. He didn't know what to unwrap first. He started with unhooking those sheer black stockings and slowly rolling them down her silky legs. When the stockings floated to the floor, he kicked off his own shoes and socks. He brushed the garter belt and panties down as she reached for his belt and started to undo his pants. He captured her wandering fingers before he embarrassed himself, and completed the job himself.

Olivia lay before him wearing only a lacy black bra, with nothing covering her thatch of black curls. He stood there gazing at her for so long that she got to her knees and stared back at him. "Is there a problem, Ethan?"

"Yeah, you're perfection, and I'm scared to death that I might break you."

Olivia smiled and pulled down the thick comforter. A couple of the pillows fell off the bed, but Olivia didn't hide beneath the blankets. She sat in the middle of the bed and took off her bra. "There is no such thing as perfection, Ethan. I'm just a woman who wants you very much."

He reached into the nightstand and with shaking fingers he rolled on a condom. The bed dipped as he got on it and leaned over her. Olivia fell to her back and lay there staring up at him. "You will never be 'just a woman,' Liv." He reached out and traced a path over her moist lips, across her chin, and down her throat. His fingers stopped just short of her breasts. He smiled when she arched her back, silently begging for more. "Do you like it when I touch you, Liv?"

Olivia gasped with pleasure as his hands gently cupped her breasts and his thumbs brushed against her nipples. "Yes," she sighed as her nipples hardened more. Her hands reached up and pulled him down on top of her. She wanted to feel the weight of his body. She wanted Ethan's mouth on her. Night after night of frustrating kissing, which Ethan never let get out of control, had taken their toll. She wanted Ethan, and she wanted him now.

Ethan's mouth crushed hers as his tongue plundered and his hands stroked everywhere at once. Her breasts, her hips, her thighs. Heat spiraled and twisted as his fingers and mouth teased and tormented.

Her hands urged him on as her mouth answered his every demand. Her fingers stroked his back and gripped his hard buttocks. She opened her thighs wider and tried to encircle his waist, but he moved lower and tugged one of her nipples deep into his mouth. She nearly climaxed. "Ethan, please."

"Please what?" Ethan's mouth captured the other nipple and proceeded to torture her out of her mind. One of Ethan's fingers skimmed her inner thigh and entered her. His mouth left her breast and he stared up into her face. "Please this?"

She shook her head as she threaded her fingers into his hair and tugged his mouth toward hers. "Please more." She bit his lip a little harder than she had planned and then instantly stroked it with her tongue. "I want all of you."

Ethan growled as she wrapped her thighs around his waist and pressed herself against the head of his hard penis. With one heavy thrust he entered her and stilled.

Olivia wrapped her legs tighter and arched her hips. She felt him slip in a bit farther. She moaned and Ethan froze.

"Liv, sweetheart, am I hurting you?" Ethan's mouth was pressed against her shoulder.

"No, but if you don't start moving, I'm going to get extremely angry." She tried to arch her hips again, but this time Ethan wasn't moving.

Ethan chuckled against her collarbone as he slowly started to pull his way out of her. Just when she thought he was going to leave her, he slowly sank back in. He filled her to the limit. Only to start the whole process over again. "You mean like this." Ethan sounded like he had just run across the state of Maine.

"There's something called payback, Ethan." She bit his earlobe and she felt his movement increase, along with his breathing. The pressure inside was building, and she knew she was about to come. "Faster, Ethan."

He pumped faster, and she came apart in his arms, shouting his name. Sadly, his ear had the bad sense of timing to be directly in front of her mouth when she screamed.

Ethan's release started the same instant he felt her go over the edge and the ringing in his ear started. He at least was gentlemanly enough to shout her name into the pillow next to her head.

Olivia pulled the two hot cake pans from the oven and placed them on top of the counter. As soon as they cooled off a bit, she would tip the chocolate cake out and onto the cooling racks.

Ethan's arms slid around her waist as he sniffed the air. "Is that what I think it is?"

"Yes, your favorite." She snuggled deeper into his arms. "Chocolate cake from scratch." She turned in his arms, brushed her mouth over his chin, and wondered when she would ever get enough of Ethan. She feared the man was in her blood and in her heart. "My grandmother's recipe."

Ethan's lips wandered up the side of her neck and teased her ear. "You smell good enough to eat." His teeth nipped playfully at her lobe. "An enticing combination of brown sugar and vanilla."

She tilted her head and gave him better access. "That would be the Christmas cookies I baked earlier." She was visiting Carol Ann tomorrow morning and she wanted to bring the kids a special treat. Carol Ann swore that Christmas cookies came from the dairy section of Barley's Food Store in those cute little rolls you cut into slices.

"God, I love your cookies." Ethan's mouth grew hungrier.

Her laugh caused him to stop his exploration of her neck. "You are so easy." She grinned seductively. "All I've got to do is offer you food, and you're mine."

"I'm yours without the food. I just need all those calories to keep up my strength." Ethan eyed the cooling cake. "How soon before I can get a piece?"

"It's for after dinner, not before." She stepped out of his arms. "So, if you don't leave me alone so I can get dinner started, it will be even longer."

"Fine, what can I do to help?"

She liked that about Ethan. He never expected her to wait on him, and he was always willing to help. She liked a lot of things about Ethan. Too many things. "You can peel a couple of potatoes and slice the cucumber for the salad. I'll do the rest."

Every night since they had become lovers, they had eaten dinner at her place, but spent the night in Ethan's queen-size bed. Ethan spent his days and a couple of evenings down at the gallery, while she had started the monumental job of going through her grandmother's things. The clothes had been the easy job. It was everything else in the house that was giving her problems. She didn't want to get rid of anything. Everything was too personal, too sentimental, or too meaningful.

A Hamilton had built this house back in the early eighteen hundreds. Amelia's bedroom set had been shipped over from England by the original builder. A Hamilton bride had slept in that bed for nearly two hundred years. How was she supposed to turn it over to some antique dealer, whose only thought would be to get the highest price possible for it?

She had spent the entire morning just going through the trunks in the attic. She hadn't seen a quarter of the treasures tucked away beneath the dormers before the tears had stopped her mental voyage into the past. Her grandmother always claimed that baking relieved stress. This afternoon she had put her grandmother's theory to a test, and she had been right. Decorating a couple dozen cookies and whipping up a cake for Ethan had made her feel better. Why didn't people bake more?

"Did you hear what I said?" Ethan gave her a funny look.

Olivia blinked and realized she was standing in front of the refrigerator with the door wide open. A package of chicken breasts was in her hand. She shook her head and closed the door. "Sorry, I was drifting again."

"You do that a lot lately." Ethan put down the peeler he had been using. "Anything I can help you with?"

"You said something about the gardens?" She glanced out the window above the sink. It was too dark to see anything out back.

"I was telling you about my trip to Karl James's place today."

"That's right. I forgot about that." Karl James was some local artist who had moved into the area about a year or so ago. Ethan was dying to carry some of his work, but it was too massive for the shop in town. "How did it go?"

"Great." Ethan resumed peeling. "He's got some pieces that blew me away. What that man can do with tree stumps and a chain saw and chisels should be classed as a miracle."

"What's that got to do with the gardens?" She seasoned the breasts and slid them into the oven.

"I'm probably going to have to call in a landscaper to change things around a little. I will need to showcase not only James's work throughout the yard and gardens, but other pieces as well."

She tried not to flinch as she stared into the oven's window at the chicken. Amelia's garden had been perfectly wonderful. Her grandmother, and her mother before her, and her mother before her, had never needed the services of a landscaper. The colorful chaos of flowers that bordered the picket fence had been planted with love, not with displaying artwork in mind.

Ethan's plans for turning the house into a gallery were wonderful. He was planning on leaving most of the house, and even some of the wallpapering, untouched. The integrity of the house would remain the same, but it would no longer be a home. It would be an art gallery. A distinguished gallery, but it would still be a shop.

The Hamiltons hadn't built this house to be a shop; they had built it to be a home. One filled with love, laughter, and the running footsteps of children. A home filled with the fragrance of bread baking in the oven and a riot of summer flowers blooming in the yard.

She realized now that was why her grandmother had left the house to her and not to her father. Amelia's son and his wife were settled in California and they were too old to have any more children. Amelia wanted Olivia to raise her family in the big wonderful home that overlooked the harbor.

She wanted the same thing as her grandmother. She had fallen back in love with the small coastal town. But how could she stay? Even with inheriting the house, she would still need an income to live on. Her heart would break every time she had to sell one of her grandmother's treasures to pay the bills. Constant repetitive heartbreak, or one quick break with the move back to California?

Where would her staying leave Ethan? He was planning on buying the house. She had already signed the contract for him to buy Amelia's house. Yellow legal pads filled with his ideas and plans were scattered all over his house, and this one. His dream was a larger gallery. Her returning home would give him that dream.

Where would her leaving leave them? Nowhere. There would be no "them." It would be her in California, miserable and lonely, and Ethan three thousand miles away. Something wonderful was happening between them, and she didn't think she had the willpower to walk away from it without discovering where it was all leading. She didn't want to leave. Not only for the house, but for Ethan. Most importantly, for Ethan.

She hadn't planned on it, but it happened anyway. She had fallen in love with Ethan. She was in love, and she now had one very big problem to solve.

Ethan stared at the woman he was falling in love with and wondered at her mood. In the past couple of days Olivia had changed. She had grown quieter, more prone to drift off into space, someplace he hadn't been able to reach her. The only time she seemed the same was when they were in bed together. Nothing had changed in that regard. She still responded to his touch. Still had the power to make him lose his control.

He never even imagined that making love with a woman could be like that. With Olivia it was more than two bodies coming together for mutual satisfaction. It was hotter, and growing almost desperate in its intensity.

Instant attraction had been his first reaction to Olivia's beauty, but it hadn't taken him long to realize there was a lot more to her than a pretty face and a killer body. He loved her laugh and the way her nose turned beet red whenever she was out in the cold. He loved the way she wasn't afraid to wear a ridiculous purple hat or spend an hour of her day down at Krup's General Store drinking hot chocolate and reminiscing with all the old timers. Olivia was generous with her time, and with her heart.

He knew she felt something for him. It was in her touch and in her eyes when she looked at him. It was in the extra-special care she went through every morning making him breakfast, no matter how many times he told her cereal was fine. It was in the way she melted beneath his kisses and wrapped her legs around his waist every night.

He knew what he felt for her. He was afraid he was no longer just falling in love with Summer Breeze. He was actually in love with the woman who once had been the biggest pain in his bottom.

In less than four weeks she would be out of his life. He had no idea how he was going to manage to breathe, let alone live, once she got on that plane. He had no idea how he was going to ask her to stay in Misty Harbor.

To stay with him.

Seven

Olivia kissed Ethan goodbye and shooed him out the front door as fast as she could. Leave it to Ethan to want to dawdle this morning of all mornings. Didn't he realize it was Christmas Eve, and she had a hundred things that needed to be done? Ethan kept giving her strange looks all morning long, but she couldn't contain her excitement.

She had solved her problem. Or at least she hoped she had figured it all out. Tomorrow morning when Ethan opened up the small present she had gotten him, she would know her answer. One of the surprises was that Ethan's presents wouldn't be under the tree in his living room. They would be under the tree in her parlor.

The seven-foot spruce was out in the garage, waiting to be dragged into the house. Five boxes of decorations were at the top of the stairs, waiting to be dragged down and put up. Christmas would be coming to Amelia's house this year.

Wasn't Ethan going to be surprised.

Olivia hurried up the steps and started to drag down the boxes one by one. She had gone through the boxes yesterday, while Ethan was at work, and figured out what else she needed. The tangled strings of lights looked old and frayed, so she had stopped at Krup's General Store and bought new lights and about fifty dollars' worth of other decorations.

The second thing she did was pull a muscle dragging the tree in from the garage, where she had hidden it from Ethan.

Getting it into the antique cast-iron stand she had found in the attic was a desperate act of brutal strength and curses. Lots of curses.

Olivia fortified herself with her fourth cup of coffee of the morning and then lit a blazing fire in the parlor fireplace. The tree branches needed to fall before she could start the decorating. With the caffeine rushing through her veins, she headed out front to drape pine garlands and red bows along the picket fence. By the time she came in from the cold, her hands were nearly frozen solid and it took a good twenty minutes standing in front of the fire to defrost them and to get feeling back into her toes.

The day was overcast and cold. Snow was once again predicted by nightfall. She turned on the porch lights and lit every candle she had bought yesterday. By late afternoon the tree was done, complete with a couple of brightly wrapped presents underneath for Ethan. The stack her parents had mailed her were neatly arranged next to Ethan's. A fire was burning brightly in both the parlor and the living room, and she had found a radio station that played continuous Christmas carols with no commercial interruptions.

The spirit of Christmas penetrated the house and filled her with hope.

All that was left was the food. Ethan was due home sometime after five. She wanted everything perfect for her surprise. She was staying in Misty Harbor.

It was nearly five-thirty when Ethan finally got to lock the doors of the Wycliffe Gallery. A couple of last minute shoppers had forced him to stay open later than he had planned. The customers had made it well worth his time, and had given him a chance to cool off. He no longer wanted to strangle Olivia.

The anger he had been feeling faded around four o'clock.

Now he was hurt and confused. Sometime after two o'clock he had gotten a call from the secretary of Olivia's lawyer. The woman wanted to verify his address for a letter she was mailing to him. He hadn't thought anything about it at first, figuring it was about the sale of the house, but then the woman said something about legal ramifications. When he questioned what legal ramifications, the woman told him that Olivia was no longer selling the house. Since Olivia had agreed in a legal contract to the sale, and she was the one breaking the contract, there obviously had to be some kind of ramifications. He couldn't remember what he had told the secretary before hanging up.

Ethan turned up his coat collar and headed for Olivia's. Snow had started to fall about an hour ago, but it wasn't sticking to the sidewalks and streets yet. By midnight he knew the worshipers at the late mass at the one and only Catholic church in town would have a hard time getting home.

How could Olivia do it? How could she sell someone else the house? It didn't make any sense. He had agreed to the price she was asking. She had sat there and listened to him as he had pointed out every improvement or change he wanted to do to the house. She had listened to his dreams for the house, and now she was selling it to someone else.

It didn't make any sense.

Olivia had been acting awfully strange and extremely happy for the past couple of days. It was as if she had a secret, a wonderful secret. He had chalked it up to Christmas and figured she had probably found him what she considered the perfect present. The only thing he had wanted from Olivia was her love. He didn't need any presents.

Now he didn't know what to think.

He slowly crossed the street, and headed up White Pine. Olivia's Christmas present lay heavy in his jacket pocket. Karen, his assistant, had come in about ten that morning and worked for a couple of hours so he could run into Bangor to pick up the gift. The tiny black velvet jeweler's box held all his hopes and dreams.

He was going to ask Olivia to become his wife and to stay in Misty Harbor with him. He loved her.

He would have sworn that Olivia loved him back. Now he wasn't too sure. How could she sell the house to someone else if she loved him? If she had wanted more money for it, all she had to do was ask. They could have worked something out.

The picket fence, with its fancy garlands and big red bows, caught his eye, but he wasn't in the mood to examine the fact that Olivia had decorated her fence. The bare porch from that morning now held a rocker piled high with foil-wrapped presents. An ancient pair of ice skates were draped across an antique sled that leaned against the siding. The most amazing decoration was the Christmas tree, fully decorated and lit, shining through the parlor's double windows.

What in the world was Olivia up to now? For weeks she had insisted she wasn't decorating her grandmother's house for the holiday. In less than nine hours she had the place looking like a magazine cover.

He opened the front door and stepped into a Norman Rockwell scene. The dark banister that soared to the second floor was wrapped in garlands and lights. Fires burned in both fireplaces, presents were under the tree, and candles were lit upon the mantels. There were even a dozen or so poinsettias scattered throughout the rooms. He could hear Christmas carols coming from the kitchen. Along with the clanging of pots and pans.

He kicked off his shoes and headed down the hallway to find Olivia. The entire house smelled of peppermint candles, pine cones, and muffins. Blueberry muffins if he wasn't mistaken. The closer he got to the kitchen, the more he smelled other fragrances. The smells of cinnamon, sizzling sausage, and French toast filled the air.

The sight of the kitchen stopped him in his tracks. It looked like the cabinetry had exploded. Pots, pans, and baking dishes were everywhere. Canisters of flour and sugar were on the counter, along with stacks of French toast, pancakes, and plates overflowing with muffins. A dozen blueberry muffins still sat in the baking tins.

Olivia, who had on a flower print apron over her demure black dress, looked like an elegant Betty Crocker standing in the midst of chaos. Baking ingredients were everywhere. The countertops and floor were dusted with flour. The sink was piled high with dirty dishes. A broken egg lay forgotten in front of the refrigerator door. Olivia stood in front of the stove flipping an omelet. She appeared to have more flour on her than in the canister.

Olivia gave him a radiant smile. "Oh, you're here." She slid the omelet onto a plate and pointed to a chair. "Quick, taste this and tell me what you think."

"What is it?" He hung his jacket on the back of a chair and sat. "What's going on, Liv?"

"It's a Western omelet." She slid the plate in front of him and handed him a fork. "Taste it before it gets cold."

The enticing aroma reminded him that he hadn't eaten any-thing since eleven-thirty. A fast-food hamburger and fries didn't even compare to what Olivia was serving him. He took a big bite and closed his eyes as he savored the taste of heaven. He opened his eyes and saw the look of anxiety on Olivia's face. She was acting as if she really cared what he thought. "It's delicious, Liv. Wonderful even." To prove his words, he took another bite.

Olivia's smile lit the room. "Do you think I can do it?" She crossed her fingers and held her breath.

"Do what?"

She glanced around the kitchen and for the first time real-ized what this must look like to Ethan. The man probably thought she was certifiable. Ethan would probably be right. Once she had started cooking up different breakfast ideas, she couldn't seem to stop. Even after she had gotten dressed, in what Ethan referred to as his favorite dress, she had to make one more batch of muffins. Blueberry muffins. Then when he had been late getting home, she had thought of a Western omelet. Thankfully he had walked in when he did. She had been contemplating Belgian waffles.

She brushed a wayward curl away from her eye, and hurriedly tugged off the flour-smeared apron. She brushed at a streak or two of flour dusting the front of her dress and wondered why Ethan hadn't gone screaming out the front door. She must look a wreck. "This wasn't exactly how I planned on telling you." She had been planning something a lot more romantic than forcing him to eat an omelet.

"Telling me what?" Ethan's voice held a strange tone. One she couldn't place. Ethan stopped eating, and stared at her.

"I'm opening a bed-and-breakfast in my grandmother's house." She took a deep breath and blurted out the rest of it. "I'm staying in Misty Harbor."

Ethan's mouth dropped open and the fork dropped to the table.

"I'm sorry about the house, Ethan." She hurried from the room and practically sprinted to the parlor. Her fingers grabbed the small gold foil–wrapped present under the tree. Her stocking-clad feet skidded across the kitchen floor. She would have fallen on top of Ethan if he hadn't pulled her down onto his lap.

Ethan's mouth found hers in a kiss that threatened to burn down the house with its heat.

She was the one to break the kiss before it got totally out of control and she ended up making love with Ethan on the kitchen table. She shoved the present into his hands and demanded, "Open it. I was going to wait until morning, but I can't now that you know about the bed-and-breakfast." She reached up and wiped a streak of flour off Ethan's jaw. She had no idea how it had got there.

"I don't care about a present, Liv. You're staying, that's all that matters to me." He tried to pull her closer, but she held her ground.

"Open it now, or no muffins." She wiggled into a more comfortable position and couldn't help but feel the bulge in Ethan's pants. The man was definitely in the holiday spirit now.

"Fine." Ethan ripped the wrapping off the small box and lifted the lid. Buried in red tissue paper was a single sheet of paper, which he slowly unfolded. It was a real estate advertisement for the old marine supply building down by the docks, but positioned almost perfectly in the center of Misty Harbor. The building had been empty for three years, but the owners had been adamant, they weren't selling. By the price listed very discretely at the bottom of the paper, they not only were willing to sell the building now, but were going to be reasonable about it. He glanced from the paper to Olivia. "What's this?"

"Right now it's an old empty building, but it could be an art gallery. Your gallery." She watched his face, trying to gauge his reaction to this sudden change in events. "I know how important enlarging your gallery is to you, and I felt so bad about taking this house off the market. I went to the local real estate office a couple days ago. This listing came in that morning and I went to see it." She worried her lip until Ethan's finger stroked her mouth. "I don't know a lot about galleries, just what you have been telling me. But I've got to tell you, Ethan, this place is perfect. It has more square footage, and is closer to the shops and the docks. It needs a lot of work, but the asking price is lower than what you were willing to pay for this place."

Ethan chuckled and tossed the paper and the box onto the table. "Liv, relax. I'll look at it later, but right now I have more important things to do."

"Like what?" What could be more important than his dream of enlarging his gallery?

Ethan stood up with her in his arms and headed for the stairs. "Like loving you in that frilly pink bed upstairs."

She wrapped her arms around his neck and smiled. "I was willing to settle for the kitchen table."

Three hours later Ethan still held her in his arms. This time they were bundled up in blankets and sitting out on the second-floor balcony. They were watching the snow fall and the boats come into the harbor for the Festival of Lights parade. Every Christmas Eve a dozen or so boats outlined themselves in Christmas lights and in the darkness they sailed into the harbor. Most of the town lined the docks and the surrounding area for the glorious and moving sight of all those lights reflecting off the water. Ethan wasn't in the mood to share Olivia with anyone tonight.

Olivia snuggled deeper into his arms. "Lord, this is beautiful."

He placed a kiss on top of her head. "Are you warm enough?" She had changed into jeans, sweatshirt, and a pair of those men's socks she had bought when she first came to town.

Olivia chuckled. "After what we just did, I don't think I will ever be cold again." She took another sip of her hot chocolate. "Need a refill yet?"

"I'm fine." They had decided to snack on blueberry muffins and hot chocolate while watching the boats, since they both hadn't had time for dinner yet. They had been too busy making love in Olivia's pink frilly bed.

Olivia was staying in Misty Harbor. He could finally catch his breath. He placed his empty cup on the wooden deck. The last boat was slowly making its way into the harbor. "Since you gave me the best Christmas present ever, I think it's only fair that you get yours tonight too." There had been more than keeping warm to his purpose of wearing his jacket up to the balcony.

"I can wait 'til morning." Olivia brushed his jaw with a kiss and then turned back to watching the boat.

He took the small box from his pocket and chuckled. "I think not." He placed it in her hand. "You demanded that I open mine, now you've got to open yours."

By the pale light coming from Amelia's old bedroom behind them, he could see Olivia's fingers tremble. She glanced from the box in her hand to his face and back several times before lifting the lid.

Whatever light there was, it seemed to hit the diamond ring perfectly. There wouldn't be a doubt in her mind as to what she was holding in the palm of her hands. His heart.

"Will you, Olivia Summer Breeze Hamilton, do me the honor of becoming my wife?"

The tears slowly rolling their way down Olivia's cheeks tugged at his heart, but her smile was radiant and filled with love. "I thought you would never ask."

As the last boat pulled up to the dock, Olivia slipped on the ring, and out of her clothes. Underneath a small mountain of blankets, on a cold snowy Christmas Eve, Ethan unwrapped the best present he had ever received.

Please turn the page for an exciting sneak peek
of Marcia Evanick' s newest contemporary romance
BLUEBERRY HILL
coming in December 2003!

One

Jocelyn Fletcher pushed the empty plate away from her and lightly patted her lips with the blue linen napkin. "There, you have fed me. Satisfied?" She studied her two sisters, Sydney and Gwen, who were sitting with her at the small table in the corner of Gwen's restaurant's kitchen. She didn't like the fact that neither of her sisters had wanted to discuss their plans for her when she'd arrived in Misty Harbor half an hour ago. All they had seemed interested in was making sure she was jamming food into her mouth. "Can we talk now?"

Gwen took the empty plate away and replaced it with another plate. This one contained a thick slice of blueberry pie. "Eat your dessert first. I made it especially for you this morning, after you called from the Connecticut rest stop."

"You never should have done that drive in one day," Sydney added. "Especially by yourself."

"Why? It's not like I could have gotten lost. You jump on Interstate 95 and head north." She reached for her fork and took a bite out of the pie. Delicious, warm, sweet blueberries melted against her tongue. She took a moment to savor the taste and then pinned both of her sisters with a knowing look. Being the youngest in the family had its drawbacks. The main one being everyone always treated her like the baby of the family. At twenty-six years old, she was hardly anyone's idea of a baby. "Both of you have made that same drive, so don't get all protective on me now." She smiled at Gwen as she forked up another mouthful. "This is delicious, Gwen, as usual. No wonder your restaurant is such a success."

"It's tourist season, and don't change the subject," Gwen said.

"Me change the subject?" Jocelyn shook her head at her sisters. "I'm trying to figure out what kind of job you've lined up for me, and you two are more concerned about my driving skills. What gives?"

"We didn't line up a job for you, Joc," Sydney said. "We lined up an interview, for tomorrow morning."

"Okay, that I can do. What about apartments? Small cottages? A place to rest my weary head after hauling in tuna all day?" Every time she had called her sisters during the past week, they had teased her about getting her a job with Bob Newman on his tuna boat. She wouldn't put it past them to actually think she was serious when she had made that comment to Sydney over the phone. Maybe she should have clarified that statement.

"The job you'll be interviewing for is a live-in position. You won't need an apartment." Gwen busied herself by pouring everyone more coffee. Sydney attacked her piece of pie like she hadn't eaten all day.

"What kind of job am I interviewing for? I didn't think governesses were much in demand any longer and I really don't think I'm merchant marine material." Her amused chuckle died in her throat when she saw the look Sydney gave Gwen. "What? What did you two do?" She was getting a horrible sinking feeling in the pit of her stomach. It was the same feeling she had when she had been four and had just eaten one of Gwen's mud pies that her sister had promised would taste exactly like a chocolate Easter bunny. It hadn't.

"Well, you're partially right," sighed Sydney.

"Partially a merchant marine? That would be what?" She stabbed at another piece of pie. "I know, a cruise ship director. I could be in charge of entertainment, right?"

"Not exactly," muttered Gwen as she glanced around the busy kitchen, keeping an eye on the staff, and avoiding making eye contact with her baby sister.

"Oh, please don't tell me that you signed me up to be the aerobics instructor. I hate aerobics. All that moving, stretching, and sweating and you never go anywhere. Now being the pool's lifeguard has possibilities."

Sydney rolled her eyes. "Jocelyn, it's not a cruise ship."

"Hell." She stared at her oldest sister. "Please tell me I'm not meeting with Bob Newman and the love of his life, his tuna boat named *Madison*, tomorrow morning."

"You're not," insisted Gwen. "The job interview we lined up has nothing to with boats or even water."

"But Sydney said I was partially right." A horrifying thought entered her tired mind. "Tell me you didn't sign me up to be some nanny or something."

Gwen and Sydney didn't so much as breathe as they stared back at her.

"No! Absolutely not!" Her voice rose dramatically. Maybe the Fletcher girls did do drama after all. Right at this moment she felt like she could try out for *Masterpiece Theater* as a homicidal maniac. She was about to strangle both of her sisters. "I would rather wrestle smelly tunas on the deck of Bob's boat all day long."

"It's only partially a nanny position." Gwen gave her a cheery smile.

"What's the other part?" She was a fool to ask, but she wanted all the facts before she killed her sisters. She was sure her brothers-in-law would want to know the reason behind their sudden status change to widowers.

Gwen looked helplessly at Sydney, who rolled her eyes and said, "Housekeeper."

"I'd rather wrestle *Bob* on the deck of his tuna boat! Are you two out of your minds? What do I know about being a nanny or a housekeeper?"

"You cleaned your own apartment, didn't you? Same thing, only more rooms." Gwen gave her a serene smile.

"You always said you wanted children one day, Joc. This would be the perfect opportunity for you to get some practice and see what it would be like." Sydney calmly finished her cup of coffee.

"I also said I wanted to get married too. That doesn't mean I'm going to go around shacking up with different guys to get some experience and practice." She shook her head at her sisters. "What were you thinking?"

"We were thinking that our sister was looking for a temporary job and a place to stay. This particular job fits both of those requirements very nicely." Gwen got up, grabbed the coffeepot, and started to refill the cups. "Quinn Larson is a very nice man who just so happens to be in a very tight spot at the moment."

"Where's Mrs. Larson? Why can't she watch her own kids and clean her own house?"

"Diane Larson was killed six weeks ago in a car accident, down in Boston." Sydney added cream and sugar to her coffee and watched her sister carefully.

"Oh, the poor man." She felt horrible for voicing her objections when he had just lost his wife. "He must be devastated."

"They were divorced," Gwen said as if that would explain it all.

"Oh." What was she supposed to say to that?

"From what we know, it was a friendly divorce. About two years ago, Diane took the three kids and moved to Boston. A year later the divorce was final. Quinn got the kids a lot during the summer months, holidays, and sometimes on long weekends. Quinn didn't seem bitter about the divorce, but he did seem to miss the kids when they weren't in Misty Harbor." Gwen glanced at Sydney. "Anything else you can think of to add?"

"The kids are in good health. Quinn brought them all in for a physical about four weeks ago."

"So, the wife picks up the kids, leaves the husband, and moves to Boston. The kids live with her full time, except when they are visiting Daddy. The ex-wife dies in some tragic car accident, so Daddy rushes to Boston to pick up his kids and bring them back to Misty Harbor?"

"That's it." Gwen frowned at her coffee. "The kids have pretty much been through hell."

"But now Larson wants to add to that hell by having some stranger move in with them and take care of the kids and the house?" Didn't sound like a smart plan to her.

"What do you expect the man to do, Joc?" Sydney asked. "He has to work to support them all."

"True, but can't he put them in day care or hire a baby-sitter?" Millions of single parents did that all the time.

"Quinn is the sheriff, which means he's on call twenty-four hours a day for six days a week. He needs someone there at night, in case he is called out. He can't be waking the kids up and taking them to his mom's."

"What's he been doing for the past six weeks?"

"He took the first week off to handle Diane's funeral and get the kids' stuff packed up and moved. Then his younger sister, Phoebe, moved back to Misty Harbor and into his house to help out."

"So why can't this aunt keep the job?"

"Phoebe is going to be opening up a stained-glass business. She's using Quinn's garage now as a studio, but she can't be doing both. Quinn doesn't want her to either. He said they are his kids, his responsibility." Sydney shrugged. "The man is going nuts trying to handle it all. So is Phoebe. No one has applied for the job yet, so Phoebe is very excited about this interview tomorrow morning with you."

"Even though I'll only be there temporarily?"

"So you are going to take the job?" Gwen asked excitedly.

"I didn't say that." Joc muttered something her sisters were better off not knowing into her cup.

"What was that?" By the sparkle in Sydney's eyes, Joc figured she had heard that word anyway.

"I asked how old were the kids. You said three, didn't you?" Three kids! What did she know about caring for one kid, let alone three? Baby-sitting never had been her favorite way to make extra money when she was a teenager. She had washed cars, mowed a few lawns, even pulled about a million weeds. But changing dirty diapers and wiping snotty noses weren't easy money in her book. If this Diane Larson had packed up the kids and moved away two years ago, the kids couldn't be that little, could they?

"Benjamin is five and will be starting kindergarten in September. I just did his physical needed for the enrollment." Sydney pushed away her empty pie plate. "Isabella and Victoria arc twin girls who just turned three last month. I remember their birthday was the day after the physical I gave them. Tori wanted a pony, and Issy wanted a mermaid."

"Did they get them?" Jocelyn remembered wanting a pony when she had been about six or so. Her parents had allowed her to take horseback riding lessons instead. She had kept up with those lessons until she discovered boys didn't appreciate a girl that smelled like a stable. A very ripe stable.

"I have no idea," Sydney said. "I think if Quinn had his way, he would have gotten the girls the moon if they had asked."

"He spoils them?"

"Wouldn't you?" asked Gwen. "Especially after what they have been through."

"Probably." She didn't like the pressure her sisters were placing on her. What did she know about raising kids? Especially those who had just lost their mother, and had been forced to move from their home and into their father's house. The poor kids' lives must be in a total upheaval. Heck, she had come to Maine to get her own life straightened out. She wasn't in any position to help ease the fears and the minds of three small children.

She looked at her two sisters, who appeared to be waiting for her to say she'd take the job. "What other kinds of jobs did you come up with?"

Disappointment flashed across Gwen's face, but Sydney just narrowed her eyes and said, "There's not much available, Joc."

"Most of the jobs are summer jobs, minimum wage, and filled by teenagers." Gwen glanced around her kitchen. "I could use an additional waitress, but it would only be part-time."

"The woman I hired to handle the phones, appointments and filing is going to be taking some time off soon," added Sydney. "I could use you in the office. I would love to redo old Dr. Jeffreys's filing system and to get more stuff onto the computer. You could help me out there."

"I don't want sympathy jobs." She shook her head at her sisters. "I appreciate the offer, but since I don't even want to live with you two, what makes you think I would work for you?"

"Fine," sighed Gwen. "Misty Harbor Motor Inn is looking for a housekeeper. You get to clean rooms all afternoon, and handle the laundry all morning. I didn't talk with Wendell Kirby yet, but maybe you can work something out with him for a room instead of a paycheck."

"Wendell Kirby? The same Wendell Kirby who proposed twice to me during my visit at Christmas?"

"The same." Sydney smiled.

"Didn't he get married yet?" Jocelyn had never seen a man so hell-bent on getting married. Someone would have thought they were giving away a free BMW with every marriage license.

"Not yet. He's still looking for wife number three. Maybe

three is his lucky number," Gwen said. "Of course he's going to be so happy once he learns you're in town for a while."

"Just think," Sydney added. "You can get to see him every day if you take the job at the Motor Inn."

Jocelyn shuddered at the thought. It had taken her a half an hour to shake Wendell from her side at Sydney's and Erik's Christmas party. Then he had left only because Gwen's husband, Daniel, had seen the hunted look in her eyes and had rescued her from the overzealous suitor. "What time did you say that interview is for tomorrow morning?"

The sick, queasy feeling returned to her gut when Gwen and Sydney shared a slow smile. She was four years old again, and she'd just been had.

Jocelyn followed Blueberry Hill Road around the bend and up the incline. The road twisted itself around what was appropriately referred to by the locals as Blueberry Hill. Sadie Hopkins's blueberry farm was on the other side of the hill, and nestled at the bottom were the crystal waters of Blueberry Cove. A few houses were scattered around the hill. It was to one of those houses she was headed. Quinn Larson's house shouldn't be that difficult to find. After all it was painted, what else, but blue.

Daniel, Gwen's husband, had drawn her a map to follow. Daniel, who had been born and raised in Misty Harbor, knew the area better than her sisters. He also knew where the Larson's house stood. He had also filled her in on the history of the house.

The house had been built two years after the Civil War ended by one of Joshua Chamberlain's lieutenants, Thomas Fuller. Thomas had purchased the entire hill, but over the generations parcels and pieces had been sold off for one reason or another. Seven years ago the last of Thomas's descendants, Ethan Fuller, had passed on, leaving the house empty. Sadie

Hopkins had bought a good chunk of the land, but Quinn and his wife, Diane, bought the run-down house and the surrounding couple of acres for a bargain basement price. Quinn had been working on the house ever since, but he had concentrated mainly on the interior. The exterior looked about the same as when they had bought it, only more faded, chipped, and worn. Daniel had warned her not to be put off by the exterior of the house.

Jocelyn slowed her car as a relatively new white mailbox came into view. Someone had taken blue paint and neatly printed the name "Larson" on the side of the box. A number 7 was below the name. Nothing was on either side of the road but trees, shrubs, and the occasional wildflower. She turned the car onto the gravel drive and headed through the trees. As she rounded a bend, she slowly stopped the car.

Before her sat a huge, at one time blue, house with wraparound porches. Most of the blue was now faded to a grayish color, but the roof looked brand new. So did most of the windows, but only half the shutters were still in place. Spots of brilliant white, where Quinn had obviously primed and replaced rotten siding and deck flooring, stuck out like zits on a teenager's nose. The outline of flower gardens could be detected skirting the porches, but the weeds had overrun them, choking most, if not all, of the flowers.

A big garage, which at one time had been painted the same shade of blue as the house, was off to one side. The garage didn't have the standard metal doors that rolled upward. Instead two sets of huge wooden doors were on horizontal tracks and had to be slid manually to the side. One of the sets of doors was open, but she couldn't see into the dim interior. Someone, probably the original owner, had attempted to landscape around the garage.

Jocelyn drove another fifty feet and parked behind a dark green SUV that had a bar holding blue and red lights bolted across the top. HANCOCK COUNTY SHERIFF'S DEPARTMENT was neatly painted across the back and the driver's door. An old white Jeep, with a ratty-looking canvas top, was parked near the garage. A shiny red wagon and two pink tricycles were on the porch. A bent basketball net was attached above one of the garage doors. A soccer ball, a baseball bat, and a catcher's mitt were lying in the grass, which looked as if it had been due for a mowing job about two weeks ago. Now the grass was due for a herd of goats.

Jocelyn made her way up onto the porch and was happy to note, while the exterior was in dire need of a paint job, it appeared structurally sound and safe. She knocked on the front door and stared at a miniature tea party that was going on in the wagon. Two Barbies were enjoying the imaginary meal. One Barbie was dressed in a whimsical gown of white satin and netting, a pearl necklace, and a shiny tiara. The other Barbie looked like she had just competed in the WWF Smackdown. In a mud ring no less. Brown gooey stuff was caked in Barbie's blond hair and across every inch of her well-endowed plastic body. Someone had dressed her in a leopard print bikini and black leather thigh-high boots. Jocelyn chuckled at the scene.

"Hi, you must be Jocelyn." A woman about the same age as herself stood on the other side of the screen door. The door was pushed open. "Come on in, I'm Phoebe Larson."

"Hi, Phoebe." She walked into the house and immediately had to step to the right to avoid a tent made out of blankets and chairs. She heard a giggle or two coming from under the blanket and grinned.

Phoebe's smile grew. "I'm sorry that the kids aren't here to meet you this morning. They went on a safari to Africa, but they promised to be back before lunch."

"Oh, that is a shame. I did want to at least meet them." She stepped around the end table that was holding down one end of the blanket. "I hope they are careful and watch out for lions and tigers. I hear that lions are particularly fond of little girls."

Phoebe led the way into the kitchen as more giggles erupted under the covers. "I heard just last week that some little boy was stepped on by an elephant. He was flatter than a pancake, and his father had to use a bicycle pump to blow him up again."

The giggles turned into full-blown laughter.

"It's good to hear their laughter." Phoebe walked over to the coffeepot. "Want a cup, it's fresh."

"Thank you." She took the cup Phoebe handed her.

"Sugar's on the counter." Phoebe opened the refrigerator and took out a carton of cream. "Quinn's upstairs on the phone. Business." Phoebe added cream to her cup and then handed Jocelyn the carton. "So I hear you're from Baltimore."

"Yes." She glanced around the recently remodeled kitchen with approval. Big and bright, with plenty of room and light. The kitchen flowed into an eating area, which flowed into a family room. Two sets of patio doors opened onto a back patio. Someone had cleared a section of trees out back. From the patio doors and the patio there was an unobstructed view of the cove below. "Wonderful view."

"It's one of the first things Quinn did when he bought this place." Phoebe joined her by the patio doors. "Gwen tells me you're a lawyer."

"You know my sister?"

"Met her a couple of times. I know Daniel better. We were in some of the same classes at school. He was a year ahead of me."

"So you grew up in Misty Harbor?"

"Born and raised." Phoebe pulled out a kitchen chair and sat. "Take a load off." Phoebe's eyes narrowed. "Even though it's not much of a load."

"Is that a comment on my height?" Being five foot, four inches in height sometimes was a disadvantage. Phoebe topped her by a good four or five inches.

"More about your weight." Phoebe chuckled. "Don't you

eat three meals a day? If you are going to be staying up here for any length of time, we need to fatten you up some. A good nor'easter will blew you clear out to Dead Man's Island."

"I'm a lot stronger than I look."

"Good, because you will need it to keep up with these kids." Phoebe gave an extravagant sigh. "It's only nine o'clock and so far I made 'smiling-face' waffles, unloaded the dishwasher, cleaned up the kitchen once, made the beds, and hung the first load of laundry." Phoebe nodded to the laundry basket filled with wet towels. "I was about to go hang the second load when you knocked."

"You obviously don't want me to take this job, do you?" She chuckled as she finished her coffee. Last night she had been bound and determined not to take the job. This morning she had pored over a stack of newspapers while sitting at Sydney's counter drinking coffee and working her way through a warm-from-the-oven Sara Lee coffee cake. None of the help wanted ads looked promising. The real estate rentals had been worse. At the height of tourist season, landlords were getting top dollar and seemed to be booked solid.

"Right now I'm desperate for you to take the job, but I wanted to be honest with you. You won't be doing anything that any other stay-at-home mom wouldn't do." Phoebe shook her head. "All these years I always envied those women who had kids and stayed at home. I thought how nice it would be to sleep late and never have to answer to a boss. The day would be yours to do with it as you please. As long as dinner's on the table for the hubby when he came home from work, your job was done."

"I take it Mr. Larson likes his dinner on the table when he walks through the door."

"With tourist season in full swing, my brother's hours are hectic and unpredictable. Usually he's reheating whatever I managed to cook for the kids earlier."

"He's not fussy?"

"Quinn fussy? Nope. Give that man the remote, clean uniforms and socks, and he's in heaven. The kids will drive you nuts, though. Benjamin doesn't like any of his foods touching each other on his plate. Issy won't eat anything green, so good luck getting her to eat her vegetables. And Tori will live on macaroni and cheese if you let her. Can you cook like Gwen?"

"Afraid not." Jocelyn chuckled as a little blond head peeked around the corner and then disappeared. "Why are you so desperate to escape? You seem to have everything under control."

"In this house, control is an illusion." Phoebe finished her coffee. "I work with stained glass. Been apprenticing for years. A couple of months ago I decided it was time for me to come home to Misty Harbor and start my own business. I was working out the last week of my notice when Diane was in the accident and Quinn needed my help. Quinn had already agreed to let me use his garage as a studio until I find something I can afford. I was supposed to move back in with my parents."

"You moved in here instead."

"Right. But the kids need a full-time keeper, and that doesn't leave me any time for my business. I have my first major load of glass being delivered this morning. My hands are itching to go, but my feet are planted here. My mom helps out as much as possible, but at her age, she shouldn't be chasing three small kids around all day and night."

"Phoebe," a deep voice shouted from the top of the stairs. "I've got to run, something has come up." Heavy footsteps thundered down the stairs. "Jocelyn Fletcher obviously doesn't want the job, or she would have been here on time. I can't hire the woman anyway. How can I trust her with the kids if she can't even be on time?"

"Daddy, Daddy, Daddy," shouted two identical little girl voices.

"Um, Dad," came a boy's voice.

Quinn Larson was swinging both of his daughters up into his arms as he stepped into the kitchen. He was glancing over his shoulder at the boy. "What is it, Ben?"

One of the little girls was trying to whisper into his ear.

Phoebe rolled her eyes then gave Jocelyn a helpless smile and mouthed the word "men." "What your son and daughters were trying to tell you is that Jocelyn arrived right on time. You were the one not here to meet her."

Quinn's gaze shot to her, and for the first time Jocelyn understood the meaning of the work "magnetism."

All I Want

Holly Chamberlin

As always, for Stephen
And this time also for Colleen
And for Monique—
all we want for Christmas is for you to be well.

Acknowledgments

The author would like to thank her editor, John Scognamiglio, for his constant encouragement. Happily, she would like to announce the much-anticipated arrival of Madison Anne. Finally, she sends warm holiday greetings to her kind readers.

Prologue

My name is Abigail Walker, Abby for short. I turned thirty-four about a month ago. I live in Boston and work at the Symphony, in development.

I'm single.

I guess that's about it. Oh, I have some family. My mother and her husband live in Lincoln. My father has been dead for many years.

And I have friends, three good ones. Erin, JoAnne, and Maggie. They make up for a lot. Like for having lost my father. And for not having a lot of self-confidence. And sometimes, for still being single.

About my not being overly confident. Maybe it comes from the way I was raised. Maybe it's just who I am. The sort of shy girl with funny little songs always running through her head. Goofy songs, like "All I Want for Christmas Is My Two Front Teeth."

I like things that aren't threatening. Things without too many hard edges.

My friends call me Pollyanna-ish or naive. But I'm neither, really, and they know that. It's just that we all make sport of each other's most obvious personality traits. It's a form of affection. JoAnne the heartless; Maggie the practical; Erin the kind.

Abby the dreamer. The fantasist. The girl with her head in the clouds.

And beyond that? Well, once Erin compared me to a steel magnolia, those Southern belles with spines of—well, steel. Except that being a New Englander, born and bred, we guessed that made me a hard-shelled lobster. Or something equally ridiculous.

But the point Erin was trying to make is true. I'm not half as fragile as I appear. Everybody who really knows me knows that. I have convictions and I'm good in a crisis. My friends can lean on me when they're not strong.

The problem is that sometimes—well, sometimes I wonder if I'm strong enough for me. I mean, when life pushes me around, most times I just collapse into someone's arms. Or want to.

JoAnne thinks I have a Cinderella complex. Maybe at one point I was hoping to just bump into my soul mate and be transformed. But lately, I'm not even sure my soul mate, my Prince Charming, exists.

Lately, I don't feel very optimistic about romance.

It saddens me to feel so hopeless. Well, not entirely hopeless. Abigail Walker is never entirely hopeless. Still, I wish . . .

I was going to say I wish I felt all bubbly with romantic expectation. But do I? Disappointment always feels keener when it follows great anticipation. So maybe this semihopeless state is, in the end, healthier. The more intelligent way to approach life.

No. I have to be honest. In my heart of hearts all I really want for Christmas this year is hope. Renewed faith in there being someone, somewhere in this world, just for me.

Someone just for me.

One

*I've changed my mind. All I want for Christmas is for every-
body to keep her good news to herself.*

It all started with a phone call from my mother one day in
mid-November. "It" being the downward slide of my spirits
into the worse holiday depression I'd ever experienced. Worse
even than the year I was quarantined with chicken pox from
December 20th through New Year's Day.

Well, not worse than the first Christmas without my father.
But almost.

It's not that I don't love my mother. It's just that—well,
sometimes I find it hard to actually like her.

Mother—Mrs. Martha (Rupert) Gilliam, formerly Mrs.
Martha (Horatio) Walker, née Martha Tinkey-Howard—is
what the kind would call a character. Not quite an eccentric
because I think that term implies someone of outstanding
intelligence along with a predisposition for odd behavior. And
Mother, while not stupid, is not exactly—intellectual.

Her friends find her charming, innocent even, and amusing. Her husband finds her adorable. I find her exasperating.
Truth be told, and without being ungrateful for all my mother
has done for me, I have often wished she were—different.
More of a traditional mother, someone I could truly rely
upon. More of an adult.

When my father died, my mother ceased to be a parental

figure. Maybe she never had been a true parent. Maybe I'd just assumed she was because my father's presence was so powerful, it spoke for her, too. But with him gone, Mother stood alone and her true nature was revealed.

Mother is what the unkind would call batty.

Anyway, back to the dreaded phone call.

I answered on the second ring.

"Dear, is that you?" a high, somewhat excited voice inquired.

I sighed. "Yes, Mother, it's me. Abigail."

"Oh," she said. "That's good."

"How are you, Mother?" I asked, bracing for a litany of inane complaints.

They came. Her stylist hadn't cut her hair in quite the same way he had the previous month, causing Mother minor heart palpitations.

The wallpaper she'd chosen for the kitchen renovation was not at all satisfactory once on the walls.

Finally, Mother had spotted a new freckle on the back of her hand, and though she'd pointed it out to the dermatologist, the doctor refused to admit he saw anything at all.

"Is it still there?" I asked, remembering the last imaginary freckle incident.

"Well, no, dear," she said. "It's the oddest thing. It seems to have disappeared!"

Rupert, Mother's husband, however, was fine. He was always fine.

"Oh, dear, Rupert is just fine," she told me. "He's such a good husband. Never a bother. And how are you, dear?"

And before I could open my mouth to say, "Just fine, Mother," she was babbling on.

"Oh, dear, you'll never guess who I ran into at the Gardners' cocktail party the other night! That darling Puffy Cochrane-Wilson and her darling husband, Scott. Puffy and Scott seem just so happy. Dear, you should see them. They just beam! And so tan! You know, dear, I prefer to stay out of the sun, what with my delicate complexion, but those two! They just glow. Those quick little trips to Tortola just do them a world of wonder. You might benefit from some sun, dear. All that vitamin D. Why don't you take a quick little trip to, say, Bermuda? Winters in New England can be so dreary."

Deep breath, Abby. I stared out at the view from my tiny kitchen window. Not more than a grim alley and rusty fire escapes.

"Mother," I said evenly, "I'd love to get away but just now I can't leave my job."

"Are you sure? Oh, I can't see why they shouldn't allow you to slip away for a few days."

Was it time to explain—yet again—the notions of responsibility and dedication? Was it time to remind Mother of the fact that I had no one with whom I could slip away to a tropical paradise? No, I decided, sure that in a moment Mother would drift on to another topic.

She did.

"Oh, dear," she blurted, "did you hear that Buffy Livingston-Hampton is having her third child? How nice for the Hamptons. Dear, why don't you have a baby?"

I swear the question was asked in all innocence. She might as well have asked why I didn't pour myself a nice cup of tea.

"Mother," I replied, struggling for calm, "I'm not married."

There was a beat during which I know Mother was processing that bit of information as if it were entirely new to her. "Oh," she said finally. "Yes. There is that. But—"

"And I'm not having a baby on my own."

"Oh. Dear, I wasn't suggesting you do! Although . . ."

Mother's thoughts had trailed off again.

"Mother, I really have to go now," I said loudly, hoping to startle her back into focus. "I'll talk to you soon, all right?"

And without waiting for her bewildered farewell, I was gone.

* * *

Whenever our schedules permitted, my three closest friends and I met for drinks or a meal.

Erin Weston, my closest friend. The friend whose father I used to date. Amazingly, our friendship survived that strange time and grew even more solid.

JoAnne Chiofalo, successful pediatrician and the most unsentimental person I've ever met. And the most fiercely protective of her loved ones.

And Maggie Branley, a professor of urban design and, along with her partner, a woman named Jan, a new parent. Maggie is one of those people you tend to overlook because they're not demanding your attention. But in the end, Maggie's the one you turn to for wisdom and good common sense.

The evening after my mother's informative phone call, the four of us met for dinner at Davio's.

"The call made me feel just a little down," I admitted. "Mother was all full of who celebrated their anniversary and who's having another baby and—"

"Down?" JoAnne said. "I'd be suicidal. I mean, I wouldn't, personally. But I could see how you might feel rotten. Wait—that didn't come out right."

"Oh, I know what you mean," I said impatiently. "But it wasn't my mother's fault. All she was doing was passing along the most recent news about my former classmates."

JoAnne raised an eyebrow. "All she was doing was trying to make you feel bad by reminding you that you're not married. And that you don't have children."

"I've never heard you call your mother a bitch," Maggie said, looking up from her menu.

"Because she's not," I insisted. "My mother is just—well, she's not always the most considerate person. But not because she's evil. It's just because she's—"

"Not the sharpest knife in the drawer?" Erin suggested with a tentative smile.

I sighed. "Yes. I mean, no, she's not. Not by far."

"So, who are these paragons of womanhood you went to school with?" JoAnne questioned. "And why haven't we met them? We haven't, have we? Am I forgetting something?"

Erin shrugged. "I've never met anyone from Abby's past. Maybe she's hiding them from us. Or us from them."

"I'm not hiding anybody!" I swore. "It's just that I didn't really keep up with the old crowd much after high school. I saw the girls a few times during college, but since then, it's more like I just run into them every couple of years. You know, at social functions. I was always kind of—different. I mean, Puffy was—"

"Puffy?"

I nodded. "Puffy. It's her nickname."

Maggie frowned. "What's it short for? Puffaret? Pufforia?"

Erin grinned. "Maybe Puffy got her nickname because she has a drinking problem. Maybe she bloats up like a bull frog with PMS. Maybe she's subject to hives!"

I sighed. Sometimes my friends had no imagination. "All right, I admit it's an unusual nickname. But just because it's different doesn't—"

"Yeah, yeah," JoAnne finished, "doesn't make it wrong or stupid. But tell us, honey, what is Puffy's real name?"

"Pamela," I answered.

"Pamela!" Erin cried. "And she prefers Puffy?"

I took a sip of my Manhattan before answering. "I guess. Back in middle school she just started calling herself Puffy and—"

"She asked to be called Puffy!" Maggie cried. "It didn't just get plastered on her by some big bully?"

"No. I remember it quite clearly."

"And no one made fun of her?" JoAnne pressed. "Man, the kids in my school would have eaten her alive."

Erin grinned. "The kids in your school didn't have mothers named Honoria and fathers named Brentwood."

"I suppose you'll be amused to learn that my other friends are named Buffy, Bitsy, and Bunny," I said stiffly, bracing for the hoots and hollers.

Maggie laid her palms flat on the table, as if preparing for disturbing news. "I know I shouldn't ask this," she said, "but I'm going for it. What's Buffy's real name?"

"Bethany. But her parents called her Buffy from the time she was a little girl."

"Better Buffy than Puffy." JoAnne finished her drink and gestured to our waiter.

"And Bitsy?" Erin asked. "She's tiny, right? Itsy Bitsy?"

"No, actually. Bitsy is a bit—well, she shops at Woman's Wisdom, that nice store for big-boned women. Her real name is Elizabeth."

The waiter took our dinner orders then. When he had gone off, JoAnne resumed the conversation. "Okay," she said, "what about Bunny?"

"Oh, she's just Bunny."

"You mean . . ."

"Just Bunny."

"Well, she can't be Catholic," Erin said dryly. " 'Cause I'm pretty sure I've never heard of a Saint Bunny."

JoAnne looked around the table. "You know, there's a theory that kids live up—or down—to their names. You name a kid Victoria or Alexandra and she grows up to be queen or CEO or something equally successful. You name a kid Brandy or Amber and there's a good shot she'll be a Playmate of the Year. So, I'm curious: Does Bunny look like a rabbit?"

"Well, she did until she got her teeth fixed!" I answered honestly.

For the first time since I've known her, JoAnne was speechless.

"I feel the need at this juncture," Erin said, "to remind us of the words of F. Scott Fitzgerald. He said, 'Let me tell you about the very rich. They are different from you and me.'"

"Those girls aren't all that rich," I corrected.

"Do they have trust funds?"

I nodded in answer to Maggie's question.

"Have they ever worked for a living?" she went on.

I shook my head.

"Then they're very rich," she said. "At least compared to me. All I inherited from my ancestors was a scratchy Chieftains album."

"No wonder you didn't keep up with that crowd," JoAnne said now, poking my forearm with a perfectly manicured finger. "If I were you, Abby, I wouldn't give them another thought. The hell with their husbands and kids and vacations."

"That's right," Maggie agreed. "We're all you need. And with friends like us—who needs more grief?"

TWO

All I really want for Christmas is a new job. Soon.

In the entire history of my career I have never, ever lost my temper with a client or spoken back to an employer.

And then, one day in November, not long after the depressing, largely one-way conversation with my mother, everything changed.

Maybe, I thought later, I should just avoid answering the phone for a while. Like, a year.

I share an office with Judy, the super administrative assistant; Jillian, a junior and very enthusiastic staff member; and whatever interns are foisted upon us. The room is just large enough to fit three desks and chairs, and one large filing cabinet. What it actually contains are three desks and six chairs; two large filing cabinets; approximately seven bulging cardboard boxes full of dusty files; two struggling potted plants of some indeterminate species; an ancient typewriting table on which sits an ancient typewriter; a wobbly coat rack which tips over on average twice a day; a microwave; a minifridge; and a crud-encrusted drip coffeemaker.

And of course, several telephones. On which the Symphony's vendors, benefactors, and hangers-on can reach us. The development staff.

Mrs. Agatha Potsdam is a minor supporter and a major troublemaker. Complaining is her forte; she's taken fault-finding to a new level of skill. Most annoyingly, while her actual monetary donations are ridiculously low, Mrs. Potsdam considers herself one of our most important supporters.

Mrs. Potsdam is wrong but protocol forbids my pointing out the truth. And it should have prevented me from commenting on her lack of intellectual powers and artistic sensibility.

The phone rang; Judy answered and put the caller on hold.

"It's Potsdam," she said, rolling her eyes. "Sounds irate."

I rolled my eyes in sympathy. "Put her through."

In place of a greeting, Mrs. Potsdam launched into a tirade about one of the upcoming programs.

"So," I said, after a solid three minutes of rant, "what you're saying is—"

"My dear, what I am saying is that I object to the Debussy piece on the basis of it's not being at all to my taste."

Too many notes? I was tempted to ask, blood boiling.

Instead, I said something much worse.

"Perhaps, Mrs. Potsdam, if you opened your mind to the beauty of the piece, you might learn something. A closed mind prevents the experience of revelation."

There was an awful beat of silence and then:

"Well, I never!" Mrs. Potsdam sputtered.

I don't know what possessed me. I swear I don't.

"Well, maybe you should!" I retorted.

Another dreadful beat of silence. Finally, Mrs. Potsdam recovered her senses.

"Young lady, your superior will hear about your insolence!" she threatened, in her shrillest voice.

Yes, she will, I thought. Because I'm going to confess all the moment you hang up, you old bag!

Mrs. Potsdam didn't wait for a reply but slammed down the receiver of what I imagined to be a pink princess phone. I'd never laid eyes on Mrs. Potsdam but I'd always imagined her as large and swathed in cotton candy pink—a color that should be illegal to wear after the age of four.

Shoving an unsettling vision of a Portly McPotsdam from my mind, I hurried out of my office, pretending not to notice the shocked stares of Judy and Jillian. Though they'd heard only one side of the conversation, they'd heard enough to know I was in trouble.

Caroline Olds was my immediate superior. She was a tough but fair boss. At least, I'd always found her to be so. Among the younger girls fresh out of college, she was known as Dragon Lady. Behind her back, of course.

I took a few deep breaths—which did absolutely nothing to ease my nervousness—knocked on Caroline's door, and once invited in, confessed.

"I'm so, so sorry," I said, wringing my hands like a silent film heroine. "It will never happen again, I promise."

Caroline gave me a look over the top of her half-glasses. It was a look that shamed me.

"It's highly unlike you, Abigail," she said, voice perfectly modulated to imply great disappointment, "to lose your temper so, especially with a patron. If you're having some problems in your personal life, perhaps—"

"No!" I protested, perhaps too forcefully.

"Generally speaking," she went on, "we don't make it a practice to offend those who finance the Symphony and its many culturally valuable programs."

"Yes, of course," I said, nodding stupidly. "I understand completely."

Caroline sighed magnificently and stood. "Well, Abigail, I trust such an incident won't happen again. I will immediately send Mrs. Potsdam a note of apology and suggest that in future, if she has any complaints, she direct them to me."

I hung my head and, with murmured assurances of good behavior and thanks for her generosity, left the office.

When I got back to my desk, still painfully aware of the

furtive looks coming my way, I yanked the To Do Whenever file toward me and pretended to study its contents closely.

The truth was that I'd begun to dislike my work. And that I was bored. The outburst with Mrs. Potsdam had demonstrated that. I was ready for a change.

But a change to what? A different organization, doing similar work? Or an entirely new direction? In which case, that meant retraining. The acquisition of knowledge.

In other words, graduate school.

Why not?

Because it would cost a lot of money. Because it would require an awful lot of hard work. Because I didn't have the dedication and perseverance it would take to go to school at night, maintain my job during the day, and spend a good part of every weekend in the library—instead of out looking for Mr. Right.

Or did I?

That evening I met Erin, Maggie, and JoAnne at Flash's Cocktails. Though I felt exhausted, I was glad to be with people who liked me. Even if they did boss me around from time to time.

"So, how was everyone's day?" Erin asked when we'd settled at a table by the windows.

"Good," JoAnne said, shrugging out of her gorgeous, full-length black leather coat. No one expected details.

"Okay." Maggie paused, then smiled. "Actually, more than okay. A student I'd pretty much given up on engaged in a class discussion. His comments were insightful. Not brilliant, but I think he might actually have a brain cell or two."

"I had a good day, too," Erin told us. "I had a fantastic ham and cheese melt from that new place, Nibbles."

"Where do you put it all?" Maggie frowned and poked at

her own thickening middle. The shaggy green sweater she wore didn't help to minimize the problem.

JoAnne shrugged. "It won't last. By forty her metabolism will be as slow as yours, Maggie. No offense."

Maggie rolled her eyes. Erin ignored the remark entirely.

"Abby?" she said. "You're oddly silent. Bad day?"

I told them about the Mrs. Potsdam incident.

"I think it might be time for a career change," I said, almost apologetically.

"I don't know about that, but I'm proud of you!" JoAnne laughed gleefully. "Standing up to that old bat. Frankly, I didn't know you had it in you."

"But I could have lost my job!" I squealed.

"Probably not," Erin said reasonably. "One slip in how many years? But I want to hear more about this idea of a new career."

"Yeah, Abby, this is exciting," Maggie said. "Any ideas?"

"Well," I demurred, "I do have a few notions—but I'd like to keep them to myself. For now. At least until I've given them some further thought. You know."

"Whatever." JoAnne picked up the tapas menu and studied it with a frown.

Sometimes it seems as if JoAnne doesn't care. But I know she does. Mostly.

Erin gave JoAnne a look.

"Well," she said to me, "when you're ready to talk about those ideas, we're ready to listen. Right, everyone?"

"Right," Maggie said promptly. JoAnne grunted but kept her eyes on the laminated card.

"I'm going to order some calamari," she announced. "And I'm hungry, so don't expect me to share."

I laughed. "Boy," I said, "I wish it had been you and not me on the phone with Mrs. Potsdam this afternoon!"

JoAnne smiled blandly. "Then you'd definitely be looking for a new job, honey."

Three

Okay. This is it. All I want for Christmas is a roach-free apart-ment. With a ceiling.

The moment I opened my front door later that night, I knew something was wrong. Not something criminal. Something—icky.

Gingerly, I stepped into the living room and scanned for evidence of trouble, but as far as I could tell, there were no dead mice or smoking electrical cords. Cautiously, I walked to the kitchen and flipped on the light. Again, nothing. The ancient fridge was humming erratically, as usual, and the backsplash displayed its usual chips and cracks.

After a quick check of the bedroom, there was only one room left to explore.

The bathroom.

My gut told me that whatever I'd find was not going to be pretty. Eyes squinted against the horror, I flipped the light switch.

And there it was.

Forty, possibly fifty roaches—big ones—were scurrying along the tiled floor and across the bathtub's rust-stained surface. Immediately, I looked at the ceiling over the shower. Yes, there it was.

A patch at least a foot in diameter was soaked through.

Plaster had already wetly fallen into the tub and more was soon to follow.

No doubt the bugs were leaving a sinking ship. That was fine for the bugs, but what about me? Where was I to go for the night?

To the otherwise empty apartment I cried, "Ew, ew, ew, ew!" Still in my coat and hat, I dashed into the kitchen and dialed the landlord's number. When I'd moved into the apartment five years earlier, I'd thumbtacked a piece of paper with the number onto a small corkboard next to the wall phone. Within months, I knew the number by heart.

Mr. Jarrens answered after twelve rings. He was not pleased. He didn't like disasters reported after his bedtime.

With grunts of impatience, he listened to my tale of woe.

"Listen, sweetheart—" he began when I'd finished.

"It's Ms. Walker," I said, hand tight around the receiver. "Abigail Walker."

"Whatever. Miss Walker. I can't do anything about it until morning. Maybe afternoon, I don't know. I gotta call my guys."

"But you don't understand," I protested. My voice was threatening to break and I struggled for composure.

"In the meantime," he went on, loudly drowning me out, "stop taking such hot showers."

"Are you saying it's my fault the ceiling is falling down!"

Silently, I plotted. I'll—I'll get a lawyer and prove I'm not responsible! But then what if Mr. Jarrens gets a lawyer and countersues me . . .

Now my hands were trembling.

With an exaggerated sigh, Mr. Lousy McLandord said, "All I'm saying is it's late. I gotta go. I'll let you know tomorrow when to expect my guys. Or the next day."

Before I could again protest the delay, the connection was severed and I was all alone with an army of fleeing roaches.

With a sigh, I surveyed the apartment. The windows that

didn't quite shut and the doors that didn't quite fit in their frames. The too-small cabinets in the kitchen and the living room's sloping floor.

There was no doubt about it. No matter how thoroughly I cleaned, no matter how nicely I decorated and maintained, this apartment would never be more than a way station. It was beyond my power to make it a real home, a place that accepted my investment and helped it grow.

After undressing, I leapt into bed, fighting a disgusting image of marauding roaches. I wondered, was I finally ready to buy a home of my own? I'd always sworn I'd never buy a place until I could buy it with a husband. But . . .

Maybe it was time to reconsider. It was possible I would never have a husband. Did that also mean I would never have a home of my own?

Four

A brand-new wish. Whoever's listening? All I want for Christmas is a boyfriend without a criminal record.

The human spirit is irrepressible. We just don't know when to quit. Sometimes this is a terrible thing.

At least, when it comes to accepting dates with creepies.

Maybe it is all about self-esteem, like JoAnne says. If you hold yourself in high regard, within reason, of course, you will demand a certain quality of person. More importantly, you will be able to recognize quality—or the lack of it—when you see it.

I'd met Patrick York at Barnes and Noble in the Prudential Mall. I was browsing the home decorating section and alternately feeling deeply depressed by the glossy photos of gorgeous mansions well beyond my financial range, and heartened by those manuals that assured me that any apartment, no matter how small or lightless, could be a paradise of domestic bliss.

Which was a good thing because the kind of condo I could afford—barely and with loans—was pretty tiny. If I stayed in Boston. And I did want to stay.

"Hi."

I looked up from a heavy tome on roof gardens to see a man in his late thirties standing just to my left. He was smiling right at me and I didn't see anyone else close by so I returned his greeting. He was nice enough-looking, in an un-remarkable way.

"What are you doing in the home decorating section?" I asked, for lack of anything better to say.

He smiled and clasped his hands behind his back. "Honestly? I was passing by on my way to the music section and I saw this lovely brunette browsing the shelves and I just had to say hello."

I smiled back and we chatted for a moment, though later I couldn't recall much of what we'd said.

Patrick York checked his watch and with an apologetic frown explained he had to run.

"Won't you have time to visit the music section?" I asked.

A look of slight confusion clouded his eyes and then he laughed, as if just getting a joke. "Oh, well, next time. I wasn't looking for anything important."

He asked if he could call me, and though some vague instinct told me to say no, I gave him my work number. I watched as he walked off—noting the unflattering cut of his leather jacket—and wondered if I'd done the right thing.

On the surface, Patrick York seemed fine. Normal. The feeling I'd gotten wasn't even all that strong. And it didn't seem to relate to any particular trait. Patrick York's eyes weren't beady and his nails weren't dirty and he hadn't used any bad language. The jacket could be a gift from his mother, something he felt compelled to wear.

With a shrug I went back to the book on roof gardens.

Patrick York called me the very next morning and asked if I'd like to meet for drinks after work. I said, sure. He asked if I'd like to pick the place, which I thought was a nice thing to do. I picked the bar at The Cheesecake Factory. It was a place I knew and liked, a place at which I felt safe.

We met at six-thirty. I wore a pair of navy wool pants and

a trim white turtleneck. Patrick York again was wearing the unflattering leather jacket—it cut his middle oddly, making him look ill-proportioned. Though he wore no overcoat, he kept the jacket on as we settled onto stools at the bar. The temperature that evening was about thirty degrees and there was an icy wind off the water. Still, I noticed that my date had come with no gloves, hat, or scarf.

After greetings, Patrick York asked me what I'd like to drink. He ordered for both of us, calling me "the lady," as in "the lady will have a cosmopolitan."

Though I do like to be treated like a lady, something about being referred to as "the" lady makes me uncomfortable.

However, I said nothing and accepted my drink. The bartender asked if we'd like to start a tab and Patrick York told him that we did. Okay, I thought. So he's not ready to run. Nothing he's seen so far has frightened him into cutting this date embarrassingly short.

The conversation was easy, if not particularly exciting. The weather. The traffic. How quickly the holidays were approaching. After a short while, I asked the perfectly acceptable question: "So, what do you do?"

"Well, truth be told," he said, leaning in toward me confidentially, "I've had a hard time getting back on my feet since getting out last June."

"Getting out?" I asked, startled. "Of rehab?" Was Patrick York a recovering alcoholic or drug addict? He was drinking nonalcoholic beer . . . Well, addiction was an illness, not a sign of moral decrepitude. There was no reason to judge.

Patrick York smiled winningly. "No," he said, "out of the slammer, actually. You know, the big house. Jail. Prison."

Oh. My. Lord, I thought. I'm having drinks with Rocky Sullivan! With Luca Brazzi! With Paulie Walnuts!

Politely, I nodded. "Oh. I see. Er . . . What . . ." Mail fraud? Embezzlement of company funds? Certainly something white collar!

"What was I in for?" Patrick York raised his hand to halt my weak apologies. "No, that's okay. I don't have a problem being honest. I'm not proud of my actions, but I'm not ashamed. Shame is a waste of time. Believe me."

And that's when Patrick York told me he had been accused of a complicated scam that resulted in several elderly people losing their life savings. Everything. All their money. Their homes. And of course, their dignity.

Not ashamed of his actions? This man should be horse-whipped, I cried silently. Whatever that means. And he should be very, very ashamed.

If he was guilty.

"So, that's that," he said, relaxing against the back of his chair.

"Were you, um, guilty?" I croaked.

Patrick York laughed quite robustly. "Oh, yeah, I was guilty."

Mr. Killer McCriminal seemed to find my shock endearing. He reached out and gently squeezed my hand. I tried not to flinch.

"Well, the way I see it," he said, his voice syrupy with sleaze, "there's no point in lying about my past. Honesty is everything in a good relationship, right?"

Right. But if honesty was so important, why hadn't Mr. Creepy McConvict told me about his criminal past when we'd met at B & N? Or when he'd called and asked me for a date?

All around me people laughed with their friends and drank colorful drinks and enjoyed mammoth portions of food. Suddenly, it seemed surreal. I felt completely separate from the crowd, suspended in a bubble of eerie stillness, just me and the sick realization that I was on a date with a crook.

Patrick York had charmed me, allowed me to relax my guard, then dropped his bombshell. Maybe he thought he was softening the blow by delaying his bombshell. I thought he was a manipulative, amoral jerk.

Suddenly, I heard JoAnne's voice in my head. This man, she said, needs to be taken down a peg or two. Now.

Patrick York smiled at me in a way he no doubt thought charming.

"So? What do you think?" he oozed. "Is everything good?"

Smoothly, I slid off the bar stool and gathered my coat and purse.

"No," I said, my voice bright, my eyes boring into his as if to pin him against a wall. "Nothing is good. See, I think it stinks. On ice. I think it stinks on ice that you didn't tell me this on the phone. You should have had the decency to do that."

Patrick York looked thoroughly surprised by my words. He put out his hand to touch my arm but I stepped out of his reach. "Hey, I—"

"I'm not finished," I said, a bit more loudly now. A few heads turned to watch the little drama. "You don't feel ashamed of your actions? Well, you should. You should feel very ashamed." And suddenly, JoAnne was at my shoulder again, whispering . . .

And the words were coming out of my mouth . . .

"You," I said, head held high, "must have a very small penis to feel the need to be such a—such an ass."

It made no real sense, but my parting blow so stunned Patrick York that while he gaped and spluttered, I made a quick and secure exit.

I got home just fine—like I was going to let Mr. Sleazy McCell Block know where I lived! It was bad enough he knew where I worked. With cell phone in hand, keyed to 911, and a stern look over my shoulder at any lurking deviants, I slipped inside the front door of my building and locked it behind me.

Home. A haven from yet another disastrous date. With a

wary eye out for a sudden infestation of flies or choking clouds of plaster dust, I undressed and slipped into bed. But sleep wouldn't come. After a frustrating half hour I got up and went for the heavy stuff.

Uncanny Cashew ice cream by Ben and Jerry. Leaning against the counter with container and spoon, I wondered why I felt so awfully alone—why I hadn't picked up the phone the minute I'd gotten home and called Erin or Maggie or JoAnne.

The sad fact was that things were changing. I was changing. I was reluctant to admit such continued failure to my three dearest friends—three women who were currently enjoying normal, committed relationships.

It wasn't that I expected them to laugh or judge. Not exactly. Maybe I expected them to be bored by me. To wish I'd just get my act together.

Truth was that in the previous weeks I'd been feeling all mean-spirited, wishing my friends would just keep quiet about their happiness. I wished Erin would keep Nick's small kindnesses to herself. I wished I didn't know how great a cook Jan was or how Merv's lack of waistline didn't seem to affect his prowess in bed.

I sighed.

How and why is this happening, I wondered, tossing the empty ice cream container in the kitchen trash, this slow disintegration of my friendships? Is it all my fault? I knew that I should trust my friends to care for me, even in bad times. I knew that I was being unfair to Erin, Maggie, and JoAnne by doubting their support.

And yet . . . I felt isolated by embarrassment, by a sense of failure. By a sense of false pride?

I wondered as I crawled back under the covers and turned out the bedside light. Did I even like myself anymore?

And if I didn't like myself, who else could?

Five

All I want for Christmas is to bump into that handsome stranger again! Please, please, please, please, please!

Where Erin says a girl can never have too many pairs of shoes, I say a girl can never have enough Christmas tree ornaments. I've been collecting them since the age of ten. Blown-glass balls inherited from my father's family; old-fashioned bubblers from my own childhood; wooden birds carved by a Maine craftsman; a variety of Victorian-style pieces; funky, papier-mâché animals.

There's a wonderful store in the Faneuil Hall marketplace called the Christmas Dove. I simply revel in the two floors of excess. Tinsel in silver and gold; garlands of shiny foil; light-bulbs in the shape of poinsettias and candy canes; Dickensian villages and elaborately embroidered stockings . . . It's a place of supreme fantasy.

One afternoon in mid-November, I made an excursion to the store. After an hour of blissful browsing, I settled on my purchases—including a beautiful, hand-carved wooden angel holding aloft a heart. After a cheery farewell to the staff, and clutching several bulky shopping bags, I made my way out the door.

And bumped smack against something large and tall.

A man. A very handsome man. A very handsome man with

a strong but gentle hand that caught my arm just above the elbow, suspecting that I might need a steadying force.

A quick glance showed a beautiful charcoal gray overcoat, thick dark hair, and truly green eyes.

"I'm so sorry," I murmured.

"It's my fault," he said, and his voice was deep and mellow.

And then our eyes met, locked, and I felt a spark sizzle between us.

But before either of us could utter another word, a storm of Japanese tourists were upon us, led by a rather large American woman in a bright red raincoat and wielding an equally red umbrella. On her head was the ugliest knit hat I've ever seen; it resembled a lump of cold oatmeal.

"Follow me!" she cried, thrusting the umbrella in the air and barreling her way between me and the handsome stranger, so that in a split second he was only a tiny spot of dark brown hair beyond the offending umbrella.

There had to be at least fifty men and women in the tour group, each armed with a camera in hand and one strung around the neck. Excited voices rose around me, and before I could shut my eyes, a flash blinded me.

"Oh!" I cried, dropping the shopping bags and clapping my hands to my eyes. I suppose I was still an interesting sight because the clicking continued for some time. Finally, finally, the horde moved on and—silence.

I lowered my hands and peeked out at the world. My shopping bags were a few feet away, slightly trampled, but Handsome was nowhere in sight.

I snatched up my shopping bags and whirled, searching.

How could a human being—a tall and noticeably handsome human being—disappear so quickly, so thoroughly, in a wide-open public space?

But it had happened. The fact was that Handsome was gone.

Six

Here's my new wish. It's important. All I want for Christmas is to be safe.

Thanksgiving—and I had plenty to be thankful for. I had a job. Okay, I didn't really enjoy it, but at least I was employed. I had my health. I had good friends. And I had an apartment. With a lazy landlord to go with it, but still, there was a roof over my head. Most times.

What more did I need? Food, shelter, friendships. What more did I want?

Love. My soul mate. My Prince Charming.

Holidays just aren't for the lonely.

My mother and her husband were heading to Colorado to stay at the luxurious ski-lodge home of some friends. I wondered what my mother would do while Rupert played in the snow. Probably skim the latest issue of *Town and Country* and sip highballs.

Erin was cooking for her boyfriend, Nick; his eleven-year-old son, David; her father, John, and his girlfriend, Marilyn; and Marilyn's college-aged son. She didn't invite me to join the party and I didn't ask for an invitation. Given the fact that I'd spent a good part of the previous year dating John Weston, it seemed best I stay away.

JoAnne and Merv were escaping to a bed-and-breakfast in Vermont.

Maggie and her partner, Jan, usually spent the day at the Women's Lunch Place, a shelter for poor, homeless, and lonely women, cooking, serving, and cleaning up breakfast and the main meal. This year, Jan was staying home with baby Jonah. In an unexpected burst of social responsibility—or severe loneliness—I asked Maggie if I could work in Jan's place. Maggie said yes, but issued a warning.

"It's hard work, Abby," she told me over the phone one night. "I'm not saying you can't handle it, I just want you to be prepared to sweat. Wear old clothes, nothing that can't be ruined. And it can be difficult emotionally, too. If you're not used to it. Some of the guests are in pretty sad shape."

I hesitated but thought of my options. Work at WLP or stay home all alone. On Thanksgiving. "I can handle it," I assured Maggie.

Six A.M., Thursday, November 24th. I hadn't been out of the house that early in years and so was terribly groggy even after three cups of coffee. As I got closer to the shelter, my stomach began to scrunch. By the time I reached the corner of Newbury and Berkeley Streets and the Church of the Covenant, I badly wanted to turn around and run home.

Instead, I took a deep breath of the chill morning air and went inside to do the job I'd promised to do.

The main room was standard church basement—plaster walls painted an inoffensive pale green, worn tile floor, and an upright piano on wheels. Colorful crayon drawings were tacked to various bulletin boards, along with notices for social worker visits and church event schedules.

The staff had decorated the room with paper turkeys, the fold-out kind with accordion tails; small centerpieces of autumn flowers; and orange streamers. The smell of roasting turkey and hot apple pie was irresistible. Except that I had no appetite.

Already there were about thirty or forty women gathered in the room, some slumped in folding chairs, many enormous with layers of random clothing, others chatting amiably to themselves. Among the crowd I saw about ten children ranging from about nine to sixteen. Without exception these were hovering around the serving tables, watching eagerly for the appearance of breakfast.

Maggie gave me the simple task of laying out napkins and checking that each table was provided with salt and pepper. With a wink she told me the tough jobs were coming later.

A tall, slim woman about sixty years old was folding paper napkins and placing them around one of the long tables. She was dressed simply in a pair of navy slacks and a striped Oxford shirt under a navy wool cardigan.

Clutching my own stack of paper napkins, I joined her. "Hi," I said, glad for the company. "I'm Abby."

The woman stopped performing her task, looked up, and smiled. "Well, hello!" she said cheerily. "My name is Marge."

I put the stack of napkins on the table and began to fold. "Do you volunteer on a weekly basis?" I asked, innocently enough.

Would that someone had warned me against asking such questions of anyone on site. I can only claim that shelter etiquette doesn't come naturally to most people. I don't know of Emily Post ever giving advice on how to make small talk while ladling soup from a massive iron pot.

The woman's face froze before relaxing into what seemed a long habit of social graciousness.

"No, I—I just like to help out when I come in," she said. I could see in her eyes and hear in her voice the effort it cost her to tell her story. "You see, I like to use the shower early in the day, before—"

Don't make a big deal about the faux pas, Abby, my smarter self advised. Just move on . . .

"This is my first time at WLP," I said, hoping my implied apology was clear. "It seems like a wonderful place."

And now, on closer observance, I saw signs of her predicament, signs I might never have noticed had I continued to assume she was a volunteer. The cuffs of her wool sweater were badly worn. The collar of her shirt was slightly grimy with repeated use.

We see only what we want to see, I reminded myself. Until somebody or something forces us to see more.

"It's a very nice place," Marge said, toying with the napkin she'd been folding. "Mostly. Some of the ladies . . ." Here she glanced around at the motley group with an expression of unease.

Marge then told me that she had gone to college, a small prestigious women's school in Vermont, and that after college she had married a man well on his way to success in business.

"We were married for almost thirty years," she said. "Until the divorce."

"Oh," I said, unsure of why she was telling me, a virtual stranger, the highlights of her life story. Unless it was to prove that she had been "somebody." "I'm sorry. About the divorce, I mean."

"Yes, yes," she replied, suddenly distracted. Then she looked closely at me. "Do you live in the city?"

I told her that I did. I was about to ask her where she lived when I realized that wasn't a question I could ask in this situation. Was it?

"I used to live in a big house," Marge said, as if in response to my unasked question. "It was very beautiful. There was a backyard, too. My friends would come over in the afternoons and we'd play cards and drink iced tea."

I imagined Marge in kinder days . . . Sun-dappled lawn, the tinkle of ice cubes in a tall glass, the ring of feminine laughter, and presiding over the gathering, a tall, slim woman in a white wicker chair . . .

"I—I'm sure that must have been lovely," I said.

"Oh, it was," Marge replied, without a trace of bitterness. "I do miss that house. I haven't lived there in such a long time."

"I'm sorry," I said again. It seemed the only safe thing to say.

Marge looked at the napkin in her hand, now crumpled and useless. Quickly she stuffed it in her pants pocket.

"I have a car," she said suddenly. "That's all that's left. Isn't that funny? I don't know how long I'll be able to keep it, though. There's an awful rattling sound but I don't have the money to take it to a mechanic . . . I so dread the idea of having to sleep in a shelter. I hear there's such violence and I'm afraid someone will try to steal my clothes."

I stood as if rooted to the earth. Marge had just told me she lived in her car. The enormity of that information didn't seem to fit the casual way in which she had related it. To Marge, *being* homeless had become a basic fact of life. To me, the notion itself was still shattering.

"Yes, I—that would be scary," I mumbled. The clatter of dishes, the din of voices harsh with illness and want, the heat from so many bodies in a windowless space, the sudden burst of wild laughter . . . My head felt all buzzy and I was sure I was about to faint.

"Oh, but it's Thanksgiving!" Marge said, laughing almost shyly. "And I shouldn't be rattling on. You're busy and so am I. I promised I'd help with the salad so I'd better get back to the kitchen."

"Okay," I managed to say. I put my hand to my forehead and felt cold sweat.

Marge gripped my other hand in hers. I glanced down to see traces of dirt in the fine lines of her fingers. Her nails were rough and poorly cut. On her right hand she wore a ring, a gold band with three small rubies. A birthday gift from long, long ago? Or maybe it had been her mother's . . .

"Will you come back another day?" she asked, her voice struggling to hide her eagerness. Her eyes held mine with fierce expectation, and beneath the months or years of shame and poverty, I saw a dim vision of the proud woman she might once have been.

And suddenly, I felt panic rising in my chest. "I—My schedule at work right now is—I'm very busy but . . ."

Marge wasn't fooled by my rambling, my hesitation.

She dropped my hand and brushed her hips with her palms, looking at the floor, at her feet—no longer at me.

"I should go and . . ." Marge's head jerked up as if she'd heard someone call her name. Without another word, she hurried off toward the kitchen, leaving me standing alone amid the swirl of women—old and young; African-American, white, Hispanic; homeless and poor; mentally ill and just plain lonely—so unlike myself.

And so just like myself.

By two o'clock I was bone tired. My back ached, my feet were swollen, and my hands red and rough. The festive sweater I'd been foolish enough to wear was ruined. Instead of feeling alive with love and goodwill, I felt heavily weighted by all the loss crammed into that stuffy basement room. The other volunteers were still bustling about, clearing tables, chatting with each other and guests, and showing no sign of sneaking off, which was what I badly wanted to do.

Maggie took pity on me. She came over to the table where I was wiping up a gravy spill and squeezed my shoulders.

"Mercy?" I whispered, fighting back tears.

"You did great, Abby. I knew you would. Go on home. And thank you."

Without another word I handed her the dirty rag and went off to find my coat.

When I got home that afternoon, I peeled off the ruined sweater and shoved it into the trash. Then I took a long, hot, soapy shower, and slipped into a flannel nightgown, robe, and slippers. I looked a sight, hair pulled into a damp ponytail, face clear of makeup, hands slathered in lotion and stuffed into white cotton gloves. But there was no one there to see me—to mock or to comfort.

Only after an hour did it occur to me to check the answering machine. No one had called. Not even my mother. But then, had I really expected her to call?

Sleep beckoned though it was not even five in the afternoon. I ignored the exhaustion and put on a DVD of *Roman Holiday*, one of my favorite movies.

But my thoughts kept wandering from the lovely black-and-white film. It was quite possible that Marge had once been as beautiful and elegant as Audrey Hepburn. But who would know that now? I wondered if Marge had photos of her former life—of her former self. Did anyone? And what about children? Marge hadn't mentioned any and I hadn't asked. In fact, I hadn't asked anything, really, except my first, blundering question.

You should go back and talk to her, I told myself, staring blankly at the screen.

Someday soon.

Seven

All right. All I want for Christmas is for every man who cheats on his wife to go to hell!

The Nantucket Walk, held the weekend after Thanksgiving, had been a longstanding tradition in my family. But after my father's passing, the tradition just fell away. One day, an excursion is laced with meaning. The next, it's simply put aside.

JoAnne was a bit testy at having been dragged along.

"Don't look now, Abby," she muttered as we stopped at a corner to wait for a light to change. "But someone's about to accost you."

JoAnne nodded in the direction of a woman and two bundled children clustered outside an old-fashioned candy shop.

"Oh," I breathed. "Rats. It's Buffy!"

"Abby!" Buffy squealed at that moment.

"I have to say hello," I whispered.

Erin sniffled and shrugged. "Sure."

We walked over to the shop, and after Buffy and I gave each other a quick hug, I introduced JoAnne and Erin to my childhood friend.

Dark circles underscored her eyes and her skin lacked luster. Her hair, once a shiny chestnut brown, was dull and pulled into a slightly messy ponytail.

Buffy had seen better days, I thought, then reminded myself that she had two young children—and according to my mother and an obvious belly, she was pregnant again. That was enough to put a strain on anyone, even someone as seemingly tireless as Buffy Livingston-Hampton.

"How long has it been?" Buffy asked, her smile as wide as ever.

"Gosh, I think it's been—well, almost two years," I said, surprising myself with this bit of information. "It was at the club's Spring Gala."

"Two years! Abby, we just have to see you more often!"

I smiled noncommittally and said, "So, how are you?"

"We're just fine!" Buffy bubbled. "This is Melissa," she said, patting the head of a blond girl in a pink snowsuit and wool hat, "and this is Melanie. They're five and seven."

"Mommy says we're going to have a brother soon," Melanie chirped. Her outfit mirrored her sister's, in purple.

"Why, that's great, Buffy," I said.

Buffy beamed. "We're six months along. Beau is just thrilled. He threatened if I didn't give him a boy this time, we'd try again and again until I got it right. He's so silly!"

The look on Erin's face told me that "silly" wasn't exactly the word she'd use to describe Beauregard Hampton. But being Erin, she just smiled politely.

JoAnne being JoAnne, she said, without a trace of levity, "He does know the male determines the sex of the child, doesn't he?"

Buffy's smile drooped and she looked from JoAnne to me in some confusion.

"So," I blurted, "what have you seen so far that we shouldn't miss?"

Buffy's face screwed up in a frown. "Well, there's a darling toy store just down the road, I think it's called—"

"The Rocking Cradle," Melissa said importantly.

"Aren't you a smart girl," I cooed and Melissa smirked.

"And who are these lovely ladies!" a falsely hearty male voice boomed.

A man joined our group. Buffy beamed at him. He was good-looking enough, but definitely going to seed in a way that made me suspect he was a heavy drinker.

"Oh, Abby," Buffy said, "you remember my husband, Beauregard. Beau, these are Abigail's friends, Erin and—oh, I'm sorry . . ."

"JoAnne," JoAnne said with a smile that could cut through a frozen steak.

"Yes, that's it, of course," Buffy babbled.

Beau grinned and nodded but something made me doubt he'd taken in my friends' names.

Buffy and I chatted about nothing for another moment or two until JoAnne cleared her throat in a not-so-subtle way.

"We really should be going," I said. "And I'm sure you have plans for the rest of the afternoon."

There followed the usual bustle of a goodbye, with empty promises of phone calls and e-mails. And somewhere in that bustle, I felt a hand touch my rear end. More accurately, I felt a hand press against it. A large hand.

And then the Hamptons moved off a few paces and for a second I thought I had imagined the touch. In the next second I thought that the touch had been accidental. Maybe Beau's hand had grazed me as he'd reached to adjust Melanie's purple hat.

Erin and JoAnne had already turned away but I remained looking after Buffy and her brood. And then—Beau looked over his shoulder and winked at me.

And I realized that he had touched me quite deliberately.

I was stunned. Sure, I'd received inappropriate passes before—once from a male colleague; once when I was fifteen, from the father of a neighbor—but something about this incident—something about Mr. Beauregard Hampton touching me with his pregnant wife and two children only feet away—simply stunned me.

And then came outrage.

I caught up with my friends and grabbed Erin's arm. "Did you see what just happened?" I demanded.

"No, what?" she asked, dabbing her nose with a tissue.

"That—pig! He just touched my butt! And then winked at me!"

"Who?" JoAnne asked with a scowl.

"Buffy's husband," I cried. "Beau!"

"Ha! I knew he was trash the minute I laid eyes on him. The part in his hair was way too neat. I never trust that in a man."

"I'm going to go after them and confront him!" I announced.

"Don't make a scene," Erin urged. "Come on, it was disgusting of him but you don't want to embarrass Buffy in front of her kids."

"It would be doing her a favor to let her know her hubby is a jerk," JoAnne said.

"While she's carrying his third child?" Erin shot back. "It's not like Buffy and Abby are close friends. Maybe then Abby would be obliged to tell her what happened."

JoAnne sighed. "Okay, Abby, make sure to get Mr. Buffy aside before telling him if he ever makes a pass at you again, you'll serve him his balls on a paper plate."

"I still say Abby should let it go," Erin argued.

Erin was right. The kindest thing would be for me to let it drop. For now.

Poor Buffy! I'd been feeling so jealous of her for having a rich husband who, I'd assumed, worshipped the ground she walked on.

"You never really know about another person's marriage, do you?" I asked rhetorically.

"No," Erin sighed, hunching her shoulders against a stiff wind that had come up suddenly, "you don't."

Eight

Okay. All I want for Christmas is for the Universe to stop teasing me!

Erin called the next morning and begged off our planned excursion to the Museum of Fine Arts, claiming she was suffering with the worst cold she'd had in years. I was disappointed but still determined to see the show I'd been so looking forward to seeing.

The show was called Impressions of Light: The French Landscape from Corot to Monet. I had bought the ticket in advance so I was able to bypass the long lines at the first-floor ticket counters. But not the crowd at the door of the exhibit itself. Grumpily, I baby-stepped along with the horde. A system of advance tickets and timed entry was supposed to help control overcrowding in the special exhibits. But every exhibit I'd ever attended had been mobbed, no matter what time of day, no matter what day of the week.

Inside the exhibit rooms the chaos was compounded. I considered turning right around and going home. It was almost impossible to view the paintings without obstruction, or for more than thirty seconds before getting shoved along by the masses.

But I stayed, figuring half a view would be better than none at all.

Just inside the second exhibit room, I spotted a Corot I'd

always wanted to see up close. I circled a band of artloving college kids until only three or four people stood between me and the work. Eagerly, I stood on tiptoe and craned my neck. Just as I did, the large man in front of me stepped back and in an effort to avoid being bumped I, too, took a step back and lost my balance in the process.

"Ooof!" said a voice from just behind me.

I regained my footing with the help of the voice's steadying hands on my arms and turned.

"I'm so sorry," I blurted into a dusky blue sweater. And then I raised my eyes. "Oh! It's you!"

It was him. Handsome! The man I'd almost knocked over outside the Christmas shop just days earlier. The man who had been swept from me by a horde of chattering, camera-wielding tourists.

"That's quite all right," he replied with a very nice smile. "And—oh, it's you!"

I laughed. Suddenly, the crowded, stuffy room seemed airy and light. Handsome and I were alone with each other, surrounded by beautiful works of art and—

"What? I can't hear you!"

I jumped at the sudden assault. A well-dressed older couple stood a few feet from my right shoulder, clutching little tape decks and squinting as if the voice in their ears somehow made it hard to see straight.

The bane of every serious museum goer! People who rent the audio tour! This particular couple were in their seventies. Clearly, the technological revolution had passed them by.

Suddenly, the couple stumbled ahead, forcing Handsome and I to take a few steps away from each other in order to avoid a crash.

"Herb, look," the woman shouted to the man only inches from her face, *"it says the brush strokes—what? No, wait, I've got it wrong—"*

I cringed. Handsome, whom I could see over the bent white

heads of the befuddled couple, cringed back. The elderly couple seemed completely oblivious to the fact that they'd wedged their way between us.

"What?" the man shouted now. *"I can't, let me turn this thing—"*

The man fumbled with the buttons on the minirecorder, face fixed in a frown. Then he looked back to his wife—who else could she be?—and shouted, *"I'm going back to that other room, Maude, do you hear me?"*

"What? It goes in order, you can't go back, all right, do what you want, get lost . . ."

The befuddled pair wandered on, each in a different direction.

"It's nice they still get out of the house," Handsome said and I laughed again.

"Do you always try for a positive spin?"

Handsome shrugged. "I find it takes less energy than being negative."

"Well," I began, "I—"

"Look out!"

Again, Handsome and I stepped back from one another as a group of about forty teens surged upon us. I assumed they were from a public high school, on a field trip. Not one face showed a spark of interest. Mouths hung open with boredom; eyes were dull with disinterest. Boys and girls shuffled along shoulder to shoulder, most in voluminous jackets and pants in a semishiny material that made an irritating swishing sound with each step. A harried, forty-something man in a worn sweater vest, tiny round glasses, and baggy chinos was trying in vain to get the kids to focus on a painting.

"Look, hey, just stop, okay?" he whined. "That's one you'd like, on the left, hey, come on!"

I wondered whose idea it had been to bring these kids to the Museum of Fine Arts. To this particular exhibit. Someone without much sense, I thought. Someone who has no idea of what interests the average urban public school teenager.

A boy who weighed at least two hundred and fifty pounds lumbered by, face set in a menacing scowl. "This shit be boring," he mumbled.

Well, maybe if you actually stopped to look at a painting, I thought crossly, you might think otherwise! Oh, get out of the way, please!

Finally, the last members of the crowd passed—but Handsome was nowhere to be seen! I scanned the room once, twice.

Where had he gone!

Braving the herd of sullen teens, the wandering elderly, the Sunday mob, and the suspicious stares of the museum guards, I hurried ahead, searching frantically for a dusky blue sweater.

The last room of the exhibit—but still, no luck. I peered through the glass doors that led into a shop featuring items related to the exhibit but saw no one that resembled Handsome. No broad shoulders, no wavy dark hair.

What to do! If I passed through those doors, I wouldn't be allowed back into the exhibit. I could go on and look for Handsome in the rooms beyond, or turn back and look for him again in the press of people gawking at the Daubigny and Gauguin. For whatever reason, I headed back to the beginning of the exhibit, murmuring apologies and ignoring annoyed glances from the crowd inching forward.

And then a horrible thought struck. Maybe Handsome had simply taken advantage of those older folk and teens to slip away, unnoticed. Maybe he'd slipped away from me that first time, too, outside the Christmas shop.

Maybe I'd been searching for someone who just didn't want to be found.

No, I decided. Handsome hadn't run away from me. Rotten luck had torn us from each other. I recalled the glint in his green eyes and the genuineness of his smile and knew he'd been pleasantly surprised to see me.

The entrance to the exhibit. I came to a breathless halt. No Handsome.

What did it matter now that he'd been pleased to see me?

I'd lost Handsome again. What were the odds I'd find him a third time?

Nine

I can't believe I'm saying this. All I want for Christmas is a boyfriend of legal age.

The Symphony's first holiday dinner dance. And while it wasn't strictly mandatory that I attend, I opted to make an appearance. I'd been less than my usual enthusiastic self in the past weeks. I felt I owed my colleagues, and Caroline, a show of support.

I'd tried to find a date for the evening, a platonic escort, but had no luck. As a last resort, I'd called Erin and asked if her friend Damion might be willing to spend an evening drinking champagne with me. But Damion was unavailable. He and his partner Frederick were going to a dinner party in Gloucester.

"I have to find more gay friends," I'd lamented. "More single ones, anyway."

"I'm sorry, Abby," Erin had said. "But I think we can cross Damion off our escort list permanently."

In the end, I took myself to the event. All dressed up in a pink satin dress and jacket from Ann Taylor, with brocade sling-backs and matching clutch. If only Handsome could see me, I thought as I stood before the full-length mirror in my bedroom. I looked—pretty.

Upon my arrival, a brief but keen glance told me that every guest was paired off. At least someone complimented my outfit. Sure, he was a very old gentleman and he did think I was his long-dead mother, but it was very sweet of him to say something.

When Mr. Gonzalez had been helped back to his table by his scowling and much younger wife, I checked in with Jillian. "Everything's fine, boss," she said perkily, eyeing the glittering room as if she were already a well-practiced hostess. "You can just relax."

"Are you sure?" I pressed. I'd been hoping to occupy myself with a small crisis or two.

"Perfectly sure," Jillian replied. "Have you tried the sushi thingies? They're awesome!"

I smiled, promised to try a sushi thingie, and walked to a far corner of the room where I could observe the crowd unobtrusively. Me and the cluster of designer-decorated Christmas trees.

If I pretend everything is okay, I told myself, it will be. I can have a good time if I want to. It's all about pretending . . .

"This thing blows."

I jumped. Someone was standing at my right. Someone all grungy looking. And mean. Someone oddly familiar.

"Pierce?" I said. "Is that you?"

Pierce grunted and poked at a fragile glass ornament on the tree closest to him. I resisted the urge to tell him to stop.

"You look so—different—from when I last saw you."

Pierce Rogers had been an intern in our office the previous year. The poor boy had had an unfortunate crush on me, made all the more painful for everyone involved by his severe social awkwardness, acne-ridden skin, and overbearing mother.

Thankfully, and not surprisingly, Pierce had gotten over his crush at about the same time another teen had come to intern with us. Lana served as just the right distraction for Pierce's youthful lust. His duties with the Symphony's development office had ended after his spring semester and I hadn't seen him since.

Until tonight. And this Pierce was nothing at all like the old Pierce. This Pierce was fierce.

"What are you doing here?" I asked. For the life of me I couldn't imagine a seventeen-year-old boy with multiple visible piercings, a tattoo on the back of each hand, electric blue hair, and motorcycle boots volunteering to spend an evening with a bunch of adults in tuxedos and gowns.

Pierce snarled. "My %%%^^^*** mother doesn't trust my ass," he told me, ignoring now the delicate ornament he'd been poking.

"Oh." I nodded as if I understood this to be a profound psychological insight.

"You wanna know why?"

Pierce's question was clearly a challenge.

What else did I have to do?

"No, why?" I asked. "Did she find you with drugs?"

Pierce opened his mouth in an exaggerated gesture of surprise. "Whoa. Yeah. Exactly. I mean, it was only pot but she, like, went all medieval on my butt. Now she won't let me out of her sight. It blows, man."

A vision of Mrs. Matilda Rogers came to me and I shuddered to imagine the loud and generally obnoxious matron watching my every move.

"Yeah," I agreed. "I bet it does."

"I mean, it's not like I can't, you know, score something, like, almost anywhere. And, like, go to the bathroom, right? But I'm really not going to the bathroom. Am I? No sir. I am going to the parking lot to get high. Dude."

"It's cold out there tonight, " I said, my attention caught by a passing waiter furtively stuffing a mini-quiche in his mouth.

"Well, I didn't say I was actually in reality going to smoke in the parking lot," Pierce responded, and for a split second I caught a whiff of the former Pierce—the kid who really was intimidated by his formidable mother. "I just said that, you know, I could. If I wanted to."

"Oh, right," I said, nodding. "Yeah. Do you want something to eat?"

Pierce shrugged. "This food is, like, not pizza."

Caviar. Bacon-wrapped scallops. Popsicle-sized lamb chops. No, it certainly wasn't pizza.

"Look at that fat dude by the bar." Pierce snorted. "Could he be any, like, fatter?"

In spite of my self, I grinned. "That's Mr. Winters," I whispered. "He's a very important contributor to the Symphony."

"Yeah, and he's fat. What a lard ass."

"Maybe he has, I don't know, a glandular problem."

Pierce fixed me with a look of such disdain I blushed.

"Oh, all right," I admitted. "The only thing wrong with Mr. Winters is a bad case of what my father called Overactive Fork."

Pierce snorted again. "Good one."

"Pierce," I observed, "you've become downright horrible." He shrugged. "Whatever."

The band struck up a traditional waltz and couples slowly began to fill the dance floor.

"This is, like, old people's music. Dead people dance to this shit."

"What kind of music do you like?" I asked. Not that I knew anything about contemporary rock. Or whatever it was called.

Pierce suddenly became animated. "Do you know the Flatheads?" he asked, bobbing on his toes. "They are so my favorite band. They so rock. And they, like, are all vegans. Except the bass guy. I think he's, like, diuretic or something, so you know how that goes."

"Totally," I said, nodding. "I mean, about—"

But Pierce was no longer listening. He was playing air guitar to some Flathead tune in his head. I turned my attention to the dance floor.

One couple in particular caught my eye. I'd seen them before at various events. They were in their early seventies, always beautifully dressed, perfectly groomed. But what was most attractive about them was the way they seemed to enjoy each other's company. A colleague had told me they'd been married for almost forty years.

Watching them waltz, my heart threatened to break.

It would be so nice to have a partner . . .

"Pierce?" I turned to find him cleaning his nails with a dinner knife. "You wouldn't want to dance with me, would you?"

"Gross," he replied, looking up from his task with a scowl.

I shrugged. "Didn't think so. Anyway, I was just testing you."

Shortly after that, Pierce eyed his mother sailing our way and ducked off to the men's room. Or so he said. I took his abandonment as my cue to leave the ball.

No Prince Charming hurried after me.

Ten

All I want for Christmas is for Christmas to go away.

The next morning I woke with a dull sense of defeat. The weak winter sun was struggling—and failing—to take hold, and a cold wind snuck into my bedroom through the poorly fitted windows.

I sighed and contemplated the ceiling, noting a new crack in the plaster just above my head. As tempting as staying in bed was—in spite of the threat of faltering plaster—I had promised JoAnne I'd attend a gingerbread house–making party at her place in Charlestown. The party had not been her idea; Merv, her fun-loving boyfriend, had foisted it upon her.

I rolled over to look at the clock on my nightstand. Already nine-thirty and I was expected at noon. Another person might have feigned illness and begged off, but there's something tenacious in me. Social training, I suppose. One of my best traits, I've been told, is that I show up.

With a sigh and a shiver, I crawled out of bed.

JoAnne and Merv had gone all out with the decorations. A fresh blue spruce stood in one corner of the living room, hung with funky glass ornaments Merv had ordered from the MOMA catalog. A bowl of fragrant pinecones, lemons, and oranges sat on the mantel of the fireplace, and a sprig of mistletoe hung in the doorway to the kitchen. Classic songs sung by classic singers—Bing Crosby and "White Christmas;" Johnny Mathis and "O Holy Night;" Louis Armstrong and "Is That You, Santa Claus?"—sounded from the CD player.

"Nice, isn't it?" Merv asked when he'd taken my coat. The man was beaming with house-pride.

"Yes," I said. "But Merv? You're not even—well, I mean, you're Jewish."

Merv shrugged. "Being Jewish doesn't mean I'm immune to all the schmaltzy stuff about Christmas. Come on, glitter crafts and caroling and candy canes? Who doesn't love this? Besides, there's a menorah in the kitchen."

I smiled an obligatory smile and Merv went off to greet more new arrivals.

The gathering was an unqualified success. Except for my own Grinch-like grumpiness, I thought, slumped on the couch next to baby Jonah in his red plastic seat, listening to the relaxed and happy voices of those gathered around the table on which sugary building materials were laid out.

"There's our lovely Miss Walker!" Merv boomed, striding across the living room with a short crystal glass in his hand. "Santa Claus told me you were fond of Brandy Alexanders," he said, smiling and handing me the creamy drink.

"You stay away from those, Merv," JoAnne hollered from across the living room. "You don't need the calories."

Merv rolled his eyes but without a trace of annoyance. "See how she loves me," he said. "Always looking out for my health."

I laughed, as was expected, but inside I felt like crying. Oh, I know I should have been happy for my friend, being in love with such a sweet man, and I was happy, really. It's just that I would have been a lot happier if I, too, were in love.

Maybe Merv knows someone for me, I thought, watching him move easily from guest to guest, patting a back here, offering a cookie there. But how could I ask him to set me up? It was too humiliating. I supposed I could ask JoAnne to ask Merv . . .

I took another sip of my drink and determined to put an end to my self-centered thoughts. This wasn't a pity party; this was a cheery holiday event at the home of a dear friend.

I stood and smiled and realized that no one was looking at me. Somehow—inevitably—everyone in the room had paired off—Erin with Nick; Maggie with Jan; Merv with JoAnne; Damion with Frederick—leaving me and a gassy baby Jonah alone together.

"Well, little guy," I said, sinking back onto the couch, "looks like it's just you and me."

Eleven

All I want for Christmas is a brain. Even a small one will do.

To borrow a tired expression, it had been the day from hell.

It started when I woke to find the ceiling over the shower leaking. Again. And a large section of plaster ready to fall on my head. Again. I called Mr. Jarrens who, conveniently, was not answering his phone at 7 A.M. and left a message in the sternest voice I could muster. Then, I took a highly unsatisfactory sponge bath.

Things got worse from there. The T was running late. When a train finally pulled into the station, there was a mad crush as commuters crammed into the cars. Clearly, no one was any happier than I was to be up close and personal with strangers . . .

Except for the creep who stuck his hand under my raised arm—I was clutching an overhead strap—and touched my breast.

I might have chosen not to publicly humiliate Beau Hampton for making an unwanted pass but this jerk was going to suffer.

"How *dare* you!" I demanded loudly.

Mr. Touchy McFeely opened his eyes wide. "I don't know what you're talking about, lady," he protested, breath foul with coffee.

"Oh, yes, you do! I'm going to call the police right now,"

I said, pulling my cell phone out of my bag. "They'll have officers waiting at the next station to arrest you, you worm!"

I pressed 9 and then—

Too late!

The train was pulling into the next station, and before the doors were fully opened, Mr. Gropey McGrabby darted out onto the mobbed platform and was lost to sight.

Not one person on that train car, male or female, offered a word of sympathy or support.

My mood simply plummeted after that. When I got to the office, I learned that Nelly from accounting had gotten engaged the night before.

"I don't know why she bothered to come in today," I said crossly, when at eleven o'clock Nelly still hadn't given me the figures I'd requested. "She's done absolutely no work. All she's done is show off that—that—ring of hers!"

"Oh, come on, Abby," Judy coaxed. "She's just excited. Can't you be happy for her?" Judy lowered her voice. "You know, her fiancé is in the Navy. He's being sent out right after Christmas. He wanted to ask her before he left in case—well, in case something happens to him . . ."

"I didn't know," I said, voice catching, sad for Nelly and embarrassed by my own selfishness. "Where is she now?"

Without waiting for an answer, I set off to find Nelly and wish her my heartfelt congratulations.

At twelve-thirty I ordered a salad from a local diner and, while eating, opened a package I'd requested from Massachusetts University, careful to keep the materials from the view of nosy colleagues.

Three pages into the brochure, my heart sank. In college I'd majored in American history. I hadn't even taken one course in economics. Now, it seemed that before I could officially start the master's in marketing program, I would need to take two introductory business courses. Two business courses! I grabbed my calculator and tapped out the cost per credit . . . There was no way I could afford the extra costs, not with an expected rent increase. I'd been so hoping I wouldn't have to apply for a loan but now it seemed I had no choice. It was either that or ask Mother—more accurately, our lawyer, Mr. Harper—for an advance on my tiny monthly income. Neither prospect was appealing.

Graduate school might have to wait. But for how long? A change in career might not be a possibility. Ever?

Suddenly without an appetite, I tossed the rest of the salad in the trash, noting that I'd just wasted six dollars. From now on, I scolded, you'll bring your lunch from home. Continuing the moment of moral firmness, I dumped five catalogs, determined to make do with my existing wardrobe, at least until spring.

The remainder of the workday passed slowly and miserably. At five o'clock all I wanted to do was head home and ease my troubled mind with a box of mini-muffins. But then it occurred to me that I still had an awful lot of Christmas shopping to do—and that Christmas was only weeks away.

For example, there was Rupert to consider. What does one give a man who has virtually everything? What does one give a man who is literally living off your mother's money?

And then there were gifts for my colleagues. Together they would cost at least two hundred dollars.

With a sigh I headed for the downtown shopping area. And then, just outside the multiplex on Tremont Street, it happened. The event I'd been hoping for . . . And the last thing I wanted to happen at that moment.

"Ooof!"

"Oooh!"

It was him! Handsome! And in my preoccupation, I'd smashed right into him. And once again, he'd reached out and set me back on my feet.

"We've got to stop meeting like this," he said, releasing me but staying close.

I managed a smile but I know it didn't quite reach my eyes.

Handsome noted this. "But seriously," he said, taking a small step back, "I'm not stalking you."

"Oh, I know." I shook my head and managed what I hoped was a more successful smile. "I know."

Handsome hesitated and then said, "Let's move out of the way. I'm taking no chances on another mob separating us."

Together we stepped out of the flow of pedestrian traffic and over to the plate-glass windows of the movie theater.

"So, what's your name?" he asked.

I noted he was wearing the same overcoat he'd worn the first time we'd crashed into each other. It suited him. An unexpected desire to rest my cheek against his chest almost overpowered me. I shoved it away.

I was supposed to be learning to stand on my own two feet. To be discriminating. To have pride. I flashed on my sagging bathroom ceiling and the morning's horrid subway guy; on Nelly's diamond and the money I'd need for school; on the notion of applying for a mortgage and carrying it alone.

"Abigail," I said flatly. "Abby Walker."

"Pleased to meet you, Abby." Handsome put out his hand and I shook it. Even through my leather glove I could feel that his bare hand was warm. "I mean, to really meet you. Not just crash into you."

He introduced himself as Greg Hanson. He explained that he was a partner in a law firm that had been started by his father, now retired. "We're on the tenth floor of a building a few blocks from here. I was just on my way back to the office. Another late night, unfortunately."

"Oh," I replied.

Oh? What kind of response is that, I scolded myself. But before I could urge my brain to kick into social gear, Greg asked, "Well, what's your excuse for being in the neighborhood?"

"I was going to do some Christmas shopping," I admitted.

"You didn't get it all done at that Christmas shop?" he said, eyes twinkling.

A sudden vision of the enormous American Express bill I'd be facing passed before my eyes and I felt sick to my stomach.

"That must mean you're a generous person," Greg added, before I could respond.

Oh, I thought, he doesn't know me at all! He doesn't know that I'm actually terribly self-centered and irresponsible . . .

I couldn't find a word to say.

Finally, Greg cleared his throat. "Look," he said, "I know this has been strange, total strangers bumping into each other three times, and I don't even know if you have someone special—"

"No." The response was automatic, and abrupt.

"Okay," he said. "Then, would you like to go out with me some time? Say, for dinner?"

If at any other time he had asked me for a date, I would have cried, "Yes!" But at the end of what had been one of the worst days of my life, conscious of smudged mascara and the onset of a pounding headache, feet frozen from the puddle I hadn't been able to avoid, self-esteem at an all-time low—

"Thank you," I said, looking just to the left of his face, unable to meet his lovely green eyes. "But I can't."

A moment of silence followed in which I felt stunned and sad and stupid.

Greg took another small step away from me. "Okay, then," he said. "I'm sorry—"

"Don't be," I mumbled, fighting back tears.

"Okay, then," he repeated. "Well, I've got to get back to the office. Have a good holiday, Abby."

He seemed disappointed and I was sorry for that but again no words came to my lips, no retraction, no apology.

I snuck a look over my shoulder at his retreating form and came very, very close to calling out after him.

And then he was gone.

That evening the reality of what I'd done slammed into me. It had been such a rotten day and I had been feeling so dejected . . .

Oh, but there was no good excuse for my stupidity! For the first time in my life I felt like screaming, like punching the wall, like tearing my hair. I settled for sitting on the couch with my face in my hands and moaning.

And then, inspiration struck. I could search for Greg on the Internet! People did that sort of thing all the time. Why, just the other day a girl at work had located her former high school history teacher through Google. That's a search engine. Or something like that. I wasn't really sure but I knew I could find out.

Hope was not lost! I went to the kitchen and prepared a cup of plum tea. While the water heated in the teapot, I pictured my wedding to Greg, an early summer event, with clusters of pink peonies and a long, trailing veil embroidered with rosebuds . . .

The teapot's whistle sounded sharply and I came out of my reverie. As I poured the steaming water into the cup, darker thoughts crept in. I wondered if Greg would think me, well, crazy, if I hunted him down.

Frowning, I brought my tea into the living room. And how, exactly, would I go about contacting Greg, assuming I found his address or phone number? This was tricky stuff, I realized. No wonder people hired private investigators to find their missing loved ones.

I sat at the computer and determined to focus. The sweet aroma of the tea calmed me and I took a sip.

Still too hot. I put the cup down and called up something

called a people finder. First name? I typed: Gregory. Last name?

Last name! I swear my heart skipped a beat when I realized I didn't remember Greg's last name! He'd told me, I was sure of it, but I'd been so wrapped up in my own misery . . .

Think, Abby, think! I did remember that Greg was partner in a law firm founded by his father, which meant his last name probably was part of the firm's name. Somebody, Somebody and Somebody.

But that didn't give me much to go on. What was I supposed to do? Call every law firm in town and ask for "Greg—you know, the tall, handsome one"?

I wondered: Would I even recognize his name if I saw it, say, in the phone book, under attorneys-at-law? Would I recognize it if I spotted it on a sign board in the lobby of a building?

And did I really have the nerve to canvass the entire downtown area looking for a law firm with a familiar-sounding name?

And if I found him, what then? Would Greg Handsome be pleased to find a crazy woman in his waiting room?

No, I decided. He would not.

I took another sip of the tea, only to discover it was now too cold. With a sigh I turned off the lights and went to bed.

Twelve

All I want for Christmas is—revenge.

My schedule that week was slow so I took a half day to visit my mother in Lincoln. Rupert was spending the day at his gym. Sometimes it was nice to be alone with my mother. Mrs. Walker. Not Mrs. Walker-Gilliam.

We spent the late morning hours in Mother's bedroom. Mother wanted to sort through her spring wardrobe and select clothes to be given on commission to The Second Act on Newbury Street. Less gorgeous, more utilitarian clothes would go to various shelters for the poor and homeless.

I don't know why my mother even bothered with a consignment shop. She certainly didn't need the money. Maybe she just needed an excuse for an excursion to Boston's most expensive shopping street.

By twelve-thirty we'd assigned four "gently worn" gowns for resale and selected two jackets, three blouses, and four pairs of slacks for donation. When Mother wasn't looking, I stuffed a pretty pink silk scarf into my purse. It was okay, I told myself. I'd given her the scarf a few years earlier for her birthday and the tags were still attached. The scarf deserved to be worn.

"What do you want to do for lunch?" I asked.

"Oh, I've taken care of that," Mother said, hands clasped as she gazed once more at the gowns. "I ordered a nice luncheon from that nice place in town, what's it called?"

"Donna's Delicacies? That's nice."

Together, Mother and I went down to the dining room where Greta, the housekeeper and maid-of-all-trades, was just laying out our meal.

Mother chattered on about the gowns as if they were children she was sending off on a dangerous journey. I winked at Greta. She raised an eyebrow in return. Greta and I had become fast friends not long after Rupert had hired her.

When we'd finished lunch and were halfway through coffee, I was surprised by the appearance of the family's lawyer. One of them, anyway. After brief greetings, Mr. Harper asked if he might speak with me in what had been my father's study. With a questioning glance at Mother—who returned it with a look of utter innocence—I followed Mr. Harper from the dining room.

Once settled in the traditionally decorated man's study— lots of dark brown leather and brass accents—I wondered if I should ask Mr. Harper if he knew a young lawyer named Greg Something and quickly discarded the idea as ridiculous.

"Abby, is something on your mind?" Mr. Harper questioned, with that sharp, lawyerly look.

"No, no, nothing," I said, smoothing my long, wool plaid skirt.

The lawyer cleared his throat and tapped a slim manila file folder on the desk.

"Okay, then," he said, "your mother and I have discussed this at some length and we think it's time you learned more of the details of your father's will. Details about the payout of your personal estate. And such."

And then Mr. Harper told me something shocking. My father had stipulated that if I married, I was to receive a rather large—no, a huge—sum of money, and a not-insignificant cash sum annually, as long as the marriage lasted.

I gripped the arms of the leather chair and noticed they'd been recently oiled.

"I'm not sure I understand," I said carefully. "If I marry . . . and stay married . . . What if my husband dies and I remarry? Wait, that's jumping ahead. If I stay single—?"

"If you don't marry," Mr. Harper replied, his silver eyebrows drawn down in a well-practiced expression of concern, "you will continue to receive your monthly allowance."

I shook my head. I could make no sense of it all. "But if I don't marry, isn't there a greater chance that I might be in more need of financial support? Especially if I remain in my line of work . . ."

Mr. Harper had the decency to look uncomfortable. "Possibly," he admitted. "But I can't argue with your father's will."

If he couldn't, then I certainly could! "What if I contested it? What if I hired a lawyer and—"

The look on Mr. Harper's face stopped me. It was pity or something very like it. I guessed he knew something I didn't about the document in question. Like the fact that it was iron-clad.

"Okay," I said, my voice barely audible. Trembling, I stood.

"Abby—" Mr. Harper began, but I cut him off.

"Goodbye, Mr. Harper," I said more loudly, and left my father's study. A million questions raced through my head but now was not the time to ask them. At least, not of Mr. Harper.

I found my mother in the sitting room. The sight of her perched on the divan made the blood rush to my cheeks. Did she know about Father's will? Had she tried to argue him out of such a ridiculous, punitive decree?

Calm down, I told myself. Slowly, the anger receded, to be replaced by something like dull defeat.

"Oh, dear, there you are!" Mother piped as I entered the room. "How was your meeting with Mr. Harper?"

I sat heavily on the overstuffed couch. "He told me," I said. "About Father's will. About me."

Mother's hands fluttered in her lap until she clasped them tightly.

"Your father," she said, looking down at her clasped hands, "was a man of very strong opinions. He was not to be reasoned with." Mother raised her eyes then and I saw an unfamiliar look of rueful sadness in them. "At least, he would never listen to his wife."

"Why did you marry him?" I blurted, shocked by my own nerve.

Mother sat up straighter and the look of sadness was gone from her eyes. "I married him because I loved him. I was in love with your father, Abigail, from the moment I laid eyes on him. It was, I suppose, my fate."

A happy one? I wondered.

And then, Mother changed the subject.

"Well, now, dear, we should talk about you. You're the one with a whole life ahead of you."

I nodded noncommittally. And then: "Mother, why didn't you tell me about Father's will years ago?"

Mother looked at me carefully, as if willing me to understand the meaning behind her next words. "Well, I suppose it didn't seem quite necessary. Until now."

Ah. "You told me now," I said, my voice oddly emotionless in spite of the frenzy in my head, "because time is running out. Because I'm already thirty-four and you think that if I don't get married soon, I'll have lost all chance of ever getting married."

"Dear," my mother replied, "I thought that if you knew about the money, you might, well, just get on with things."

"I'm not in love, Mother," I said. "My fate hasn't found me, like yours found you."

"My dear," Mother went on, "you must remember that people marry for all sorts of reasons. Love is only one of them. Romantic love, I mean."

"What other reasons are there?" I muttered.

My mother's answer came promptly. "Companionship."

Or social status, I thought. Or money. But I said nothing. For all I knew, Rupert had married for companionship as well as for social status and money.

For all I knew. Which didn't seem to be much. I wondered what other secrets about my family were still to be unveiled.

"Now, take Dean Widermeyer," Mother said brightly. "He's an upstanding member of the church, and since his wife died last year, he's been just so lonely. He's let Mrs. Gardner know he's looking for a new mother for those adorable children."

My head began to pound and I leaned farther into the couch. "Are you saying I should date Dean Widermeyer?" I asked. I'd never been drawn to men who were fond of three-piece suits. And his "adorable" children were in reality insufferably spoiled.

My mother pondered this for a moment. "No, actually, I don't think he's quite the right husband for you. But you see my point, dear? Perhaps you haven't been considering marriage in just the right light. You're searching the horizon for Prince Charming when perhaps a perfectly nice husband is living just next door."

There really was little point in arguing with my mother. In some ways, we were just so different. "Thank you, Mother," I said. "I promise I'll think about what you've said."

Mother smiled, and in that moment, she looked so very young. "I'm glad, dear. I so want you to be happy. I want you to know the happiness I know with my Rupert!"

Soon after, I left for home.

Thirteen

Now this is serious. All I want for Christmas is for my girl-friends to be with me always.

The bizarre afternoon with my mother and Mr. Harper had forced my thoughts back to Marge. I wondered what the important men in her life—her father and husband—had thought of women, how they had regarded her, in particular. Had they really taken good care of her? Or had they destroyed her with their so-called protection?

I decided to go to the Women's Lunch Place during my lunch hour and see Marge.

I thought about bringing her something but couldn't decide what might be appropriate. And then I wondered if there was some policy that might forbid the giving of personal gifts to guests. I vowed to learn more about the etiquette of shelters and set out empty-handed.

As I passed through the first door of the church basement, I wondered what I would say to Marge. "See, I told you I'd come back!" was out as I'd never promised to return. "How are you?" was surely an acceptable question with which to begin a conversation, though I couldn't imagine Marge's answer would be a happy one.

Then again, she hadn't really complained when we'd spoken briefly on Thanksgiving. In fact, it seemed that all Marge had really wanted was to have a conversation with another woman—plain and simple.

And really, Abby, I scolded, it won't kill you to listen to a few complaints and offer some sympathy or advice. That's what friends are for.

Friends?

"Can I help you?"

The abrupt tone of the woman's voice startled me until I realized that she might be suspicious of my presence. The volunteers at WLP were protective of the guests, and of the safe space they had provided for them.

"Oh, yes," I said quickly. "I'm looking for someone I met here. On Thanksgiving. Her name is Marge."

"Why do you want to find her?" she asked. "Who are you?"

"My name is Abigail Walker," I said. "Abby. I just want to say hello. Really. Marge and I chatted a bit and I was just wondering how she was doing."

A moment of silence followed as the volunteer considered my story. Finally, she said, "Well, we have a few guests named Marge. What does your friend look like?"

Friend. There was that word again.

"Um, let's see. She's about my height, maybe a bit taller," I said, working hard to recall outstanding details of Marge's appearance. "Her hair is short with gray roots, as if she hasn't been to the beauty parlor in a while."

The inanity of that last remark hit me and my cheeks burned. But the volunteer, clearly used to such casual insensitivity, simply nodded.

"Anything else?" she asked.

"Well, yes," I said, suddenly remembering the gold and ruby ring on Marge's right hand. I described the ring to the volunteer, then added the final piece of information. "And she told me she was living in her car."

"Yup, I know that Marge, all right." The volunteer shifted

the stack of dirty dishes in her arms, and sighed. "But I haven't seen her since Thanksgiving. Nobody has."

The possibility of Marge having disappeared simply hadn't occurred to me. "But maybe someone knows about the car," I pressed, "what kind it is or where she parks it?"

"Marge didn't talk much," the woman noted. "If you had a conversation with her, she must really have liked you."

"You're using the past tense," I said almost angrily. "You said 'Marge didn't' instead of 'Marge doesn't.'"

The volunteer looked at me closely, as if trying to understand why I cared. "I'm sorry," she said finally. "I didn't mean anything by it. Look, I've got to get these dishes into the dishwasher. If Marge shows up, you want me to tell her you came by? Abby, was it?"

I nodded. The volunteer walked away. Ducking my head to hide the tears pricking at my eyes, I hurried from the room and out onto Newbury Street. Directly across from the church was Louis of Boston, a mecca of retail indulgence.

What irony.

A recent study conducted at UCLA revealed that there's something uniquely special about women's friendships with other women. It seems that women respond to stress partly by producing certain chemicals in the brain that cause them to make and maintain friendships with each other.

None of the information in the study really came as a surprise to me—or to any of my women friends—but it was nice to see our native wisdom formally acknowledged.

So now, rather than fight or flee, I was going to befriend—if not tend—in the hopes of relieving some of the stress I'd been experiencing since my meeting with Mr. Harper.

Erin, JoAnne, Maggie, and I gathered at the bar in the Ritz Hotel at the corner of Newbury Street and the Boston Gardens. With a roaring fireplace, shiny brass wall sconces, and a highly polished dark wood bar, it seemed a bastion of an old-money, male-dominated world, similar to my father's study—an interesting choice for a meeting of women, one of whom was about to reveal her father's antiquated notions of feminine intellect.

As simply as I could, I explained the terms of my father's will. Before I could finish speaking, JoAnne's face had grown dark.

"He *what*?" she cried.

Erin flinched. Several people in the well-appointed room stared disapprovingly and I tried to take on a general air of apology.

Maggie laid a hand on JoAnne's arm.

"The man is dead, okay?" she said calmly. "You can't hit him so just calm down."

JoAnne shifted noisily in her chair, unwilling to let her anger go.

"I know it seems odd," I said, keeping an eye on the bartender, who looked poised to bounce the perpetrator of the next outburst.

"Odd? It's outright insulting! It's stupid. It's—"

Erin interrupted. "I think we all agree Mr. Walker's attitude toward women was somewhat—archaic—but there's nothing we can do now but help Abby deal with this—this stunning news."

"Let's just drop it, please," I begged.

"I thought you wanted to talk," Erin said, leaning toward me.

"I did," I admitted. "I just didn't want to start a riot. I don't hate my father, you know. I loved him. I guess it's just that I didn't know him very well."

"And he didn't know his daughter very well, either," JoAnne observed.

"Abby," Maggie said, "is there a time limit on this deal? I mean, do you have until, say, forty to marry and get the money?"

"No," I said, thinking of this new twist. "At least, I don't think there's a time limit."

"Too bad," JoAnne grunted. "You could just wait until the day before you turn forty, drag some unsuspecting hottie idiot down the aisle, grab the money, and slap the guy with a divorce the very next day. Bet Daddy Dearest didn't think of that!"

I wrinkled my nose. "No, that's horrible," I said. "I could never do something so—cold."

JoAnne shrugged.

"Abby," Maggie asked now, "did the lawyer tell you what happens to the money if you never get married? Does the money just sit around doing no one any good until you're dead? And then—what?"

My stomach sank. I hadn't stayed around to ask Mr. Harper about all the contingencies. Reluctantly, I admitted as much to my friends. "I was just so shocked," I told them. "I know that's not an excuse for ignorance . . ."

Erin patted my arm. "You have nothing to apologize for. You can always find out the details later. With the help of your own lawyer."

I nodded. There was so much to understand. "I guess," I said finally, "that my being an only child . . . My father had no son to carry on the business—or the family name. I guess that meant something to him. I just don't know."

JoAnne slammed her empty glass of scotch on the table. "Please don't tell me there's a bonus if you reproduce!"

Oh, Lord, I hadn't thought to ask Mr. Harper about that, either! I made a mental note to call him very soon with a long list of questions for which I would demand answers.

"Let's call a halt to this discussion," Erin said then. "It's beginning to make me sick."

I readily agreed.

JoAnne summoned our waiter and we ordered another round of cocktails. When he'd served us and gone off,

JoAnne, who'd been peeking in the direction of the bar, turned to Maggie with a sly smile.

"Okay, honey, don't turn around, just trust me. There's a rich old guy at the bar and he's been eyeing you for the past five minutes. In that way."

"Me!" Maggie blushed crazily. "No way. "

"Yes, way," Erin teased.

"Can you believe this?" Maggie squeaked. "Isn't this so typical of the way life works? Why couldn't I have snagged a rich old guy when I was dating men? Now that I'm happily with a woman, the sugar daddies come out of the woodwork!"

"There's been more than one?" I asked, glad for the silly turn of topic.

"Well, no," Maggie admitted. "Just this one guy. But you get my point."

"Yup. Timing is everything," Erin pronounced.

Thinking suddenly of Handsome, I silently agreed.

Fourteen

Okay. Here goes. All I want for Christmas is a man who refuses to wear green tights. Ever.

The effect of my father's decree from beyond the grave was the opposite of what he might have wished. Knowing what I knew about my potential inheritance didn't make me intensify the search for a husband. It made me consider—briefly—a life of celibacy.

And then it left me with a slightly dirty feeling. I wondered how long it would take for the specter of Greed to recede enough so that I could look at a man for who he was, not for what he might get me through marriage.

Answer: About three days.

Judy, our administrative assistant, is a motherly type. She's always baking cookies for the staff, selling wrapping paper for her children's school, and trying to fix up the single women. Where she meets single men, I have no idea, what with living out in Framingham, driving three kids to and from soccer practice, covering for a husband who travels, and keeping an eye on a mother-in-law in assisted living.

Still, she's made a few successful matches, so when she told me about Walt Stewart, banker, I halfheartedly agreed to go out with him. After all, I thought, what did I have to lose? I'd already thrown away my chance with Greg Handsome.

Walt Stewart and I met right after work. I didn't bother to

change into an outfit more appropriate for a date but wore what I'd worn to the office: a navy skirt suit; a cream-colored high-necked blouse; sensible navy pumps; pearl earrings and necklace. Finally, I reanchored my hair into a bun.

The evening was doomed from the start.

The second nail in the coffin: Walt Stewart appeared at Joe's American Bar and Grill in chinos about an inch too short, an ancient barn jacket, and a baseball cap worn backward. There's something a bit sad about a sartorially mismatched couple.

Not that we were a couple, exactly.

Maybe he had the day off, I thought, noting a large expanse of dingy white socks. Still, he might at least have turned the hat forward before meeting me.

We were seated at a table in the dining area, and while we waited for menus, I determined to give Walt the benefit of the doubt.

"So," I said, feigning interest, "Judy told me you work for Investors Capital?"

"Actually, I don't work for them anymore," Walt said brightly.

"Oh, I'm sorry," I replied automatically. "The economy is so bad . . ."

Walt laughed. "Oh, no. I didn't get laid off. I quit."

"You quit?" I repeated, perhaps a bit too loudly. "For a better job?"

"Nah. 'Cause I want to be an actor."

Here was an unexpected bit of news. Walt Stewart had to be in his late thirties. And he was just starting a career in acting?

"Oh," I said. "I see. Do you, um, have an agent?"

"Nope. But I've got a few leads," Walt said, scratching his neck with vigor.

Ten minutes. I'd been on this date for ten minutes and already I wanted to run. It was the clothes. The profession. And now, it was the trickle of blood on his neck. Walt Stewart had torn open a pimple with his intense scratching.

The menus arrived and I was able to look away from Acne McActor. "So," I said, "have you actually—um, acted?"

"Sure!" he boomed. "I've done some TV work."

I glanced up at that bit of news. "Oh. That's great."

Walt Stewart leaned across the table and I instinctively leaned back in my chair. "Hey," he said, ignorant of my discomfort, "my piece runs between five and seven each evening. We can catch it now. I mean, if you'd like to see it?"

Oh, I thought. Between five and seven. Just when the evening news airs. Maybe Walt Stewart was a special reporter on a cable news station . . .

"Okay," I said, and followed him back to the bar area. I took my purse and coat with me.

Walt Stewart asked the bartender, a funky-looking guy about twenty-five, if he would turn to a particular cable channel.

"What do you want to see?" the bartender asked, aiming the remote at the television suspended at the far corner of the bar. "There's no game tonight."

Walt Stewart winked at me. "This is way better than a game, trust me. Ssshhh! Here it comes!"

And there it was. There he was. Walt Stewart, my date, leaping manically across the screen in a pair of baggy green tights, a lopsided cap with a jingle bell at the end, and a mock-medieval tunic.

Walt Stewart's television work was a commercial for a furniture warehouse. You know the kind of commercial. Bad script. Lame jokes. Poor production. Tinny music.

Mesmerized, I stared at the screen as Greenie McGruesome capered and shouted.

"Eldridge the Elf wants you all to be good little boys and girls and come on down to our Christmas blowout warehouse sale . . ."

When the commercial was over, I cringed. It wasn't a choice.

Walt, however, seemed blissfully unaware of his mortified date. And the smirking bartender.

"Well?" he asked, beaming. "Whaddya think?"

"Um, how—how did you get that—gig?" I squeaked.

"My uncle owns the store," Walt explained unabashedly. "I figure if I do a whole series of commercials for him, I've got the start of a real portfolio. Or whatever actors call their, like, résumé. I'm still learning the lingo, you know."

"Then, you'll probably be thinking of moving to New York," I said casually, noting that the front door was very, very close.

"L.A.," Walt corrected. "I'm shooting to be settled out there this time next year. After the next round of Eldridge Christmas ads are filmed."

Did Judy know all this when she set me up with Walt, I wondered. And if so, why, why had she done so?

"Um, Walt?" I said, faking a smile. "Why don't you go back to our table while I run to the ladies' room, okay?"

"Sure," he said, fingering the crusting pimple on his neck. "Don't be long."

When he was out of sight, the bartender—my sudden coconspirator—gave me a nod and I ran. I didn't stop running for blocks.

When I got home, I called Judy to apologize. I'd decided she couldn't have known about Walt Stewart's new "career." Judy was out so I left a message with her oldest daughter, a girl of fourteen.

"All guys suck," Lola told me knowingly. "I'm so totally sure it wasn't your fault."

After thanking Lola for her support, I dialed Erin's number, half hoping she'd be out. But she wasn't so I gathered my courage and told her about my recent disastrous dates—as well as about Greg. About how we'd met a magical three times. About how I'd felt such a spark. And about how I'd blown it all by being such an idiot.

"Maybe you're aiming too low," Erin suggested when she'd finished laughing about the Eldridge the Elf episode. "Maybe you should raise your expectations."

"Why?" I replied sulkily. "So I have even farther to fall when they don't come true?"

Erin laughed. "Oh, come on, Abby! With that kind of attitude—"

"Well," I blurted, sudden anger boiling in my chest, "what kind of attitude am I supposed to have? All happy and optimistic and la-de-da when I'm all alone and it's Christmastime and—"

"Hey," Erin said forcefully. I closed my mouth but the awful out-of-control feeling was still there.

"Look, Abby," she went on. "I'm sorry, I shouldn't throw platitudes at you. You have the right to feel crappy when you need to feel crappy. Everybody needs a good bout of self-pity now and then. But please, do me a favor and never, ever say you're all alone. That is ridiculous. You are not all alone. You have me and JoAnne and Maggie, and that's an awful lot. Do you hear me?"

"Yes," I mumbled. "I know. It's just—"

Tears prevented me from going on.

Erin sighed. "I know, Abby. I do understand. I've been there. Every woman has. With all three of us hooked up, you feel—like an extra."

"I don't want to interfere," I managed to croak. "I don't want to ruin your happiness. But I miss you all . . ."

"And we miss you! God, there are times when all I want to do is hang with my girlfriends, even when things are great with Nick. Face it, honey. Guys aren't enough, even the sweetest, sexiest guys in the world. We need each other.

Women need women. And you have me and JoAnne and Maggie and we have you and that's the end of that. All right?"

"All right," I whispered. I knew Erin was right. I'd known before I'd called and forced her to lecture me. But I'd needed to hear that lecture.

"Good," Erin replied. "Now, about that Greg guy. I thought you believed in fate."

"I do. I think."

"Good. If it's meant to be with him, it's meant to be."

"Or not," I said.

"Or not. And then there'll be someone else. Don't lose faith in your soul mate, Abby. He needs you believing in him because that belief is going to shine out like a beacon and guide him to you."

I burst out laughing. "Do I really sound so ridiculous?"

"Yeah," said my best friend. "But I tolerate you anyway."

Fifteen

Please. All I want for Christmas is something nice to happen. Anything.

I try to be a good daughter. I do. Most times, I'm not sure my mother even notices my presence in a room, let alone my larger efforts. But that's another story.

This story is about how I agreed to attend the Winthrops' annual Christmas tree–decorating party as the family representative. Mother had come down with a bad flu and Rupert wasn't in the habit of attending parties without her. So, reluctantly, I agreed to attend, though I'd never liked Mrs. Alberta Winthrop in the least. She was overbearing and snobby and, in my opinion, the sole reason poor Mr. Harlan Winthrop spent much of his day propped up in a corner, sipping from a large glass of bourbon and nodding benignly.

Dressed in a pair of winter-white slacks and a red silk blouse, I arrived at the Winthrop home to find the usual—music too low to be identified; a sullen housekeeper pressed into service as waitress; and several yapping, rat-like dogs nipping at exposed ankles.

No one was even remotely interested in trimming the tree, a white plastic monstrosity. Mrs. Winthrop, I thought, eyeing the hot-pink foil star atop the tree, must have been sneaking sips from Mr. Winthrop's glass when she made such an outrageous error in taste.

As was typical of these parties, the men stood in small clusters, downing glasses of brown liquor on ice and talking in low, self-important tones.

The women, meanwhile, paid court to Mrs. Winthrop. That day she sat squarely on an overstuffed, chintz-covered couch, a self-satisfied smile on her face, a boxy tweed suit emphasizing her bulk. Though I'm sure she thought she presented a magnificent picture, to me she seemed like a giant toad squatting on a slimy rock.

Dutifully, I joined the group. The conversation rapidly turned to the upcoming nuptials of Mrs. Webster's daughter, Charlotte. And from there, to the engagement of Bunny Smith's sister, Suze. I had nothing to add, having been so out of touch with these women for the past years, but I nodded and murmured when it seemed appropriate. Like when Mrs. Webster whispered—as if she really wanted the information kept secret!—that Charlotte's ring was a full three and a half carats.

Suddenly, Mrs. Winthrop turned to me with a piercing eye. Not for the first time I noted that she had a full three chins— and that her daughter, Alice Winthrop-Graham, was about to come into her own inheritance.

"Abigail, you've been awfully quiet," Mrs. Winthrop said with a syrupy smile and a not-subtle glance at my left hand. "Dear, I must ask. Why aren't you married yet?"

An expectant hush fell over the group. Mouths salivated, eyes narrowed, nerves tingled for the kill.

Mother, I thought, gripping my glass of eggnog tightly, the things I do for you.

Formerly, my answer to this incredibly insensitive question had been: "Because I'm waiting for my soul mate." But now, I gave her the reply Erin offers in such a situation.

"Because," I said, sweetly and wide-eyed, "no one has asked me."

By the way, I added silently, your Christmas tree is ugly.

An uncomfortable murmur rose around me. Mrs. Webster

scooted her chair away a few inches and Mrs. Gardner, seated to my left, showed me her bony, brocade-covered back. Mrs. Winthrop glared. Interestingly, the only one who seemed mildly amused by my reply was Mrs. Winthrop's daughter, Alice. She gave me a look I couldn't quite interpret, though it definitely wasn't hostile, and a small smile played briefly on her lips.

"If you'll excuse me," I said, my best social smile well in place. I rose and made my way to the dining room, where the table was laid with a spectacular buffet. But I had little appetite.

Just as I was contemplating another glass of eggnog—

"Well, hello!"

I whirled, startled, incredulous—

It was him! Handsome. Gregory. Greg.

God—the Universe—Somebody!—was giving me another chance! All I want, I prayed silently, is not to blow it!

"Are you sure you're not stalking me?" I asked, feeling my cheeks flood with heat.

Greg laughed merrily, as if he were truly happy to see me again. The woman who'd knocked a shopping bag out of his hand, stepped on his toes, and turned him down so unceremoniously on a street corner.

"I think I'm not," he said. "But this is getting spooky!"

"Spooky in a good way," I replied boldly, noting that once again Greg was beautifully dressed. His style was manly and classic. I liked that. No dirty white socks. No ill-fitting leather jackets. No green tights.

Greg nodded. "Definitely."

"So, you know the Winthrops," I said, desperate for a conversation to develop.

"For years," he said. "My father used to do some business for Mr. Winthrop. My family moved to Atlanta some time ago but I came back to Boston after law school. Making me the New England rep of the Hansons. I tolerate these parties for my parents' sake."

Hanson, Hanson, Hanson. The name was now burned into my brain.

I told Greg that I was attending in place of my mother—another little link in the chain I hoped was binding us close.

"Dutiful children," he said.

"Most times."

There was a natural pause in our conversation and it felt anything but awkward. We looked at each other, smiling, appreciating. I was almost reluctant for that comfortable moment to end.

"What do you do, Abby?" Greg asked finally.

"I work in development at the Symphony," I told him.

"Sounds like interesting work."

"It's not," I said, so abruptly we both laughed. "Well, maybe it was, once. But I've been bored with my job for quite some time now."

"Time for a change of career?"

"It might be." And then, though I'd not even told my best friends, I told Greg: "I know it sounds silly but I've been toying with the idea of going to graduate school. For a degree in marketing."

"What's silly about that?" Greg replied. "Education is never a waste."

"True," I said. "But I don't know if I could be successful in graduate school now."

"Why not?" Greg asked bluntly. "You're obviously intelligent. And something tells me you're not the lazy type."

I laughed. "How could you know that?"

A shrill feminine voice distracted us and we both peered into the living room.

"I noticed no one has been trimming the tree," Greg said dryly.

I made a face.

Greg mimicked my look of disgust. "I know. What was she thinking?"

"I'm not a snob, really," I blurted, grinning in spite of myself. "It's just that—just that a Christmas tree should be real. At the very least it should be green!"

"I wonder what Mr. Winthrop has to say about his wife's taste." Greg nodded in the direction of the far corner of the dining room. True to form, our host sat in an armchair, clutching a glass of bourbon and smiling amiably at no one in particular.

"I can't imagine she cares what he thinks," I said, then clapped a hand to my mouth. "Oh, I can't believe I said that!"

Greg reached out and gently brought my hand away from my mouth. He held it a moment before letting it go.

"You spoke what we know to be the truth," he said. "Whatever the Winthrops have is not my idea of a marriage, either."

And at that moment, I fell in love. With Greg Hanson's body and soul, his words and touch, with everything about him, what I knew and what I didn't yet know.

Gazing into his wonderful green eyes, I knew. He gazed back and I just knew—

"Gregory?"

"Huh?" I said eloquently.

"What?" he added.

Suddenly, Greg and I were no longer alone. Shaken back to the larger world, we found ourselves with—another woman.

She was near-perfect. Her features were even, symmetrical, perfectly proportioned. She was tall but not too tall. Taller than me. Her hair was thick and straight and icy blond. She was thin. But not emaciated. Oh, no. I would have liked to think she'd had a breast enlargement but her breasts were all too obviously natural—and the wraparound dress she was wearing showed them to full advantage.

"Abby," Greg said, clearing his throat, "this is my—"

The goddess stuck out her hand and said, "Valerie. Nice to meet you."

My voice caught and I swallowed before croaking, "Nice to meet you."

Her handshake was brutally strong and I winced.

Well. I'd been put in my place.

"Greg, we really should be going," Valerie said, taking his arm, still smiling brightly at me.

Greg's eyes went dark. I wasn't sure if he sensed my discomfort or simply was thinking of a pressing appointment.

"You're right," he said, to Valerie, but looking at me. "We'll be late for—Abby, it was so good to spend time with you . . ."

He put out his hand and I took it reluctantly, thinking it would all be much easier if he'd just leave. So that I could crumple up and die.

I mumbled a few words in parting. Then Greg Hanson and his date were gone and I was left alone by the platter of bloody roast beef.

All the way home on the commuter rail I berated myself. How could I have thought that someone as handsome and funny and smart as Greg was at a party alone! Of course he'd be with a woman. And of course she'd be stunning!

I convinced myself that I must have imagined the electricity between us. I'd done it before, imagined a level of intimacy that didn't actually exist. God, I'd thought John Weston was about to propose when what he really was about to do was break up with me!

Later that evening, in a futile effort to get my mind off Greg and the Bombshell, I called Maggie, hoping to learn something more about Marge.

Maggie answered.

"Hey, Abby, what's up?" She sounded hassled.

"Oh, nothing," I said hurriedly. "You sound tired."

"I am. I'm always tired. Not much I can do about it, either."

"Are you sure I'm not bothering—"

"It's bothering me that you're being so skittish! Talk."

I did. I asked if she had seen Marge at the WLP since Thanksgiving. She hadn't.

"Oh," I said. "Well, I think she was about to lose her car. She told me she had no money for a mechanic."

"That's too bad."

"Isn't there anything anyone can do?" I pleaded.

"For Marge," Maggie said, "or for all the women like her? It's a big problem, Abby. And there are no easy answers. People far smarter about this stuff than me are stumped beyond a certain point. I don't know what I can tell you."

"I guess I wanted to hear something that would make me feel better," I admitted. "Not so—guilty."

"Why do you feel guilty?" Maggie asked. "I can't imagine you said anything to Marge that—"

"No," I interrupted. "I didn't say anything bad. I'm just being silly. I'll let you go now, okay?"

I could picture Maggie shrugging, her mind already on to the next task in her busy life. "Okay," she said. "Sleep tight."

"Kiss the baby for me," I said and hung up the phone.

Sixteen

All I want for Christmas is a new family. Now.

The club's annual Christmas Ball. The last place I wanted to spend an evening was with the Winthrop set, especially after the fiasco that was the tree-trimming party. But once again, at my mother's request, and strangely this time at Rupert's as well, I agreed to attend.

I chose to wear a basic black, cocktail-length gown, with a portrait neckline and three-quarter sleeves. Elegant, but not outstanding. And on the off chance that Greg Hanson made an appearance—well, what did that really matter? He had Valerie.

Mother, Rupert, and I arrived at the club shortly after seven o'clock. I spotted the Winthrops immediately—Mrs., Mr., and Alice, but no Peter, her husband. I determined not to seek them out and felt pretty sure they would avoid me as well.

After settling at our table, I excused myself and went off to the ladies' lounge to check my makeup. While reapplying, my mind was set at ease—at least on the topic of running into Greg and his Barbie doll—by a conversation between two matrons sneaking a cigarette.

"Well," said the mauve-clad woman after a long drag, "I'm sure I don't know how successful this evening will be, what with so many of our men missing."

"Dear," her rust-covered friend replied, "don't remind me!

The Balder brothers are traveling. Something to do with the Alps. And that adorable Gregory Hanson is said to be out of town on business of some sort. I'm just sick about it. I was so looking forward to a dance! Why work has to interfere with pleasure, I'll never know."

Mauve dropped the butt of her cigarette into a glass of water and sighed. "Well, I suppose we'll just have to make do with our husbands."

Rust shook her head ruefully. "At least your Robert doesn't tromp on your feet like my George. One would think the man was raised in a cave, the way he capers on the dance floor!"

Lord, save me from such a fate, I prayed as I returned to the ball. Were all marriages horrible compromises?

At our table I found Mother and Rupert engaged in amiable conversation with a stranger. He introduced himself to me as Clive Whitaker. I placed him in his early forties. He was quite slim and I wondered if he was a runner. His hair was slicked back but not overgelled and the fit of his tuxedo, impeccable.

Something about Clive Whitaker was vaguely familiar but I couldn't quite put my finger on what. It didn't bother me much, because in spite of his charming manners, good conversational skills, and neat appearance, I felt no chemistry between us.

When he asked me to dance, however, I accepted. It had been a long time since I'd been on the dance floor in the arms of a man.

"You're a natural," Clive said as we waltzed across the polished floor.

"Oh," I demurred, lowering my eyes coquettishly, "anyone can waltz."

"Perhaps," Clive murmured. "But not everyone can do it with such grace."

Appropriately, I blushed. For about an hour I enjoyed myself enormously. Clive and I danced and flirted and sipped

champagne until I almost forgot—almost—my general loneliness and heartache.

Eventually, Clive returned me to Mother, and the men of
our party—Rupert, Clive, and a Mr. Breen—excused themselves. It was time for a cigar on the terrace.

"Clive is such a darling!" Mrs. Breen enthused with a wink
in my direction. "I must say, the Gilliam family grows them
quite impressively!"

Perhaps it was the look of shocked horror on my face that
sent her scurrying, but Mrs. Breen was soon gone and I was
left alone with Mother.

"The Gilliam family?" I repeated. "Mother, what's going
on?"

Mother's eyes grew wide with phony innocence. "Why,
nothing's going on, dear."

I grabbed her bejeweled hand. "Mother, tell me the truth.
Are Rupert and Clive related?"

Mother seem flustered for a second, then regained her
usual composure. "Well, yes, dear. It turns out that the men
are cousins."

"It turns out? You knew that from the start, didn't you?" I
demanded.

Mother yanked her hand from mine and drew herself tall
in her chair. "Why, of course, dear," she answered, blandly
as you please.

A setup. The whole evening had been a setup!

"Whose idea was it to set me up with Clive?" I asked. My
cheeks burned with anger—and embarrassment.

Mother pretended to consider. "Well, let me see. Yes, I
think it was Rupert who first suggested the notion. And I
thought it a lovely one."

So that was why Rupert had personally requested I attend
this stupid ball!

"My dear, by all accounts," Mother went on, "Clive is a
wonderful young man. And just look how happy I am with

my Rupert! If Clive is anything like his cousin, why, he'll make a fine husband."

"Husband!" I cried, jumping to my feet.

"You know, dear," Mother said in a low voice, as if about to impart words of great wisdom, "it's wise to keep things in the family."

Keep what in the family, I thought. Money-grubbing lotharios? Smooth-talking gigolos?

"Tell me something, Mother," I asked, gathering my purse and shawl. "Do you even love Rupert?"

I'd never seen my mother's eyes grow so dark. "What a question, Abigail," she replied, and her voice, too, betrayed her anger. "Of course I love him. He's my husband."

I was unable to reply. Turning on my heel in true outraged heroine fashion, I hurried from the ball before Clive could return from his cigar break.

Tears threatened. I'd been having a fine time dancing, chatting, and ever so slightly flirting with Clive. And now it was all spoiled.

I wondered: Had Clive been attracted to me at all? Or had he simply been playing a part in the interesting little family drama directed by his dear cousin?

What did it matter, I thought, waiting out front for my mother's car and driver to appear. It's not Clive my heart pines for.

The cold air worked to clear my head and after a moment I realized I should never have challenged my mother's love for Rupert.

To be fair, Rupert was awfully kind to Mother. To me, he'd never been less than a perfect gentlemanly acquaintance. It was all I could have hoped for from such a stepfather.

And my mother's marriage was her business.

As my marriage—or my lack of one—was my own.

Seventeen

All I want for Christmas is . . .

It started out to be an unremarkable day. I like unremarkable days. Especially when compared to days that include dates with criminals, elves, and gigolos.

But at 10:30 A.M., everything changed.

"Abby," Judy said, "there's a Mr. Hanson on the line for you."

"Excuse me, what now?" I said, brilliantly dropping my pen.

"A Mr. Hanson? Should I just take a—"

"No," I cried, "I'll take the call!" I took a deep breath and lifted the receiver. "Hello?"

"Is this Abigail Walker?" a male voice asked. "This is Greg Hanson. We met at Mrs. Winthrop's party last Sunday."

I swung my desk chair to face away from Judy and Jillian, who were both grinning, having realized that this was not a work-related call.

"Oh, hi. How are you?" I squeaked.

"I'm just fine, thanks. I hope you don't mind my calling . . ."

"No, not at all," I replied less squeakily.

"Good," he said. "I have to admit I asked Mrs. Winthrop for your home number but she claimed not to have it."

That old cow!

"But I did remember you worked at the Symphony so . . ."

"Oh," I said inanely. "Right."

Greg was undeterred by my sudden lack of conversational

skill. "I was hoping you might like to have dinner with me," he said.

The specter of his personal Valkyrie rose before me . . .

"See," Greg went on, "I was talking to my mother and I discovered that years ago our parents were close. Back before we moved to Atlanta. And," he added, "before your father passed away."

"Oh, were they?" I said.

What is his point, I thought, imagining his lovely eyes, his broad shoulders. He's with Valerie. Why does he want to talk about old times neither of us remember?

"I know it's last minute," Greg pressed, "but would you be available tonight? I could make a reservation at Locke-Ober. They're usually booked far in advance but I know one of the managers . . ."

I stared blankly at the piles of folders and loose papers before me. I should say no, I thought. I really should.

"Yes," I said. "Yes, I'd love to have dinner with you tonight."

Later that afternoon I called my mother and asked her about the Hansons. Even though I hadn't yet forgiven her for the Clive incident.

"Why haven't you ever mentioned them?" I asked.

"Oh, I don't know," she said. "I guess I just forgot about them somewhere along the line. After your father died. They were quite a nice family, though."

"So, do you know anything about the son? Greg?"

"Well," she replied, "I seem to recall someone mentioning a Gregory. Was it Mrs. Winthrop? Or maybe Trish Bushnell . . . Oh, I just can't—"

"That's okay, Mother," I interrupted.

"Oh. All right, then. Have a nice day, dear," she said and hung up the phone before I could respond.

Eighteen

All I want for Christmas is for this dream never to end . . .

After work I dashed home to change into a body-skimming dress in cocoa-colored silk. Because I intended to take a cab to the restaurant, I was able to forgo snow boots and wear sling-backs with a two-and-a-half-inch heel.

At six-thirty my stomach began to knot and I reached for the phone to call Erin. I wanted to share the good news. I wanted to mention Valerie. I wanted to hear that I was doing was the right thing.

I resisted the impulse.

At six-forty-five, I called for a cab and ten minutes later was on my way.

Locke-Ober is a Boston institution, recently revived. It's a wonderfully romantic spot, warm and cozy and not in the least intimidating, in spite of its illustrious history.

Greg couldn't have known, but Locke-Ober is my favorite restaurant in the world.

Greg was at the bar when I arrived. I thought he'd never looked more handsome in a black suit and French blue shirt. He greeted me with a glad smile, and after checking my coat, we were seated.

"I have a confession to make," he said as soon as we'd ordered a bottle of wine.

Here it is, I thought. I felt my lips tighten.

"I lured you here on a pretense."

"Oh?" I crumpled the napkin in my lap into a ball.

"Yes. When I asked you to meet me to talk about our families, well, that's not really why I asked you."

"It isn't?" I said warily.

"No. I asked you to meet me because I really like you, Abby. I want to get to know you. I'm sorry."

"Don't be," I said, laughing, releasing the napkin, pleased. But what about Valerie?

I had to know. While Greg studied the menu, I gathered my courage.

I am a strong, independent woman, I reminded myself. I am taking control of my life. I am billing my landlord for the work his "guys" never did. I have demanded a full explanation of my father's will. I will hire a financial planner to help me negotiate grad school and a mortgage.

And I will learn the truth about this blond hussy!

"So," I said calmly.

Greg looked up from his menu. "Yes?" he asked.

He didn't *seem* like a liar or a cheat . . . Courage, Abby!

"That woman you were with at the Winthrops'. Is she your girlfriend?"

"Not at all," he answered promptly. "I was afraid you'd gotten that impression."

Happiness bloomed . . .

"Valerie and I are friends," he went on. "On occasion, we've helped each other out when one of us needed a date for an event. Sometimes you just can't walk into a room alone."

"I didn't know men felt that way," I commented, trying not to whoop with glee.

"Sometimes. Take Mrs. Winthrop's party. I knew that if I showed up alone, every matron there would be trying to set me up with her daughter. And I strongly prefer to choose the people in my life."

"No blind dates?"

Greg winced. "One. And it was so bad it turned me off fix-ups forever."

"Unfortunately," I admitted, "I've been on more than one awful blind date. But no more."

"It's much better this way, isn't it?" Greg said softly.

"Mmm," I agreed, taking a sip of wine.

"Honestly," Greg said then, "if I'd known you'd be at the Winthrops', I wouldn't have asked Valerie to join me. Frankly, while you and I were talking, I forgot all about her. And that I was obliged to leave with her. "

"Oh," I said, "you did the gentlemanly thing, taking her home."

"I did what any friend would do." Greg grinned. "Besides, if I'd ditched her, she would have made me pay!"

From there, the evening progressed enjoyably.

"How could we have lost each other twice," I said when our entrées had been served. "That first time was just so odd! Once the crowd of tourists was gone, I looked all over for you—"

"I thought maybe you'd ducked back into the Christmas shop while everyone was still snapping away," Greg said. "When I didn't see you on the first floor, I ran upstairs, but no luck."

"Oh, no! Timing is everything, isn't it?"

"Timing is all. Now, what about the museum? When that crowd of kids moved on, I couldn't see you anywhere, so I headed back to the entrance—"

"And I headed toward the exit! We were like two ships passing in the night . . ."

"But now we've dropped anchor and sounded a salute. Or something like that. I'm not good with extended similes."

Whew, I thought. Neither am I.

Suddenly, I had the courage to say something that had been on my mind all evening.

"Um, Greg?" I began. "I want to explain why I didn't accept your invitation to dinner. That time outside the movie theater."

Greg nodded encouragingly.

"Well, it sounds silly but I'd had an awful day and—" I sighed. "The moment you were out of sight, I regretted saying no. I couldn't even understand why I had! The truth is—well, I'd been hoping to bump into you again."

"Thank you for telling me," Greg said simply. "I'm glad we're here together now."

It was that easy. Any residual awkwardness was over. We ate and talked and laughed, and by the time we left the restaurant, I felt as if I'd known Greg for a long, long time.

Greg hailed a cab and together we drove to my apartment. I wondered if I should invite him in. I didn't want the evening to end but instinct told me there was no need to rush this relationship.

When we reached my building, Greg got out of the cab to open the door for me. He asked the driver to wait and walked me to the door.

"Thank you for seeing me tonight," he said. His eyes held mine and we moved closer.

"Thank you for asking me," I replied.

Very easily, we kissed. It was teasingly soft and very exciting.

"I'd like to call you tomorrow," Greg said when our lips parted.

"Yes, please," I replied, still under the influence of his touch. "I mean, okay."

Greg waited until I was safely inside before returning to the cab. I watched from my bedroom window as he disappeared into the night.

"I'm in love," I said to the four walls. "And this time, I think it's real."

* * *

True to his word, Greg called the very next morning and asked if we might meet for a quick lunch. At noon we met at Sonsi and, over bowls of leek and potato soup, continued where we'd left off the night before. We talked, laughed, kissed upon parting. Greg claimed a late night at the office but promised to call very soon.

That evening Erin phoned; Nick was spending Friday night with his son and a bunch of David's buddies at a sports arcade.

Excitedly, I told her the wonderful news about me and Greg.

"See," she said teasingly. "I told you that if you kept sending out hopeful energy, something good would happen."

"It really has! Oh, Erin, I know I've said this before, but I think I've finally met my soul mate."

There was silence.

"Don't say it, Erin!" I begged. "This time I know what I'm doing."

After another moment, she sighed and said, "Okay. You know what, Abby? I believe you. And even if I didn't, it shouldn't matter. You need to follow your heart."

Suddenly, I felt unnerved. "That's what I've been doing all my life," I admitted. "Maybe . . . maybe I am making another big mistake . . ."

"Abby," Erin said, "sometimes following your heart can get you into trouble. But other times, it leads you right where you need to be."

"Did you follow your heart with Doug?" I asked, curious, though knowing the subject of Erin's married lover was a delicate one for my friend.

"Honestly, Abby, I don't know," she said. "From this perspective, happy with Nick, I think maybe I wasn't following my heart as much as I was working through something. Like anger over my parents' divorce. I don't know. I don't blame

Doug for anything. I blame myself for not having enough self-respect. And self-control," she added with a rueful laugh.

"That's the Catholic in you," I said, teasing.

"Maybe," she admitted. "And maybe that's not a bad thing after all. Sometimes what we do is wrong. Guilt reminds us of the social contract."

"Well," I amended, "guilt is okay as long as it eventually lifts. So that you can get on with life. Right?"

"Right," she agreed. "And you have nothing to feel guilty about. So, Abby? Enjoy this. I'm so happy for you."

"Thanks," I said. "I'm happy for me, too."

Nineteen

All I want for Christmas is for every woman to have a home of her own.

The following days were magic. I felt happy all the time, even when a call from the querulous Mrs. Potsdam was mistakenly directed to me; even when the official notice of a rent increase was slipped under my front door; even when Clive Whitaker called me at home, admitting he'd gotten my number from Rupert.

When I was with Greg, I felt energized. When we were apart, I felt good just knowing he was alive.

One evening we drove to Concord to attend a candlelit Christmas concert in an old Lutheran church and then to have dinner at a small, cozy restaurant Greg had heard about from a colleague.

Just over the Concord town line, I saw it.

"Look!" I cried. "That big white house up ahead, pull over!"

Greg pulled to the side of the road and looked worriedly at me. "Are you okay?"

"Just fine. I want to show you something. This house," I said, pointing to the huge, late-Victorian-style structure, "means a lot to me. When I was a little girl, I used to fantasize about living here when I grew up. "

"All alone?" Greg asked. "It's a pretty big house."

"Oh, no! I lived with my wonderful husband and our three adorable children." I thought hard. It had been a long time since I'd considered this childhood dream. "And a German shepherd named Buster and a big gray cat named Fluff. Who had kittens and we kept them all. Pretty silly, isn't it?"

Greg shrugged. "Sounds normal to me. Who doesn't want to be surrounded by love? Hey," he asked, trailing a finger along my cheek, "do you have a pet now?"

I made a rueful face, in spite of the thrill of his touch. "My nasty landlord doesn't allow pets. But just as soon as I move—"

"Tell me more about this fantasy," Greg said.

"Well, in the summer we would sleep in hammocks out back. And at Christmastime we would string the entire house with teeny white lights and there'd be a big tree set right inside that window there, see? And we were all happy. Well," I added, "I guess that goes without saying. About being happy. No one fantasizes about divorce and unemployment and kids on drugs. But there's so much tragedy all around . . . Oh, I didn't mean to sound so negative!"

Greg leaned forward and touched his lips to my forehead. The kiss was so gentle and yet so sexy.

"Sometimes it's hard not to be negative," he said. "At least, scared and confused. The important thing is to keep sight of all the good. Now I sound all preachy."

"Not at all," I assured him, pressing a kiss on his forehead.

Greg started the engine, and as we pulled away, he commented that the house seemed empty.

Maybe it's up for sale, I thought, though there was no visible realtor's sign.

We drove on to the little white church at which the concert was being held. The best part about it all was not the music but sitting in the dark lit only by candles, inhaling the spicy sweet scents of pine and incense, Greg's hand clasping mine, our bodies close.

We remained in the church, silently, comfortably, until everyone else had gone. Finally, the minister appeared near the altar and gave a polite cough. Greg and I left and emerged into the cold, brittle air, to a night filled with stars. I shivered and Greg pulled me close and kissed me like I'd never been kissed before.

"Wow," I said eloquently when we drew apart. "That was neat!"

Greg burst out laughing. "You are priceless, Abigail Walker," he said, hugging me closer. "Absolutely without price."

I might be priceless, I thought the next morning, but these shoes are going to cost a fortune to fix!

I frowned at a treasured pair of black satin pumps, now sadly nibbled. As if by mice. Who had eaten right through the cardboard box in which the pumps had been stored.

I knew what I'd be doing on my lunch hour.

At twelve-thirty I bundled up and headed for the shoe repair shop. It was a bitterly cold day but I decide to walk for the exercise. And as I walked, my mind wandered—from bittersweet memories of my father, to an oddly pleasant memory of my mother's wedding to Rupert, to thoughts of my last long-term relationship. That had been with Erin's father, John Weston.

John was kind and intelligent and accomplished; I'd convinced myself I was in love. When he ended our relationship, I felt just awful. But time healed my wounds and I came to realize that John really had known what was best for us. And now, I thought, I'm with the man I was meant to be with, forever. Everything had turned out fine.

I was just passing the Rattlesnake on Boylston Street when my thoughts were interrupted by the sound of unmistakably cruel laughter. The source? Two teenaged boys with the bulk and dull look of bullies were passing a shuffling figure they found amusing. As I gained on the figure and the bullies loped past me, instinct identified the unfortunate figure as a woman.

She was carrying a huge black plastic bag, the kind used for yard work. It brushed along the sidewalk as she walked. That bag will rip open before long, I thought, almost absent-mindedly. What could she possibly have in there?

And then—Marge? Could it possibly be Marge? My mind rebelled at the thought. This woman was in far worse shape than Marge had been at Thanksgiving . . .

Could someone fall so far in so short a time?

I stopped short.

Marge. I'd seen her indoors, without a coat, without a scarf over her head, and only once. Of course I might have trouble recognizing her right off. But now I knew.

The woman was at least half a block ahead and I began to hurry after her. "Marge?" I called. "Marge!"

The woman grabbed the plastic bag with both hands so that it was inches above the pavement and began a stumbling run.

"Marge, it's Abby," I called again, hoping my tone conveyed friendship.

The woman glanced over her shoulder and I caught a glimpse of terrified eyes. It was Marge, no doubt at all.

Had she recognized me? If not, who did she think was pursuing her? An enemy.

With a speed surely born of panic, Marge rounded the corner and was lost to sight. As fast as I could run in heavy-duty winter boots, I followed. At the corner, I stopped and scanned all directions. But Marge was gone. Maybe into the Gardens, maybe down into the T station, maybe into the dark sanctuary of the church.

It was up to me to follow or to let her be. For a moment more I stood on the corner, my breath coming in short gasps. And then, I headed on my own way.

Twenty

All I want for Christmas is a new life.

Erin and Nick were scheduled to have dinner with Greg and me the following night. I was excited about introducing Greg to my friends and not in the least worried he would make anything other than a wonderful impression. I envisioned the four of us vacationing together; standing up for one another at our weddings; living in the same town so that our children could grow up to be friends—and maybe even fall in love!

"Your mother," Judy announced, scattering my reverie to the wind.

Mother rarely called me at the office. She must be totally bored, I thought. Maybe the cable is out.

"Hello, Mother."

"Oh, hello, dear," she replied, as if surprised to hear my voice. Nothing new there.

"Is anything wrong?" I asked, flipping absentmindedly through a file.

"What could be wrong, dear," Mother answered. "Everything is just fine. Though I do wish the holidays weren't so stressful! Oh, my dear, I just heard the nicest news!"

Here comes the gossip, I thought, prepared to tune out completely.

"Mrs. Winthrop's daughter, Alice, is getting a divorce!"

The mention of Alice's name caused me to refocus. At her mother's tree-trimming party, she'd been the only one not to express disapprobation at my reply to Mrs. Winthrop's rude question. And she'd been alone at the club's Christmas Ball.

"Gee, that's too bad," I said, wondering what was "nice" about this news. Alice was my age and had been married for almost ten years. She had no children.

Mother went on. "Peter Graham filed for divorce sometime last month. He and Alice have been living apart since then. Poor thing! I can't imagine her rattling around in that big house all by herself! It's a good thing she's got Gregory. Of course—"

"Who?" I said sharply.

"Why, Gregory Hanson, dear. Now, of course, it's all hush-hush until Alice's divorce is final. We don't want anything muddying her settlement. But once all the unpleasantness is over, Alice will be free to marry Gregory."

A buzzing began in my ears and spread like wildfire through every inch of my body. I vibrated with anger. With hurt. I felt sick, sick, sick.

I did not, for one moment, experience disbelief.

"Mother," I demanded, "where did you hear this?"

"Why, everyone knows about Gregory and Alice. Her mother's sworn us all to secrecy, but . . . oh, dear, perhaps I shouldn't have told you . . . By the way, didn't you ask me something about the Hanson boy, dear? Well, I'm sure—"

I couldn't listen to another word. "Mother," I said abruptly, "I have to go."

You can fall very far, very fast.

As soon as both Judy and Jillian were away from the office, I dialed Greg's office and asked to be connected to his voice mail. The receptionist told me that he was in but I insisted I didn't want to speak with him directly.

I left a terse message canceling our dinner plans with Erin and Nick. I could barely speak through the pain and fury.

"And don't ever call me again, Gregory Hanson," I said finally.

I gave no explanation.

It was over.

Greg called three times that afternoon but I refused to talk to him. About four o'clock, Jillian came rushing into the office with the news that a Mr. Hanson was downstairs, asking to see me.

"Oh, honey," Judy said, "maybe you should just talk to him."

"You don't know what happened!" I cried.

I grabbed my coat and purse and made for the back stairs. Once outside the building I hailed a cab and directed the driver to my street.

My heart beat wildly. I sank back against the torn leather seat and tried to slow my breathing, but to no avail. I felt pursued and it frightened me, though I'd set the game in motion. In Greg's position, just cut off, I'd want an explanation, too.

But Greg is guilty, I reminded myself. You wouldn't have done what he did.

"Miss? Miss!"

I startled back to the moment. "Yes?"

"Is it left or right at the light, miss?" the driver asked.

"Left," I said, looking out at the grim, gray winter afternoon. Suddenly—

"Wait!" I cried. "Keep going straight!"

"But you—"

"I know what I said! Please, just keep going!"

As the cab continued on, I watched Greg Hanson come to a halt in front of my building. Over my shoulder, I saw him run up the stairs . . .

"Miss? Is everything all right?" the driver asked. "Are you sick?"

"No, I'm fine," I lied. "I just—I just remembered I have to be somewhere." I gave him Erin's address and prayed she wouldn't mind an unexpected overnight guest.

Twenty-one

All I want for Christmas is . . . what used to be.

The next few days were the absolute worst, in some ways harder to bear than the days just after my father's death. I was barely able to do my job; I was alternately lethargic and jittery, weepy and manic. Judy and Jillian were sympathetic in an unobtrusive way, for which I was glad.

I still hadn't spent the night in my apartment. But that situation wasn't going to last.

Erin and Nick confronted me one night after dinner. I sat on the couch, Erin's fawn Abyssinian cat, Fuzzer, purring against my leg.

"Abby," Erin began gently, "you know you're welcome here as long as you need to stay."

I nodded, knowing what was coming next.

"But I really think you should go back to your apartment. You can't hide from Greg forever. Or from—from yourself. You want to be a strong, independent woman? Well, be that woman and go home."

I rubbed Fuzzer's head and pouted.

"He's been leaving messages on my machine," I said. "If I go home, I'll hear his voice."

"Abby," Erin said firmly, "that makes no sense. How many times have you called home for messages? Come on. If you really don't want to hear from Greg, you'll go home and disconnect the answering machine. Or change your number. You'll *do* something."

Erin was right. I was sunk in avoidance and denial.

"Abby," Erin said now, "maybe you should talk to Greg."

"Why?" I cried, and Fuzzer leapt away, royally annoyed. "What will that do?"

Erin scooted closer to me and took my hand in hers. "Abby, from everything you've told me Greg sounds like a good guy. Come on. You know how batty your mother can be. Maybe she got the story all wrong."

Of course, the possibility had occurred to me. Still, I'd made no move to find and verify the truth. Why?

Deep in the night something disturbing had come to me. Maybe—just maybe—I was afraid of something so real—my relationship with Greg, communion with my soul mate—that the moment it seemed threatened, I'd taken the easy way out and run.

A small voice, but one impossible to ignore, had asked: Do you really want what you say you want, Abby? Are you willing to accept the joys and responsibilities of true and lasting love?

Nick's voice brought me back to the moment.

"At least listen to his side of the story," he urged. "If he turns out to be full of crap, at least you'll have the opportunity for closure. You can throw a drink in his face or call him a bad name."

I sat and thought. Erin and Nick were right. At least about my going home. Home was where I belonged. About that other stuff—talking to Greg, confronting myself—well, about those things I didn't yet know.

"Okay," I said. "I'm going home."

There were five messages on the answering machine. Four were from Greg. One was from Mr. Jarrens. He wanted to be sure I'd received the rent increase notice.

I'd listened to three of Greg's messages from Erin's apartment. They were short, careful, and urgent. Now, I played the fourth message. It had come in earlier that evening.

"Abby. I'm worried. Please, let me hear from you, just to know you're all right. Send me a note if you won't talk to me. I don't want to bother or frighten you. I won't call again. Just know that—okay? I have to respect your choice. Good night."

I saved the message, as I'd done with the others. And then I sat, trembling. His voice . . . I'd heard despair. And concern. And finally, just a trace of—exasperation.

"What am I supposed to do?" I whispered to no one, tears sliding down my cheeks.

Later that night, I lay in bed, unable to sleep. My brain raced around the situation, refusing to confront real options, real feelings.

If Greg was guilty of courting Alice Winthrop-Graham behind my back, was he also guilty of keeping his true relationship with Valerie a secret? Maybe, I thought, clutching the sheets, he was dating both women and lying to all three of us!

I could confront Alice with what I knew. After all, if Greg was cheating on Alice with me, wouldn't she want to know? I tossed onto my side, wide-eyed. Unless, I thought, unless they'd made an agreement that he should be seen with other women until her divorce was final . . .

I tossed onto my back. Oh, what a tangled web I was imagining!

Maybe I'd call Buffy! She was sure to know the gossip! But would I be obliged to tell her about the incident with Beau?

With a sigh I threw back the covers and sat on the edge of my bed. This is ridiculous, Abby, I told myself. This is all so ridiculous.

Just walk away. Leave it all in the past. Forget you ever met Greg Hanson.

As if I ever could.

Twenty-two

All I want for Christmas is . . . Everything!

Christmas Eve.

Erin and Nick had invited me over for the evening but I'd declined the invitation. They'd seen enough of me in the past days.

Besides, I needed to be alone.

There had been no phone message from Greg for the past two days. No e-mail, no letter, no Christmas card.

And I'd done nothing.

Six in the evening. I sat alone in my apartment, surrounded by a pile of holiday cards and glossy color photos of babies, children, and golden Labs. Normally, I enjoyed receiving such photos. That night, I felt hurt by the bounty they represented.

Still, I retained enough self-awareness to recognize the result of self-pity. I picked up the photo of Buffy and her beautiful family gathered around the Christmas tree. Poor Buffy. Maybe, I thought, I should just crop her miserable husband right out of the picture!

I didn't have a husband. But I did have my dignity. Didn't I?

I curled up on the couch in my robe and slippers. The apartment looked nice, all candlelit. The compact Douglas fir I'd wrestled up three flights of stairs to my apartment stood proudly by the window. On a side table stood the wooden angel holding aloft a heart.

I wish Greg could see this, I thought.

Why can't he? that small, impossible-to-ignore voice piped.

I didn't answer. Instead, I went to my bedroom closet to choose an outfit for Christmas Day.

The next morning I would drive to Lincoln. Mother, Rupert, and I would host an open house for the twenty or so Walker cousins who regularly surfaced at Christmas. Though Mother had suggested I spend the night, my plan was to come back to Boston by evening.

After laying out my clothes, I returned to the living room. What I saw was the one glass on the coffee table. The one teacup next to it. The one napkin, neatly folded. Who knows, I thought. Maybe I will stay with Mother.

Thoughts of Mother's house led to thoughts of owning my own home. Which led to thoughts of my financial future.

Right then I made my first New Year's resolution. To follow up with Mr. Harper. Better yet, to hire an attorney so he'd be forced to return calls.

And then, thinking of attorneys and unreturned calls, I thought again of Greg and my heart constricted. Oh, it was going to be a long, lonely Christmas.

"*Bzzzzzzzzzzzz!*"

I jumped. The intercom buzzer.

Who would be stopping by on Christmas Eve?

"Hello?" I said, pushing the Talk button.

"Abby, it's me. Please, don't go away."

Greg!

"What do you want?" I asked. Thrilled to hear his voice. Amazed that he hadn't given up. Thankful, too.

"I want to talk to you, Abby. Please. Not over the intercom."

"I'm not sure I want you in my apartment," I said, lying madly.

"That's fine. Actually," he said, "I thought we could go for a drive."

"Can't we just go for coffee?" I countered, untying the belt of my robe.

"Uh, sure, of course," Greg said. "But I think a drive might be nice, too. It's a clear night, and, uh—"

"Fine," I said, flipping off my slippers. "I'll be down in ten minutes."

Greg was waiting in the lobby. The sight of him made my knees weak.

"Hello, Abby," he said. "You look—very pretty. In that color."

Around my neck I'd tied the pink silk scarf I'd given my mother, the one she'd never worn. I don't know why I should have thought it would bring good luck.

"Thank you," I said, slipping my hands in my coat pockets.

For a moment I thought he was going to kiss me, but the moment passed. I didn't know whether to feel offended or glad.

Silently, we left the lobby; Greg was double-parked just outside. Once settled, he tuned to a classical music station. "Is this okay?" he asked.

I told him it was. Neither of us spoke again until we were getting on Storrow Drive.

"Where are we going?" I asked.

"You'll see." Greg flashed me a smile. He had no idea he'd given the wrong answer.

"Don't do that to me!" I said fiercely. "My father never used to give me a straight answer. It was always 'we'll see' or 'just wait' or 'you don't need to know.' It makes me feel like a stupid little kid when someone refuses to answer my questions."

"Abby, I'm sorry," Greg said. "I just wanted it to be a surprise. I thought we'd go to Concord."

"Why?"

"You really won't let me surprise you?" he asked.

"Okay," I agreed finally. "But if I say enough—"

"I'll come clean. Deal."

For a while we drove in silence. I tried to focus on the music but it was impossible. Where is all this leading, I wondered, dreading, anticipating.

"There's something I want to tell you," Greg said suddenly.

"Go ahead." I folded my hands in my lap. Tightly.

"Abby, I was frantic. You wouldn't take my calls. I had no idea what I'd done wrong and I was desperate to know so that I could make it right. Finally, I called your mother. I remembered that at the Winthrops' we'd talked about being dutiful children. I figured if anyone knew where you were and if you were all right, it would be your mother."

I murmured to indicate I was listening.

Greg went on. "Imagine my surprise when she congratulated me on my engagement to Alice Winthrop-Graham."

"So it's true!" I blurted. Suddenly, the lights of the cars around us seemed too bright. Loud. Offensive.

"God, no, Abby, it's not true! I've spoken maybe twenty words to Alice in my entire life. She'll confirm there's nothing between us but I'd rather if you just believed me."

"So," I said slowly, "you're sure you were never engaged to Alice?"

Greg laughed. "Abby, a man knows when he's proposed to a woman and when he hasn't. Unless he was drunk at the time and I haven't been that drunk since college."

"Oh, my God," I breathed. "But then why did Mother—"

"Oh, I'll tell you why. That evening I paid a little visit to the Winthrops'. Here's the long story short. It seems someone saw you and me together and told Mrs. W., who, all on her own, had decided I was perfect for her daughter. So she started a rumor—sure to get back to you—that Alice and I were secretly engaged, hoping that you'd dump me—which you did—leaving me free again for Alice."

"That's so stupid!" I blurted.

"Yeah, well," Greg said, "the woman isn't known for her brains. By the way, I promised I'd take Mr. W. out for dinner next week. He got a big kick out of my telling his wife to mind her own business."

I smiled, thinking of poor, harmless Mr. Winthrop. Maybe his years of suffering under the yoke of his horrid wife were finally over!

I noted the sign for the Concord exit. We were close to the end of our journey.

Or were we?

Minutes later we were in the heart of the beautiful, historic town. Greg pulled up outside a big white house.

The fantasy house.

My house.

"What are we doing here?" I asked.

Greg didn't answer. Instead, he cut the engine, got out of the car, and came around to open my door. Together we stood at the edge of the snow-covered lawn.

"Greg, what—"

"There is someone I love, you know," he interrupted. "And her name is not Alice Winthrop-Graham."

I steeled myself.

"And it's not Valerie Murphy," he went on. "In fact, I ended our friendship. I went to her for advice on winning you back and she told me she had feelings for me. It wasn't a pleasant scene."

"Oh," I whispered. Elation!

Greg took a step closer. My head went all fuzzy.

"The person I love is you, Abby Walker. I am madly and truly and deeply in love with you. There is no one else and there never will be. Abby, I was beginning to think I'd never meet my soul mate. And then I met you. Well," he laughed, "bumped into you. You're beautiful and kind and funny.

You're the best thing that's ever happened to me. I hope you can say the same about me someday."

I grabbed Greg's hands. "Oh, I love you, too," I said, eyes filling with tears. "I'm sorry I doubted you."

"You don't need to apologize, Abby."

"I want to," I insisted. "You've never done or said anything to make me so afraid."

"Fear is natural. It's a protective thing. You'd been hurt in the past, so it was natural for you to throw up a wall when you thought I might be a bum."

I grinned. "Are you always this understanding? And sensitive. And wonderful."

"Oh, sure," he said, mock serious. "Just not before my morning cup of coffee."

"I'll remember that," I promised.

And then, it happened. Gregory Hanson got down on one knee on the snow-covered lawn and presented me with a black velvet ring box.

"Abigail," he said, and my name had never sounded so sweet. I began to tremble and Greg took my hand in his free one.

"Abigail Walker," he began again, "will you do me the honor of becoming my wife?"

"Oh, yes!" I cried. "But please, get up or you'll catch your death of cold!"

Greg laughed and stood and opened the ring box for me to see an antique cushion-cut diamond in a pavé band.

"It was my grandmother's," he said and there was a catch in his throat. "I hope you—"

"Oh, Greg, it's the most beautiful ring I've ever seen!" And it was. Because it was Greg's gift.

I tore off my left glove and let Greg slip the ring onto my finger.

"A perfect fit," he murmured. "But now we should get inside. Your hands are like ice."

I made a move back toward the car. Greg's hand on my arm stopped me.

"No," he said. "Look."

I looked in the direction he was pointing—at the house. Suddenly—it was illuminated by hundreds of tiny white lights! And through the living room window, I saw a tall Christmas tree . . .

"How—"

Greg put something into my hand and it was a moment before I could focus on what it was.

And then—

"It's a key," I said. "I don't understand."

"The house is ours, Abby," he told me. "If you want it."

I nodded, crying now too hard to speak. Greg led me across the snowy ground and into the beautiful old house—our house. A fire roared in the fireplace and champagne was chilling in a silver bucket. A buffet was spread on a blanket by the fire. Silently, we settled there until I was able to talk.

"I'm sorry," I mumbled, blowing my nose. "I must look a sight!"

Greg laughed. "You look just fine. But we'll wait a few minutes before we take photos. You told me you kept scrapbooks so I brought this."

Greg held up a throwaway camera.

"You think of everything," I said, pointing to the top of the tree. "How did you know I love angels?"

"I caught a glimpse of what was in your shopping bags the day we first met. Before we were separated by that mob."

"Please tell me there are no more surprises! I've got nothing for you!"

Greg grinned. "Your happiness is the only gift I want. And it's a good thing too, because—"

Greg dashed from the room and returned a moment later with a handful of gray kitten.

"You can call her Fluff," he said as I leapt to my feet. "Ow! Claw might be a better name!"

The kitten mewed and I snuggled it to my breast. "Kitties are never as helpless as they appear," I said. "That's part of their appeal."

"If you say so. I'm a dog man myself."

"Oh, I'm going to explode with happiness," I said, looking up at the man who was going to be my husband.

Greg grimaced. "Please don't do that!"

Still holding the now purring kitten, I wrapped my arm around Greg. "No more being separated by hordes of tourists or school kids or by women who are so miserably bored with their own lives they have to manipulate the lives of others who seem happy and busy and fulfilled."

"Right," Greg agreed, pulling me closer. "From now on, we stick together."

"Like best friends."

"Like lovers," he whispered and the words made me tingle.

"Like family."

We kissed and the promise it held was unmistakable.

"So, did you get what you wanted for Christmas?" Greg whispered, smoothing my tousled hair.

I thought about Greg's question.

A home. A new career. A husband. Children. A cat. A dog. And me.

"Yes," I said, pulling away just enough so I could look deeply into Greg's lovely green eyes. "I most certainly did."

Please turn the page for an exciting sneak peek
of Holly Chamberlin's
LIVING SINGLE
currently available in trade paperback and
coming in mass market in March 2004!

Prologue

This is the story of a year in the life of a thirty-two-year-old single woman. It's my story and I'm telling it because I need to tell it. Also, because I want to.

Consider it a cautionary tale. Consider it a good laugh. Consider it a little of both.

My name is Erin Weston. I recently celebrated—a slightly optimistic way of putting it—my thirty-third birthday.

Jesus Christ was crucified at the age of thirty-three. Not being a rabble-rouser, I'm hoping for a far less spectacularly troublesome year. After last year, I could use the rest.

Anyway, I made it out alive and, yes, even well. Imagine that.

Overall, life's been good to me, though on occasion its macabre sense of humor is distressing.

But enough summarizing. My story begins last January, exactly a year ago to this day.

I hope you like it.

One

January in Boston is probably like January everywhere in America. At least in the sense of it being a month of grand resolutions and well-meant gestures—as well as a month of postholiday disappointment and incipient depression as the resolutions and gestures begin to break down.

Nice time of the year to be born.

I'd just turned thirty-two. And I was a workaholic.

Not really. Though sometimes, especially on those days when I was the only one left in my downtown Boston office after six-thirty, I'd get all panicky and think that if I wasn't very careful I could very easily slip over the line and go from being your typical hardworking single woman to being a painfully skinny spinster, scarily devoted to her filing system and not so secretly in love with her abusive, Scotch-swilling boss.

Or, maybe I would go the other way. Maybe I would wind up a coldhearted, hard-assed, too-tanned, slave-driver-type female executive with helmet hair, no husband, and surprisingly few girlfriends.

But I was determined not to allow that slippage to occur, either way. Absolutely not. Because I'd decided I wanted something significantly different for my life.

I wanted legitimacy. The kind that, for a woman, doesn't come even with a solid career.

And my career was solid. In fact, my annual review was scheduled for the following day. If it went well, there was a chance—slim, but I was hoping—that I would be named a senior account executive at East Wind Communications. That's the marketing/PR firm where I'd worked for the past five years. It's a smallish firm, owned by a guy named Terry Bolinger, and its work focuses on nonprofits and organizations that barely make a profit.

I liked being at East Wind.

More information. I lived—and still live—in the South End, officially an historic district of Boston. I own a condo in what was once, way back in the nineteenth century, a single-family brick house. Think New York brownstones but brick. Thanks to the building department's controls, the structure is still charming, as is the entire block, with its brick sidewalks, huge old trees, and lovely, well-tended front gardens.

I had—and still have—a cat named Fuzzer. And yes, on occasion I was definitely frightened of becoming a looney cat lady. Especially if the single situation persisted for much longer.

Which, I vowed upon turning thirty-two, it wouldn't. It couldn't. Because things were going to change. Five, ten, twenty years ahead when I looked back on my life, I was going to refer to this as The Year. The year I met my husband, the man of my dreams.

Tall or medium height, it didn't matter. Neither did hair or eye color. He'd have a fine intelligence and a large sense of humor, i.e., he would appreciate the Three Stooges as well as Jerry Seinfeld, and Margaret Cho as well as Monty Python's Flying Circus. He would be kind and loving and he'd be a hardworking man, as laziness is, for me, the ultimate turnoff. Above all he would have a huge capacity for love and devotion and treat me like a great gift and be respectful of my parents and tolerate with grace—if not really like—my more difficult friends and family members.

The man of my dreams.

Well. That was the hope, anyway. That I'd meet my husband in the very near future. I didn't have much of a plan. I didn't even make an official resolution. I'd never gotten very far with resolutions. In fact, the last official resolution I'd made—at least, the last resolution I'd remembered making— was during my sophomore year in college when for some unaccountable reason I was dating a born-again Christian and inspired by lust I resolved to spend by life as a missionary in some "godless savage land." Those were his words.

Okay, I knew why I was dating the guy. He was gorgeous. Extremely disturbed, but very, very nice to look at. Which is pretty much all I got to do because, you know, those born-again Christian types aren't into premarital sex. Catholics aren't either, but we all cheat. We're all going to hell, but it just might be worth it.

Anyway, though my common sense and my experience in the dating trenches and my recently acquired cynicism about everything romantic told me I was nuts to be thinking in terms of finally meeting Mr. Right, my heart, that disturbingly powerful organ, told me otherwise. It told me that if I just approached it with openness, I would, indeed, meet my very own hero.

Okay, sure, delude yourself. Knock yourself out. It's your funeral, Erin.

That was Reason. It spoke to me several times a day. Often, it interrupted my sleep. It just had to share its opinions; it just had to pass judgment.

It was one of those workaholic days.

The phone rang just as I was about to pack up for the fifteen-minute walk home. I debated whether to answer it. I checked my watch. Six-forty-five. Not an unheard-of time for a disgruntled client to call and lodge a lengthy complaint. Then again, maybe it was bad karma not to take the call, being on the verge—possibly—of becoming a senior account executive. I was—am—nothing if not responsible.

I picked up on the fourth ring.

"Erin Weston."

"Hi. It's me, Abby."

Relief.

"Hi. I wasn't going to pick up the phone. After-hours cranky clients."

Abby laughed. "Tell me about it."

Abby worked—and still works—as a fund raiser for the Boston Symphony Orchestra. A career in development or, if you like, advancement, sounds all sophisticated and civilized until you start to hear stories about the people Abby has to deal with on a daily basis. Mainly, the outrageously childish women of the Brahman set. My take on the situation is that these women have far too much money and far too much free time on their hands. My Grandmother Morelli had a favorite saying, one she usually delivered with an ominous look at my habitually out-of-work cousin Buster: "The devil finds work for idle hands."

Anyway, how Abby hadn't already put one of those vicious, gossipy, nastily meddlesome ladies—potential donors, all—out of her misery, I just didn't know.

Well, I did know. Abby was genuinely nice. The genuinely nice person is a rarity. I am nice but perhaps not genuinely. I mean, I'd never laugh openly at someone with a silly walk but you can be sure I'm guffawing inside.

"What's up?" I said.

"I thought you might want to have dinner. I know it's last minute, but . . ."

"I'd love to," I said and I meant it. Spending time with Abby would be a great way to ignore my mounting nervousness about the next day's review. It also would be a chance to talk about my mother and her latest escapades. Selfish reasons, mostly, for wanting to get together with a friend, but understandable.

"Great," she said. "I was thinking Biba. Is that okay?"

It was. I agreed to meet Abby in half an hour—she was cabbing over to Boylston Street from Huntington and Massachusetts Avenue—and hung up.

From my office on Boylston Street, Biba was only a three-minute walk. I decided that instead of hanging around the deserted office, I'd take a brisk walk through the Common. Not that my office was in any way unpleasant. The entire East Wind Communications floor had been redesigned about a year earlier. The space was well-lit and nicely decorated in calming beige and taupe with artful splashes of warm colors, deep reds and yellows. My own office boasted a hypermodern beechwood and black leather couch and two matching chairs for clients. And I had a large, south-facing window with a ficus jungle in colorful Aztec-influenced pots.

Still, I was a big fan of walking, not as much for the exercise as for the stimulation of urban sights and sounds. Plus, the Common is such a beautiful place to walk, rich with history. Back in colonial seventeenth century, the land was the common grazing ground for local farmers. As Boston grew and became less rural, more urban, somebody had the wisdom to preserve the land as a public park. Now, it's laced with tree-lined paths, scattered with monuments to the heroes of liberty, and largely safe at night.

I bundled into my brown mouton coat, a piece I'd bought ten years before in The Antique Boutique in New York. The coat, which I call The Bear, is the warmest coat on the face of this Earth. Over the years I'd managed to find an almost perfectly matching hat. A cream-colored wool scarf, brown leather gloves, and I was ready.

The air was cold and clear, and even though the holiday

lights had been removed from the trees, and the annual ice sculptures had melted or been chipped away by bored kids, there lingered the scent of celebration. And the enticing, romantic scent of smoke from the fireplaces in the homes along Beacon Street. It's one of the few joys of winter in Boston: a lungful of cold, crisp air laced with a hint of cozy hearth.

I was not alone in enjoying the evening. It seemed lots of people had chosen to cut through the Common on their way home or to meet friends. In spite of the freezing weather, a couple embraced on the little bridge. In the spring and summer, tourists ride the stately swan boats back and forth under that bridge. I imagined for a moment that the scene was frozen on canvas. I even gave the painting a title: "The Dream."

Sentimental? Sure.

Then—I heard excited shouts and laughter coming from the Frog Pond, frozen over for late fall and winter. It's the city's most popular and picturesque skating venue, a brainchild of our mayor.

I decided to watch the skaters for a few minutes. It had been a long time since I'd worn skates—white, with rabbit fur pom-poms—and it would probably be a long time before I ever wore them again. When it comes to most sports, I am strictly a spectator. I do après-ski quite skillfully.

The Frog Pond was jammed with skaters. Lots of couples. Mostly young, one probably in their seventies, looking spry and healthy, typical hardy New Englanders. A boy about twelve, wearing a striped Dr. Seuss *Cat-in-the-Hat* hat, shot around the slower skaters, zipping backward, then forward again, making loop-the-loops. A girl about ten in a fancy red velvet skating costume, trimmed in white fur, did careful pirouettes at the exact center of the rink. A group of teenagers, baggy pants wet from trailing on the ice, hauled each other around the rink by the hand. Fell on each other. Screamed and hooted with hormonal glee.

It made me smile. Fun is catching. Two golden retrievers bounded around and around the frozen pond, barking excitedly, agreeing with me.

Then, I spotted a family of four. Father, mother, two little kids, maybe five and seven. All members of the same team, all bundled to the teeth in shiny ski jackets and mile-long scarfs and fuzzy woolen mittens and goofy, brightly colored knit hats. Laughing. Hanging on to each other, grabbing arms and legs. The father catching the mother as she slipped, kissing her on the nose.

And suddenly, I didn't feel like smiling anymore. This happy family had so much. I didn't begrudge them their riches. I just . . .

So simple. It should have been so simple to fall in love, marry, build a family. But sometimes it seemed so impossible, such a faraway dream. How did you start the process? Was there a magic word or ritual? Did you just have to want it badly enough?

Would it be too insane, I wondered, to go up to the wife/mother of that happy family and ask her for some pointers?

Reason told me, Sure. Go ahead. Make a jerk of yourself.

Here's the bitch of it. At twenty-one, the dream—husband, family, a lovely house with a dog in the yard, a cat on the hearth, an antique mirror over the beautifully upholstered couch—seemed too mundane and dead-end to consider.

I was different.

It wasn't something I could explain very easily. I just wanted something—else.

That dream of husband and house seemed so easy to acquire, so unquestioned. Everybody did it. Why would I want what everybody else had? Wasn't I glad to be different, to go my own way, make my own life, all independent?

Okay. I was young. I thought I'd chart a new course. I thought I'd be some kind of new woman. I thought too many women fell for the dream that started with the white gown, princess for a day, and ended bitterly in divorce court. Didn't almost all women fall into marriage and family, only to learn that the dream's daily trappings were stifling to the self and the soul?

Yes, maybe my mother taught that to me, often, though obliquely, hinting that this was the case with her. She'd married at twenty-one and I'd never seen her happy, only put upon, and used up. Or, it occurred to me, much, much later, acting that way.

Okay. So I had made my own way, built a career, traveled, dated a fair share of exciting, interesting men. In retrospect: self-centered artists; self-absorbed Internet gurus; self-aggrandizing brokers—none with an ounce of energy for anyone but themselves.

And then I'd turned twenty-eight. And the pangs began. Mild yearnings at first, for what, exactly, I couldn't even name.

Just something—else.

Suddenly, going to a friend's wedding dateless didn't seem like striking a blow for the happy, independent woman.

It just seemed—lonely.

Lacy white gowns and sparkling headpieces are fun!

That was Romance speaking up. It was new in town. Reason had tried to shut it down. But the yearning was big and clear and specific and Romance would not be silenced. It had appeared to remind me that I wanted to be married to that intelligent, funny, kind, and hardworking man. Okay, with brown eyes. It had appeared to remind me that I wanted to have children. Two, maybe three, healthy and happy and bright-cheeked. It had appeared to remind me I wanted a big, Victorian-style house on a tree-lined street, with a backyard big enough for a picnic table and a swing set and, of course, a barbecue. It had appeared to remind me I wanted there to be a little white church in the center of town—not Catholic—

where my beautiful husband and children and I would attend Christmas Eve services. It had appeared to remind me I even wanted to be a soccer mom—as long as I didn't actually have to play.

But Reason mocked me. There's just one little problem, Erin, it would say. Time's running out. Your biological clock is ticking away. Did you know that a woman who gives birth at the age of thirty-five and older is considered to be of Advanced Maternal Age? AMA. And therefore she and her baby are at much greater risk for all sorts of calamities than, say, a twenty-five-year-old and her baby. So get a grip. Accept the reality. The door's just about to close.

I looked at the mother/wife and her brood. It was hard to tell at that distance, with her face mostly covered by her scarf, but when she laughed, her voice sounded young and clear. I guessed she was about my age. Give or take a year. Which meant that she'd had her children in her twenties.

Let's face it, Erin. Reason again. If a man can date a twenty-five-year-old, he will. Even if the twenty-five-year-old makes less money and has less experience than the thirty-two-year-old he thought he might want to ask out. Until the twenty-five-year-old came along. Oh, sure, in the man's mind, the thirty-two-year-old woman definitely has something the twenty-five-year-old doesn't. Wear and tear.

I didn't want to feel bitter, really.

And I couldn't even blame anyone for my being in that place. I'd made the decisions all along the way. The decisions that got me where I was—thirty-two, single, and with no good prospect on the horizon.

I loved my job and I was proud of my career and my condo and my travels. But at the same time, I wanted what I suspected might have been too late for me to have.

I wanted to fall in love. I wanted it to be real. And I wanted it to last forever.

I watched as the skating family tumbled off the ice. For a

moment, I listened to the laughter and shouts of the other skaters, to the excited barking of the dogs.

Then I pulled my coat closer around me and walked on.

Merry, Merry

Fern Michaels

Andi Evans stared at the light switch. Should she turn it on or not? How many kilowatts of electricity did the fluorescent bulbs use? How would it translate onto her monthly bill? She risked a glance at the calendar; December 14, 1996, five days till the meter reader arrived. The hell with it, the animals needed light. She needed light. Somehow, someway, she'd find a way to pay the bill. On the other hand, maybe she should leave the premises dark so Mr. Peter King could break his leg in the dark. Breaking both legs would be even better. Like it was really going to happen.

Maybe she should read the letter again. She looked in the direction of her desk where she'd thrown it five days ago after she'd read it. She could see the end of the expensive cream-colored envelope sticking out among the stack of unpaid bills. "Guess what, Mr. Peter King, I'm not selling you my property. I told that to your forty-seven lawyers months ago." She started to cry then because it was all so hopeless.

They came from every direction, dogs, cats, puppies and kittens, clawing for her attention, their ears attuned to the strange sounds coming from the young woman who fed and bathed them and saw to their needs. They were strays nobody wanted. This was what she'd gone to veterinarian school for. She even had a sign that said she was Andrea Evans, D.V.M. Eleven patients in as many months. She was the new kid on the block, what did she expect? Because she was that new kid, people assumed they could just dump unwanted animals on her property. After all, what did a vet with only eleven patients have to do?

Andi thought about her student loans, the taxes on her house and three acres, the animals, the bills, the futility of it all. Why was she even fighting? Selling her property would net her a nice tidy sum. She could pay off her loans, go to work for a vet clinic, get a condo someplace and . . . what would happen to her animals if she did that? She wailed louder, the dogs and cats clambering at her feet.

"Enough!" a voice roared.

"Gertie!"

Tails swished furiously; Gertie always brought soup bones and catnip. Andi watched as she doled them out, something for everyone. She blew her nose. "I think they love you more than they love me."

"They love what I bring them. I'd like a cup of tea if you have any. It's nasty out there. It might snow before nightfall."

"Where are you sleeping tonight, Gertie?"

"Under the railroad trestle with my friends. Being homeless doesn't give me many choices."

"You're welcome to stay here, Gertie. I told you the cot is yours anytime you want it. I'll even make you breakfast. Did you eat today?"

"Later. I have something for you. Call it an early Christmas present. I couldn't wait to get here to give it to you." Gertie hiked up several layers of clothing to her long underwear where she'd sewn a pocket. She withdrew a thick wad of bills. "We found this four weeks ago. There it was, this big wad of money laying right in the street late at night. Two thousand dollars, Andi. We want you to have it. We watched in the papers, asked the police, no one claimed it. A whole month we waited, and no one claimed it. It's probably drug money, but them animals of yours don't know that. Better to be spent on them than on some drug pusher. Doncha be telling me no now."

"Oh, Gertie, I wouldn't dream of saying no. Did you find it in Plainfield?"

"Right there on Front Street, big as life."

Andi hugged the old woman who always smelled of lily of the valley. She could never figure out why that was. Gertie had to be at least seventy-five, but a young seventy-five as she put it. She was skinny and scrawny, but it was hard to tell with the many layers of clothing she wore. Her shoes were run-down, her gloves had holes in the fingers, and her knit cap reeked of moth balls. For a woman her age she had dewy skin, pink cheeks, few wrinkles and the brightest, bluest eyes Andi had ever seen. "Did you walk all the way from Plainfield, Gertie?"

Gertie's head bobbed up and down. "Scotch Plains ain't that far. I left my buggie outside."

Translated, that meant all of Gertie's worldly possessions were in an Acme shopping cart outside Andi's clinic.

"Here's your tea, Gertie, strong and black, just the way you like it. It's almost Christmas; are you going to call your children? You should, they must be worried sick."

"What, so they can slap me in a nursing home? Oh, no, I like things just the way they are. I'm spending Christmas with my friends. Now, why were you bawling like that?"

Andi pointed to her desk. "Unpaid bills. And a letter from Mr. Peter King. He's that guy I told you about. His forty-seven lawyers couldn't bend me, so I guess they're sending in the first string now. He's coming here at four-thirty."

"Here?" Gertie sputtered, the teacup almost falling from her hand.

"Yes. Maybe he's going to make a final offer. Or, perhaps he thinks he can intimidate me. This property has been in my family for over a hundred years. I'm not selling it to some lipstick mogul. What does a man know about lipstick anyway?

Who cares if he's one of the biggest cosmetic manufacturers on the East Coast. I don't even wear lipstick. These lips are as kissable as they're going to get, and his greasy product isn't going to change my mind."

"I really need to be going now, Andi. So, you'll tell him no."

"Gertie, look around you. What would you do if you were me? What's so special about this piece of property? Let him go to Fanwood, anywhere but here. Well?"

"Location is everything. This is prime. Zoning has to be just right, and you, my dear, are zoned for his needs. I'd tell him to go fly a kite," Gertie said smartly. "I hear a truck. Lookee here, Andi, Wishnitz is here with your dog food."

"I didn't order any dog food."

"You better tell him that then, 'cause the man's unloading big bags of it. I'll see you tomorrow. Greasy, huh?"

"Yeah. Gertie, I wish you'd stay; it's getting awfully cold outside. Thanks for the money. Tell your friends I'm grateful. You be careful now."

"Hey, I didn't order dog food," she said to the driver.

"Bill says it's a gift. Five hundred pounds of Pedigree dog food, sixteen cases of cat food and two bags of birdseed. Sign here?"

"Who sent it?"

"Don't know, ma'am, I'm just the driver. Call the store. Where do you want this?"

"Around the back."

Andi called the feed store to be sure there was no mistake. "Are you telling me some anonymous person just walked into your store and paid for all this? It's a fortune in dog and cat food. No name at all? All right, thanks."

A beagle named Annabelle pawed Andi's leg. "I know, time for supper and a little run. Okay, everybody *SIT!* You know the drill, about face; march in an orderly fashion to the pen area. Stop when you get to the gate and go to your assigned dishes. You know which ones are yours. No cheating, Harriet," she said to a fat white cat who eyed her disdainfully. "I'm counting to three, and when the whistle blows, *GO!* That's really good, you guys are getting the hang of it. Okay, here it comes, extra today thanks to our Good Samaritan, whoever she or he might be."

"Bravo! If I didn't see it with my own eyes, I wouldn't have believed it. There must be thirty dogs and cats here."

"Thirty-six to be exact. And you are?" Andi looked at her watch.

"Peter King. You must be Andrea Evans."

"Dr. Evans. How did you get in here? The dogs didn't bark." Andi's voice was suspicious, her eyes wary. "I'm busy right now, and you're forty-five minutes early, Mr. King. I can't deal with you now. You need to go back to the office or come back another day." The wariness in her eyes changed to amusement when she noticed Cedric, a Dalmatian, lift his leg to pee on Peter King's exquisitely polished Brooks Brothers loafers.

The lipstick mogul, as Andi referred to him, eyed his shoe in dismay. He shook it off and said, "You might be right. I'll be in the waiting room."

Andi raised her head from the sack of dog food to stare at the tall man dwarfing her: Thirty-six or -seven, brown eyes, brown unruly hair with a tight curl, strong features, handsome, muscular, unmarried: no ring on his finger. Sharply dressed. Pristine white shirt, bold, expensive tie. Very well put together. She wondered how many lipsticks he had to sell to buy his outfit. She debated asking until she remembered how she looked. Instead she said, "You remind me of someone."

"A lot of people say that, but they can never come up with who it is." He started for the waiting room.

"It will come to me sooner or later." Andi ladled out food, the dogs waiting patiently until all the dishes were full. "Okay, guys, go for it!" When the animals finished eating,

Andi let them out into their individual runs. "Twenty minutes. When you hear the buzzer, boogie on in here," she called.

Andi took her time stacking the dog bowls in the stainless steel sink full of soapy water. She'd said she was busy. Busy meant she had to wash and dry the dishes now to take up time. As she washed and dried the bowls, her eyes kept going to the mirror over the sink. She looked worse than a mess. She had on absolutely no makeup, her blond hair was frizzy, her sweat shirt was stained and one of her sneakers had a glob of poop on the heel. She cleaned off her shoe, then stacked the dishes for the following day. "When I'm slicked up, I can look as good as he does," she hissed to the animals and let the dogs into their pens. The beagle threw her head back and howled.

"I have five minutes, Mr. King. I told your forty-seven lawyers I'm not selling. What part of no don't you understand?"

"The part about the forty-seven lawyers. I only have two. I think you mean forty-seven letters."

Andi shrugged.

"I thought perhaps I could take you out to dinner . . . and we could . . . discuss the pros and cons of selling your property." He smiled. She saw dimples and magnificent white teeth. All in a row like matched pearls.

"Save your money, Mr. King. Dinner will not sway my decision. You know what else, I don't even like your lipstick. It's greasy. The colors are abominable. The names you've given the lipsticks are so ridiculous they're ludicrous. Raspberry Cheese Louise. Come *onnnnn.*" At his blank look she said, "I worked at a cosmetic counter to put myself through college and vet school."

"I see."

"No, you don't, but that's okay. Time's up, Mr. King."

"Three hundred and fifty thousand, Dr. Evans. You could relocate."

Andi felt her knees go weak on her. "Sorry, Mr. King."

"Five hundred thousand and that's as high as I can go. It's a take it or leave it offer. It's on the table right now. When I walk out of here it goes with me."

She might have seriously considered the offer if the beagle hadn't chosen that moment to howl. "I really have to go, Mr. King. That's Annabelle howling. She has arthritis and it's time for her medication." She must be out of her mind to turn down half a million dollars. Annabelle howled again.

"I didn't know dogs got arthritis."

"They get a lot of things, Mr. King. They develop heart trouble; they get cancer, cataracts, prostate problems, all manner of things. Do you really think us humans have a lock on disease? This is the only home those animals know. No one else wanted them, so I took them in. My father and his father before him owned this kennel. It's my home and their home."

"Wait, hear me out. You could buy a new, modern facility with the money I'm willing to pay you. This is pretty antiquated. Your wood's rotten, your pens are rusty, your concrete is cracked. You're way past being a fixer-upper. You could get modern equipment. If you want my opinion, I think you're being selfish. You're thinking of yourself, not the animals. The past is past; you can't bring it back, nor should you want to. I'll leave my offer on the table till Friday. Give it some thought, sleep on it. If your decision is still no on Friday, I won't bother you again. I'll even raise my price to $750,000. I'm not trying to cheat you."

Andi snorted. "Of course not," she said sarcastically, "that's why you started off at $200,000 and now you're up to $750,000. I didn't just fall off the turnip truck, Mr. King. Let's cut to the chase. What's your absolute final offer?"

It was Peter King's turn to stare warily at the young doctor in front of him. His grandmother would love her. Sadie would say she had grit and spunk. Uh-huh. "A million," he said hoarsely.

"That's as in acre, right? I have a little over three acres. Closer to four than three."

King's jaw dropped. Annabelle howled again. "You want three million dollars for this . . . hovel?"

"No. Three plus million for the *land.* You're right, it is a hovel; but it's my home and the home of those animals. I sweated my ass off to keep this property and work my way through school. What do you know about work, Mr. Lipstick? Hell, I could make up a batch of that stuff you peddle for eight bucks a pop right here in the kitchen. All I need is my chemistry book. Get the hell off my property and don't come back unless you have three million plus dollars in your hand. You better get going before it really starts to snow and you ruin those fancy three-hundred-dollar Brooks Brothers shoes."

"Your damn dog already ruined them."

"Send me a bill!" Andi shouted as she pushed him through the door and then slammed it shut. She turned the dead bolt before she raced back to the animals. She dusted her hands dramatically for the animals' benefit before she started to cry. The animals crept from their cages that had no doors, to circle her, licking and pawing at her tear-filled face. She hiccupped and denounced all men who sold lipstick. "If he comes up with three million plus bucks, we're outta here. Then we'll have choices; we can stay here in New Jersey, head south or north, wherever we can get the best deal. Hamburger and tuna for you guys and steak for me. We'll ask Gertie to go with us. I'm done crying now. You can go back to sleep. Come on, Annabelle, time for your pill."

Andi scooped up the pile of bills on her desk to carry them into the house. With the two thousand dollars from Gertie and the dog and cat food, she could last until the end of January, and then she'd be right back where she was just a few hours ago. Three million plus dollars was a lot of money. So was $750,000. Scrap that, he'd said a cool million. Times three. At eight bucks a tube, how many lipsticks would the kissing king need to sell? Somewhere in the neighborhood of 375,000. Darn, she should have said two million an acre.

It might be a wonderful Christmas after all.

Peter King slid his metallic card into the slot and waited for the huge grilled gate to the underground garage of his grandmother's high rise to open. Tonight was his Friday night obligatory dinner with his grandmother. A dinner he always enjoyed and even looked forward to. He adored his seventy-five-year-old grandmother who was the president of King Cosmetics. He shuddered when he thought of what she would say to Andrea Evans's price. She'd probably go ballistic and throw her salmon, Friday night's dinner, across the room. At which point, Hannah the cat would eat it all and then puke on the Persian carpet. He shuddered again. Three million dollars. Actually, it would be more than three million. The property on Cooper River Road was closer to four acres. He had two hard choices: pay it or forget it.

Who in the hell was that wise-ass girl whose dog peed on his shoe? Where did she get off booting him out the door. Hell, she'd pushed him, shoved him. She probably didn't weigh more than one hundred pounds soaking wet. He took a few seconds to mentally envision that hundred-pound body naked. Aaahh. With some King Cosmetics she'd be a real looker. And she hated his guts.

"Hey, Sadie, I'm here," Peter called from the foyer. He'd called his grandmother Sadie from the time he was a little boy. She allowed it because she said it made her feel younger.

"Peter, you're early. Good, we can have a drink by the fire. Hannah's already there waiting for us. She's not feeling well."

Sadie's voice turned fretful. "I don't want her *going* before me. She's such wonderful company. Look at her, she's just lying there. I tried to tempt her with salmon before and she wouldn't touch it. She won't even let me hold her."

Peter's stomach started to churn. If anything happened to Hannah, he knew his grandmother would take to her bed and not get up. He hunched down and held out his hand. Hannah hissed and snarled. "That's not like her. Did you take her to the vet?"

Sadie snorted. "He went skiing in Aspen. I don't much care for all those fancy vets who have banker's hours and who don't give a damn. Hannah is too precious to trust to just anybody. Let's sit and have a drink and watch her. How did your meeting go with Dr. Evans?"

"It was a bust. She wants a million dollars an acre. She means it, too. She booted my ass right out the door. I have a feeling she's a pretty good vet. Maybe you should have her take a look at Hannah. One of her dogs squirted on my shoe."

"That's a lot of money. Is the property worth it?"

"Hell yes. More as a matter of fact. She ridiculed my low-ball offer. Hey, business is business."

"We aren't in the business of cheating people, Peter. Fair is fair. If, as you say, Miss Evans's property is the perfect location, then pay the money and close the deal. The company can afford it. You can be under way the first of the year. I know you had the attorneys do all the paperwork in advance. Which, by the way, is a tad unethical in my opinion. Don't think I don't know that you have your contractor on twenty-four-hour call."

"Is there anything you don't know, Sadie?"

"Yes."

Peter eyed his grandmother warily. God, how he loved this old lady with her pearl white hair and regal bearing. It was hard to believe she was over seventy. She was fit and trim, fashionable, a leader in the community. She sat on five boards, did volunteer work at the hospital and was an active leader in ways to help the homeless. Her picture was in the paper at least three days a week. He knew what was coming now, and he dreaded it. "Let's get it over with, Sadie."

"Helen called here for you about an hour ago. She quizzed me, Peter. The gall of that woman. What do you see in her? I hesitate to remind you, but she dumped you. That's such an unflattering term, but she did. She married that councilman because she believed his PR campaign. She thought he was rich. The man is in debt over his ears, so she left him. Now, she wants you again. She's a selfish, mean-spirited young woman who thinks only of herself. I thought you had more sense, Peter. I am terribly disappointed in this turn of events."

He was pretty much of the same opinion, but he wasn't going to give his grandmother the pleasure of knowing his feelings. She'd been matchmaking for years and was determined to find just the right girl for him."

"We're friends. There's no harm in a casual lunch or dinner. Don't make this into something else."

"I want to see you settled before I go."

"You can stop that right now, Sadie, because it isn't going to work. You're fit as a fiddle, better than a person has a right to be at your age. You can stay on the treadmill longer than I can. You aren't going anywhere for a very long time. When I find the right girl you'll be the first to know."

"You've been telling me that for years. You're thirty-six, Peter. I want grandchildren before . . . I get too old to enjoy them. If you aren't interested in Helen, tell her so and don't take up her time. Don't even think about bringing her to your Christmas party. If you do, I will not attend."

"*All right,* Sadie!"

Sadie sniffed, her blue eyes sparking. "She just wants to be your hostess so she can network. Men are so stupid sometimes. Tell me about Dr. Evans. What's she like?"

Peter threw his hands in the air. "I told you she kicked me

out. I hardly had time to observe her. She has curly hair, she's skinny. I think she's skinny. She had this look on her face, Sadie, it . . . Mom used to look at me kind of the same way when I was sick. She had that look when she was with the animals. I was sizing her up when her dog squatted on my shoe. The place is a mess. Clean, but a mess."

"That young woman worked her way through school. She worked at a cosmetic counter, did waitressing, sometimes working two jobs. It took her a while, but she did it. I approve of that, Peter. That property has been in her family for a long time. Both her parents were vets, and so was her grandfather. No one appreciates hard work more than I do. Take a good look at me, Peter. I started King Cosmetics in my kitchen. I worked around the clock when your grandfather died and I had three children to bring up. I read the report in your office. I can truthfully say I never read a more comprehensive report. The only thing missing was the color of her underwear. I felt like a sneak reading it. I really did, Peter. I wish you hadn't done that. It's such an invasion of someone's privacy."

"This might surprise you, Sadie, but I felt the same way. I wanted to know what I was up against, financially. For whatever it's worth, I'm sorry I did it, too. So, do we buy the property or not?"

"Are you prepared to pay her price?"

"I guess I am. It's a lot of money."

"Will she hold out?" Sadie's tone of voice said she didn't care one way or the other.

"Damn right. That young woman is big on principle. She's going to stick it to me because she thinks I tried to cheat her."

"You did."

"Why does it sound like you're on her side? What I did was an acceptable business practice."

"I'm a fair, honest woman, Peter. I don't like anything unethical. I wish this whole mess never happened. Why don't you invite Dr. Evans to your Christmas party. If you got off to a bad start, this might shore up things for you. I think you're interested in the young woman. I bet she even has a party dress. And shoes. Probably even a pearl necklace that belonged to her mother. Girls always have pearl necklaces that belonged to their mothers. Things like pearl necklaces are important to young women. Well?"

"Before or after I make the offer?" Jesus, he didn't just say that, did he?

"If you're going to make the offer, call her and tell her. Why wait till Monday? Maybe you could even go over there and take Hannah for her to check over. That's business for her. Then you could extend the invitation."

Peter grinned wryly. "You never give up, do you?"

"Then you'll take Hannah tomorrow."

"For you, Sadie, anything. What's for dinner?"

"Pot roast," Sadie said smartly. "I gave the salmon to Hannah, but she wouldn't eat it."

"Pot roast's good. We settled on the three million plus then?" His voice was so jittery-sounding, Sadie turned away to hide her smile.

"I'd say so. You need to give Dr. Evans time to make plans. Christmas is almost here. She'll want to spend her last Christmas at her home, I would imagine. She'll have to pack up whatever she's going to take with her. It's not much time, Peter. She has to think about all those animals."

"Three million plus will ease the burden considerably. She can hire people to help her. We're scheduled to go, as in *go,* the day after New Years. I hate to admit this, but I'm having second thoughts about the contractor I hired. I think I was just a little too hasty when I made my decision, but I signed the contract so I'm stuck. Time's money, Sadie. If the young lady is as industrious as the report says, she'll have it under control."

Sadie smiled all through dinner. She was still smiling when she kissed her grandson good night at the door. "Drive carefully, Peter, the weatherman said six inches of snow by morning. Just out of curiosity, do you happen to know what kind of vehicle Dr. Evans drives?"

"I saw an ancient pickup on the side of the building. It didn't look like it was operational to me. Why do you ask?"

"No reason. I'd hate to think of her stranded with those animals if an emergency came up."

"If you want me to stop on my way home, just say so, Sadie. Is it late? Why don't I call her on the car phone on the way?"

"A call is so impersonal. Like when Helen calls. You could tell Dr. Evans you were concerned about the animals. The power could go out. She might have electric heat. You could also mention that you'll be bringing Hannah in the morning. If she doesn't like you, this might change her mind."

"I didn't say she didn't like me, Sadie," Peter blustered.

"Oh."

"Oh? What does oh mean?"

"It means I don't think she likes you. Sometimes you aren't endearing, Peter. She doesn't know you the way I do. The way Helen did." This last was said so snidely, Peter cringed.

"Good night, Sadie." Peter kissed his grandmother soundly, gave her a thumbs-up salute, before he pressed the down button of the elevator.

As he waited for the grilled parking gate to open, he stared in dismay at the accumulated snow. Maybe he should head for the nearest hotel and forget about going home. What he should have done was bunk with Sadie for the night. Too late, he was already on the road. The snow took care of any visit he might have considered making to Scotch Plains. He eyed the car phone and then the digital clock on the Mercedes walnut panel. Nine o'clock was still early. Pay attention to the road, he cautioned himself.

In the end, Peter opted for the Garden State Parkway. Traffic was bumper-to-bumper, but moving. He got off the Clark exit and headed for home. He could call Dr. Evans from home with a frosty beer in his hand. When the phone on the console buzzed, he almost jumped out of his skin. He pressed a button and said, "Peter King."

"Peter, it's Helen. I've been calling you all evening. Where have you been?"

He wanted to say, what business is it of yours where I was, but he didn't. "On the road," he said curtly.

"Why don't you stop for a nightcap, Peter. I'll put another log on the fire. I have some wonderful wine."

"Sorry, I'm three blocks from home. The roads are treacherous this evening."

"I see. Where were you, Peter? I called your grandmother, and she said you weren't there."

"Out and about. I'll talk to you next week, Helen."

"You're hanging up on me," she said in a whiny voice.

"Afraid so, I'm almost home."

"I wish I was there with you. I didn't get an invitation to your Christmas party, Peter. Was that an oversight or don't you want me there?"

Peter drew a deep breath. "Helen, you aren't divorced. I know your husband well. We play racquet ball at the gym. He's a nice guy and I like him. He's coming to the party. It won't look right for you to attend."

"For heaven's sake, Peter, this is the nineties. Albert and I remained friends. We're legally separated. He knows it's you I love. He's known that from day one. I made a mistake, Peter. Are you going to hold it against me for the rest of my life?"

"Look, Helen, there's no easy way to say this except to say it straight out. I'm seeing someone on a serious basis. You and I had our time, but it's over now. Let's stay friends and let it go at that."

"Who? Who are you seeing? You're making that up, Peter. I would have heard if you were seriously seeing someone. Or is she some nobody you don't take out in public? I bet it's somebody your grandmother picked out for you. Oh, Peter, that's just too funny for words." Trilling laughter filled Peter's car.

Peter swerved into his driveway just as he pressed the power button on the car phone, cutting Helen's trilling laughter in mid-note. He waited for the Genie to raise the garage door. The moment the garage door closed, Peter's shoulders slumped. Who *was* that woman on the phone? Jesus, once he'd given serious thought to marrying her. He shook his head to clear away his thoughts.

How quiet and empty his house was. Cold and dark. He hated coming home to a dark house. He'd thought about getting an animal, but it wouldn't have been fair to the animal since he was hardly ever home. He slammed his briefcase down on the kitchen counter. Damn, he'd forgotten the report on Andrea Evans. Oh, well, it wasn't going anywhere. Tomorrow would be soon enough to retrieve it.

Peter walked around his house, turning on lights as he went from room to room. It didn't look anything like the house he'd grown up in. He leaned against the banister, closing his eyes as he did so. He'd lived in a big, old house full of nooks and crannies in Sleepy Hollow. The rug at the foot of the steps was old, threadbare, and Bessie, their old cocker spaniel had chewed all four corners. She lay on the rug almost all her life to wait for them to come home, pooping on it from time to time as she got older. When she died, his parents had buried her in the backyard under the apple tree. Jesus, he didn't think there was that much grief in the world as that day. He thought about the old hat rack with the boot box underneath where he stored his boots, gloves and other treasures. The hat rack and boot box were somewhere in the attic along with Bessie's toys and dog bones. He wondered if they were still intact.

Peter rubbed at his eyes. He'd loved that house with the worn, comfortable furniture, the green plants his mother raised, and the warm, fragrant kitchen with its bright colors. Something was always cooking or baking, and there were always good things to eat for his friends and himself after school. The thing he remembered the most, though, was his mother's smile when he walked in the door. She'd always say, "Hi, Pete, how's it going?" And he'd say, "Pretty good, Mom." They always ate in the kitchen. Dinner hour was long, boisterous and memorable. Even when they had meatloaf. He tried not to think about his younger brother and sister. He had to stop torturing himself like this. He banged one fist on the banister as he wiped at his eyes with the other. He looked around. Everything was beautiful, decorated by a professional whose name he didn't know. Once a week a florist delivered fresh flowers. The only time the house came alive was during his annual Christmas party or his Fourth of July barbecue. The rest of the time it was just a house. The word nurture came to mind. He squeezed his eyes shut and tried to imagine what this perfectly decorated house would be like with a wife, kids and a dog. Maybe two dogs and two cats.

"Five thousand goddamn fucking square feet of *nothing*." He ripped at his tie and jacket, tossing them on the back of a chair. He kicked his loafers across the room. In a pique of something he couldn't define, he brushed at a pile of magazines and watched them sail in different directions. Shit! The room still didn't look lived in. Hell, he didn't even know his neighbors. He might as well live in a damn hotel.

On his way back to the kitchen he picked up the portable phone, asking for information. He punched out the numbers for the Evans Kennel as his free hand twisted the cap off a bottle of Budweiser. He wondered if her voice would be sleepy sounding or hard and cold. He wasn't prepared for what he did hear when he announced himself.

"I don't have time for chit-chat, Mr. King. I have an emergency on my hands here and you're taking up my time. Call me on Monday or don't call me on Monday." Peter stared at the pinging phone in his hand.

Chit-chat. Call or don't call. *Emergency.* Sadie's dire warnings rang in his ears.

Peter raced up the steps. So there was a sucker born every minute. Sadie would approve. He stripped down, throwing his clothes any which way as he searched for thermal sweats, thick socks and Alpine boots. His shearling jacket, cap and gloves were downstairs in the hall closet.

Emergency could mean anything. She was handling it. Oh, yeah, like women could really handle an emergency. Maybe his mother could handle one, or Sadie, but not that hundred pound prairie flower. He raced to the garage where all his old camping gear was stored. Blankets and towels went into the back of his Range Rover. He threw in two shovels, his camp stove, lanterns, flashlights. The last things to go in were Sterno lamps and artificial fire logs. What the hell, an emergency was an emergency.

It wasn't until he backed the 4 by 4 out of the garage that he questioned himself. Why was he doing this? Because . . . because . . . he'd heard the same fearful tone in Dr. Evans's voice that he'd heard in his mother's voice the day Bessie couldn't get up on her legs anymore.

Driving every back street and alley, over people's lawns, Peter arrived at the Evans Kennel in over an hour. Every light appeared to be on in the house and the kennel. There were no footprints in the snow, so that had to mean the emergency was inside the house. Even from this distance he could hear the shrill barking and high-pitched whine of the animals that seemed to be saying, intruder, intruder.

Peter walked around to the door he'd been ushered out of just hours ago. His eyebrows shot up to his hairline when he found it unlocked. He felt silly as hell when he bellowed above the sound of the dogs, "I'm here and coming through!"

In the whole of his life he'd never seen so many teeth in one place—all canine. "You need to lock your goddamn doors is what you need to do, Dr. Evans!" he shouted.

"You!" She made it sound like he was the devil from hell making a grand entrance.

"Who'd you expect, Sylvester Stallone? You said it was an emergency. I react to emergencies. My mother trained me that way. I brought everything. What's wrong?"

Andi, hands on hips, stared at the man standing in front of her, the dogs circling his feet. She clapped her hands once, and they all lay down, their eyes on the giant towering over them.

"I had to do a cesarian section on Rosie. Her pups were coming out breach. Come here. Mother and puppies doing just fine, all eight of them. God, eight more mouths to feed." Andi's shoulders slumped as she fought off her tears.

"I'll take two. Three. I love dogs. It won't be so hard. I'm going to meet your price. Three million plus, whatever the plus turns out to be. It's fair. You'll be able to do a lot if you invest wisely. I can recommend a pretty good tax man if you're interested. You might even want to give some thought to taking payments instead of one lump sum. You need to talk to someone. Am I getting girls or boys? Make that four. I'll give one to my grandmother. That's another thing, her cat Hannah is sick. I was going to call you in the morning to ask if you'd look at her. Their regular vet is away on a winter vacation."

"Oh, my. Listen, about this afternoon . . ."

"You don't have to apologize," Peter said.

Andi smiled. "I wasn't going to apologize. I was going to try and explain my circumstances to you. I appreciate you coming back here. It's the thought that counts. Are you serious about the pups?"

Was he? "Hell yes. Told you, I love dogs. Isn't it kind of cold out here for the new mother and my pups?"

"No. Actually, dogs much prefer it to be cooler. I was going to take Rosie into the kitchen, though. I leave the door open, and if the others want to come in, they do. At some point during the night, when I'm sleeping, three or four of them will come in and sleep outside my door. There's usually one outside the bathroom when I shower, too. They're very protective; they know when you're bathing and sleeping you're vulnerable. It's really amazing."

"Bessie was like that. Do you want me to carry the box?"

"Sure. Can I make you some coffee? I was going to have a grilled cheese sandwich. Would you like one or did you have your dinner?"

Peter thought about how he'd pigged out on his grandmother's pot roast. "I'm starved. Coffee sounds good, too. I brought a lot of blankets and towels with me. I thought maybe your heat went out."

"I could really use them. My washer goes all day long, and like everyone else in this house, it's getting ready to break down. My furnace is the next thing to go."

Peter's face turned ashen. "Your furnace? Don't you check it? You need to call PSE&G to come and look at it. My parents . . . and my brother and sister died from carbon monoxide poisoning. Turn it off if it's giving you trouble. Use your fireplace. I can bring you electric heaters. Is the fireplace any good?"

Andi stared at the man sitting at her table, a helpless look on her face. "I . . . I 'm sorry. I don't know the first thing about the furnace except that it's very old. The fireplace is in good condition; I had it cleaned in September. I'd probably be more at risk using electric heaters; the wiring and the plumbing are . . . old. I guess I just have to take my chances. It's only another two weeks. You said you wanted to . . . start . . . whatever it is you're going to do right after the first of the year."

"Tomorrow when I bring Hannah I'll bring you some of those detectors. I have one in every room in my house. I was away at school when it happened. All you do is plug them in."

"I appreciate that. I won't charge you for Hannah, then."

"Okay, that's fair." He wasn't about to tell her each detector cost eighty-nine dollars. She would need at least four of them for the sprawling house and kennel.

"Want some bacon on your sandwich? Ketchup?"

"Sure."

"I made a pie today. Want a piece?"

Peter nodded. "Your house smells like the house I grew up in. It always smelled like apples and cinnamon. At Christmastime you could get drunk on the smell. Speaking of Christmas, I give a party once a year, would you like to come? I think you'll like my grandmother. It's next Thursday."

"I don't know . . . I hate to leave the animals. I haven't been to a party in so long, I don't think I'll remember how to act. Thank you for asking, though."

"Don't you have a pair of pearls?" he asked, a stupid look on his face.

"What do pearls have to do with it?"

"Your mother's pearls." Jesus, he must have missed something when Sadie was explaining party attire. She was staring at him so intently he felt compelled to explain. "You know, pearls to go with the dress. Your mother's pearls. If you have that, you don't have to worry about anything else. Right? Can I use your bathroom?"

"Upstairs, third door on the right. Don't step on the carpet at the bottom of the steps. Annabelle lies there all the time. She pees on it and I didn't have time to wash it. She chewed all the fringe off the corners. She's getting old, so I can't scold her too much."

Peter bolted from the room. Andi stared after him with puzzled eyes. She scurried into the pantry area where a mirror hung on the back of the door. She winced at her appearance. She didn't look one damn bit better than she had looked earlier. "What you see is what you get," she muttered.

Andi was sliding the sandwiches onto plates when Peter entered the room. "This must have been a nice house at one time."

Andi nodded. "It was a comfortable old house. It fit us. My mother never worried too much about new furniture or keeping up with the neighbors. It was clean and comfortable. Homey. Some houses are just houses. People make homes. Did you know that?"

"Believe it or not, I just realized that same fact today. Every so often I trip down memory lane."

"I don't do that anymore. It's too sad. I don't know how I'm going to walk away from this place. My mother always said home was where your stuff was. Part of me believes it. What's your opinion? By the way, where do you live?"

"In Clark. It's a new, modern house. Decorated by a professional. Color-coordinated, all that stuff. I don't think you'd like it. My grandmother hates it. I don't even like it myself. I try throwing things around, but it still looks the same."

"Maybe some green plants. Green plants perk up a room. You probably need some junk. Junk helps. I'll be throwing a lot away, so you can help yourself."

"Yeah? What kind of junk? My plants die."

"You need to water plants. Get silk ones. All you have to do is go over them with a blow dryer every so often. Junk is junk. Everybody has junk. You pick it up here and there, at a flea market or wherever. When you get tired of it you throw it away and buy new junk."

Peter threw his head back and laughed until his eyes watered. "That's something my grandmother would say. Why are you looking at me like that?"

"I'm sorry. You should laugh more often. You take yourself pretty seriously, don't you?"

"For the most part, I guess I do. What about you?" He leaned across the table as though her answer was the most important thing in the world. She had beautiful eyes with thick lashes. And they were her own, unlike Helen's.

"I've been so busy scrambling to make a go of it, I haven't had the time to dwell on anything. I guess I'm sort of an optimist, but then I'm a pessimist, too, at times. What will be will be. How about some pie? I can warm it up. More coffee?"

"Sure to everything. This is nice. I haven't sat in a kitchen . . . since . . . I left home. We always ate in the kitchen growing up."

"So did we. Are you married?"

"No. Why do you ask? Do you have designs on me?"

"No. I just want to make sure Rosie's pups get a good home. Who's going to take care of them when you work?"

"I already figured that out. I'm going to hire a sitter. I'll have her cook chicken gizzards and livers for them. My mother used to cook for Bessie. She loved it. You're very pretty, Dr. Evans. Why aren't you married?"

"Do you think that's any of your business, Mr. King?"

"As the owner of those dogs, of which I'm taking four, I should know what kind of person you are, marital status included. Well?"

"I was engaged, not that it's any of your business. I wanted to come back here; he didn't. He wanted to work in a ritzy area; I didn't. He was in it for the money. I wasn't. I don't know, maybe he was the smart one."

"No, you were the smart one," Peter said quietly. "It's rare that the heart and mind work in sync. When it does happen, you know it's right."

"Your turn."

Peter shrugged. "I run my grandmother's business. She tells me I'm good at it. She's the only family I have left, and she's up in years. I always . . . take . . . introduce her to the women I, ah, date. I value her opinion. So far she hasn't approved of anyone I've dated. That's okay; she was on the money every single time. Guess I just haven't met the right girl. Or, maybe I'm meant for bachelorhood. Would you like to go out to dinner with me to celebrate our deal?"

"Under other circumstances, I'd say yes, but I have too

much to do. I also want to keep my eye on Rosie and the pups. If you like, you can come for dinner tomorrow."

"I'll be here. I'll bring in the towels and blankets and shovel you out before I leave."

"I'll help you. Thanks."

It was one o'clock in the morning when Andi leaned on her shovel, exhaustion showing in every line of her face. "I'm going to sleep like a baby tonight," she panted.

"Yeah, me, too. Tell me, what's it like when you operate on one of the animals, like you did tonight?"

"Awesome. When I saw those pups and when I stitched up Rosie, all the hard years, all the back-breaking work, it was worth every hour of it. Guess you don't get that feeling when you label Raspberry Cheese Louise on your lipsticks."

Suddenly she was in the snow, the giant towering over her. She stretched out her foot, caught him on the ankle and pulled him down in an undignified heap. He kissed her, his mouth as cold and frosty as her own. It was the sweetest kiss of her life. She said so, grinning from ear to ear.

"Sweet?" he asked.

"Uh-huh?"

"Didn't make you want to tear your clothes off, huh?"

"You must be kidding? I never do that on a first date."

"This isn't a date." He leered at her.

"I don't do that on pre-dates either. I don't even know you."

"I'll let my hair down tomorrow, and you can *really* get to know me."

"Don't go getting any ideas that I'm easy. And, don't think you're parading me in front of your grandmother either."

"God forbid."

"Good night, Mr. King. You can call me Andi."

"Good night, Dr. Evans. You can call me Peter. What are we having for dinner?"

"Whatever you bring. Tomorrow is bath day. I'm big on fast and easy. What time are you bringing Hannah?"

"How about ten? Our attorney will be out bright and early for you to sign the contract. Is that all right with you?"

"Okay. Good night."

"I enjoyed this evening. Take good care of my dogs."

"I will." Suddenly she didn't want him to go. He didn't seem to want to go either. She watched the 4 by 4 until the red taillights were swallowed in the snow.

He was nice. Actually, he was real nice. And, he was going to give her over three million dollars. Oh, life was looking good.

The following morning, Andi woke before it was light out. She threw on her robe and raced down the stairs to check on Rosie. "I just want you to know I was having a really, that's as in *really,* delicious dream about Mr. Peter King." She hunched down to check on the new pups, who were sleeping peacefully, curled up against their mother.

While the coffee perked, Andi showered and dressed, taking a few more pains with her dress than usual. Today she donned corduroy slacks and a flannel shirt instead of the fleece-lined sweats she usually wore in the kennel. Today she even blow dried her hair and used the curling iron. She diddled with a jar of makeup guaranteed to confuse anyone interested in wondering if she was wearing it or not. A dab of rouge, a stroke of the eyebrow pencil and she was done. She was almost at the top of the steps when she marched back to her dressing table and spritzed a cloud of mist into the air. She savored the smell, a long-ago present from a friend. She told herself she took the extra pains because it wasn't every day she signed a three-million-plus deal. As she drank her coffee she wondered what the plus part of the contract would net her.

Andi thought about Gertie and her friends under the railroad trestle. Where did they go last night during the storm? Were they warm and safe? As soon as everything was tended to and she checked out Hannah the cat, she would drive into Plainfield and try to locate Gertie and her friends. Now that she had all this money coming to her, she could rent a motel for them until the weather eased up, providing the manager was willing to wait for his money.

The notebook on the kitchen table beckoned. Her list of things to do. Call Realtor, make plans to transport animals. Her friend Mickey had an old school bus he used for camping in the summer. He might lend it to her for a day or so. She could pile Gertie and her friends in the same bus.

Andi's thoughts whirled and raced as she cleaned the dog runs and hosed them out. She set down bowls of kibble and fresh water, tidied up the kennel, sorted through the blankets and towels. The heavy duty machines ran constantly. Her own laundry often piled up for weeks at a time simply because the animals had to come first. She raced back to the kitchen to add a note to her list. Call moving company. She wasn't parting with the crates, the laundry machines or the refrigerator. She was taking everything that belonged to her parents even if it was old and worn-out. The wrecking ball could destroy the house and kennel, but not her *stuff.*

She was on her third cup of coffee when Peter King's attorney arrived. She read over the contract, signed it and promised to take it to her attorney, Mark Fox. Everything was in order. Why delay on signing. The plus, she noticed, amounted to $750,000. That had to mean she had three and three-quarter acres. "Date the check January first. I don't want to have to worry about paying taxes until ninety-seven. Where's the date for construction to begin? Oh, okay, I see it. January 2, 1997. We're clear on that?"

"Yes, Dr. Evans, we're clear on that. Here's my card; have Mr. Fox call me. Mark is the finest real estate attorney in these parts. Give him my regards."

"I'll do that, Mr. Carpenter."

The moment the attorney was out of her parking lot, Andi

added Mark Fox's name to her list of things to do. She crossed her fingers that he worked half days on Saturday. If not, she'd slip the contract, along with a note, through the mail slot and call him Monday morning.

Andi's eyes settled on the clock. Ten minutes until Peter King arrived with his grandmother's cat. She busied herself with phone calls. Ten o'clock came and went. The hands of the clock swept past eleven. Were the roads bad? She called the police station. She was told the roads were in good shape, plowed and sanded. Her eyes were wet when she crouched down next to Rosie. "Guess he just wanted my signature on the contract. My mother always said there was a fool born every minute. Take care of those babies and I'll be back soon."

At ten minutes past twelve, Andi was on Park Avenue, where she dropped the contract through the slot on Mark Fox's door. She backed out of the drive and headed down Park to Raritan and then to Woodland, turning right onto South Avenue, where she thought she would find Gertie and her friends. She saw one lone figure, heavily clad, hunched around a huge barrel that glowed red and warm against the snow-filled landscape. Andi climbed from the truck. "Excuse me, sir, have you seen Gertie?" The man shook his head. "Do you know where I can find her? Where is everyone?" The man shrugged. "I need to get in touch with her. It's very important. If she comes by, will you ask her to call me? I'll give you the quarter for the phone call." She ran back to the truck to fish in the glove compartment for her card, where she scrawled, "Call me. Andi." She handed the card, a quarter and a five-dollar bill to the man. "Get some hot soup and coffee." The man's head bobbed up and down.

Her next stop was Raritan Road and her friend Mickey's house. The yellow bus was parked in his driveway next to a spiffy hunter green BMW.

Mickey was a free spirit, working only when the mood

struck him. Thanks to a sizable trust fund, all things were possible for the young man whose slogan was, "Work Is A Killer." She slipped a note under the door when her ring went unanswered. Her watch said it was one-thirty. Time to head for the moving company, where she signed another contract for her belongings to be moved out on December 22nd and taken to storage on Oak Tree Road in Edison. Her last stop was in Metuchen, where she stopped at the MacPherson Agency to ask for either Lois or Tom Finneran, a husband/wife realty team. The amenities over, she said, "Some acreage, a building is a must. It doesn't have to be fancy. I'm going to build what I want later on. Zoning is important. I was thinking maybe Freehold or Cranbur. You guys are the best, so I know you can work something out that will allow me to move in with the animals the first of the year. Have a wonderful holiday."

There were no fresh tire tracks in her driveway and no messages on her machine. "So who cares," she muttered as she stomped her way into the kennel. The kitchen clock said it was three-thirty when she put a pot of coffee on to perk. When the phone shrilled to life she dropped the wire basket full of coffee all over the floor. She almost killed herself as she sprinted across the huge kitchen to grapple with the receiver. Her voice was breathless when she said, "Dr. Evans."

"Andi, this is Gertie. Donald said you were looking for me. Is something wrong?"

"Everything's wrong and everything's right. I was worried about you and your friends out in the cold. I wanted to bring you back here till the weather clears. I signed the contract this morning. For a lot of money. Oh, Gertie, what I can do with that money. You and your friends can come live on my property. I'll build you a little house or a big house. You won't have to live on the street, and you won't get mugged anymore. You can all help with the animals, and I'll even pay you. I'll be able to take in more animals. Oh, God, Gertie, I almost forgot, Rosie had eight puppies. They are so beautiful. You're going to love them. You're quiet, is something wrong?"

"No. I don't want you worrying about me and my friends. I'll tell them about your offer, though. I'll think about it myself. How was . . . that man?"

"Mr. King?"

"Yeah, him."

"Last night I thought he was kind of nice. He came back out here later in the evening and shoveled my parking lot. He was starved, so I gave him a sandwich and we talked. I invited him to dinner tonight. He was supposed to bring his grandmother's cat for me to check and he was a no-show. I even let him kiss me after he pushed me in the snow. You know what, Gertie, I hate men. There's not one you can trust. All he wanted was my signature on that contract. He had this really nice laugh. We shared a few memories. As far as I can tell the only redeeming quality he has is that he loves his grandmother. Oh, oh, the other thing was, he was going to bring me some carbon monoxide things to plug in. He was so forceful I agreed and said I wouldn't charge for Hannah. That's the cat's name. He even invited me to his Christmas party, but he never even told me where he lived. Some invitation, huh? I should show him and turn up in my rubber suit. He acted like he thought I didn't know how to dress and kept mumbling about my mother's pearls. You're still coming for Christmas, aren't you? You said you'd bring all your buddies from the trestle. Gertie, I don't want to spend my last Christmas alone here in this house with just the animals. If they could talk, it would be different. Promise me, okay?"

"I can't promise. I will think about it, though. Why don't you hold those negative thoughts you have for Mr. King on the side. I bet he has a real good explanation."

Andi snorted. "Give me one. Just one. The roads are clear. Alexander Bell invented this wonderful thing called the telephone, and Mr. Sony has this machine that delivers your messages. Nope, the jerk just wanted my signature. I'll never see him again and I don't care. Do you want me to come and get you, Gertie? It's supposed to be really cold tonight."

"We're going to the shelter tonight. Thanks for the offer. Maybe I'll stop by tomorrow. Are the pups really cute?"

"Gorgeous. That's another thing; he said he was taking four, three for him and one for his grandmother. On top of everything else, the man is a liar. I hate liars as much as I hate used car salesmen. You sound funny, Gertie, are you sure you're all right?"

"I'm fine. Maybe I'm catching a cold."

"Now, why doesn't that surprise me? You live on the damn streets. I'll bet you don't even have any aspirin."

"I do so, and Donald has some brandy. I'll talk to you tomorrow, Andi. Thanks for caring about me and my friends. Give Rosie a hug for me."

"Okay, Gertie, take care of yourself."

Andi turned to Rosie, who was staring at her. "Gertie was crying. She's not catching a cold. She's the one who is homeless, and she's the one who always comes through for us. Always. I can't figure that out. She's homeless and she won't let me do anything for her. I hope somebody writes a book about that someday. Okay, bath time!"

Andi ate a lonely TV dinner and some tomato soup as she watched television. She was in bed by nine o'clock. She wanted to be up early so she could begin going through the attic and packing the things she wanted to take to storage. If her pillow was damp, there was no one to notice.

Less than ten miles away, Peter King sat on the sofa with his grandmother, trying his best to console her. He felt frightened for the first time in his life. His zesty grandmother was falling apart, unable to stop crying. "I thought she would live forever. I really did. My God, Peter, how I loved that animal.

I want her ashes. Every single one of them. You told them to do that, didn't you?"

"Of course I did, Sadie. I'm going to bring them by tomorrow. Do you want—"

"Do not touch anything, Peter. I want all her things left just the way they were. I wish I'd spent more time with her, cuddled her more. Sometimes she didn't want that; she wanted to be alone. She was so damn independent. Oh, God, what am I going to do without Hannah? She kept me going."

"It can't be any worse than when Bessie died. I still think about that," Peter said past the lump in his throat.

"She just died in her sleep and I was sleeping so soundly last night. What if she needed me and I didn't hear her?"

"Shhhh, she just closed her eyes and drifted off. That's how you have to think of it."

"Don't even think about getting me another cat. I won't have it, Peter. Are you listening to me?"

"I always listen to you, Sadie."

"Did you call Dr. Evans?"

"No. She'll understand. She loves animals. She's nice, Sadie. I really liked her. She forced a sandwich on me and I ate it to be polite. I shoveled her parking lot and pushed her in the snow." At Sadie's blank stare, his voice grew desperate. "I kissed her, Sadie, and she said it was a sweet kiss. Sweet! It's too soon to tell, but I think she might be *the one.* Did you hear me, Sadie?"

"I'm not deaf."

"I invited her to the party, but she doesn't want to come. I screwed up the pearl thing. She thought I was nuts." Sadie's eyes rolled back in her head. "Okay," Peter roared, "that's enough, Sadie, pets die every day of the week. People and children grieve, but they don't go over the edge. You're teetering and I won't have it."

Sadie blinked. "Oh, stuff it, Peter. This is me you're talking to. I need to do this for one day, for God's sake. Tomorrow

I'll be fine. Why can't I cry, moan and wail? Give me one damn good reason why I can't. I just want to sit here and snivel. You need to make amends to that young veterinarian, and don't go blaming me. I didn't ask you to stay here with me. You didn't even like Hannah and she hated you. Hannah hated all men. I never did figure that out. Go home, Peter. I'm fine, and I do appreciate you coming here and staying with me. It might be wise to send the young lady an invitation. I'd FedEx it if I were you."

"Do you want me to call that guy Donald you're always talking about?"

"Of course not. He's . . . out and about . . . and very hard to reach."

"Why don't you get him a beeper for Christmas."

"Go!"

"I'm gone."

Peter had every intention of going home, but his car seemed to have a mind of its own. Before he knew it he was on the road leading into the driveway of Andi's clinic. What the hell time was it anyway? Ten minutes past ten. It was so quiet and dark he felt uneasy. Only a dim light inside the clinic could be seen from the road. The rest of the house was in total darkness. If he got out to leave a note, the animals would start to bark and Andi would wake up. Did he want that? Of course not, his mother had raised him to be a gentleman. He felt an emptiness in the pit of his stomach as he drove away. He couldn't ever remember being this lonely in his entire life. Tomorrow was another day. He'd call her as soon as the sun came up, and maybe they could go sleigh riding in Roosevelt Park. Maybe it was time to act like kids again. Kids who fell in love when they were done doing all those wonderful kid things. One day out of their lives, and it was a Sunday. Just one day of no responsibilities. He crossed his fingers that it would work out the way he wanted.

* * *

Andi rolled over, opening one eye to look at the clock on her nightstand. Six o'clock. How still and quiet it was. Did she dare stay in bed? Absolutely not. She walked over to the window and raised the shade. It was snowing. Damn, her back was still sore. Maybe she could call one of the companies that plowed out small businesses.

She was brushing her teeth when the phone rang. Around the bubbles and foam in her mouth, she managed to say, "Dr. Evans."

"This is Peter King. I'm calling to apologize and to invite you to go sleigh riding. Hannah died in her sleep. I spent the day with my grandmother. I'm really sorry. Are you there?"

Wait." Andi rushed into the bathroom to rinse her mouth. She sprinted back to the phone. "I was brushing my teeth."

"Oh."

"You should have called me. It only takes a minute to make a phone call." Hot damn, he had a reason. Maybe . . .

"I came by last night around ten, but everything was dark, and I didn't want to stir up the animals so I went home."

He came by. That was good. He said he was sorry. He was considerate. "I went to bed early. It's snowing."

"I know. Let's go sledding in Roosevelt Park. My parents used to take me there when I was a kid. I have a Flexible Flyer." He made it sound like he had the Holy Grail.

"No kidding. I have one, too. Somewhere. Probably up on the rafters in the garage."

"Does that mean you'll go? We could go to the Pancake House on Parsonage Road for breakfast."

"Will you pull me up the hill?"

"Nope."

"I hate climbing the hill. Going down is so quick. Okay, I'll go, but I have things to do first. How about eleven o'clock?"

"That's good. What do you have to do? Do you need help?"

This was looking better and better. "Well, I have to clean the dog runs and change the litter boxes. I was going to go through the things in the attic. You could see if you can locate someone to plow my parking lot and driveway. Don't even think about offering. I know your back is as sore as mine, and my legs are going to be stiff if we climb that hill more than once. It's going to take me at least two hours to find my rubber boots. Is your grandmother all right? I have some kittens if you're interested."

"It was a real bad day. She doesn't want another cat. Hannah is being cremated so she'll have the ashes. She'll be okay today. Sadie is real gutsy. I know she'll love it when I give her one of Rosie's pups. She'll accept the dog but not a cat. I understand that."

"Yes, so do I."

"What did you have for supper last night? I'm sorry about standing you up. I mean that."

"Tomato soup, a TV dinner and a stale donut. If you do it again, it's all over." She was flirting. God.

She was flirting with him. Peter felt his chest puff out. "Bundle up."

"Okay. See you later."

"You bet. Don't get your sled down; I'll do that."

"Okay." A gentleman. Hmmnn.

Peter kicked the tire of his Range Rover, every curse known to man spitting through his lips. How could a $50,000 year-old truck have a dead battery? He looked at his watch and then at the elegant Mercedes Benz sitting next to it. The perfect vehicle to go sledding. "Damn it to hell!" he muttered.

He was stomping through the house looking for his keys when the doorbell rang. Expecting to see the paperboy, he opened the door, his hand in his pants pocket looking for money. "Helen!"

"Peter! I brought breakfast," she said, dangling a Dunkin Donuts bag under his nose, "and the *New York Times*. I thought we could curl up in front of a fire and spend a lazy day. Together."

He wanted to push her through the door, to slap the donut bag out of her hand and scatter the paper all over the lawn. What did he ever see in this heavily made up woman whose eyelashes were so long they couldn't be real. "I think one of your eyelashes is coming off. Sorry, Helen, I have other plans. I'm going sledding."

"Sledding! At your age!" She made it sound like he was going to hell on a sled.

"Yeah," he drawled. "Your other eyelash is . . . loose. Well, see you around."

"Peterrrrr," she cried as he closed the door.

He was grinning from ear to ear as he searched the living room, dining room and foyer for his keys. He finally found them on the kitchen counter right where he'd left them last night. She really did wear false eyelashes like Sadie said. He laughed aloud when he remembered the open-toed shoes she had on. "My crazy days," he muttered as he closed the kitchen door behind him.

In the car, backing out of the driveway, he realized his heart was pounding. Certainly not because of Helen. He was going to spend the whole day with Andrea Evans doing kid things. He was so excited he pressed the power button on his car phone and then the number one, which was Sadie's number. When he heard her voice he said, "Want to go sled riding? I'll pull you up the hill. I'm taking Dr. Evans. You won't believe this, but she has a Flexible Flyer, too. So, do you want to come?"

"I think I'll pass and watch a football game. Don't forget to bring Hannah's ashes. I don't want to spend another night without her. I don't care, Peter, if you think I'm crazy. Be sure you don't break your neck. Are you aware that it's snowing outside? I thought people went sled riding when it *stopped* snowing."

"I don't think you're crazy at all. I know it's snowing. I

think there's at least three inches of fresh snow. You know how you love a white Christmas. I'll be sure not to break my neck, and I think you can go sledding whenever you want. Mr. Mortimer said I could pick up the ashes after five this afternoon. I'll see you sometime this evening."

"Peter, does this mean you're . . . interested in Dr. Evans?"

"She's a real person, Sadie. Helen stopped by as I was leaving—I'm talking to you on the car phone—and she had open-toed shoes on, and both her eyelashes were loose at the ends. How could I not have seen those things, Sadie?"

"Because you weren't looking, Peter. Do you think Dr. Evans is interested in you?"

"She agreed to go sledding. She wasn't even mad about yesterday. I like her, Sadie. A lot."

"I love June weddings. Six months, Peter. You have to commit by six months or cut her loose. Women her age don't need some jerk taking up their time if you arcn't serious."

"How do you know her age?"

"Well . . . I don't, but you said she put herself through vet school and the whole education process took ten years. That should put her around thirty or so."

"I don't remember telling you that."

"That's because you were rattled over Helen. It's all right, Peter, I get forgetful, too, sometimes. Now, go and have a wonderful time."

Peter pressed the end and power buttons. He decided his grandmother was defensive sounding because of Hannah. He wished the next eight weeks were over so he could present her with one of Rosie's pups.

Peter was so deep in thought he almost missed the turnoff to the Evans Kennel. He jammed on his brakes, the back end of his car fishtailing across the road. He took a deep breath, cursing the fancy car again. Shaken, he crawled into the parking lot and parked the car. He wondered again if the Chevy pickup actually worked.

"I saw that," Andi trilled. "It's a good thing there was no one behind you. Where's your truck?"

"Dead battery."

"We can take my truck. It's in tip-top shape. Turns over every time. No matter what the weather is. It was my dad's prized possession. The heater works fine and we can put our sleds in the back." Andi dangled a set of car keys in front of him. She was laughing at him, and he didn't mind one damn bit. "Those boots have to go. When was the last time you went sled riding?"

"Light-years ago. These boots are guaranteed to last a life-time."

"Perhaps they will. The question is, will they keep your feet dry? The answer is no. I can loan you my father's Wellingtons. Will you be embarrassed to wear yellow boots?"

"Never!" Peter said dramatically. "Does the rest of me meet with your approval?"

Andi tilted her head to the side. "Ski cap, muffler, gloves . . . Well, those gloves aren't going to do anything for your hands. Don't you have ski gloves?"

"I did, but I couldn't find them. Do you have extras?"

"Right inside the yellow boots. I figured you for a leather man. I'm a mitten girl. I still have the mittens my mother knitted for me when I was a kid. They still fit, too. When you go sled riding you need a pair and a spare. I bet you didn't wax the runners on your sled either."

"I did so!"

"Prove it." Andi grinned.

"All right, I didn't. It was all I could do to get the cobwebs off."

"Come on," Andi said, dragging him by the arm into the garage. Neither noticed a sleek, amber-colored Mercury Sable crawl by, the driver craning her neck for a better look into the parking lot.

"Here's the boots. They should fit. I'm bringing extra thermal socks for both of us, extra gloves and mittens. There's nothing worse than cold hands and feet. I lived for one whole winter in Minnesota without central heat. All I had was a wood-burning fireplace."

"Why?"

"It was all I could afford. I survived. Do they fit?"

"Perfectly. You should be very proud of yourself, Andi."

"I am. My parents weren't rich like yours. Dad wasn't a businessman. There's so much money on the books that was never paid. He never sent out bills or notices. I'm kind of like him, I guess."

"My parents weren't rich. My grandmother is the one with the money. My dad was a draftsman; my mother was a nurse. You're right, though; I never had to struggle. Did it make you a better person?"

"I like to think so. When you're cold and hungry, character doesn't seem important. You are what you are. Hard times just bring out the best and worst in a person. Okay, your runners are ready for a test run."

"Do you ski?"

"Ha! That's a rich person's sport. No. I'm ready."

"Me, too," Peter said, clomping along behind her.

"You look good in yellow," Andi giggled.

"My favorite color," Peter quipped.

"That's what my mother said when she presented my father with those boots. The second thing she said was they'll never wear out. My dad wore them proudly. How's your grandmother today?"

"Better. I promised to stop by this evening with Hannah's ashes. My grandmother is a very strong woman. She started King Cosmetics in her kitchen years ago after my grandfather died. I'd like you to meet her."

"I'd like that. Do you want to drive or shall I?"

"I'll drive. Sleds in the back," he said, tossing in both Flexible Flyers.

An hour later they were hurtling down the hill, whooping and hollering, their laughter ringing in the swirling snow.

On the second trek up the hill, Peter said, "Have you noticed we're practically the only two people here except for those three kids who are using pieces of cardboard to slide down the hill?"

"That's because we're crazy. Cardboard's good, so is a shower curtain. You can really get some speed with a shower curtain. A bunch of us used to do that in Minnesota."

Peter clenched his fists tightly as he felt a wave of jealousy river through him. He wanted Andi to slide down a hill on a shower curtain with him, not some other guy, and he knew it had been a guy on the shower curtain next to Andi. He asked.

"Yeah." He waited for her to elaborate, but she didn't.

"Hey, mister, do you want to trade?"

Peter looked at Andi, and she looked at him. "The cardboard is big enough for both of us to sit on. Wanna give it a shot?" he asked.

"Sure. You sit in the front, though, in case we hit a tree."

"Okay, kid." He accepted their offer, then turned to Andi. "Did you notice they waited till we dragged these sleds to the top of the hill?" Peter hissed.

"I don't blame them. I think this is my last run. My legs feel numb."

"Sissy," Peter teased. "Cardboard's easy to drag. We've only been here two hours."

"It seems like forever," Andi said. "I can't feel my feet anymore. How about you?"

"Hey, mister, where'd you get them yellow boots?" one of the kids asked.

"Macy's. Neat, huh?"

"They look shitty," the kid said.

"That, too. You kids go first and we'll follow."

"Nah, you go first. You might fall off and we'll stop and pick you up. You might break a leg or something. You're old."

Peter settled himself on the slice of cardboard that said Charmin Tissue. "Hang on, Andi, and sit up straight."

They were off. Andi shrieked and Peter bellowed as they sailed down the steep hill. Midway down, the cardboard slid out from under them. They toppled into the snow, rolling the rest of the way down the hill. The kids on the sleds passed them, waving and shouting wildly. Andi rolled up against Peter, breathless, her entire body covered in snow.

"Now *that* was an experience," Peter gasped as he reached for Andi's arm to make sure she was all right.

"I feel like I'm dead. Are we?"

"No. Those little shits are taking off with our sleds!" Peter gasped again.

"Who cares. I couldn't chase them if my life depended on it. Every kid needs a sled. Let them have them."

"Okay. Are you all right?"

"No. I hurt. This wasn't as much fun as I thought it would be. God, I must be getting old. My eyebrows are frozen to my head. They crunch. Do yours?"

"Yep. C'mon, lets get in the truck and go home. The first run was fun. We should have quit after that." He was on his feet, his hand outstretched to pull Andi to her feet. "Ah, I bet if I kissed your eyebrows they'd melt."

"Never mind my damn eyebrows, kiss my mouth, it's frozen."

"Hmmmnn. Aaahhh, oh, yes," Andi said later.

"Was that *sweet?* I have a kiss that's a real wake-up call."

"Oh, no, that one . . . sizzled. Let's try it out," Andi said.

"Oh, look, they're kissing. Yuk. Here's your sleds, mister."

"I thought you stole those sleds. Your timing is incredible. Go away, you can have the sleds."

"My mother ain't never gonna believe you gave us these sleds. You gotta write us a note and sign your name."

"Do what he says." Andi giggled as she headed for the truck, and Peter hastily penned a note.

"Guess you're gonna have to wait for my wake-up call," he said when he caught up to her.

"How long?"

Peter threw his hands up in the air. "I have all the time in the world. You just let me know when you're ready."

"Uh-huh. Okay. That sounds good. I had a good time today, Peter, I really did. I felt like a kid for a little while. Thanks. Time to get back to reality and the business at hand."

"How about if I drop you off, go pick up Hannah's ashes, take them to my grandmother and come back. We can have dinner together. I can pick up some steaks and stuff. I want to get those carbon monoxide units for you, too."

"Sounds good."

"It's a date, then?"

"Yep, it's a date."

"I'll see you around seven-thirty."

Inside the kennel the animals greeted their owner with sharp barks and soft whines, each vying for her attention. She sat down on the floor and did her best to fondle each one of them. "I smell worse than you guys when you get wet," she said, shrugging out of her wet clothes. "Supper's coming up!"

With the door closed to the outside waiting room, Andi paid no mind to the excessive barking and whining from the animals; her thoughts were on Peter King and spending the night with him. She had at least two hours, once the animals were fed, to shower and change into something a little more *romantic*.

Outside, Helen Palmer watched the dinner preparations through the front window. When she was certain no one else was in attendance, her eyes narrowed. She walked back to the office, a manila folder in hand, the detective's report on one Dr. Andrea Evans that she'd taken from Peter King's car when she'd backtracked from Roosevelt Park where she'd spied on her old lover.

She eyed the messy desk with the pile of bills. On tiptoe,

she walked around the back of the desk to stare down at the piles of bills. With one long, polished nail, she moved the contract to the side so she could see it better. Three million, seven hundred and fifty thousand dollars! For this dump! She tiptoed back to the door and let herself out. Miss Girl Next Door would know there was no manila envelope on the desk. Better to drop it outside where Peter's car had been parked. "She'll think it fell out when he got out of the car. Perfect!" she muttered.

Her feet numb with cold, Helen walked out of the driveway to her car parked on the shoulder of the road in snow up to her ankles. She'd probably get pneumonia and all of this would be for naught. One way or another she was going to get Peter King for herself.

Inside the house, Andi climbed the stairs to the second floor to run a bath. She poured lavishly from a plastic bag filled with gardenia bath salts. It was the only thing she consistently splurged on. She tried to relax, but the dogs' incessant barking set her nerves on edge. What in the world was wrong with them today? Maybe they were picking up on her own tenseness in regard to Peter King. And she was tense.

"I hardly know the man and here I sit, speculating on what it would be like to go to bed with him." The bathtub was the perfect milieu for talking to herself. She loved this time of day when she went over her problems, asked questions of herself aloud and then answered them in the same manner. She wondered aloud about what kind of bed partner he would make. "Shy? No way. Lusty? To a degree. Wild and passionate? I can only hope. Slam, bam, thank you, ma'am? Not in a million years. A man with slow hands like the Pointer Sisters sang about. Oh, yeahhhhh."

Puckered, hyped and red-skinned, Andi climbed from the tub, towel dried and dressed. She fluffed out her hair, added makeup sparingly. The gardenia scent stayed with her.

Andi eyed the bed. When was the last time she changed the

sheets? She couldn't remember. She had the bed stripped and changed inside of eight minutes. "Just in case."

Downstairs, the dogs milled around inside the house, running back and forth to the waiting room and her tiny office area. Susy, a long-haired, fat, black cat, hissed and snarled by the door, her claws gouging at the wood. "Okay, okay, I get the message, something's wrong. Let's do one spin around the parking lot. When I blow this whistle, everyone lines up and comes indoors. Allow me to demonstrate." She blew three short blasts. "Everybody line up! That's the drill. If you don't follow my instructions, you're out for the night. Let's go!" She stood to the side as the dogs and cats stampeded past her. She'd done this before, and it always worked because Beggin Strips were the reward when everyone was indoors. She waited ten minutes, time for everyone to lift their leg or squat, depending on gender. The floodlights blazed down in the parking lot, creating shimmering crystals on the piled-high snow. Now it was speckled with yellow spots in every direction.

Andi blew three sharp blasts on the whistle as she stepped aside. One by one, the animals fell into a neat line and marched to the door. "C'mon Annabelle, you can do it!" Andi called encouragingly. "You can't sit down in the middle of the parking lot. All right, all right, I'll carry you. Move it, Bizzy," she said to a cat with two tails. The cat strolled past her disdainfully. Andi gave one last blast on the whistle for any stragglers. Satisfied that all the animals were indoors, she walked over to Annabelle to pick her up. She noticed the folder then and picked it up. She stuck it under her arm as she bent to pick up the beagle. "I swear, Annabelle, you weigh a ton."

Inside, she did one last head count before she doled out the treats, the folder still under her arm. "My time now!"

Andi did her best not to look at the clock as she set the table and layered tin foil on the ancient broiler. Candles? No, that would be too much. Wineglasses? She looked with disgust at the dust on the crystal. How was it possible that she'd been here almost a year and a half and hadn't used the glasses, much less washed them? That was going to change now. The wineglasses were special, and there were only two of them. She remembered the day her father had presented the Tiffany glasses to her mother and said, "When we have something special to celebrate we'll use these glasses." To her knowledge, nothing special had ever occurred. Well, tonight was special. She liked the way they sparkled under the domed kitchen light. Peter probably used glasses like this to gargle with every day.

He was late. Again. Her insides started to jump around. What should she do now to kill time? What if he didn't show up? "Oh, shit," she muttered. No point in letting him think she was sitting here biting her nails waiting for him. Only desperate women did things like that. In the blink of an eye she had the dishes back in the cabinet and the wineglasses in their felt sacks with the gold drawstrings. She refolded the tablecloth and stuck it in the drawer. She eyed the manila folder as she slid the drawer closed. It must have fallen out of Peter's car because it wasn't hers and no one else had been at the kennel today.

Eight o'clock.

Andi moved the folder. She moved it a second time, then a third time. She watched it teeter on the edge of the kitchen counter. She brushed by it and it slid to the floor. Now she'd have to pick up the papers and put them back in the folder. When she saw her name in heavy black letters on the first page, she sucked in her breath. Her heart started to pound in her chest as she gathered up the seven-page report. Twenty minutes later, after reading the report three times, Andi stacked the papers neatly in the folder. From the kitchen drawer she ripped off a long piece of gray electrical tape. She taped it to the folder and plastered it on the door of the clinic. She locked the doors and slid the dead bolt into place. She turned off all the lights from the top of the steps. Only a dim hall light glowed in the house.

She made her way to the attic. The small window under the eaves was the perfect place to watch the parking lot. Sneaky bastard. The report chronicled her life, right down to her bank balance, her student aid, her credit report, and her relationships with men. Her cheeks flamed when she remembered one incident where her landlady said Tyler Mitchel arrived early in the evening and didn't leave for three days. The line in bold letters that said *"The lady uses a diaphragm"* was what sent her flying to the attic. That could only mean someone had been here in her house going through her things. Unless Tyler or Jack or maybe Stan volunteered the information.

"You son of a bitch!"

Headlights arched into the driveway. Andi's eyes narrowed. Down below, the animals went into their howling, snarling routine.

Andi nibbled on her thumbnail as she watched Peter walk back to his car, the folder in his hand. Her phone rang on the second floor. She knew it was Peter calling on his car phone. She sat down on the window seat and cried. The phone continued to ring. Like she cared. "Go to hell, Mr. Lipstick!"

When there were no more tears, Andi wiped her eyes on the sleeve of her shirt. She had things to do. Empty cartons beckoned. She worked industriously until past midnight, packing and sorting, refusing to go to the window. Tears dripped down her cheeks from time to time. At one-thirty she crept downstairs for a soda. She carried it back to the attic and gulped at it from her perch on the window seat. He was still there. He was still there at four in the morning when she called a halt to her activities.

Andi curled herself into a ball on top of the bed with a comforter where she cried herself to sleep. She woke at seven and raced to the window. "We'll see about that!"

With shaking hands, Andi dialed the police, identified her-

self and said in a cold, angry voice, "I want you to send someone here right now and remove a . . . person from my parking
lot. He's been sitting there all night. You tell him he's not to
dare set foot on my property until January. If I have to sign
something, I'll come down to the police station. Right now. I
want you to come here right now. My animals are going
crazy. I have a gun and a license to use it," she said dramatically. "Thank you."

Her heart thundering in her chest, Andi raced back to the
attic. She knew the dirt and grime on the window prevented
Peter from seeing her. She clenched her teeth when she saw
the patrol car careen into her driveway, the red and blue lights
flashing ominously. She just knew he was going to give the
officers a box of Raspberry Cheese Louise lipsticks for their
wives.

Five minutes later the Mercedes backed out of her parking lot. It didn't look like any lipstick had changed hands.
"He's probably going to mail them," she snorted as she raced
down the steps to answer the door, the din behind her so loud
she could barely hear the officer's voice.

"Do you want to file a complaint?"

"You're damn right I do," Andi screamed.

"All right, come down to the station this afternoon."

"I'll be there."

Andi closed the door and locked it. She tended to the animals, showered and ate some cornflakes before she resumed
her packing. "You are dead in the water, Mr. Lipstick," she
sniveled as she started to clean out her closet and dresser
drawers.

At ten o'clock she called the Finnerans. "You really and truly
found something in Freehold! . . . I can move in on Sunday?
That's Christmas Eve! . . . Move-in condition! Fifteen acres! A
heated barn for the animals. God must be watching over me.
How much is fenced in? . . . Great. That's a fair price. . . . The
owners are in California. . . . I knew you could do it. . . . Okay.

I'll drive down this afternoon and look at it. . . . The last of their things will be out by Saturday. I'm very grateful, Tom." She copied down directions. Her sigh of relief was so loud and long she had trouble taking a deep breath.

Andi's second call was to her friend Mickey. "Can you bring the bus by today? Thanks, Mickey. I owe you one."

Her third call was to her attorney, who admonished her up one side and down the other for signing the contract before he had a chance to go over it. "You're lucky everything is in order. Congratulations. I'm going to set up a payout structure you'll be able to live with." Andi listened, made notes, gave the attorney her new address and told him to check with information for her new phone number.

The phone started to ring the moment she hung up from the attorney. The answering machine clicked on. If it was a patient she'd pick up. A hang up. Mr. Lipstick. "Invade my privacy, my life, ha! Only low-life scum do things like that. Well, you got your property, so you don't have to continue with this charade. It doesn't say much for me that I was starting to fall for your charms." Her eyes started to burn again. She cuddled a gray cat close to her chest, the dogs circling her feet. "So I made a mistake. We can live with it. We'll laugh all the way to the bank. The new rule is, we don't trust any man, ever again."

The elaborate silver service on the mahogany table gleamed as Sadie King poured coffee for her nephew. "You look like you slept in a barn, Peter. Calm down; stop that frantic pacing and tell me what happened. You've never had a problem being articulate before. So far all I have been able to gather is someone stepped on your toes. Was it Dr. Evans? I'm a very good listener, Peter."

"Yesterday was so perfect it scared me. She felt it, too, I could tell. Somehow, that goddamn investigative report fell out of my car and she found it. When I went back later for dinner, after I left you, she had it taped to the door. Obviously she read it. I called on the car phone, I banged on the door, but she didn't want any part of me. I sat in her parking lot all night long. This morning the police came and ran me off her property. Their advice was to write her a letter and not to go back or they'd run me off. I think I'm in love with her, Sadie. I was going to tell her that last night. I think . . . thought she was starting to feel the same way. My stomach tightens up when she laughs and her laughter shines in her eyes. She gave me her father's boots that were bright yellow, and his gloves. She's so down to earth, so real. I even started to wonder how our kids would look. What should I do? How can I make her understand?"

"A letter isn't such a bad idea. You could enclose it with the invitation to your Christmas party and send it Federal Express or have a messenger deliver it. I'd opt for the messenger because he could deliver it today. If you choose Federal Express she won't get it until tomorrow."

"What's the use, Sadie? I don't blame her. Jesus, the guy even . . . a diaphragm is pretty goddamn personal. I didn't want that kind of stuff. I didn't ask for it either. All I wanted was her financials and a history of the property. I have that same sick feeling in the pit of my stomach I used to get when I was a kid and did something wrong. I could never put anything over on my mother, and Andi is the same way."

"There must be a way for you to get her to listen to you. Apologies, when they're heartfelt, are usually pretty good. Try calling her again."

"I've done that. Her answering machine comes on. I know she's there listening, but she won't pick up. I told you, I don't blame her."

"Maybe you could disguise yourself and ride up on a motorcycle with . . . someone's animal and pretend . . . you know, it will get you in the door. She'll have to listen if you're face-to-face."

"Sadie, that's probably the worst idea you ever came up with. Andi Evans is an in-your-face person. She'll call the cops. They already gave me a warning. I don't want my ass hauled off to jail. They print stuff like that in the papers. How's that going to look?"

Sadie threw her hands up in the air. "Can you come up with a better idea?"

"No. I'm fresh out of ideas. I have to go home to shower and shave. Then I have to go to the office. I have a business to run. I'll stop by on my way home from the office." Peter kissed his grandmother goodbye, his face miserable.

Sadie eyed the urn with Hannah's ashes on the mantel. "Obviously, Hannah, I have to take matters into my own hands. Men are so good at screwing things up, and it's always a woman who has to get them out of their messes. I miss you, and no, I'm not going to get maudlin. I now have a mission to keep me busy."

Sadie dusted her hands before she picked up the phone. "Marcus, bring the car around front and make sure you have my . . . *things*. Scotch Plains. The weather report said the roads are clear." She replaced the receiver.

"They're meant for one another. I know this in my heart. Therefore, it's all right for me to meddle," Sadie mumbled as she slipped into her faux fur coat. "I'm going to make this right or die trying."

Andi had the door of the truck open when she saw Gertie picking her way over the packed-down snow. "Gertie, wait, I'll help you. If you tell me you walked all the way from Plainfield, I'm going to kick you all the way back. You're too old to be trundling around in this snow. What if you fall and fracture your hip? Then what? Where's your shopping cart?"

"Donald's watching it. I wanted to see Rosie and her pups. Can I, Andi?"

"Of course. Listen, I have some errands to run. Do you want to stay until I get back? I can drive you home after that."

"Well, sure."

"Rosie's in the kitchen, and the tea's still hot in the pot. Make yourself at home. I might be gone for maybe . . . three hours, depending on the roads. You'll wait?"

"Of course."

"Gertie, don't answer the phone."

"What if it's a patient?" Gertie asked fretfully.

"If it is, you'll hear it on the machine. Pick up and refer them to the clinic on Park Avenue. My offices are closed as of this morning. I called the few patients I have and told them."

"All right."

"I'll see you by mid-afternoon."

Ninety minutes later, Andi pulled her truck alongside Tom Finneran's white Cadillac. "Oh, it's wonderful, Tom! The snow makes it look like a fairyland. I love the old trees. Quick, show me around."

"Everything is in tip-top shape. Move-in condition, Andi. The owners' things are packed up ready for the mover. All the walls and ceilings were freshly painted a month ago. There's new carpet everywhere, even upstairs. Three bathrooms. A full one downstairs. Nice modern kitchen, appliances are six years old. The roof is nine years old and the furnace is five years old. The plumbing is good, but you do have a septic tank because you're in the country. Taxes are more than reasonable. I have to admit the road leading in here is a kidney crusher. You might want to think about doing something to it later on. Fill the holes with shale or something. It's a farmhouse, and I for one love old farmhouses. A lot of work went

into this house at one time. Young people today don't appreciate the old beams and pegs they used for nails back then."

"I love it," Andi said enthusiastically.

"The owner put down carpeting for warmth. Underneath
the carpeting you have pine floors. It was a shame to cover
them up, but women today want beige carpets. The blinds
stay, as do the lighting fixtures and all the appliances. You'll
be more than comfortable. Take your time and look around.
I'll wait here for you. The owner agreed to an end of January
closing, so you'll be paying rent until that time."

"It's just perfect, Tom. Now, show me the barn."

"That's what you're really going to love. It's warm and
there's a mountain of hay inside on the second floor or whatever they call it in barns. Good electricity, plumbing, sinks.
There's an old refrigerator, too, and it works. The stalls are
still intact. You can do what you want with them. There's a
two-car garage and a shed for junk. The owner is leaving the
lawnmower, leaf blower and all his gardening stuff. Any questions?"

"Not a one. Where do I sign?"

"On the dotted line. You can move in on Sunday at any
time. I probably won't see you till the closing, so good luck.
Oh, Lois took care of calling the water company, PSE&G and
the phone company. Everything will be hooked up first thing
Monday morning. You can reimburse us at the closing for the
deposits."

Andi hugged the realtor. She had to remember to send him
a present after she moved in.

The clock on the mantel was striking five when Andi
walked through the doors of the kennel. "I'm home," she
called.

Gertie was sitting at the kitchen table with three of the pups
in her lap. "Rosie is keeping her eye on me. It almost makes
me want to have a home of my own. Did you give them
names?"

"Not yet. Did anyone call?" Andi asked nonchalantly.

"Mr. King called; his message is on the machine. He sounded . . . desperate."

"And well he should. Let me tell you what that . . . lipstick person did, Gertie. Then you tell me what you think I should do. I hate men. I told you that before, and then I let my guard down and somehow he . . . what he did . . . was . . . he sneaked in. I let him kiss me and I kissed him back and told him I liked it. Do you believe that!"

Gertie listened, her eyes glued to Andi's flushed face.

"Well?"

"I agree, it was a terrible thing to do. Andi, I've lived a long time. Things aren't always the way they seem. Everything has two sides. Would it hurt you to hear him out? What harm is there in listening to him? Then, if you want to walk away, do so. Aren't you afraid that you're always going to wonder if there was an explanation? You said he was nice, that you liked him. He sounded like a sterling person to me."

"Listen to him so he can lie to my face? That's the worst kind of man, the one who looks you in the eye and lies. That's what used car salesmen do. Sometimes lawyers and insurance men do it, too. I called the police on him this morning. He sat in my parking lot all night, Gertie."

"How do you know that?"

"Because I watched him. You know what else? I even changed the sheets on the damn bed because I thought . . . well, what I . . . oh, hell, it doesn't matter."

"Obviously it does matter. Your eyes are all red. You really sat up watching him sit in your parking lot! That's ridiculous!"

"I was packing my stuff in the attic. I looked out from time to time," Andi said defensively. "I guess he wasn't who I thought he was. I swear to God, Gertie, this is it. I'm not sticking my neck out, ever again."

"Don't business people do things like that, Andi? I'm not

taking sides here, but think for a moment; if the situation was reversed, wouldn't you want to get the best deal for your company?"

"Does that mean he and his company need to know about my love life, that I use a diaphragm? No, it does not. He had no damn right."

"Maybe it's the detective's fault and not Mr. King's. Maybe Mr. King told him to do a . . . whatever term they use, on you, and the man took it further than he was supposed to. That's something to think about," Gertie said, a desperate look on her face.

"Whose side are you on, Gertie? It sounds like you favor that war-paint king."

"I believe in giving everyone a fair hearing."

"Is that why you refuse to call your children and live in a ditch?"

"It's not the same thing, and you know it."

"There's no greater sin in life than betrayal. I could . . . can forgive anything but betrayal."

Gertie's tone turned fretful. "Don't say that, Andi. There's usually a reason for everything if you care enough to find out what it is. I've lived a long life, my dear, and along the way I learned a few things. An open mind is a person's greatest asset in this world."

"I don't want to hear it, Gertie, and my mind just shut down. I know his type; he was just playing with me in case I changed my mind about selling. I would have gone to bed with him, too. That's the part that bothers me. Then, one minute after the closing, it would be goodbye Andi."

"He's not like that at all, Andi. You're so wrong." At Andi's strange look she hastened to explain. "What I meant was . . . from everything you said, from what I've seen in the papers, Mr. King is a gentleman. You said so yourself. I really should be going. Someone's pulling into your driveway. I'm going to walk, Andi. I've been cooped up too long in the shelter." Gertie held up her hand. "No, no, I do not want a ride. You still have packing to do. Thanks for the tea and for letting me hold these precious bundles. When are you going to name them?"

"I was thinking of giving them all Christmas names. You know, Holly, Jingle, et cetera. Just let me get my coat; it's too cold, and there's ice everywhere. I refuse to allow you to walk home, wherever home may be today."

"I'm walking and that's final," Gertie said, backing out the door. "Besides, I have some thinking I have to do. I do thank you for caring about this old woman. I'll be fine. It's a messenger, Andi, with a letter. I'll wait just a minute longer to make sure it isn't an emergency."

Andi stared after her, a helpless look on her face. She knew how important it was for the seniors to feel independent. She reached for the envelope and ripped at it. "Ha!" she snorted. "It's an invitation to Mr. Lipstick's Christmas party."

"Guess that makes it official. Change your mind and go. Is there a note?"

"Yep. It says he's sorry about the report and all he had requested were the financials, none of the personal stuff. He said he meant to destroy it once he met me, but time got away from him. He also says he had more fun yesterday than he's had in twenty years, and he thinks he's falling in love with me. He's very sorry. Please call."

"So call and put the poor thing out of his misery. That certainly sounds contrite to me. Everyone makes mistakes, Andi, even you. I would find it very heartwarming to hear someone tell me they think they're falling in love with me. Think about that, Andi. Have a nice evening."

"Goodbye, Gertie. Be careful walking."

"I will, my dear."

Andi read the note and the invitation until she had them both memorized. She ran the words over and over in her mind as she finished packing up the attic. At one point, as she descended the attic steps, she put the words to music and sing-songed her way through her bedroom as she stuffed things in cartons.

Andi stopped only to feed the animals and eat a sandwich. The telephone continued to ring, the answering machine clicking on just as the person on the other end hung up. At eleven o'clock she carried the last of the boxes downstairs to the garage where she stacked them near the door. By three o'clock she had her mother's china packed as well as all the pictures and knickknacks from the living room sealed in bubble wrap. These, too, went into the garage.

At three-thirty, she was sitting at the kitchen table with a cup of tea, the invitation to Peter King's party in front of her and his letter propped up against the sugar bowl. Believe or not believe? Go to the party, don't go to the party? Call him or not call him? Ignore everything and maybe things would turn out right. Like thirty-year-old women with thirty-six animals were really in demand. Was Gertie right? Was she acting like some indignant teenager?

There were no answers in the kitchen, so she might as well go to bed and try to sleep. Was this how it felt to be in love? Surely love meant more than a sick feeling in the stomach coupled with wet eyes and a pounding headache.

Andi felt as old as Gertie when she climbed the stairs to the second floor. She blubbered to herself as she brushed her teeth and changed into flannel pajamas. She was asleep the moment she pulled the down comforter up to her chin.

Even in her dream she knew she was dreaming because once before, in another lifetime, she'd slid down the hill on a plastic shower curtain with a colleague named Tyler. The same Tyler she'd had a two-year relationship with.

> *She fell sideways, rolling off the frozen plastic, to land in a heap near a monstrous holly bush. The wind knocked out of her, she struggled to breathe.*
> *"You okay, Andi?"*

"Sure. Bet I'm bruised from head to toe, though. How about you?"

"I'm fine. You really aren't going with me tomorrow, are you?"

"No. I'll miss you. Let's stay in touch, okay?"

"People promise that all the time; they even mean it at the time they say it, but it rarely happens. I'll be in Chicago and you'll be in New Jersey. I want the big bucks. I could never be content living in some rural area counting my pennies and practicing veterinarian medicine for free. Right now you're starry-eyed at taking over your family's old practice, but that's going to get old real quick. You're gonna be the new kid on the block. Who's going to come to your clinic? Yeah, sure, you can board dogs, but how much money is there in that? Not much I can tell you. Let's go home and make some magic. We're probably never going to see each other again. We'll call at first and even write a few letters, and then it will be a Christmas card once a year with our name printed on it. After that it will be, Tyler who? Andi who?"

"Then why do you want to go to bed with me?"

"Because I think I love you."

"After two years you think you love me? I want to go home and I want to go by myself. I don't want to go to bed with you either because you remind me of someone I don't like. He makes greasy lipstick. I changed the sheets and everything, and then he found out, probably from you, that I use a diaphragm. That was tacky, Tyler, to tell him something that personal."

"I never told him any such thing."

"Liar, liar, your pants are on fire. Get away from me and don't think I'm going to your stupid Christmas party either. Take this damn shower curtain with you, too."

"All right, all right. You came with me, how are you going to get home?"

"I have two feet, I'll walk. When you're homeless that's how you get around. I hope you make your three million plus. Goodbye, Peter."

"My name isn't Peter, it's Tyler."

"Same thing, birds of a feather flock together. All you're interested in is money. You don't care about me. The fact that you're taking this so well is suspect in my eyes. And another thing, I wouldn't let you see me wear my mother's pearls even if you paid me my weight in gold. One more thing, don't for one minute think I'm giving one of Rosie's pups to you to give your grandmother. She'll sneeze from all of that Lily of the Valley powder."

Andi rolled over, her arm snaking out to reach the phone. She yanked it back under the covers immediately. Six-thirty. She'd only had two and a half hours of sleep, and most of that had been dream time. Damn.

Andi struggled to remember the dream as she showered and dressed.

The animals tended to, Andi sat at the table sipping the scalding hot coffee. She frowned as she tried to remember what it was in her dream that bothered her. It didn't hit her until she finished the last of the coffee in the pot. Lily of the Valley. Of course. "When you're stupid, Andi, you're stupid." A moment later the phone book was in her hands. She flipped to the Ks and ran her finger down the listing. She called every S. King in the book until she heard the voice she was expecting. She wasn't sure, but she thought her heart stopped beating when she heard Gertie's voice on the other end of the line. *Sadie King, Peter King's grandmother, was the homeless Gertie.*

Blind fury riveted through her. Shaking and trembling, she

had to grab hold of the kitchen counter to steady herself. A conspiracy. If the old saying a fool is born every minute was true, then she was this minute's fool. Of all the cheap, dirty tricks! Send an old lady here to soften me up, to spy on me so I'd spill my guts. You son of a bitch!

Andi fixed another pot of coffee. Somewhere in this house there must be some cigarettes, a filthy habit she'd given up a year ago. She rummaged in the kitchen drawers until she found a crumpled pack pushed way in the back. She lit one, coughed and sputtered, but she didn't put it out.

Promptly at nine o'clock she called King Cosmetics and asked to speak to Peter King. "This is Dr. Andrea Evans and this call is a one-time call. Tell Mr. King he doesn't get a second chance to speak with me. It's now or never."

"Andi, is it really you? Listen I'm sorry—"

"Excuse me, I called you, so I'm the one who will do the talking. Furthermore, I'm not interested in any lame excuses. How dare you send your grandmother to spy on me! How dare you! Homeless my ass! She said her name was Gertie and I believed her. I didn't get wise till this morning. It was that Lily of the Valley. *That always bothered me.* Why would a homeless lady always smell like Lily of the Valley? She should have had body odor. All those good deeds, all those tall tales. Well, it should make you happy that I fell for it. You have to sink pretty low to use an old lady to get what you want. Don't send her back here again either. My God, I can't wait to get out of here so I don't ever have to see you or your grandmother again. She actually had me feeling sorry for her because her children, *she said,* wanted to slap her in a nursing home. This is my R.S.V. P. for your party. I'll leave it up to you to figure out if I'm attending or not."

"What the hell are you talking about. Who's homeless? My grandmother lives in a penthouse, and she works to help—"

Andi cut him off in mid-sentence, slamming down the phone. She zeroed in on Rosie, who was watching the strange goings-on with puzzlement. Her owner rarely raised her voice. It was rarer still that she cried. "Do I care that his grandmother lives in a penthouse? No, I do not. Do I care that she sneaked in here and . . . took care of us? No, I do not. I bet that old lady came here in a chauffeur-driven limousine and parked it somewhere, and then she trundled over here in her disguise. I am stupid, I admit it. Well, my stupid days are over."

Andi cried then because there was nothing else for her to do.

"Sadie!" The one word was that of a bellowing bull.

"Peter! How nice of you to come by so early. Did you come for breakfast?"

"Sadie, or should I call you Gertie? What the hell were you trying to do, Sadie?"

"So you found out. I only wanted to help. Who told you?"

"Guess!"

"Not Andi? Please, don't tell me Andi found out. So, that was who called this morning and hung up without speaking. I thought it might be Donald."

"Who the hell is Donald?" Peter continued to bellow.

"He covered for me. He's a homeless man I befriended. How did she find out?"

"I have no idea. She said something about you always smelling like Lily of the Valley."

"Yes, I guess that would do it. Was she very upset?"

"Upset isn't quite the word I'd use. She thinks I put you up to it. She thinks we had a conspiracy going to get her property."

"Well, I certainly hope you explained things to her. I'll go right over there and make amends."

"I wouldn't do that if I were you. I couldn't explain; she hung up on me. Don't meddle, Sadie. I mean it."

"She's so right for you, Peter, and you're perfect for her. I wanted you two to get together. When the men found homeless animals, I had them take them to Andi. They told me how nice and kind she was. I wanted to see for myself what kind of girl she was. I want you to get married, Peter, and I don't want you marrying someone like Helen. That's why I did it."

"Couldn't you trust me to find out for myself, Sadie? Why couldn't you simply introduce me or in this case leave me to my own devices? I met her on my own."

"No, I couldn't trust you. Look how long it took you to figure out Helen wore false eyelashes." She watched her grandson cringe at her words. "I just wanted to help so you would be happy. I'm sorry, but I'm not taking all the blame, Peter. You screwed it all up with that report."

"That's another thing. That report was on the backseat. The day we went sledding I didn't have anything in the backseat. I didn't even open the back door. All my stuff was in the trunk. How'd it fall out?"

"It doesn't matter now how it fell out. It did, and Andi found it and read it. End of story," Sadie said.

"I'm not giving up. I like her spunk."

"She hates your guts," Sadie said. "By the way, she isn't going to your party. I was there when the messenger brought your invitation. Peter, I'm so sorry. I just wanted to help. Where are you going?"

"To correct this situation."

"Peter, Andi is very angry. Don't go on her property again unless you want to see yourself and this company on the six o'clock news."

"Then what the hell am I supposed to do?"

"Does that mean you want my advice?"

"Okay, I'll try anything."

"Go to the police station and increase your Christmas donation to the Police Benevolent Association. Then ask them if they'll loan you one of their bullhorns. Talk to her from the road. She'll have to listen, and you aren't breaking any laws. I'm not saying it will work, but it's worth a try."

"Sadie, I love you!" Peter said as he threw his arms around his grandmother.

Peter King, the bullhorn next to him on the front seat, pulled his car to the curb. He felt stupid and silly as he climbed from the car. What to say? How to say it? Apologize from the heart. You know Spanish and French and a smattering of Latin. Do it in four languages. That should impress her. Oh yeah.

Peter took a deep breath before he brought the horn to his mouth. "Dr. Evans, this is Peter King. I'm outside on the road. I want you to listen to me. When I'm finished, if you don't want me to bother you again, I won't, but you need to hear me out. You can't run and hide, and you can't drown this out."

Peter sensed movement, chattering voices and rock music. Disconcerted, he turned around to see a pickup truck full of skis, sleds, and teenagers, pulling a snowmobile, drive up behind his parked car. "Shit!" Like he really needed an audience. Tune them out and get on with it.

"Andi, listen to me. Don't blame my grandmother; she only wanted to help. She wants to see me married with children before she . . . goes. I didn't know she was pretending to be a bag lady, I swear I didn't. As much as I love her, I wanted to strangle her when I found out."

"That's nice, mister," shouted a young girl in a tight ski suit and hair that looked like raffia. "You should always love your mother and grandmother. You're doing this all wrong. You need to appeal to her basic instincts."

"Shut up, Carla," a pimple-faced youth snarled. "You need to mind your own business. Yo, mister, you need to stand tall here and not beg some dumb girl for . . . whatever it is you want out of this scene."

"Listen, Donnie, don't be telling me girl stuff. You're so ignorant you're pathetic. Listen to me, mister, tell her she has eyes like stars and she's in your blood and you can't eat or sleep or anything. Tell her all you want in life is to marry her and have lots of little girl kids that look just like her. Promise her anything, but you better mean it because us women can spot a lie in a heartbeat."

Peter turned around. "She thinks I cheated her or tried; and then I did something really stupid, but I didn't know it was stupid at the time. Well, I sort of knew, but I didn't think anyone would ever find out. How do I handle that one?" he asked the girl with the three pounds of makeup and raffia hair.

"Tell her what you just said to me. Admit it. It's when you lie and try to cover up that you get in trouble."

"Don't listen to Carla, man; that chick in there is gonna think you're the king of all jerks."

"You're a jerk, Donnie. Listen to me, mister, what do you have to lose?"

Peter cleared his throat. "Andi, I'm sorry for everything. I was stupid. I swear to God, I'll never do another stupid thing again. I tried to explain about the business end of things. I want to marry you. I'll do anything you want if you'll just come out here and listen to me or let me come in and talk to you. Sadie says we're meant for each. She's hardly ever wrong. What's ten minutes out of your life, Andi? I admit I'm dumb when it comes to women. I don't read *Cosmo,* and I don't know diddly squat about triple orgasms and such stuff; but I'm willing to learn. I'll use breath mints, I'll quit smoking, I'll take the grease out of the lipstick. Are you listening to me, Andi? I goddamn well love you! I thought I was falling in love with you, but now I know I love you for real."

"Mister, you are a disgrace to the male race," Donnie said.

"Oh, mister, that was beautiful. You wait, she's coming out.

Give her five minutes. No woman could resist that little speech. You did real good, mister. My sister told me about triple orgasms. I can explain . . ."

"Oh, jeez, look, she's coming out. That's who you're in love with?" There was such amazement in the boy's face, Peter grinned.

"Oh, she's real pretty, mister. I know she loves you. You gonna give her something special for Christmas?"

"Yeah, himself," Donnie snorted.

"You know what, kid, they don't come any better than me. You need to get a whole new attitude. Carla, we're looking for teenage models at King Cosmetics. Here's my card; go to personnel and arrange a meeting with me for after the first of the year. Dump that jerk and get yourself a real boyfriend. Here's the keys to my car. My address is in the glove compartment. Drop it off for me, okay? That way she'll have to take me home or else allow me to stay. Thanks for your help. Can you drive?"

"Now you got it, mister. I can drive. Remember now, be humble, and only the truth counts from here on in."

"Got it," he said as he moved toward the house.

Inside the kennel, Andi said, "You got the dogs in a tizzy. I'm in a tizzy. You're out of your mind. I never heard of a grandmother/grandson act before."

"It wasn't an act. Everything I said was true. I do want to marry you."

"I hardly know you. Are you asking me so the three million plus stays in the family?"

"God, no. I feel like I've known you all my life. I've been searching for someone like you forever. My grandmother knew you were the one the moment she met you. She adores you, and she feels terrible about all of this. Can we start over?"

Well . . . I . . . we're from two different worlds. I don't think it would work. I'm not giving up my life and my profession. I worked too hard to get where I am."

"I'm not asking you to give up anything. I don't much care for the life I move around in now, but it's my job. I can make it nine-to-five and be home every night for dinner. If you're busy, I can even cook the dinner or we can hire a housekeeper."

"I'm moving to Freehold Christmas Eve."

"Freehold's good. I like Freehold. It's not such a long commute. Sunday's good for me. I'm a whizbang at putting up Christmas trees. Well?"

"Were you telling me the truth when you said you couldn't eat or sleep?"

"Just look at the bags under my eyes. How about you?"

"I cried a lot. I would have cried more, but the animals got upset so I had to stop."

"So right now, this minute, we're two people who are starting over. All that . . . mess, it never happened. Your money will always be your money. That was a business deal. What we have is personal. So, will you marry me? If you don't have pearls, Sadie will give you hers. This way they'll stay in the family. That kid who took my car knows more than I do. I'll tell you about her later. Was that a yes or a no?"

"It's a maybe. We haven't even gone to bed yet. We might not be compatible."

"Why don't we find out."

"Now? It's morning. I have things to do. How about later?"

"Where we're concerned, later means trouble. Now!"

"Okay. Now sounds good. I put clean sheets on the bed on Sunday. You were a no-show. That didn't do anything for my ego," Andi said.

"I dreamed about it," Peter said.

"You said you didn't sleep."

"Daydreamed. There's a difference. In living color."

"How'd I look?"

"Wonderful!" Peter said. "Want me to carry you upstairs?"

"No. I'm the independent type. I can be bossy."

"I love bossy women. Sadie is bossy. People only boss other people around when they love them. Sadie told me that."

"You are dumb." Andi laughed.

"That, too. I sleep with my socks on," Peter confided.

"Me, too! I use an electric blanket."

"You won't need it this morning." Peter laughed.

"Pretty confidant, aren't you?"

"When you got it you got it."

"Show me," Andi said.

"Your zipper or mine?"

"Oh the count of three," Andi said.

Zippppppppp.

He showed her. And was still showing her when the sun set and the animals howled for their dinner. And afterward, when the kennel grew quiet for the long evening ahead, he was still showing her. Toward midnight, Andi showed him, again and again. He was heard to mutter, in a hoarse whisper, "I liked that. Oh, do that again."

She did.

"I hate to leave. Oh, God, I have to borrow your truck, do you mind?"

"Of course I mind. You sport around in a fifty-thousand-dollar truck and a ninety-thousand-dollar car and you want to borrow my clunker!"

"I'll have someone drive it back, okay? Is this going to be our first fight?"

"Not if I can help it. I do need the truck, though. I have some errands to do, and I'm not driving that bus."

"Are you going to call Sadie?"

"Not today. She needs to sweat a little. Are you going to tell her?"

"Not on your life. Well, did that maybe turn into a yes or a no? What kind of ring do you want?"

"I don't want an engagement ring. I just want a wide, thick, gold wedding band."

"Then it's yes?"

Andi nodded.

"When?"

"January. After I get settled in."

"January's good. January's real good. Jesus, I love you. You smile like my mother used to smile. That's the highest compliment I can pay you, Andi. She was real, like you. I don't know too many real people. When you stop to think about it, that's pretty sad."

"Then let's not think about it," Andi said as she dangled the truck keys under his nose.

"I can't see you till tomorrow. I'll call you tonight, okay? Some clients are in town, and the meetings and dinner are not something I can cancel. You're coming to the party?"

"Yes."

"What about the pearls?" Peter asked fretfully. "You have to explain that to me one of these days."

"I have my mother's pearls."

"God, that's a relief"

He kissed her then until she thought her head would spin right off her neck.

"Bye."

Andi smiled, her eyes starry. "Bye, Peter."

Thursday morning, the day of Peter King's Christmas party, Andi climbed out of bed with a vicious head cold. Her eyes were red, her nose just as red. She'd spent the night propped up against the pillows so her nasal passages would

stay open. If she'd slept twenty minutes it was a lot. The time
was ten minutes to eight. In her ratty robe and fleece-lined
slippers she shuffled downstairs to make herself some hot
coffee. She ached from head to toe. Just the thought of cleaning the dog runs made her cringe. She shivered and turned up
the heat to ninety. She huddled inside the robe, trying to quiet
her shaking body as she waited for the coffee to perk.

Cup in hand at fifteen minutes past eight, she heard the
first rumblings of heavy duty machinery in her parking lot.
The knock on the door was louder than thunder. She opened
the door, her teeth chattering. "What are you doing here?
What's all that machinery? Get it out of here. This is private
property. Is that a wrecking ball?"

He was big and burly with hands the size of ham hocks, the
perfect complement to the heavy duty monster machinery behind him. "What do you mean what am I doing here? I'm
here to raze this building. I have a contract that says so. And,
yeah, that's a wrecking ball. You gotta get out of here, lady."

"Come in here. I can't stand outside; I'm sick as you can
see, and I'm not going anywhere. I, too, have a contract, and
my contract says you can't do this. Mine, I'm sure, supersedes
yours. So there. I have thirty-six animals here and no place to
take them until Sunday. You'll just have to wait."

"That's tough, lady. I ain't comin' back here on Sunday;
that's Christmas Eve. I have another job scheduled for Tuesday. Today is the day for this building."

"I'm calling the police; we'll let them settle it. You just go
back outside and sit on that ball because that's all you're
going to do with it. Don't you dare touch a thing. Do you hear
me?" Andi croaked. She slammed the door in the man's face.
She called the police and was told a patrol car would be sent
immediately.

Andi raced upstairs, every bone in her body protesting as
she dressed in three layers of clothing. She had to stop three
times to blow her runny nose. Hacking and coughing, she ran

downstairs to rummage on her desk for her contract to show the police. While she waited she placed a call to both Peter and Sadie and was told both of them were unavailable. Five minutes later, her electricity and phone were dead.

Two hours later, the electricity was back on. Temporarily. "I don't know what to tell you, ma'am. This man is right and so are you. You both have signed contracts. He has every right to be here doing what he's doing. You on the other hand have a contract that says he can't do it. Nobody is going to do anything until we can reach Mr. Peter King, since he's the man who signed both these contracts."

"Listen up, both of you, and watch my lips. I am not going anywhere. I'm sick. I have thirty-six animals in that kennel, and we have nowhere to go. Based on my contract, I made arrangements to be out of here on Sunday, not Saturday, not Friday and certainly not today. Now, which part of that don't you two men understand?"

"The part where you aren't leaving till Sunday. This is a three-day job. I can't afford to lose the money since I work for myself. It's not my fault you're sick, and it's not my fault that you have thirty-six animals. I got five kids and a wife to support and men on my payroll sitting outside in your parking lot. Right now I'm paying them to sit there drinking coffee."

"That's just too damn bad, mister. I'm calling the *Plainfield Courier* and the *Star Ledger.* Papers like stories like this especially at Christmastime. You better get my phone hooked up again and don't think I'm paying for that."

The afternoon wore on. Andi kept swilling tea as she watched through the window. The police were as good as their word, allowing nothing to transpire until word came in from Peter King. Her face grew more flushed, and she knew her fever was creeping upward.

Using the police cell phone, Andi called again and again, leaving a total of seven messages on Sadie's machine and nine messages in total for Peter at King Cosmetics. The receptionist logged all nine messages, Mr. King's words ringing in her ears: "Do not call me under *any* circumstance. Whatever it is can wait until tomorrow. Even if this building blows up I don't want to know about it until tomorrow."

At five o'clock, Andi suggested the police try and reach Mr. King at his home. When she was unable to tell them where he lived, the owner of the wrecking equipment smirked. It wasn't until six o'clock that she remembered she had Peter's address on the invitation. However, if she kept quiet she could delay things another day. Besides, his party was due to get under way any minute now. He would probably try and call her when he realized she wasn't in attendance.

The police officer spoke. "You might as well go home, Mr. Dolan. We'll try and reach Mr. King throughout the evening and get this thing settled by morning."

Cursing and kicking at his machinery, Dolan backed his equipment out of the parking lot. The officer waited a full twenty minutes before he left. Andi watched his taillights fade into the distance from the kitchen window. The yellow bus was like a huge golden eye under her sensor light. Large, yellow bus. Uh-huh. Okay, Mr. Peter King, you have this coming to you!

"Hey you guys, line up, we're going to a party! First I have to get the location. Second, you need to get duded up. Wait here." The Christmas box of odds and ends of ribbon and ornaments was clearly marked. Spools of used ribbon were just what she needed. Every dog, every cat, got a red bow, even Rosie. The pup, smaller, skinnier ribbons. "I'm going to warm up the bus, so don't get antsy. I also need to find my mother's pearls. I don't know why, but I have to wear them." Finally, wearing the pearls, wads of tissue stuck in the two flap pockets of her flannel shirt, pups in their box in hand, Andi led the animals to the bus. "Everybody sit down and be quiet. We're going to show Mr. Peter King what we think about the way he does business!"

Thirty-five minutes later, Andi swung the bus onto Brentwood Drive. Cars were lined up the entire length of the street. "This indeed poses a dilemma," she muttered. She eyed the fire hydrant, wondering if she could get past it and up onto the lawn. Loud music blasted through the closed windows. "It must be a hell of a party," she muttered as she threw caution to the wind and plowed ahead.

Andi grabbed the handle to open the door. "Ooops, wait just one second. Annabelle, come here. You, too, Cleo." From her pocket she withdrew a tube of Raspberry Cheese Louise lipstick and painted both dog's lips. Annabelle immediately started to lick it off. "Stop that. You need to keep it on till we get to the party. Okay, you know the drill, we move on three. I expect you all to act like ladies and gentlemen. If you forget your manners, oh, well." She blew her nose, tossed the tissue on the ground and gave three sharp blasts on the whistle. "We aren't going to bother with the doorbell, the music's too loud."

"Party time!"

"Eek!" "Squawk!" "Oh, my God! It's a herd!" "They're wearing lipstick! I don't believe this!"

"Hi, I'm Andrea Evans," Andi croaked. "I think I'd like a rum and Coke and spare the Coke." Her puffy eyes narrowed when she saw her intended lounging on a beautiful brocade sofa, his head thrown back in laughter. He laughed harder when Cedric lifted his leg on a French Provincial table leg. Not to be outdone, Isaac did the same thing. Annabelle squatted in the middle of a colorful Persian carpet as she tried to lick off the lipstick.

"Now, this is what I call a party," Peter managed to gasp. "Ladies and gentlemen, stay or go, the decision is yours. It ain't gonna get any better than this! Wait, wait, before you go, I'd like to introduce you to the lady I'm going to marry right after the first of the year. Dr. Andrea Evans, meet my guests. I don't even want to know why you did this," he hissed in her ear.

"You said you wanted a lived-in house. Myra is going to get sick from all that paté. Oh, your guests are leaving. By the way, I parked the bus on your lawn."

"No!"

"Yep. Don't you care that your guests are leaving? I'm sick."

"And you're going right to bed," Sadie said, leaning over Andi. "You can forgive me later, my dear. Oh, my, you are running a fever. Isn't this wonderful, Peter? It's like we're a real family. Your furniture will never be the same. Do you care?"

"Nope," Peter said, wrapping his arm around Andi's shoulders. "Do you want to tell me what prompted this . . . extraordinary visit?"

Andi told him. "So, you see, we're homeless until Sunday."

"Not anymore. My home is your home and the home of these animals. Boy, this feels good. Isn't it great, Sadie? That guy Dolan is a piece of work. It's true, I did sign the contract, but it was amended later on. I don't suppose he showed you a copy of that."

"No, he didn't. It doesn't matter. I thought you'd be angry. I was making a statement."

"I know, and I'm not angry. You did the right thing. You really can empty a room. Look, the food's all gone."

"Do you really love me?"

"So much it hurts."

"I'm wearing my mother's pearls. I think I'd like to go to bed now if you don't mind. Will you take care of Rosie and her pups?"

"That's my job," Sadie chirped. "Peter, carry this child to bed. I'll make her a nice hot toddy, and by tomorrow she'll be fine. Trust me."

Andi was asleep in Peter's arms before he reached the top of the steps. He turned as he heard steps behind him. "Okay, you can all come up and stand watch. By the way, thanks for coming to the party. I really like your outfits and, Annabelle, on you that lipstick looks good."

Peter fussed with the covers under Sadie's watchful eye. "I meant it, Sadie, when I said I love her so much it hurts. Isn't she beautiful? I could spend the rest of my life just looking at her."

"Ha! Not likely, you have to work to support all of us," Andi said sleepily. "Good night, Peter. I love you. Merry Christmas."

"Merry Christmas, Andi," Peter said, bending low to kiss her on the cheek.

"Ah, I love it when things work out," Sadie said, three of Rosie's pups cradled against her bony chest." I think I'd like five grandchildren. Good night, Peter."

"Thanks, Grandma. It's going to be a wonderful life."

"I know."

Christmas Eve

Virginia Henley

One

Eve Barlow was naked.

Her towel had slid to the floor with a whisper and here they stood, finally alone together, staring at each other. She posed provocatively, lifting her long blond hair and letting it waterfall to her shoulders.

"Am I beautiful?" she asked. "Am I sexy?"

The questions proved she was vulnerable, which was the very last thing she wanted to be.

Was that a critical look she detected? Silence filled the bedroom. If the answer to her questions took this long, perhaps the answer was *no!*

She looked straight into the green eyes, saw the humor lurking there, and her exuberant self-confidence came flooding back.

"Yes, you're beautiful; yes, you're sexy! You are also intelligent, successful, and independent," came the answer. The green eyes assessed the full, ripe breasts and watched as the nipples turned to spikes.

"You forgot *crazy,*" she told her reflection as her body shivered with gooseflesh. "Anyone who would stand naked before a mirror when it's below zero outside has got to be crazy!"

Eve knew Trevor Bennett's Christmas present would be a diamond ring. As she drew on her pantyhose, she asked herself if she was ready to be engaged. The answer came back *yes.* She was twenty-six years old—the perfect age for marriage. Everything else in her life was just about perfect, too.

Her career was in high gear, her finances were rock-solid, and her fiancé had all the qualities that would make him a perfect husband: sensitivity, kindness, and understanding. Trevor was an English professor at Western Michigan University and often quoted poetry to her.

Eve chose a red wool suit, then pulled on black, high-heeled boots. Even with a power suit she always wore heels. There were no rules that said a career woman couldn't have sexy-looking legs. The minute she picked up her briefcase, the telephone rang.

"Eve? You didn't give me a definite answer about coming home for Christmas, dear."

"Hi, Mom. I sent you an answer on E-mail last night."

"Oh honey, you know I don't understand that computer stuff. Daddy's tried to explain it to me, but I feel so much more comfortable on the phone."

"Of course Trevor and I are coming for Christmas dinner. It's my turn and I would love to take everyone out to The Plaza—I hate to see you cooking all day. But since you insist on a traditional, home-cooked turkey, I capitulate."

"You know it's fun for me. I just love doing all the things that make Christmas special."

"I know you do, Mom. That's why we all love you so much. I have to run—I have the keys to the office and have to open up today. See you Christmas morning."

"Drive carefully, dear."

Eve sighed. There was absolutely no point in trying to change Susan this late in life. Her mother was a perfectly contented housewife, an angel of domesticity who'd been kept in her place by the men in her life. She had no idea there were worlds to conquer out there.

Susie, as Eve's father insisted on calling her, had made a happy home for her air force family, no matter where they'd been stationed. It hadn't mattered much to Susie where she was; Ted was the center of her life and her two children orbited closely around him.

Ted was the macho major who wisecracked about everything, but ruled his family with an iron hand. She had gotten her name from one of her father's wisecracks. He had wanted a brother for his firstborn, Steven, but when Susie had a girl, he grinned good-naturedly and said, "Now it's Eve 'n' Steven!"

Her brother had followed in his father's footsteps, joining the military and becoming a macho ace before he was twenty. But Eve was determined not to become a clone of her mother. She avoided dominant, controlling men who thought a woman's place was in the kitchen, *unless she was in the bedroom*.

Eve pulled her Mercedes into the parking space that had her name on it, then unlocked the front door of Caldwell Baker Real Estate. Within six months she hoped to be a full partner in the privately owned company.

Before she read all the faxes, the other agents started to arrive. Bob and George arrived together because Bob had cracked up his Caddy on an icy road and it was in the shop awaiting parts. When Eve started working at the agency, they had joked about her aggressive salesmanship, calling her a ball-breaker, but now that her sales topped theirs, they gave her the respect she had earned.

"I'm sorry about your accident, Bob. It must be milder today—the ice was melting when I drove in."

"Warm enough to snow," predicted George, who tended to look on the dark side.

"Congratulations on breaking into the President's Circle, Eve," Bob said.

She had been in the Multimillion-Dollar Club for the last

two years, but now that she was selling commercial as well as residential properties, she had reached new production levels. "I haven't quite made it yet, Bob, but thanks."

"Oh hell, it's only December twenty-third. Still nine days left before the year ends," he said, winking at George.

The sons-of-bitches hope I don't make it, Eve suddenly realized.

Other agents began arriving and the first thing they did was glance toward the coffee urn beside the bank of filing cabinets. When they saw there was nothing brewing, the second thing they did was glance at Eve. Well, they could wait until their Grecian Formula wore off before she would make coffee, she decided, going into her office to go over the listings. She was two hundred thousand dollars short, and determined to reach her goal if it was humanly possible.

When the secretary arrived, the men heaved a collective sigh of relief. They fell over each other helping her off with her coat and boots, then followed her en masse to the coffee urn. *Bo Peep has suddenly found her sheep,* Eve thought sarcastically.

Someone came through the front door. Since all the agents were at the back of the premises, Eve came out of her office to attend to the prospective customer. He was tall with jet black hair, wearing a heavy blue shirt and a leather vest with decorative bullet-holder loops above and below the pockets. This guy apparently didn't know they were decorative; they held real bullets.

"I'm Eve Barlow. May I help you?"

The man's deep blue eyes stared at her mouth, lingered on her breasts, went down to her legs, then climbed back up her body to her blond hair and, finally, to her eyes.

Why don't you take a bloody picture? It'll last longer, she thought silently.

"I don't think so. I'm looking for Maxwell Robin."

He had the deepest voice Eve had ever heard.

"Maxwell has an early appointment; he won't be here until ten. Are you sure I can't be of some service?"

"I can think of a dozen, none of them appropriate for a real estate office." He gave her a lopsided grin.

Eve did not smile back. She turned on her heel and walked back toward her office.

"You could get me a cup of coffee while I'm waiting for Max."

Eve stopped dead in her tracks and turned to give him a look that would wither a more sensitive male. She bit back the cutting retort that sprang to mind and said coolly, "Feel free to help yourself."

"Don't tempt me." He winked at her.

The sexist son-of-a-bitch actually winked at her! Eve went into her office and slammed the door. She turned on her computer, saw that she had E-mail and accessed it. The message was from Trevor, who stayed many weeknights at the university in Kalamazoo. *No classes Friday, so I'll see you tomorrow night. Would you like to go to Cygnus and dance under the stars?*

Eve answered in the affirmative.

Trevor, I would love to go to Cygnus for dinner, on condition we don't stay too late. I'm probably working Friday.

Within half an hour, Trevor replied. *I understand. It's a date!*

Eve smiled at the words on her computer screen. Trevor Bennett was the most understanding man in the world. He had no problem with her assertiveness, her career, or the fact that she made more money than he. She wondered briefly if she would keep her own name when they married. Eve Barlow Bennett . . . it sounded good to her and Trevor would never object. So why not?

Maxwell's voice came over the intercom, cutting her reverie short.

"Eve, are you free to come into my office?"

As she opened her door, she heard the deep voice say, "I don't want a female agent. I want you, Max."

"The property you're interested in is Eve Barlow's listing. It's exclusive."

She gritted her teeth and walked into the owner's office.

"Ms. Barlow, this is Mr. Kelly. He's interested in the lakefront property you have listed up past Ludington. I've just been explaining that's your exclusive."

Eve shook hands with Action Man, as she had already dubbed him, making sure her grip was firm. She knew Max was being generous. The listing *was* hers, given to her by a friend in Detroit who had been left the property by her late parents. However, there was no reason why Maxwell couldn't have sold it—except, of course, he wanted her to qualify for the President's Circle this year.

"I'd like to take a look at it." Kelly turned from Eve to address Maxwell. "Can you go with me?"

"I told you, it's Ms. Barlow's listing. I have appointments all day."

"I'll take you to see it, Mr. Kelly. Are you free to leave now?"

The rugged-looking man drew dark brows together in a frown. "It's a hundred miles."

Eve failed to see his point. "Slightly more. It's a two-hour drive, two-and-a-half in bad weather. Perhaps you don't have time today."

"I have all the time in the world."

"Well, that's terrific, Mr. Kelly. Just let me get my briefcase."

In spite of the fact that he resented dealing with a female agent, Kelly helped her on with her camel-hair coat and held the door open for her.

The condescending gestures were politically incorrect in this day and age. Any woman breathing could put on her own coat and open her own doors. Kelly had either been living under a stone, or was being deliberately annoying. She suspected it was the latter.

Eve walked toward her Mercedes, but he did not follow her.

"We'll use my vehicle," he stated.

"It's part of my job to provide the transportation, Mr. Kelly."

"We'll use my vehicle," he repeated.

Eve glanced at the Dodge Ram four-wheel drive truck and repressed a shudder. They were already in a tug-of-war. "The Mercedes will be more comfortable," she asserted.

"This is a rough terrain vehicle," he pointed out.

"You don't trust my driving?"

"I have nothing against women drivers, but I wouldn't let a woman drive me unless I had two broken arms."

That could be arranged, you sexist swine!

He gave her a meaningful look. "Whatever happened to the idea that the customer is always right?"

Eve decided if she wanted this sale, she had better do things his way. She walked toward the Dodge Ram. It had flames painted across the doors, as if they were coming from the engine.

The first thing she saw when she climbed in was a gun rack holding a rifle. Action Man was obviously a hunter. She liked him less and less. He drove aggressively. He didn't race, but nothing passed him. Before they got out of the city, it began to snow-flurry.

"So, talk to me, tell me about yourself," he invited. He sounded patronizing.

I'm a feminazi who loathes macho men, she thought, then remembered her six percent commission. "My name is Eve Barlow. I was an air force brat. Lived in Germany, then the Orient. When my dad retired, we moved back to Detroit where he was born, but the crime rate spurred my parents to move to a more wholesome city. They chose Grand Rapids."

"I moved here from Detroit, too, a few years ago. My dad and brothers were police officers, so I know all about the crime rate."

Kelly. Irish cops. Tough as boiled owl, she thought. *Born with too much testosterone!*

"How did you get into real estate?"

"I chose it very deliberately. It's a field where women can excel. I didn't want to spend years at university, living at home. I wanted to be independent. I'm on my way to breaking the glass ceiling."

"Glass ceiling?" he puzzled.

He's got to be kidding; the man's a Neanderthal!

"Is that some sort of feminist term?"

"Yes. It's a ceiling erected by the men who run the corporate world, to keep women from high earnings and from achieving their potential."

"Bull! If a woman doesn't reach her full potential, she has only herself to blame."

Eve tended to believe that, yet she had an overwhelming urge to oppose him. He had a dark, dangerous quality about him, as if he could erupt. She turned away to look out the window. It was snowing harder now. It seemed to Eve that the harder it snowed, the faster he drove.

"Where's the fire?" she asked.

He began to laugh. His teeth were annoyingly white.

"Let me in on the joke."

"I'm a fire captain."

"You're kidding me! You're a fire fighter?"

He nodded. "I'm a captain, studying for my chief's exams."

"The flames!" she said, suddenly comprehending.

"My attempt at humor."

Until this moment, Eve had had no idea one had to sit exams to fight fires. The property he was interested in was listed at a quarter of a million dollars. Did Action Man have this kind of money, or was she on a wild goose chase? Eve cleared her throat. "How do you know Maxwell?" she probed.

"I teach scuba. He's in my diving class."

"Really?" Eve was a city girl. Scuba diving was out of her depth of comprehension. It was too physical, too dangerous, too unnatural somehow. Encasing yourself in rubber, sticking a breathing tube in your mouth, then isolating yourself fathoms deep in murky water was not her idea of fun.

"That's one of the reasons I'm interested in the lakefront property. Michigan offers nine underwater preserves. There are miles of bottomland for exploring shipwrecks."

"I see. Wouldn't a summer cottage do just as well? This is a year-round log home." She was trying to hint at the price.

"I need something year-round for ice diving."

"Ice diving?" She said it with abhorrence as if he had said grave-robbing.

"You cut a hole in the ice with an auger. Of course, you tie yourselves together with a safety rope."

"You do this for pleasure, or as some sort of penance?"

"If that's a jab at my being Catholic, I believe you're being politically incorrect, *Miz* Barlow."

Eve stiffened.

"I'm astounded you even know what political correctness is, Mr. Kelly. You make sexist remarks every time you open your mouth!"

His eyes were like blue ice. His glance lingered on her hair and mouth, dropped to her breasts, then lifted to her eyes. "What a waste; you obviously hate men."

"Your father, the cop, must have shot you in the arse . . . *you* obviously have brain damage!"

"There you go again. He was a police officer, not a cop." She saw the amusement in his eyes.

"You have a wicked tongue. I could teach you sweeter things to do with it than cutting up men, *Miz* Barlow."

"Don't call me that," she snapped.

"All right. I'll call you Eve. My name's Clint. Clint Kelly."

"Clint? My God, I don't believe it. You've made that up."

His bark of laughter told her that her barbs didn't penetrate his thick hide.

The visibility was deteriorating rapidly. "The weather's closing in. Would you like to turn back?" he asked.

His tone of voice was challenging, almost an insult.

She replied, "If I couldn't handle snow, I wouldn't live in Michigan."

He shrugged. "The decision's yours."

"Good. I like making decisions. And I don't have much use for macho males."

"That's all right, Eve. I don't have any at all for feminists."

Two

Eve lit up a cigarette. She was trying to stop smoking, but tended to reach for one when she was annoyed.

Clint frowned. "That's a dangerous habit."

"That's all right—if I set myself on fire, you're obviously qualified to put it out."

He refused to lecture her.

By twelve-thirty they reached Ludington, a thriving tourist port in the summertime but quiet in winter. Two hours was terrific time in adverse weather conditions.

Clint stopped at a service station for gas; Eve used the ladies' room.

"How about some lunch before we leave civilization?" he asked.

The town had two good restaurants, but both were closed for Christmas week. "I don't usually eat lunch," Eve said, relieved that she didn't have to sit across a table from Clint Kelly. All she wanted to do was show him the property and get back to Grand Rapids.

There was a fast-food place open as they pulled out of town. Clint stopped the truck. "Can I get you a burger? You should eat something."

"No, thanks. That stuff is incredibly bad for you."

Clint laughed. "And cigarettes aren't?"

She almost asked him to bring her a coffee, but remembered that she had not brought him one earlier.

Clint came back with two hamburgers and a milkshake. He raised his eyebrow, offering her one. When she shook her head, he devoured them both.

Highway 31 turned into an undivided road and Eve recalled that they would have to turn off in just a few miles. She remembered Big Sable River, but couldn't recall if they had to turn off before or after they crossed it.

Clint turned on the radio, but not many stations came in clearly. He found one that was playing country music. "You like country music?"

"Actually, I loathe it." The moment the words were out of her mouth, she suspected she had made an admission she would regret. He made no effort to change the station; in fact, he turned up the volume.

Eve put up with the torture for five minutes, then reached out decisively to shut it off. She cut the announcer off in midsentence as he said, "I have an updated weather—" Then she had to do an about-face and turn it back on.

"—Snow, and lots of it. Blizzard conditions will prevail. Travellers are advised to stay off the roads unless it's an emergency."

"Where is that station?" she asked the air.

"Don't panic. It could be across the lake in Wisconsin, or it could even be Canada."

"I'm not the type to panic," she said coolly.

He gave her a fathomless look. "What type are you, Eve?"

"What type do you think I am, Kelly?"

"You're difficult to read. I can't decide if you're an ice queen or simply unawakened."

"You're not difficult to read. You're an arrogant, sexist swine!"

He grinned. "You sure have a short fuse; I was teasing."

"For your information, I'm engaged to be married."

His eyes looked pointedly at her hands.

"I'm getting my ring for Christmas," she explained, then

wondered why in hellfire she found it necessary to explain herself to this insufferable devil.

"I take it he's the sensitive type."

"He's an English professor." Why did that sound so wimpy? "An intellectual," she added. "Trevor is the opposite of you. Yes, he's sensitive—and understanding."

"He's passive and I'm aggressive . . . he's a sheep and I'm a wolf."

Eve narrowed her eyes. "He doesn't drive a truck with flames on it."

"I bet he doesn't drive a Mercedes, either."

His arrow hit its target. "He isn't threatened by the fact that I earn more than he does."

"Then he should be. You intend to wear the pants in the family?"

"No, I intend to be an equal partner. But I admit I'm not domesticated. I don't cook, I don't sew, and I don't cower."

"I bet you even carry your own condoms."

Eve blushed. She had a couple in her shoulder bag. The fact that he could make her blush threw her off balance. "Oh, I think we should have turned off back there."

"You *think?*" He found a place where he could turn around, and showed no impatience. They drove down the snowy road for a couple of miles, but Eve saw nothing that looked familiar. She gave directions, but they were tentative. Finally, she admitted she was hopelessly lost, but only to herself.

"You don't know where this place is, do you?"

"We should be there. You must have passed it."

"Have you actually been to this property?" he asked.

"Of course I have, but it was in the fall. Everything looks different covered with snow. Go back across the river and—"

He held up a commanding hand. "Don't help. I'll find it myself."

By using logic and old-fashioned common sense, he

wound his way down a couple of unplowed sideroads until he came to the lake. Then he drove slowly along the lakeshore road until Eve finally recognized the private driveway. It was almost two-thirty. They were no longer making good time.

Eve took the keys from her briefcase and followed Clint Kelly from the truck. The winter winds from Lake Michigan had piled up a huge snowdrift across the front entrance to the house. Clint walked back to his truck, opened the hard box on the back, and pulled out a shovel. "Looks like we'll have to dig our way in," he said without rancor.

"If you had two shovels, I could help."

"Shifting light snow won't exactly prostrate me," he explained.

No, I'd have to hit you over the head with the shovel to do that, she thought.

By the time they got inside the house, it was three o'clock. Eve stamped the snow off her boots and shook it from her shoulders, but she didn't take off her coat because the log house was freezing. She walked straight to the telephone to call her boss to tell him they were running late.

"Damn, the phone's been put on holiday service; no calls can go in or out." She gave him a scathing look. "I have a car phone in my Mercedes."

"That isn't going to help you one bit."

"Exactly!" She threw up her hands.

"Can't you survive without a telephone?"

Eve didn't have to call the office. She lived alone; no one was expecting her. Trevor was in Kalamazoo. "If you don't need to call anyone, I certainly don't."

"If you mean, am I married, the answer is no. Both my brothers are divorced, so I'm wary of women."

"I meant no such thing! I'm not the least bit interested in your personal life."

"Curiosity's written all over your face. You're wondering if I can afford this place."

Damn you, Clint Kelly, you're too smart for your own damn good.

"You turn on the water and I'll check the electrical panel. It'll be dark before we know it."

Eve went downstairs to the basement in search of the water valve. She couldn't find it. She found laundry tubs, a washer and dryer, a water heater that was turned to *off.* She went into the basement washroom. It had a shower, a sink, and a toilet; it even had a shut-off valve, but only for the toilet it was connected to. Without lights, the basement was very dim. She looked under the stairs and finally admitted defeat.

"I couldn't find it," she said lamely.

He gave her a pitying glance.

"If you'd turned on the electricity, I might have been able to see down there!"

"The electricity's been cut off," he said shortly. "You start a fire; I'll find the water valve."

Eve stared at the small stack of logs beside the massive stone fireplace. There were no matches. She opened her purse, took out her lighter, and looked about for an old newspaper. Nothing! Paper, where could she get paper? She opened her briefcase and crumpled up some 'Offer to Purchase' forms. Kindling, now she needed kindling. She couldn't start a fire with only paper and logs. Eve spied a basket of pine cones used for decoration and felt quite smug as she carried them to the fireplace. She piled up a pyramid atop the crumpled paper and set her lighter to it. It blazed up merrily, but gradually smoke billowed out at her and she began to cough.

A powerful hand pulled her out of the way, reached up the chimney and pushed an iron lever. "You have to open the damper," he explained.

"Did you locate the water valve?" she challenged.

"Of course."

He had the ability to make her feel useless. He soon had the logs in the fireplace blazing and crackling. "As soon as you get warm, you can give me the tour."

The log house was truly beautiful. It was a full two storeys. Four bedrooms and two baths opened onto a balcony that looked down on the spacious open-concept living room and kitchen. The bedrooms also opened onto an outside balcony that ran around the entire perimeter of the house.

The views over the lake and forest were breath-stopping. Clint lifted his head and breathed deeply, drawing in the smell of the lake and the woods. She watched, fascinated, as his eyelashes caught the snowflakes.

"Last night was a full moon. It had a ring around it; that always predicts a change in the weather."

"Been reading the *Farmers' Almanac,* have we?"

"I suppose yuppies find folklore exceedingly quaint, but I've learned not to scoff at it."

They went back inside to explore the rooms downstairs. A cobalt blue hot tub had been built into a glass-enclosed room along with a sauna.

How romantic, Eve thought.

"Decadence," Clint said, grinning.

Eve quickly switched her thoughts to the business at hand. "As you know, the asking price is a quarter of a million, but that's furnished. A lot of this furniture is hand-crafted. Isn't it lovely?"

"It is. I make furniture like this. In fact, that sleigh bed upstairs is one of my pieces. Sorry, I digress."

Why was she surprised? The man was an entity unto himself. She began to believe Clint Kelly could very well afford the property.

"I want to look over the acreage before the light goes."

Eve groaned inwardly; it was a blizzard out there.

"Do you have a survey of the property in that briefcase of yours, or is it just for show?"

Eve snapped open the case and rifled through the papers. She pulled out the survey and thrust it at him. "I didn't think you'd be able to read anything so technical," she said sweetly.

Clint ignored the barb. "We'd better hurry. If much more of this comes down, we might not get out of here tonight. I can look around by myself, if the elements are too fierce for you," he goaded.

"Is that more Clint claptrap? You don't have to keep proving what a physical man you are."

"If I intended to prove how physical I can be, I'd have you down to your teddy by now."

Why did her mouth go dry at his provocative words?

Outside, he opened his truck, pulled out a down-filled jacket, and shrugged into it. Then he took a big steel tape from his toolbox. As they set off through the trees, she thought, *Surely he's not going to take measurements in the snow? Please don't let him expect me to hold the other end of the tape. From now on, I'll stick to my own turf: good old city property.*

As if he could read her thoughts, he said, "This is the reason I would have preferred Maxwell to come with me. This isn't a woman's job."

Eve ground her teeth. "There are no such things as *men's* jobs and *women's* jobs."

"Bull! The world has gone nuts. They're even telling us women can be firefighters!"

"You sound like my father: air force women shouldn't fly combat jets."

"Your father is right. Women are perfectly capable of flying jets, but they shouldn't allow them into combat zones."

Eve had walked out on an argument with her father and brother on this subject, and she was close to walking out on Clint Kelly. *That would be gutless,* she decided. *I'll make this sale if it kills me!*

The barn loomed before them. Clint used his booted feet to kick the drift of snow from the entrance, then they went inside to look around. The first thing Eve noticed was the smell. The scent of hay and straw mingled with the lingering miasma of horses, who had occupied the stalls once upon a time. How was it barns and hay always conjured fantasies of lovemaking, Eve wondered? She'd certainly never had a romantic encounter in a barn . . . yet.

"This place has amazing possibilities."

She turned away quickly so he wouldn't see her blush. She knew perfectly well that his thoughts did not mirror hers; it was simply because of his overt masculinity, and their close proximity in the romantic setting.

All too soon, Clint was again ready for the great outdoors. After they tramped what felt like miles through the deep snow, he selected a spot beside a wire fence and began to dig with his hands.

He had big, strong, capable hands that were well-calloused. Eve reluctantly admitted to herself that she found them strangely attractive.

Clint found what he was looking for—a one-inch square iron surveyor's bar. He didn't ask her to hold one end of the tape, as she expected; instead he began to follow the fenceline, counting his strides.

Eve pulled up her collar and jammed her hands into her pockets. She was freezing. Clint, hatless, didn't even seem to notice the cold.

"An abundance of wildlife here . . . raccoon, weasel, fox, deer, even elk."

Eve hadn't noticed the animal tracks until he pointed them out. He didn't miss much, she decided. *I bet women fall all over him.* Where the devil had that thought come from? It certainly didn't matter to her what effect he had on women! He had a decidedly abrasive effect on her, yet she didn't think the abrasiveness would affect the sale. He seemed to enjoy sparring with her.

Suddenly, as they came upon a bushy undergrowth, a covey of pheasants flew up into the trees. One bird huddled on the ground.

"It's caught in a snare," Clint said. "Its leg's broken." He immediately wrung the pheasant's neck, then ripped the snare apart in anger and flung it away. "Goddamn snares are as bad as leg-hold traps."

Eve stared at him in horror. "You cruel bastard! Why did you do that?"

"I'm not cruel, nature is. The bird's leg was broken. As soon as it's full dark, a fox would have eaten it."

"We could have taken it with us and nursed it back to health."

"The cold's getting to your brain."

"And you're suffering from necrosis of the cranium! Too bad you didn't have your gun—you could have shot them all." She turned away furiously and hurried in the direction of the house.

"Eve, get back here." It was an order.

Eve kept on going.

"Don't you dare go off on your own." This time it was more than an order, it was a command. She took great satisfaction in defying it.

Darkness was descending rapidly, but because of the white snow he could see her figure disappearing through the trees. Her black coat soon blended in with her surroundings, however, so that he could no longer see her.

"Bloody women! Can't live with 'em, can't shoot 'em." He tucked the bird inside his jacket and set off after her.

Eve had a soft spot for animals, especially injured ones.

She and her mother had once nursed their cat back to health after it had been poisoned. They'd stayed up with it night after night, soothing it, trying one food after another, until they found something its stomach would not reject. The only thing that worked was honey, a dab at a time on its paw. The cat licked it off, again and again, and was able to stay alive.

Looking after injured animals took a great deal of patience and time. Patience she had in abundance—much more for animals than humans—but these days, time was in short supply.

Eve was totally preoccupied with her thoughts and as a consequence, she paid little attention to where she walked. She was going in the general direction of the house and when she saw a clearing where the trees thinned out, she crossed it. Suddenly, a crack like a rifle shot rent the air and Eve felt the ground give way beneath her.

She cried out in alarm, not knowing what was happening. Then ice-cold water closed over her head. Dear God, she had walked out onto the pond and gone through the ice!

Three

"Help! Help me!" Eve screamed, then the icy water covered her mouth, effectively cutting off her cries. She knew the water was deep. Her feet touched bottom once before she struggled to the surface and grabbed hold of the ice at the edge of the hole she had made. Eve could swim, but her soaked coat and boots felt ten times heavier.

There was no time to pray, no time even to think coherently; sheer panic took control. The more she struggled to grab hold of something, the more ice broke from the edges, until the hole gaped wide. Eve had never experienced cold like this in her entire life. It penetrated her skin, seeped into her blood, froze her very bones to the marrow.

Clint heard her screams—a sound with which he was on intimate terms. He ran through the dusk on the path she had taken, knowing not to run across the open clearing. He saw nothing until she surfaced and cried out again. His eyes went swiftly to the hole in mid-pond—he was alarmed to see Eve was submerged to her neck.

"I see you!" he shouted. "Try not to panic."

"Clint," she wailed. Her voice a mixture of relief and hope.

"Can you stand up?" Clint demanded.

"No!" came the urgent reply.

"Can you swim?" His deep voice carried well.

"My coat is too heavy!"

"Remove it!" he ordered sternly.

Clint's mind flashed about like mercury. He knew if the ice wouldn't support her, it would never hold him. He remembered seeing a long wooden ladder in the garage. He had rope in his truck; he never travelled without it. The danger was two-fold: she could drown or she could die from hypothermia.

He would try to rescue her with rope and ladder. If that failed, he would have to go in after her. Clint preferred to keep his clothing dry. He knew he would need to keep himself warm during the long night that loomed ahead.

He focused all his attention on Eve. "Take off your coat!" he ordered a second time.

Eve's fingers were numb. She fumbled with the buttons. "I can't!" The water closed over her again as she struggled.

"Keep your head up. Concentrate on those buttons. Rip it off!" If she did not get the coat off, she could die, but he hesitated to tell her.

Finally, miraculously, the waterlogged coat came off and immediately sank from its own weight. Eve felt even colder without the blanket-like coat, but she could move her arms and legs easier.

"I have to get a rope from the truck. Stay afloat, no matter what. Try not to flounder about and break any more ice!"

Clint lunged off toward the house. Inside the garage, he removed his down jacket and threw the dead pheasant on the floor. Then he took the wooden ladder that lay against the wall and carried it outside. He got the long rope from his truck, tied it to the ladder, then raced back to the pond.

When he was halfway there, he began shouting encouragement for her to hang on. His heart started hammering when he got no reply. It was full dark now as he peered across the snow-covered pond to the gaping black hole. He saw nothing!

"Eve! Eve!" he bellowed. Then he heard a whimper and knew she was still alive.

"Hold on, sweetheart, I'm coming. You're so damn brave. I'll have you out in a minute." His voice exuded total confidence, though Clint felt no such thing. It was something he had learned to do over the years. Confidence begot confidence!

Eve could no longer speak. She could only gasp and make small animal sounds every once in awhile. She could no longer feel her arms and legs, and the rest of her body was also slowly becoming numb. She was on the brink of total exhaustion—the icy-cold water had numbed her thought processes as well. She kept her mouth above water by sheer instinct alone, but was dangerously close to the edge of unconsciousness.

Clint Kelly carefully laid the ladder across the ice of the pond, making sure the end of it stopped well back from the black hole. He took the rope firmly in both hands and lay down flat on top of the ladder.

Slowly, inch by inch, he moved his body toward the hole. He was totally focused—there was no room in his mind for failure. He intended to get her out, one way or another. The tricky part was to get her out before it was too late.

When he was halfway along the ladder, he heard a faint cracking noise, but resolutely ignored it and inched forward. He braced himself for the big crack that would sound like a rifle shot. Clint held his breath in dreaded anticipation and forced himself to breath normally.

The crack did not come while his full weight was distributed on the ladder. It came when he slithered his torso across the bare ice, keeping his feet and knees hooked onto the rungs. Clint did not hesitate; he was too close to back off now. With a superhuman effort he lifted her enough to loop the rope around her body, beneath her arms. Only then did he back off, slithering as swiftly as a serpent.

When his whole weight was back on the ladder, he wound the rope around his body, then hauled as he slowly crawled backward. Sounds of splintering ice filled the darkness, but it didn't matter now. She was anchored firmly to him.

When Clint threw off the rope, then lifted her high against his chest, he saw that Eve was unconscious. He refused to panic, telling himself that this was only to be expected. The falling snow looked like big white goose feathers, blanketing everything it touched. Their tracks were filled in, but by now Clint could have found the house if he'd been blindfolded.

He laid Eve facedown on the floor before the dying embers of the fire. Then he straddled her, splayed his large hands across her rib cage, and pressed and released in a rhythm that simulated natural breathing. In less than a minute, Eve coughed up water, gagged up more, then groaned. She opened her eyes briefly, then closed them again, but Clint was satisfied that she was breathing normally.

They needed heat and they needed it now. He immediately piled the remaining wood on the fire and poked it up into a blaze. He gathered half a dozen towels from the linen closet and three large blankets from the bedroom and brought them to the fire. Before Clint went out to his truck, he glanced at Eve to make sure the bluish color was leaving her face.

Clint brought in his tackle box, his rifle and ammunition, and a forty-ounce bottle of whisky he had picked up for a raffle at the firehall. He spread out the towels and began undressing her. He removed her boots first and set them on the hearth. While she was still facedown, he pulled off her suit skirt, then peeled off her pantyhose.

Clint rolled her onto the towels so that she lay faceup. His sure fingers unbuttoned the red jacket, deftly removed it, and tossed the icy wet object beside the fire. A curse dropped from his lips as he noted the logs were already half burned away. He glanced at the girl who lay helplessly before him in a short red slip and bra.

Eve's face and hair had a delicate, unearthly fairness about them that stirred a deep protectiveness within him. Clint tried to crush down the personal feelings she aroused, trying to be detached and totally professional. When he peeled off her wet undergarments, he tried not to stare at her nakedness. He covered her with a towel and began to rub her limbs briskly.

After a couple of minutes, he had her completely dry, but he did not succeed in warming her body. The glowing logs were giving off their last heat, so he knew the fire would be of little use in raising her body temperature. He thanked Providence for providing the whisky and for teaching him emergency techniques. He opened the bottle, poured the amber liquid into his cupped palm, and applied it to her neck and shoulders.

With long, firm strokes he massaged her with the whisky. He had once seen an older firefighter revive a newborn baby with this technique even after oxygen had failed. Clint pulled the towel completely away from her upper body, palmed more whisky and stroked down firmly over her breasts, then between them, across her heart.

Eve opened her eyes and threw him a frightened look. "Don't!"

"Eve, I have to. This is no time for false modesty. I *must* raise your body temperature. You have no food inside you for fuel, you have exhausted all your energy, and we have no wood left."

Eve stiffened.

"No, no, don't be afraid. Relax! Trust me, Eve, trust me. If you can feel what I'm doing to you, that's good. Relax . . . give yourself up to me . . . feel it, feel it."

He poured some of the amber liquid onto her belly, then swept his hands in firm circles, rubbing, massaging, kneading it into her flesh, so that her circulation would improve.

When Clint lifted her thigh and began to stroke it firmly, the word *silken* jumped into his mind. He tried valiantly not to become aroused, but failed miserably! Resolutely, he lifted her other thigh and repeated the ministrations. Clint had never done anything like this before, but it was suddenly brought home to him how pleasurably erotic a body massage could be. If you substituted warm oil, or perhaps champagne, for whisky, you could have one helluva sensual celebration!

He censured himself for his wicked thoughts and gently turned her over. On Eve's back, his strokes became longer, reaching all the way from her shoulders to her buttocks. He bent over her with tender solicitude. "Eve, are you any warmer?"

"Colder." Her voice was a whisper.

As he massaged the backs of her legs he said, "That's because your skin is getting warmer and the alcohol feels cold as it evaporates. It's a good sign that you can feel the surface of your skin."

He sat her up. "I want you to drink some of this. It will warm up your insides."

Eve nodded. She had no energy to protest, no will to object; all she wanted to do was obey him.

There was no time to search for a glass. Etiquette went the way of her modesty as he held the bottle to her lips and she took a great gulp. It snatched her breath away and she began to cough.

"Easy, easy does it." His powerful arm about her shoulders supported her until she could breathe again. Then he gently tipped the bottle against her lips so she could take a tiny mouthful.

By the third or fourth sip she felt a great red rose bloom in her chest; by the eighth, she felt a fireglow inside her belly. Clint moved her from the damp towels onto a blanket and starting again at her neck and shoulders, gave her a second whisky rubdown.

As Eve lay stretched before him, she gradually became euphoric. She thought Clint Kelly's hands were magnificent, and she wanted him to go on stroking her forever. As she watched him beneath lowered lids, a nimbus of light seemed to surround his dark head. She pondered dreamily about what it could be. Was it magic? Was it his aura? Did he emanate goodness and light? Then suddenly it came to her, and the answer was so simple. It was energy! This man exuded pure energy.

When Clint had anointed every inch of her with the warm, tingling whisky, he wrapped her up in the blanket and lifted her to the couch. "Eve, listen to me. I have to leave you for a while. I imagine we're snowed in here for a couple of days and there are things I need to do."

Eve was far too languorous to speak. Instead she smiled at him, giving him permission to do anything he had to. The smile made her face radiant. Clint knew she was intoxicated and would be asleep in minutes.

He retrieved his jacket from the garage and cut a length of green garden hose that was stored inside for the winter. Then he hiked to the barn to get a milk pail he had seen. He carried both to his Dodge Ram and proceeded to siphon the gasoline from the truck. Clint hated the taste of petroleum in his mouth, but he knew of no other way to siphon gas. He spat half a dozen times, then took a handful of fresh snow to his mouth.

He carried the pail of gasoline very carefully to the generator that stood inside a cupboard in the kitchen. Fortunately it had a funnel beside it. *Winter storms in this area must make a generator a necessity,* he concluded.

Clint opened his tackle box and removed a stringer with several large hooks and lures on it, then slipped the box of ammunition into his pocket and picked up his rifle. He shut the front door quietly and went in the direction of the lake. The snow was coming down heavier than ever and the visibility was zero. He stepped cautiously when he sensed he was on the edge of Lake Michigan. He knew it would be frozen, but if the ice on the pond hadn't held Eve, the ice on the great lake couldn't be very thick.

Noting the formation of the trees, he kicked a hole through the ice and set the stringer, then fastened the other end to the closest tree. He turned up the collar of his jacket and set off toward the bush at the back of the property where he had seen a wild apple tree. In the heavy snow, it took him quite some time to locate it, but when he did, he loaded his rifle and hunkered down with his back against a tree trunk to wait.

Eve slept deeply for two hours, then she drifted up through a layer of sleep and began to dream. She was in her parents' house where the air was filled with delicious smells and the atmosphere was warm and inviting. Her mother was cooking, while her father decorated the Christmas tree.

"Susie, can you help me with this?"

When Susan came into the living room wearing oven mitts, Ted grabbed her and held her beneath the mistletoe.

"You devil, Ted Barlow. This is just one of your tricks; you don't need help at all!"

"I couldn't resist, sweetheart; you're so easy to fool."

Eve saw her mother's secret smile and realized she knew all about the mistletoe. Susan went into her husband's arms with joy. The kiss lasted a full two minutes. She looked up at him. "Do you remember our first Christmas?"

"I love you even more than I did then," he whispered huskily, feathering kisses into Susie's hair.

"We had no money, no home; I was pregnant with Steven, and you'd just been posted overseas."

"What the hell did you see in me?" Ted asked, amusement brimming in his deep blue eyes.

"I was so much in love with you, I couldn't think straight, fly boy."

Ted's hands slipped down her back until his hands came to rest on her bottom cheeks. "But why did you love me?" he pressed.

"It was your strength. You were my rock; you made me feel safe. Even though we had almost nothing, I wasn't afraid to go halfway around the world with you."

He kissed her again. "That's the nicest thing anyone ever said to me."

"It's true, Ted. You inspire confidence. Now, it's true confession time for you. What did you see in me?"

"Besides great legs? You were willing to give up everything for me. I made the right choice. We're still lovers, aren't we?"

"Passionate lovers," she agreed.

"Do you think Eve is serious about Trevor Bennett?"

"I think so."

"You don't think she'll marry him, do you?" he asked, untangling a string of lights.

"Don't you like him?"

"Oh sure, I like him well enough, but I don't think he's right for Eve."

"Why not?" Eve demanded, but they couldn't hear her. Eve realized she was invisible. Her parents had no idea she was in the room with them.

"He's one of these sensitive, modern types, always politically correct. He even teaches courses where men get in touch with their feminine side."

Susan laughed at her husband. "And you don't believe you have a feminine side?"

"Christ, if I did, I'd leave it in the closet where it belongs!"

"You worry too much about Eve. She isn't your little girl anymore."

"Oh, I know she does a terrific impression of being able to take care of herself, but she has a vulnerable side."

Am I that transparent? Eve asked.

"And don't kid yourself . . . she'll be my little girl until I give her away—hopefully to a real man."

"What I meant was, don't worry about her making the

wrong choice. Eve knows exactly what she needs. And remember, it's her choice, not yours, fly boy!"

Ted grinned at her. "I just want her to have skyrockets, like we do."

Eve was no longer at home. She was somewhere dark and cold, in deep water, and she was desperately searching for a rock.

Four

Clint Kelly held his breath as he saw a shadow move. He had waited two hours because he knew they would come. Deer loved apples. The shadow separated into three when it reached the trees. He selected his target, a young buck, then lifted his rifle and squeezed the trigger. The two does flew past him, sending down an avalanche of snow from the overhanging branches; the buck dropped.

When Clint stood up from his cramped position, he stretched up to fill his pockets with apples; he could hardly feel his feet. He stomped about for a few minutes to restore his circulation before he hoisted both rifle and carcass to his shoulders. Their food worries were over—now he could concentrate on providing fuel.

For the last two hours, thoughts of Eve had filled his head. He knew she would recover from her ordeal, but worried about the pond water she had ingested. Bacteria from the murky water could make her very sick. If luck was with them, however, the germs may have been killed off by the cold.

Clint's thoughts had then drifted along more personal lines. He couldn't lie to himself; he found Eve Barlow extremely attractive in spite of their differences. Perhaps it was even *because* of their differences. She was a new experience for Clint; independent, assertive, competitive, even combative. A far cry from the clinging types he had dated recently.

Eve was an exciting challenge. Beneath the polished veneer, he might find a real flesh-and-blood, honest-to-God woman! All his thoughts were sexual now. In retrospect, giving Eve the whisky massage had been a very erotic experience. When he had his hands on her body, he had tried to be detached. Now, however, he relived every stroke, every slide of skin on skin. She was ice, he was fire—a combustible combination!

Hers was probably the loveliest female form he had ever seen or touched. She had everything to tempt a man: long blond hair, silky skin, nipples like pink rosebuds, and a high pubic bone covered by pale curls. And long, beautiful legs.

Back in the garage, with axe and hunting knife, Clint skinned the carcass, then dressed and hung the venison. He was considerably warmer by the time he finished. He glanced ruefully along the wall where the woodpile was customarily stacked. All that remained were wood chips, evidence that split logs were usually stored in abundance.

He saw a wooden pallet marked "Evergreen Sod Farm" and speculated that there must be a lawn buried deep beneath the snow. The wood from the pallet wouldn't last an hour, but perhaps he could put it to better use than burning. The beams and column supports in the barn were fashioned from whole trees. If he used the pallet as a sled, perhaps he could drag a tree trunk up here to the garage where he could axe it into logs, then split the logs into firewood. He looked about for his rope, then remembered it was still at the pond with the ladder. *Necrosis of the cranium*—wasn't that what Eve had flung at him? Perhaps she was right, he thought wryly.

Eve stirred in her sleep, then awoke with a start. She felt disoriented for a moment. She knew she had been dreaming, but as she tried to call back the dream, it danced out of her reach. Then she remembered where she was.

The room was silent, dark and very cold. For a moment,

panic assailed her. Had he gone off and left her here? Had he abandoned her? Then she laughed at her own foolishness. Clint Kelly wasn't the kind who would desert a damsel in distress. He had rescued her from a watery grave and was probably out gathering wood. He would relish the challenge of being snowbound.

Eve's belly rolled. Lord, she was hungry. She struggled to sit up and realized she had no strength. Her head dropped back to the couch cushion as she drew the blanket closer and closed her eyes. Clint would take care of everything.

The task of dislodging one of the upright tree trunks was more difficult than Clint had anticipated. None of them budged even a fraction, in spite of the stout shoulder he pressed upon them. He selected the one closest to the barn door, wedged the ladder against a beam, then chopped with his axe until he felled it.

He knew the hardwood would have made a fine piece of furniture and under any other circumstances it would be sacrilege to burn it. But it was exactly what they needed. Hardwood burned longer and gave off a fiercer heat than other timber, and even more to the point, it was dry.

Try as he might, Clint could not lift the tree trunk. He decided that expending his energy was foolish. After studying the problem for a moment, once more he put the rope to good use. He tied it to the tree trunk, threw the other end over a barn beam and used it as a pulley to lift the huge log onto the pallet.

With the rope around his chest, he pulled the makeshift sledge through the snow. Fancifully, he realized he was doing what men had done in past centuries: bringing home the Yule Log. The only difference was that he had to do it alone.

Clint needed a rest to catch his breath before he started cutting wood. He slipped quietly into the living room to check on Eve. Though he didn't feel it after his strenuous exertion, he knew the room was far too chilly for someone who needed to keep her body temperature from falling again.

He bent over her with concern. He heard her even breathing and saw the crescent shadows of her lashes as they lay upon her cheeks. Two fingers to her forehead told him that she wasn't fevered. A proprietary feeling stole over him as he stood close to her. Who the devil was this Trevor guy who wanted to marry her? He sure as hell wouldn't be able to give her an engagement ring for Christmas. It was way past midnight, already Christmas Eve.

Clint flexed weary muscles as he thought of all the wood that needed to be chopped, but strangely, he knew he would rather be here tonight than anywhere else on earth.

Clint spent the next three hours alternately sawing the tree into huge rounds and splitting them into logs that would fit in the fireplace. He only stopped working once, and that was to build a roaring fire in the living room.

By the time he was finished, he vowed the first thing he would buy for the new house was a chain saw, and the second, a log-splitter. He lifted the long axe handle behind his head to stretch the kinks out of his shoulder muscles and yawned loudly. Food! His body needed refuelling. Clint carved some thin slices of venison and went in search of a frying pan. He set it on the flames, cut up an apple amongst the meat and sat down on the hearth.

"Mmm, that smells heavenly."

He turned to the couch in time to see Eve stretch and open her eyes. "How do you feel?" he asked, hiding all trace of anxiety.

"Hungry," she replied, eyeing the contents of the pan. "Thanks for cooking my breakfast," she teased, "but what are you going to have?"

He laughed, but warned, "You're going to have to take it easy. If you eat too much or too fast, your stomach will reject it." He searched her face; it didn't look flushed.

"Don't stare! I know I must look a damned fright."

Clint was so relieved she wasn't fevered, he was perfectly happy to let her have the food and cook more for himself. He found her a plate and took the empty pan into the garage with him. When he returned, she said, "This is absolutely wonderful. What is it?"

"Meat," he said evasively, knowing her aversion to guns.

"What kind of meat?"

"Venison."

She went all quiet, but kept on chewing. *He went hunting last night when I fell asleep.* It wasn't a question, it was a deduction. Her gaze moved from Clint to the fireplace. *I woke up about two o'clock. The fire was almost out. He chopped wood after he bagged the deer. He hasn't slept all night!*

Eve was deeply impressed by what he had done for her. From the moment she had gotten herself into such dire peril, all her ideas about this man had been turned upside down. She experienced an overwhelming gratitude. He had saved her life. He had warmed her and sheltered her and fed her. She hadn't had to lift a finger.

Eve felt more than gratitude; she felt respect and admiration. As she searched her emotions, it suddenly hit her like a bolt of lightning. What she felt was desire!

She put her fork down. Damnation, she mustn't let him see how she felt about him.

"Something wrong with the food?"

"It needs salt . . . and you could use a shave," she said.

"Thankless little bitch," he murmured. He wasn't smiling, but Eve saw that he couldn't hide the amusement in his eyes.

"Why are you always laughing at me?"

"Because you're an impostor."

"What the devil do you mean?"

"You want the world to think you're the competent, self-sufficient, woman-of-the-year type, but it's just a facade. Scratch the surface and you're a little girl who needs some-one to take care of her. A little girl from hell perhaps, but nevertheless—"

"You're wrong!" Eve interjected.

"Am I? Even your clothes give you away."

"My clothes?" She became conscious of the fact that she wasn't wearing any beneath the blanket.

"The briefcase and the power suit present a false image. Once I stripped them away, what did I expose? The most fem-inine lingerie I've ever seen. It's not just Victoria's Secret, it's also Eve's Secret."

"You're crazy!"

Clint rubbed his backside. "Brain damage from when my father—"

"Shot you," she finished. Suddenly, she began to laugh. Clint joined in.

"I like to see you laugh," he told her. "It really suits you. You should let your hair down and have fun more often."

"Fun—what a concept. I haven't had any in so long, I've forgotten how."

"I could teach you."

She lowered her lashes. He was too damned tempting. "Having my eye on advancement and my nose to the grind-stone is very demanding."

"It's also a helluva funny position to go through life in. I could teach you other positions."

Her lashes swept up; green eyes met blue.

"I just bet you could, Action Man."

Clint had to call on all his willpower not to kiss her. His need to taste her was so overpowering at that moment, he had to physically remove himself from her space. He could not make love to her right now—it would be taking advantage of her vulnerability. When he made love to Eve, and he fully intended to, he wanted her to be able to give as good as she got. He wanted her energy to be high voltage.

"I need something to wear." She looked at the red heap on the hearth that had once been an Alfred Sung suit. Oh well, perhaps her underwear could be salvaged.

"I'll see what I can find in the bedrooms," Clint offered.

The moment he disappeared upstairs, she struggled into her bra and short satin slip, shoved the mangled pantyhose and briefs beneath the red heap and pulled the blanket back around her.

"Lean pickings, I'm afraid." Clint presented her with his findings, a pair of red longjohns and some ski socks. "Here, take my shirt—it'll cover the longjohns."

He stripped off vest and shirt before she could protest. Eve's eyes slid across the wide expanse of muscled chest, covered by a thick mat of black hair. He put the leather vest back on, leaving his hard biceps exposed.

She simply couldn't help staring at him. "What do you do to keep in shape?" she asked in wonder.

"Nothing. My job and my hobbies do it for me."

There was absolutely no point in her asking him if he would be warm enough. A man like this couldn't possibly feel the cold. He looked like the Marlboro Man!

"I'll bring in more wood while you get dressed," he said tactfully. "There's water, but it's cold. Don't stand under a cold shower long, Eve," he cautioned.

She was devoutly thankful that she had left her shoulder bag with her briefcase when they went out to look over the property yesterday. In the bathroom, she took the shortest shower on record and pulled the longjohns over her satin slip. When she turned to the mirror she was dismayed to see that she looked like a hillbilly from an old "Hee-Haw" rerun.

Eve quickly covered the red longjohns with Clint's blue wool shirt. His male scent enveloped her. She closed her eyes, trying to define its essence. It was a combination of apples and woodsmoke mixed with honest-to-God sweat. It was like an aphrodisiac!

She pulled on the thick socks and ran her comb through her hair. Miraculously, the pond water hadn't done much damage. If anything, her hair was curlier than usual. The only makeup she had with her was a lipstick. She had chosen it to match the Alfred Sung; now it matched the longjohns.

When she came out of the bathroom, he was waiting for her. She said quickly, "Let's go on a scavenger hunt and see if we can turn up anything at all that will be useful."

He grinned at her. "Brilliant as well as beautiful."

When they entered the kitchen, Clint opened a cupboard and showed her its hidden treasure. "This is a generator. I siphoned the gasoline from the truck so we can have electricity. We should ration it, though. Tonight, when it gets dark, we can have lights, use the stove to cook something, and maybe listen to the weather reports on the radio."

Eve grinned at him. "Brilliant as well as handsome."

Inside the numerous kitchen cupboards they found every pot and pan known to man. There was china, silverware, glasses and mugs, but almost nothing edible. There was a rack that contained fifteen different herbs and spices, a box of candles, some tinfoil, a package of napkins from Valentine's Day, and a lone package of Kool Aid that lay forgotten in an empty drawer.

The last cupboard produced a half-jar of instant coffee. To Eve and Clint it was like finding a gold nugget in an abandoned mine.

"Coffee!" they chorused with joy. Clint filled the kettle and set it on the fire. Eve measured a spoonful of the magic brown powder in each of two mugs, then they sat by the fire with bated breath, waiting for the water to boil.

"They say anticipation is the best part," she teased.

"Don't you believe it." His voice was so deep, his double

entendre so blatantly clear, a frisson of pleasure ran down her spine.

When he poured the boiling water into her mug, Eve closed her eyes and breathed in its aroma. To Clint, it was a sensual gesture, revealing her passion for everything in life. When he added a drop of whisky to his coffee, Eve held out her mug. When she tasted it, she rolled her eyes. "Now that *is* decadent!" She took two big gulps. "My God, it's better than sex."

Clint laughed. "If that's true, you've had very inadequate lovers, Eve Barlow."

She wondered if that were true. Until yesterday she would have vehemently denied that, but after spending twenty-four hours with Clint Kelly, her perceptions about a lot of things were changing. She looked him straight in the eye. "I think it's time for your cold shower."

Clint knew it would take more than a cold shower to cure his condition. It would take an ice dive, at least. Then he remembered his fishing line. He picked up his coat.

"Where are you going?"

"To check on my stringer."

When she was alone, she wondered what the devil a stringer was. She also wondered why she had brought up the subject of sex. She must be out of her mind. Then she recalled she had read somewhere that female captives always became enamored of their abductors. It was some sort of syndrome.

Suddenly, Eve began to laugh. Clint Kelly had not abducted her. The captor/captive scenario was a fantasy. *Quit kidding yourself! He's the most desirable man you've ever met in your life, and the attraction is definitely mutual.*

Five

Clint took his axe with him to the lake because the temperature had plummeted and he knew the ice would be thicker now. The snow was still coming down, but it had changed to fine stuff that never seemed to melt.

He followed the line from the tree, taking great care not to walk out onto the lake. When he chopped open the hole, he was gratified to see that he had hooked two walleyes. He carefully removed the lures and set the stringer back in the lake.

Eve's eyes widened when she saw the fish. "You *are* a magic man!"

He held them up by the mouth. "Hocus pocus, fish bones choke us."

She followed him to the kitchen and watched, fascinated, as he skinned and filleted the walleyes. When he was finished, he said, "Now I need that shower."

When Clint came downstairs, she noticed how his black hair curled when it was wet. He hadn't been able to shave and the blue-black shadow on his jaw added to his overt masculinity. With effort, Eve forced herself to stop staring at him.

She busied herself spreading tinfoil to wrap the fish. They selected the herbs together. It seemed a great luxury to have so many choices in the spice rack. They finally decided to sprinkle the fillets with chervil, basil, and dried parsley. Then he sealed the tinfoil and set it amid the smouldering logs.

When the tantalizing aroma of the herbs began to permeate the air, both of them realized how hungry they were.

"I'm drooling," Eve breathed.

Clint's glance flicked over her mouth. "Me, too," he confessed.

The amused look she threw him told him she understood exactly what he meant. She waited most patiently for the fish to cook and then she thought she smelled it burning. They both reached out at the same time. Eve pulled the tinfoil from the fire, but it burned her fingers. With a yelp, she hastily dropped it into Clint's calloused palms.

He set it on the hearth and reached for her hands. His face exuded tenderness as he examined her fingers.

"It's all right, I didn't get burned," she assured him. *Not yet, at least,* she added silently, as she felt heat leap from him into her hands and run up her arms. He gave her back her hands, but not her heart.

When she tasted the walleye, she knew it had been worth waiting for. The delicate flavor was ambrosia to the palate.

"I ate a whole fish, all by myself!"

"Your body needed the nourishment. I'm going to make a spit and roast us a haunch of venison for dinner."

"I'm profoundly grateful to you, Clint Kelly."

"Why do I get the feeling you're going to add a *but* to the end of your sentence?"

"You're a perceptive man. It's time we got down to business."

For one split second his mind went blank. She had the power to make him forget there was anything beyond this moment. Then he realized she wasn't talking about them, she was talking about the house.

"Are you sure you're up to this?"

"I'm positive," she assured him.

"Okay, I make an offer of one hundred and fifty thousand."

"Please be serious, Mr. Kelly."

"I'm deadly serious, Ms. Barlow. My offer is one-fifty."

"You're wasting my time."

That's a moot point, he thought, but kept a wise silence.

"The asking price is *two* hundred and fifty thousand."

"You surely don't expect me to offer the asking price?"

"Well no, but one-fifty is simply unacceptable."

"To whom? You? You aren't the owner, Ms. Barlow. You merely present the offer."

"I won't present an offer of one-fifty on a property that's worth *two*-fifty!"

"Just a moment. No one said anything about how much this property is worth. We're discussing the asking price. It isn't worth anywhere near two-fifty."

Eve had heard those words before, from her longtime friend who owned the property. She could hear Judy's voice now. *"It can't be worth more than about one hundred and eighty thousand, Eve. Let's list it for two hundred."*

Eve had replied, *"No way. They aren't making any more lakefront property, you know. If you aren't in a hurry for the money, I'd like to list it at two-fifty and see what happens."*

Actually, nothing had happened. The property had been for sale for nine months without a single offer. Eve knew what she could get for a city property within a few dollars, but country places were not her bailiwick.

"In your exalted opinion, Mr. Kelly, what do you think it is worth?"

He didn't beat about the bush. "It's worth a hundred and eighty thousand."

With all she had learned about him, why had she underestimated his business acumen? "You're wrong, Mr. Kelly. It's worth two hundred and twenty-five. Lakefront property is at a premium and this place is furnished."

"What was the last offer you received, Ms. Barlow?"

"That's privileged information, Mr. Kelly."

Clint grinned. "You've had no offers on this place!"

Eve could have kicked herself for being so transparent.

"How long has it been on the market?" he demanded. "I bet it's been over a year."

"Only nine months!" There was a pregnant pause. "Damn you, Clint Kelly." Eve's resolve hardened. She needed another two hundred thousand to make the President's Circle and she'd get that much if it killed her!

"Write up an offer for one-fifty and I'll sign it."

"No. The asking price is two-fifty and I've already admitted it's only worth two-twenty-five. I've come down, but you haven't budged!"

"I don't have to budge until the seller rejects my offer."

"Mr. Kelly—"

"Clint," he amended.

"Clint, let me explain about real estate. There's a leeway of about five percent. It's like an unwritten law."

"Thanks for the economics lesson. Now let me teach you poker."

"You're laughing at me again."

"Eve, you're required by law to make out an Offer to Purchase. I *have* bought real estate before, you know."

"A cemetery plot?"

"Sarcasm is the lowest form of wit. As a matter of fact, when my dad retired from the force, we became partners in a sports bar."

Eve stared at him. "Not Kelly's?"

"Afraid so," he said, grinning. "Business is my long suit."

"Then you can bloody well afford two hundred."

"I can, but I won't."

"*Why* won't you make me a counteroffer?"

Clint's grin widened. "I don't have to; you keep dropping the price."

She covered her ears and screamed in frustration.

"I was afraid you weren't up to this," he said softly.

"Of course I'm up to it . . . well, maybe I'm not." Eve decided to throw herself on his mercy. "Clint, let me be honest with you. If I make a sale of two hundred thousand my earnings for the year will get me into the President's Circle, a very prestigious achievement."

"Now, let me get this straight," he said, trying not to show his amusement. "You want me to up my offer from one-fifty to two hundred because you need the sales figures? Your logic escapes me. We have an impasse. I suggest we take a time-out."

"Do you have to talk to me in sports terms? I know nothing about football."

"We must have something in common. How about hockey?"

"I loathe it!"

Clint brought in firewood and stacked it by the hearth. The fire had to be kept at a constant temperature to roast the venison. The pile of wood that had seemed so large was half gone. Timber on the property was mostly pine that burned too fast, but it was better than nothing. He decided to cut some and bring it into the garage so it could dry a little.

Clint cut a haunch from the deer, found a meat spit in the barbecue, and wedged it in the fireplace, over the glowing logs. "You decide what flavor you'd like."

Eve studied the bottles in the spice rack and came back with fennel and garlic powder. Almost as soon as they were sprinkled on the meat, the air became redolent with a piquant aroma that awoke their tastebuds.

"Call me if the fire burns low."

Eve was restless. She was in a tug-of-war with herself, wanting Clint Kelly to come close, yet keep his distance at the same time. She felt extremely guilty—when Trevor arrived to take her dancing, she wouldn't be there.

To stop her outrageous thoughts about Kelly, Eve went in

search of something to read. She was delighted to find a book; when she discovered it was a collection of O. Henry stories, she took the precious volume back to the fire and lost herself in its pages.

Throughout the afternoon, Clint came in and out. He tended the fire and turned the spit, then returned to his wood-cutting. The atmosphere between them was cozy and companionable. Eve was palpably aware that they were forging a bond. Strangely, she didn't feel guilty that he was working so hard. He was a man, she a woman; it felt right.

She saved "The Gift of the Magi" for last. It was a Christmas story, a love story so poignant that it evoked tears. When she came to it, however, she found that she could not read it. It was simply too sentimental, too emotional.

Clint removed his jacket and turned the venison, which had crisped to a delicious deep brown. He immediately sensed Eve's melancholy and set about banishing it. He put a couple of apples to roast, then went into the kitchen and flipped the electrical switch to "generator." Light flooded the living room, dispelling all real and imaginary shadows.

Clint brought a carving board to the hearth. When he cut into the venison, succulent juices ran from the pink slices. Eve brought plates, cutlery, and napkins, and filled crystal goblets with water.

As they sat before the fire to dine, Clint lifted his goblet. "Happy Christmas, Eve."

She touched her glass to his. "Happy Christmas, Clint."

They ate in companionable silence, paying tribute to the food. When they were almost done, Clint set about amusing her. "We must have something in common, let's find out what it is." He deliberately suggested something he knew she would hate. "How about camping?"

She grimaced. "How about shopping?"

He shuddered. "Darts?"

She shook her head. "Chess."

"Read the comics?"

"Poetry," she said softly.

"Phil Collins?" he suggested.

"Barbra Streisand," she countered.

Clint chuckled and turned on the radio. Between Christmas carols, the only topic of conversation was the weather. They described how many inches had fallen and how many more were expected. They warned drivers to stay off the roads and told of flight cancellations. They reported power failures, downed lines, and overloaded telephone circuits. They asked everyone to exercise patience. They announced that the snow plows would be working all night.

Clint tried every station. The reports were identical. He switched it off just as Nat King Cole's beautiful voice sang, *Unforgettable, that's what you are.* He and Eve looked at each other, knowing they were exactly where they wanted to be.

"Coconut cream pie?" he suggested.

She shook her head. "Lemon."

"Baseball?"

Eve got to her feet. "Yes!"

"Detroit Tigers!" Clint shouted.

"Yes! Yes!" Eve's face was radiant. "Blame it on my father—it's in my genes."

"Cecil Fielder," he said with reverence.

"Mickey Tettleton," she enthused.

Clint took hold of her hands. "One hundred and seventy-five thousand."

"You devil, you know I need two hundred!"

"I know what you need," he said huskily, drawing her into his arms and covering her mouth with his.

The way he kissed made her weak at the knees. There was nothing tentative about it. He kissed the same way he did everything else; he simply took charge. His mouth was firm and demanding and possessive. His mouth was . . . perfect.

He kissed her the way a man should kiss a woman, but seldom did.

Clint did not try to part her lips with his tongue. He was in no hurry. Even kissing had its foreplay. Her mouth was soft and yielding and told him without words that she loved what he was doing.

Clearly, he enjoyed kissing; probably because he was so good at it. His hands cupped her face and he lifted it for another kiss. He did it reverently as if he held something delicate and priceless. Clint's hands were just as sensual as his mouth. They were calloused, capable, and downright carnal as they caressed her skin. His fingertips explored her features, and the backs of his fingers stroked across her cheekbones.

"Sweet, sweet," he murmured, seeing how her lashes were tipped with gold, seeing the fine down upon her brow, seeing her cheeks tint shell-pink, seeing everything.

Her breath came out on a sigh. How beautiful he made her feel, how utterly lovely. He conveyed with a look, with a touch, how special he found her. He kissed her eyelids and the corners of her mouth, delighting when they turned up with pure pleasure. And then his whole focus centered on her mouth, and she opened to him as a flower being worshipped by the sun.

He outlined her lips with the tip of his tongue. When the tip of her tongue touched his, a tremor of need made her throat and breasts quiver. His fingers slid into her hair, holding her, then his tongue mastered hers. This was only the first part of his body to enter hers, but she moaned low with the deeply erotic sensations it evoked.

Her hands moved from his leather vest to grip his bare arms where his biceps bulged so boldly. She clung to him, relishing his strength, loving his hardness, both above and below. She longed for more. It was her first experience with raw lust. She was already love-drunk, and all he had done was kiss her!

His lips were against her throat. "Evie," he murmured. How the diminutive pleased her; she never wanted to be called Eve again. How feminine it made her feel. He was teaching her the nuances of domination and submission, the sheer bliss that transforms a female who yields all to the male.

She stood obediently while his powerful hands removed the shirt and stripped the long red undergarment from her slim body and long legs. She was impatient for him to remove his own clothes, but she didn't paw at him; she waited, knowing it would be worthwhile.

With the lights blazing, they stood and looked at each other. Really looked. His body tapered down to slim hips. His flanks were long and hard. The dark pelt on his chest narrowed to a line of black hair that ran down his flat belly, then bloomed like a blackthorn bush. His manroot stood up, thick and powerful—a testament to her breathstopping beauty.

Clint's eyes licked over her like a candle flame. "Have you any idea how lovely you are?"

Truly, she could not answer his question. He took hold of her hand and traced her own fingertips from her temple to her lips. "Your eyes are Irish green, your mouth tastes like honeyed wine." He drew her fingertips slowly down the curve of her throat, then down to her breast, where a golden tress lay curled. "Your hair is the color of moonlight."

His voice, so low, so deep and masculine, did glorious things to her. He drew her fingers across the swell of her breast to the nipple. He drew her fingers down her body. "Your body is like silk." He touched one fingertip to her navel. "It has hidden depths."

Eve caught her breath. Surely he wouldn't make her touch herself? But he did. He held their hands so that their fingers threaded through the curls of her mons. Then he traced one of her fingertips along the folds of her pink cleft, then slipped it inside to touch the center of her womanhood. "A rosebud drenched with dew." He brought her fingers to his mouth and tasted them.

Eve was adrift on a sea of sensuality. His powerful hands cupped her shoulders to steady her. "I'm going to turn out the lights now to conserve our fuel. Don't move; I want to see you by fireglow. Then I'm going to pull down the couch. It has a bed inside."

Nothing escapes him, she thought dreamily. She knew she didn't have to worry about protection; Clint was the kind of man who took care of everything.

Six

Clint set lighted candles on the hearth before he came back to her. After he kissed her, he placed her in front of him so that she faced the fire. She leaned back, revelling in the solid feel of him. His hands were free to seek out all her secret places. He warmed her at the fire before he lifted her to their bed.

But Eve was already on fire. His arousal made her feel as if she were smouldering, longing for the moment she would burst into white hot flame. When the firestorm came, and she knew it would, it might consume her. But she was ready, nay eager, to go up in smoke.

He never left her mouth for long. In the first hour, they shared what seemed like ten thousand kisses. One powerful arm enfolded her as his calloused palms cupped her breasts, and then he began to focus all his attention upon her nipples.

Clint knew that when he licked, some sensation would be lost as it moved back and forth under his tongue. To prevent this, he placed his fingers on either side of her nipple and pressed down, not hard, but firmly. Then he spread his fingers apart, holding it totally immobile, and lowered his lips to her.

Her nipple swelled up into his mouth like a ripe fruit. When he began to slowly lick her, Eve went wild! She covered his breastbone with tiny love bites, then took his other hand to her mouth, drew one of his fingers inside, and began to suck, hard. His love-play made her drown in need. She writhed against him. The friction of sleek skin on skin made her flesh feel like hot silk.

He knew she needed immediate release. Then he would be able to start again, building her passion slowly, so they could make love for hours. He moved her up in the bed until his cheek lay against her silken thigh. Then she felt a wet slide of tongue, followed by a deep thrust. His tongue curled about her bud exactly as it had her nipple, and she was undone. She cried out into the flickering shadows that hid their secret rites, and arched herself into his masterful mouth.

Clint moved up in the bed so that he could catch her last soft cry with his mouth. Eve tasted herself on his lips and felt delicious as original sin. Most of the sensations she experienced were new to her, and Clint's earlier words drifted through her consciousness: "I can't decide if you're an ice queen or if you're simply unawakened." *Obviously, I was both!*

She couldn't believe how highly aroused he had made her or how she had peaked so beautifully, and they hadn't even completed coitus. That adventure still lay ahead. She wanted to scream from excitement.

Now he began to whisper love words, each phrase more erotic than the last. She would never have guessed he could be poetic. But had she not underestimated everything about him?

Clint expected her second arousal to be slow, but it was not. She became wildly inquisitive about his body—the feel of it, the man-scent of it, the salt taste of it. The masculine roughness of his beard sent thrills spiralling through her consciousness, driving her to touch his male center, to stroke, squeeze, play and tease. His testes were big and heavy, more than a handful for her. How she loved the feel of this big, hard man.

Clint slipped a finger into her sugared sheath. This was the second part of his body he'd put inside her, and it was every bit as exciting as the first. He withdrew it slowly, and she gasped as he slid two fingers into her. Her sheath pulsated and clung to him tightly. When she became slippery, he knew she was ready.

He positioned the swollen head of his shaft at the opening of her cleft, then pushed up gently, inch by inch, until he was fully seated. Then all semblance of gentleness fell away. His lovemaking became fierce and savage. She adored every rough, elemental stroke as he anchored deep in her scalding body, then pulled all the way out so he could repeat the deep penetration over and over until her nails raked him. He took her to the edge of sanity. She became aware of every pulse-point on her body.

The moans in his throat were raw and it came as a blinding revelation that he was receiving as much pleasure as he gave. Then suddenly the night exploded for both of them. They keened and arched as they spent, and she mourned that she could not fully feel his white-hot seed spurt up inside her.

Eve thrashed her head from side to side with the intensity of her release, and Clint's hand came up to cup her cheek and hold her still. Then his mouth joined hers in a deep kiss.

When he rolled from her, he brought her against his side possessively. Eve had never felt more alive in her life. Her eyes sought his, but they were closed and she realized he was asleep. Her face softened as she gazed at him. He hadn't slept in over forty hours.

Eve lay entranced for a long time, savouring the feel of her body, watching the play of firelight make strange shadows on the ceiling. Their lovemaking had been a ballet of domination and submission, yet the strange thing was, they had each given and taken in equal measure. Male and female were only halves of one magnificent whole. *Equal* halves! She had not been diminished in any way; she had been exalted.

Inevitably, reality stole into her consciousness. She pushed away all thought of Trevor. She would deal with it later. In this isolated haven, where the pristine snow lay all about them, she wanted no footprints of others to mar the beauty that enfolded them. At least for tonight, the world must be held at bay.

Eve, a million miles from sleep, brought book and candle back to the bed. She propped herself up quietly and turned to "The Gift of the Magi." She was transported back in time to another Christmas Eve. The couple in the story were so real, she was in the room with them.

O. Henry's words brought her deep pleasure. When she finished the story, her eyes were liquid with unshed tears. The young man had pawned his watch to buy combs for his wife's beautiful hair; she had sold her hair to buy him a watch chain. The objects in the story were symbols. What they had really given each other were gifts of love.

More than anything, she wanted to give Clint Kelly a gift of love, and she knew exactly what it would be. She slipped from the bed, opened her briefcase, and removed an Offer to Purchase form. Then she made out the offer in the amount of one hundred and seventy-five thousand dollars. She knew Judy would accept it and the knowledge filled her with joy. He belonged here; this house and property were already a part of him.

That she would not qualify for the President's Circle seemed unimportant when she compared it to making him happy. She blew out the candles and curled up beside him. This Christmas Eve had been pure magic.

The first sound Eve heard on Christmas morning was a groan. She sat up quickly and looked down at Clint stretched beside her. He looked flushed. "Are you all right?"

"I'm fine," he croaked.

His beautiful, deep voice had been replaced by a rasp.

"You're not fine at all! You have laryngitis at the very least." She touched his brow. "You're warm; you have a fever."

"I never get sick," Clint protested in a hoarse whisper.

"You mean, you never admit you get sick."

"Same thing." He gave her a lopsided grin and threw back the covers.

"Oh, no, you don't," Eve said, pushing him back down and covering him with the blankets. "You're sick because you overtaxed yourself, hunting and cutting wood and going without sleep."

He laughed at her. His throat sounded like he'd been gargling with gravel. "It was child's play compared to a twelve-hour night shift, fighting a fire in below-zero temperatures."

Eve glared at him, daring him to make a move from the warm bed. "Wasn't it another Clint who said, *A man should know his limitations?* It's my turn to take care of you."

She took a one-minute cold shower, pulled on her satin slip, then stepped into the red longjohns and blue wool shirt. She felt Clint's amused eyes on her as she built up the fire. In the kitchen she turned on the generator just long enough to boil the kettle for coffee. She mixed up the orange Kool-Aid, sliced some cold venison from the haunch, and carried a tray to the bed.

His dark eyebrow lifted at the glass of Kool-Aid.

"It's pretend orange juice. Didn't you ever play pretend?"

"I played house, too," he croaked.

She made sure he ate everything, then poured the last of the whisky into his coffee. "I want you to go back to sleep."

"It's Christmas Day—there's stuff that needs doing," he protested.

"And I'm the one who's going to do it," she said flatly.

As Clint sipped his coffee, he took delight in looking at her. He didn't know what had brought about this transformation to domesticity. Perhaps his slight ailment brought out a need to nurture him. It felt strange to be pampered. He handed her his empty mug, pulled up the covers, and turned over.

By the time she finished her breakfast, she heard his even breathing and knew he was asleep. Eve's mind overflowed with plans for their Christmas Day. She pulled on her boots, ignoring the fact that the insides had hardened as they had dried by the fire. She slipped into Clint's down jacket and went to the garage for his axe.

When she went outside, she saw that it had stopped snowing and the sun was turning the landscape into a glittering fairyland. She didn't have to venture far to find a small pine tree. The one she selected was literally buried beneath the snow, with only its growing point sticking up. It took her quite a while to scoop away the snow so that she could reach its trunk with the axe. Her hands were freezing by the time she chopped it free and dragged it up to the house.

Eve warmed her hands at the fire, glancing at Clint's unmoving form in the bed. When he awoke, he would be surprised. It was fun trying to make their Christmas special. Eve needed something that would act as a tree stand. She went into the garage and looked about carefully, knowing she had to use her ingenuity. There was a cement block, probably used as a door prop, and she decided that would do the trick.

When her eyes fell on the pheasant, she felt a pang of regret that the poor creature had been caught in a snare. That thought drifted away as she realized, here was their Christmas bird! Eve had not lived years in the Orient without learning how to pluck and clean fowl.

She hummed to herself as she boiled the water and performed the odorous chore. A flash of remembrance came to her. Hadn't she seen a few onions hanging in the basement when she'd been searching for the water valve? She went downstairs to retrieve them, wondering how she'd overlooked such a treasure.

Eve sprinkled the bird with sage and thyme, set it in a shallow roasting pan with a square of tinfoil over it, and put the pan on the logs. Then she carried in the cement block and stuck the tree upright in it. She certainly didn't have much in the way of decorations, but again she used her ingenuity. She took the red Valentine napkins and fashioned paper flowers of a sort.

She had seen some old dried corncobs in the barn. She wondered if she could pop the kernels and string some popcorn. It wouldn't be edible, but it would be okay for decorating the tree. Nothing seemed too much trouble. Once more she slipped on the boots and coat and plodded off to the barn.

Stable smells assailed her as she entered, and it was suddenly brought home to her that this day was celebrated because of the Christ Child born in a manger. She thought of Mary giving birth in such a place, and then she thought of her own mother. How worried Susan must be because Eve hadn't shown up this morning. They would be searching for her, and it would very likely ruin their Christmas.

She felt guilty. She loved them very much and regretted causing them worry. It was so frustrating when she could do nothing about it, but Eve had learned to accept things that couldn't be altered.

Back in the kitchen, she cut the kernels from the old corncobs and turned on the generator long enough to pop the corn on the stove. She carried the big bowl to the living room and opened Clint's tackle box, thinking to thread the popcorn on fishing line. Some of his lures were so colorful that she hung them on the tree.

Before she sat down to thread the popcorn, she basted the pheasant, leaving the tin foil off so it would brown. The onions in the roasting pan gave off a tantalizing aroma. Eve offered up a prayer of thanks.

In Grand Rapids, Susan Barlow was also praying. She had called her daughter to wish her a happy Christmas, but there had been no answer. She assumed Eve was already on her way, but when half an hour elapsed and she didn't arrive, a vague uneasiness touched her. After a whole hour, she voiced her worry to her husband, who had just finished shovelling the driveway.

"Ted, I called Eve over an hour ago. When she didn't answer, I assumed she was on her way, but she should be here by now."

"The main streets are all plowed, so she shouldn't have had any trouble. Maybe she and Trevor are stopping somewhere before they come here."

Susan pulled back the sheers. "Oh, here's Trevor's car now. Thank heavens!"

Still wearing his boots, Ted went outside to greet them. Trevor was alone. "Where's Eve?"

"I couldn't get her on the phone and when I got to her apartment, the Mercedes was gone. I assumed she was here."

"No," Ted said, shaking his head. "We're worried about her."

"Oh, I wouldn't worry too much, Mr. Barlow. Eve can take care of herself."

Ted frowned at Trevor, but bit back a retort. When they went inside, Ted got on the computer. *Eve, if you're there, please answer. If you're sick, let us know. If you can't start your car and are waiting for the Motor League, send a message.*

Susan brought them coffee and hot muffins with homemade jam. Trevor had just taken his first bite when Ted said, "I'm going over there. Come on." He touched his wife's cheek to reassure her. "Don't worry, sweetheart, we'll find her."

When Ted saw that Trevor was right and his daughter's Mercedes was not in the parking lot of her apartment building, he went upstairs and banged on her door. Then he banged on the superintendent's door and insisted he open up Eve's apartment. At first the man said he couldn't do that, but he hadn't reckoned with Ted Barlow. Reluctantly, he finally agreed to use his master key.

Trevor demurred. "I don't really think this is wise . . . you're violating Eve's privacy."

"Bullshit!" Ted replied shortly.

Inside the apartment, everything was in its place but her winter coat, her purse, and briefcase were missing. As they looked about, Trevor said, "See how efficient and organized she is? By the time we get back to your house, she'll be there."

Her father decided to drive to Eve's office; she was a voracious worker. A lone car sat in the parking lot. When he brushed off the foot of snow, he saw it was Eve's Mercedes. Ted was really worried now and even Trevor was beginning to feel uneasy. "There has to be a logical explanation for this," he assured her father.

Ted drove back home and got on the phone to Maxwell Robin. "Max, Eve's missing! Her car is parked at the office. Do you know where she is? Have you spoken with her?"

"No, Ted. The last time I saw her was the day before yesterday. She drove a client up to that country property she has listed for that friend of hers. Well, actually, now that I think of it, the client did the driving."

"Damn, they must have got caught in the storm. It's been a real blizzard north of here. Who is the client? Do you know anything about him?"

"Yes, I know him personally. Name's Clint Kelly. He's a diving instructor and also a fire captain. In an emergency situation she couldn't be in better hands."

"Thank God for that. Where exactly is the property?"

"I don't know off the top of my head, but it has to be in the files at the office. I'll meet you there."

"I'll call her friend Judy and get it from the horse's mouth.

Your kids probably haven't opened their presents yet," Ted said.

"You've got to be kidding; they were up at six o'clock! Listen, Ted, call me if you need me."

Ted Barlow telephoned Eve's friend in Detroit and got directions to the log house, while Susan silently prayed that her daughter was safe. When Ted got off the phone he announced, "I'm on my way!"

"I think we should call the police," Trevor advised.

"The police won't even file a missing person's report until after seventy-two hours."

"The State Troopers then. They'll search the highways. They'll have any accident reports and can check out the hospitals."

"That's a great idea, but I'm still going," Ted insisted.

"Leave it to the professionals. It's too risky in blizzard conditions. You could get stuck or lost and that would just compound the problem."

Susan looked at Trevor bleakly. He might as well save his breath to cool his soup. If Eve needed rescuing, Ted Barlow would be in the vanguard!

Seven

When Clint awoke, he felt miraculously restored. He threw off the blanket and stretched. Before he could lower his arms, the mouthwatering aroma of roasting game assaulted his senses. He sat up and blinked his eyes. Where the devil had the Christmas tree come from, or its decorations?

"Evie," he bellowed. His throat was much improved, sounding only slightly husky.

She had been waiting for him to awake, anticipating his re-action to her surprise. She pulled off his blue shirt and stood in front of the bathroom mirror in the red longjohns. She stuffed the cushion down the front and fastened the buttons over the bulge. She had taped her blond curls across her face as a makeshift beard and mustache, and knew she looked ridiculous. But Eve didn't care; inside, her silly juices were bubbling.

She took a deep breath and bounded into the living room. "Ho! Ho! Ho! Merry Christmas!"

Clint began to laugh. If he hadn't, Eve would have been devastated. She joined in the laughter, holding her cushion belly with both hands.

"I see you're feeling better."

His eyes glittered with amusement. "You were so much woman, you almost finished me off."

Eve's blush competed with her longjohns, but she needed

the acknowledgment that he remembered last night's glow—
that she lingered in his consciousness, as he did in hers.

"You went out and cut a tree all by yourself, then thought
up these ingenious decorations."

"I'm not just a hairy face," she beamed.

"And the pheasant! I thought you told me you couldn't
cook."

"No, I told you I *didn't* cook, not that I couldn't. My
mother was Susie Homemaker—I had to learn how to cook."

"Santa Claus, you're full of surprises."

She handed him an envelope.

Clint opened it and read the Offer to Purchase. "What's
this?" he asked softly.

Eve smiled into his eyes. "I know the seller will accept a
hundred and seventy-five."

"What about your President's Circle?"

"My gift to you means more than the President's Circle."
She bent down to kiss him.

"Germs," he warned huskily.

"Santa is immune," she whispered.

He took her in his arms and brushed her curls away from
her mouth. Then he claimed it, kissing her thoroughly.

In the same husky voice he had used last night, she repeated his words: "I know what you need."

"What?" he murmured, wanting her to say it.

"A sauna."

Clint groaned with anticipation.

"I've already stacked the wood into it. After we eat our
pheasant, all we have to do is light that fire."

"All these gifts for me. What can I give you, Evie?"

She almost melted with desire. "I'll think of something,
Action Man," she whispered.

"I was going to give you scuba lessons, but it pales in com-
parison to your generosity."

Suddenly, she began to laugh. Her pillow belly bobbed up

and down. She pulled it from her longjohns and threw it at him. "Only an insensitive male could offer diving lessons to a woman who almost drowned in murky pond water!"

He gave her a lopsided grin, his teeth showing white against his dark, unshaven jaw.

Eve realized that with Clint Kelly beside her, she wouldn't even be afraid of being submerged underwater. She set the table as elegantly as she could for their Christmas dinner, with crystal goblets of water and lighted candles.

Clint donned his leather vest and held out her chair with a flourish. The flesh of the pheasant, seasoned with the sage and thyme, tasted better than any turkey she could ever remember. The roasted onions were elevated from common vegetables to savory delicacies.

Clint was beguiled by Eve's transformation from career woman to chatelaine. The role suited her to perfection, in his eyes. He speculated on what had brought it about. Was it the Christmas season, being snowed in, or a direct result of what had happened between them last night? He had known from the moment he undressed her that she was a real flesh and blood woman.

Eve watched the man sitting across the table from her. What was it about him that brought out her domesticity? She believed his masculinity called out to her femininity. She had no desire to compete with him; she had only the desire to nurture him and make him happy.

Her thoughts drifted to her mother and father, and she realized that was the kind of relationship they had. Susan was fulfilled as a woman and her contentment and happiness was visible to everyone. It was a heady sensation to have the power to make a man completely happy. She was revelling in that new-found power at the moment. Their time together here would be so short.

When they finished dinner, Eve picked up an apple and held it out to him. The picture she made entranced him. In the

Bible, Adam said, *The woman tempted me.* Well, if Adam's Eve was anything like his Eve, no wonder he had succumbed.

"We can have dessert in the sauna," he said, rising and taking her hand. She knew he had something more exotic than apples in mind. "I'll light the fire so the logs will have a chance to glow, while we undress."

Eve wrapped her nakedness in a towel; Clint was less modest. He opened the sauna door and peered into its dark interior. "We'll need a candle." There was no way he was going to make love to her without being able to see her.

When Eve stepped inside, the aromatic cedar wood of the walls and seats gave off a heady scent that filled her senses. It was already deliciously warm and inviting, like a cocoon that enveloped them in a small, private world. Along two of the walls, the bench seats were normal height, while the third wall had a very low one, so you could stretch out your legs across the floor. The remaining wall had just the opposite, a bench seat set high so it could be used as a ledge to set things on, or to perch upon for maximum heat.

Clint set the candle on the ledge and lifted off her towel. Eve had no objections. When Clint lifted her against him, she cried out with excitement; she wrapped her arms around his neck, clinging to him as he took total possession of her mouth.

"Wrap your legs around me," he demanded. Eve obeyed willingly, loving the feel of his big calloused hands beneath her bottom. When beads of moisture formed along his collarbone, she licked them off playfully at first, then sensually, as she became more highly aroused.

The feel of her rough pink tongue gave Clint desires of his own. He lifted her high until she was perched on the shelf, opened her thighs and stepped between. His mouth was on a level with her belly. He trailed kisses down it, taking the drops of moisture onto his tongue. Then with his fingers, he opened the delicate pink folds between her legs and gazed at her woman's center. He worshipped her with his eyes, then dipped his head and made love to her with his mouth. With his lips against her cleft, he murmured, "God, you're so hot inside."

She was hot because she was on fire. Eve knew it had very little to do with the sauna. She writhed and arched, threading her fingers into his black hair and holding him to her center, faint with the ravishing. He swung up to perch beside her, gathering her close to watch her green eyes glitter with passion.

Eve needed to vent that passion in an abandoned act of worship. She slid down from the high seat. Her head was on the level of his knees. She parted them and stepped close. Standing on tiptoe, she delicately licked the tiny opening at the tip of his phallus, then drew its swollen head into her hot mouth. She swirled her tongue, spiralling it around and beneath the ridge of his cock.

"Enough, Evie, or I'll spill." It was all new to her. She was receiving as much pleasure as she was giving. Clint slid from his high perch. "No, sweet, I don't want it that way."

Dimly, she realized that though Clint had loved what she was doing, he could not spend in such a passive manner.

He stood her on the low seat, pressed her against the wall and thrust up inside her. The savage force of his entrance lifted her, and he took her hips in powerful hands to anchor her in place for his plundering. Their bodies, drenched with moisture, slid against each other like wet silk, driving them wild. He slowed his thrusts deliberately to draw out the loving. Then he told her in that dangerous, deep voice all the things he was going to do to her that night, when they went to bed.

Ted Barlow decided to take his snowmobile with him on his drive north. Pulling a trailer would slow him down and even add to the hazard of driving, but he had a gut feeling it would come in very handy if the roads to the property had not been plowed out.

Trevor was on the telephone to his mother. He was about to tell her that Eve was missing, but he detected such a plaintive note in her voice, that he hesitated. "Are you all right?" he asked anxiously.

"Oh, I'll be all right, Trevor. Don't worry about me being here alone—I'm used to it. Just so long as you're enjoying your Christmas; that's all that matters to me, dear."

Trevor was covered with guilt. He was torn between conflicting duties, as usual. Being in the middle was so unfair. He had given up his date with Eve last night to stay at his mother's. Thank heavens her illness had turned out to be merely indigestion. In retrospect, things had worked out for the best, because Eve apparently wasn't here anyway.

She had a tendency to be willful and impulsive and as a result had gone dashing off to show a property a hundred miles away. She certainly wouldn't appreciate his rushing after her. Eve Barlow had a mind of her own. That's what attracted him, however. His mother was so clinging, he only sought out independent females.

Trevor glanced through the window and saw Ted Barlow hook up his trailer and snowmobile. God, the man was so gung-ho! He'd flown rescue missions during the Korean War and had obviously bought into the hero syndrome. Now he was off on a wild goose chase that would physically exhaust a much younger man. Into the phone he said, "You sound like you need my company, Mother. I'll be there in about an hour."

Trevor went outside and stood beside Susan Barlow. "My mother's not very well."

"Oh, Trevor, I'm so sorry."

Ted rolled down the van window and said to Trevor, "Are you coming?"

Susan spoke up quickly. "His mother is ill. He has to go to Kalamazoo, honey."

"Oh, sorry. Susie, I'll call the minute I have news. Try not to worry, love."

She waved until he was out of sight. "I'll call you right away, if there's any news, Trevor."

He took her small hand in his. "Thanks, Mrs. Barlow. I'm so sorry about all the food you cooked."

"Don't give it a second thought. The people we love come first."

For the most part the highways had been plowed up as far as Ludington. It took Ted Barlow over three hours to cover the hundred miles. Everything was closed for Christmas Day, even the gas stations; it was a good thing he carried extra cans in the van.

The highway ended north of Ludington where the forests began. Ted located a State Troopers' Headquarters and explained the situation. They told him they had been in constant communication with the Department of Highways, who'd had their plows out since the blizzard began, as well as Michigan Power who had their linemen on overtime.

Ted Barlow showed them a sketch he'd made of Judy's property.

"Back on the twenty-third, traffic was still going in and out of that particular area until late afternoon. After that, anything that went in didn't come out."

They put in a call to the Department of Highways to see when the lakeshore road leading to this property would be plowed out, and then sipped coffee and waited for the information to be relayed to them.

It occurred to Ted Barlow that he should take advantage of a telephone while there was one available. He asked the clerk for a phone directory and began calling hospitals. None of them had admitted a young woman by the name of Eve Barlow. That was good, he told himself, that was very good news indeed.

The State Troopers' office checked over all the accident reports filed in the area since the twenty-third of December. Ted cursed himself for not finding out what Clint Kelly was driving, but at least neither the name Kelly nor the name Barlow showed up in any of the reports. Ted was an optimist and honestly believed his daughter and her client were holed up at the property, safe and sound. They had simply been snowed in and knew they wouldn't get out until the roads were cleared. The alternative was unthinkable.

Finally a report came in from the Department of Highways. Though they would be working all night, they wouldn't get to isolated roads until morning. It was strictly a matter of priorities. Ted Barlow was faced with two choices. He could stay at the troopers' headquarters tonight and follow the first plow in the morning, or he could head out on his snowmobile.

It was one of the easiest decisions he'd ever made. He took an extra gas can from the van and put it under the seat of the snowmobile in the storage compartment. A State Trooper tried to talk him out of it, but realized if his own daughter were missing, he'd do exactly the same thing.

Ted changed into his snowmobile suit, then put on his goggles and heavy leather gauntlets. The visibility was good, but his progress was slower than usual. A snowmobile was at its peak performance on fresh powder or when a crust of ice had formed on top of the snow. Today, the sun had produced a partial thaw and as a result, the snow was wet and heavy.

He kept his goal foremost in his mind, telling himself over and over that it was less than twenty miles. When his snowmobile hit a particularly slushy patch and bogged down, he got off the machine and dug it out with his hands.

He shook his head and chuckled at the irony. His son couldn't come home this Christmas. Steven was halfway around the world in a new posting at Camp Page in South

Korea. Although there was no war, he flew jets very close to the border of the unpredictable North Koreans. Up until today, Ted's thoughts had been preoccupied with the danger his son might be in this Christmas season, so far away from his family and his country. Then, wouldn't you know it? It was Eve, who lived in little old Grand Rapids, a place renowned for its safety and security, who was missing!

Ted offered up a prayer for both of his children as he restarted the stalled machine and set off again with renewed determination.

Eve yawned as she sat before the fire. She was so relaxed after the sauna and Clint's lovemaking, she couldn't lift a finger, and what was more, she didn't wish to. *It should be against the law to feel this content,* she thought. Eve had never been cut off from the world before; it certainly had its advantages.

Although she hadn't been too keenly aware of it before, now she realized she'd been on edge lately. The stress of city living and constantly competing in a man's world had made her uptight. Now she felt at peace with herself; she felt happy.

Clint stood gazing out the window. He realized their idyll would soon be over. It hadn't snowed all day, and by tomorrow at the latest, the roads would likely be plowed out and they would be connected with civilization again.

His gaze travelled possessively over the landscape. He felt elated that it would soon be his. No matter the asking price, he had decided this property would belong to him. He had discovered something precious here—a peace and quiet that had a healing quality about it. He loved his job and would have no other, but it was said that the constant flow of adrenaline brought on by danger was addictive.

After fighting a great conflagration, when he had beaten it and knew his men were safe, he felt totally drained. This house, this land not only cleansed him, it renewed his vitality and filled him with strength and power. The woman in the room with him had a similar effect. She filled him with a glorious feeling of omnipotence.

Clint wondered why he was so pensive. He had just found his dream home—why wasn't he dancing an Irish jig? The answer was simple; his heart was sinking because there was a piece missing from his happy picture. At the moment everything was perfect, but once Eve departed and took up her life where it had left off, there would be a hole in his future existence.

He didn't want their time together to end.

He didn't want to let her go!

Clint turned from the window. His face softened as he watched her sitting curled up, dreaming and drowsing before the fire.

"I love this place . . . share it with me, Evie."

Eight

Eve's lashes flew up. The magic spell was broken. Their idyll was over. He'd said the words that rang the death knell to their intimate interlude. Reality suddenly raised its unwelcome head and rushed in upon her.

She leapt off the couch and took two steps toward him. By that time, Clint had reached her. She raised her fingers to his lips as if to stay his words, but of course it was too late. They had been uttered and could not be recalled.

Eve agonized over her reply. The last thing on earth she wanted to do was hurt this man who had saved her life, fed her, warmed her, and loved her. She had to find the right words. Guilt assailed her from all sides. Not guilt over what they had done—she would never feel even the smallest pang for that, nor one tiny shred of regret. But guilt because she had somehow conveyed the possibility that what they had shared could go beyond this time, beyond this place.

And terrible guilt toward Trevor. She had betrayed his trust and in doing so had discovered another man who eclipsed him in her eyes. What made it worse, unforgivable almost, was the undeniable fact that the things she found irresistible were Kelly's dominance, macho attitude, and strength. Poor Trevor with his gentleness, kindness, and understanding came off a poor second.

Clint watched the play of emotions cross her lovely features, one after another. He had known from the outset that this woman was committed to another, yet he had deliberately set out to seduce her. To him she had been fair game. He was a man, she was a woman; they were alone together. To a male predator, that was all that counted.

She had been a great challenge to him, with her feminist attitudes. Then Providence had tipped the scales in his favor. By almost drowning, she had become completely vulnerable. Then he was able to shine at all the things he did best. But, underneath her polished veneer, he had found trust, generosity, and an innocence that captured his heart.

At first, he had thought, if he couldn't steal this female from a passive professor of English who spouted poetry, he wasn't worth his salt as a red-blooded American male. But the seduction had backfired. Once he stole her, he wanted to keep her.

Eve took a tremulous breath. "Clint . . . I can't," she said softly.

His face seemed to harden.

"You have such formidable attributes, Clint. I'm attracted to everything about you. I'm racked with guilt, but I could never leave Trevor."

Clint's bright blue eyes took on the cold gray of Lake Michigan.

"Trevor is such a fine person, so completely understanding and sensitive. I can't just leave him and come to you. I couldn't be that cruel!"

"You don't think you're capable of cruelty?" he asked drily.

She tried desperately to make him understand. "We have an understanding, a commitment. God help me, Clint, I can't walk out on him. I have too much compassion for that."

Clint was acutely aware that she made no protestations of love.

Eve avoided speaking of love; did not dare even think of love. It would open a door she wished to keep firmly closed. Her gaze slipped from his hard mouth to his powerful shoulders, then down to his big, calloused hands. *He's so tough, I bet he's never cried in his life.*

"Clint, you do understand?" she agonized.

"No." Silence filled the room and stretched to the breaking point. "I've asked you once. I won't beg," he said quietly.

Their heads turned at the same time as they heard a noise.

"That's some sort of machine. Is it a plow?" she asked.

Clint went to look out the window. "I don't think so. The sound of the motor is too high-pitched." He went to the door and opened it. "It's a snowmobile," he said over his shoulder. "We have company."

Eve peeped out from behind Clint, not wanting anyone to get a clear view of her in the red longjohns. "It's my father!" she cried.

Removing his boots and snowmobile suit, Ted Barlow began to joke. "Since you didn't show up for Christmas, the mountain decided to come to Mohammed."

"Oh, Dad!" She threw her arms around him, knowing how worried he must have been, and how he must have struggled for hours to get to her. His wisecracks camouflaged his enormous relief.

Still holding her hands in his, he held her away from him and looked askance at her red suit. "Did you mug Santa?"

"Dad, this is Clint Kelly, who intends to buy the house; Clint, this is Ted Barlow."

The men shook hands, assessing each other in the first thirty seconds. Both liked what they saw. Ted realized Clint had given the shirt off his back to his daughter and he wondered what had happened to her clothes.

"We wouldn't have been snowed in if it hadn't been for my stupidity. We were out on the property Thursday afternoon, just before it got dark, when I walked straight onto the pond and went through the ice."

"Is the pond deep?" Ted asked.

"About fifteen feet. I almost drowned, but Clint saved my life!"

Ted looked from one to the other. "How did you manage to rescue her?"

"With a rope and a ladder. I'm a firefighter; I know rescue techniques."

"Thank God you were with her."

"He didn't just rescue me from the pond. I was unconscious from the cold water. He revived me and spent the rest of the night chopping wood for the fire."

Ted's eyes showed his admiration. They all moved to the fireplace and sat down to recount the rest of what happened.

"Was there stuff here to eat?" Ted inquired.

"No. Clint hunted for food. I've dined like a queen on venison and pheasant—oh, and walleye . . . he fished, too!"

"Walleye? Lord, I haven't had a feed of walleye in a donkey's age. My mouth is watering."

"There's probably some out there on my stringer now. I'll go take a look." Clint knew father and daughter might want a private conversation. He put on his jacket and disappeared through the door.

When they were alone, Eve's father asked, "Are you okay, honey? You weren't afraid of this guy, were you?"

"No, I wasn't afraid of him. At first we rubbed each other the wrong way. He wanted Maxwell to show him the property, hated like hell having a woman agent. I didn't like him any better. He was so damn macho, I called him Action Man. But Dad, when I got into trouble, he really came through for me. I stopped laughing at his muscles when he used them to save us."

Ted observed her closely, wondering what had gone on between them. A man and woman isolated together for days was tempting, intimate, even romantic. He didn't ask; it was none of his business, and he wouldn't be upset if Eve did form a romantic attachment to someone like Clint Kelly.

"I'm sorry I couldn't call you. The telephone service has

been temporarily discontinued. Even the electricity is off. Clint siphoned gas from his truck to run the generator, but we've had to ration it." She asked the question uppermost in her mind. "Did I really upset Mom?"

"She was worried, but she hides it real well. She's had a lot of practice with some of my hare-brained adventures, and Steven's."

"How did you find me?"

"Well, Trevor arrived without you this morning, so we drove back to your place and when your car wasn't there, I went to your office. Then I called Max and told him your Mercedes was still at work. He told me the last time he saw you, you were driving up here to show this guy the property. I phoned Judy to get directions, and here I am!"

"I ruined your Christmas."

"Like hell you did! Instead of sitting around eating my head off and being a couch potato in front of the television set, I had a great snowmobile adventure! And the best part is, it had a happy ending . . . I found you safe and sound."

Eve grinned at her father. "Actually, it was a great adventure for me, too. Don't breathe it to a soul, especially Trevor, but I wouldn't have missed it for the world. I learned so many survival techniques." Eve blushed because of the other techniques she'd learned.

"Trevor didn't come because his mother was ill. But he was reluctant anyway. Some bull about you not appreciating him running after you. Is he afraid of you, Eve?"

She smiled. "Aren't most men afraid of women when it comes right down to it?"

"Most," he acknowledged, "but not all." He winked at her. "Action Man doesn't look like he'd intimidate easily."

Clint returned with five beautiful walleyes. Ted couldn't believe their size.

"It won't take me long to clean them and we can cook them

on the fire," Clint offered. "You probably haven't eaten since breakfast."

"That's too tempting to refuse," Ted admitted.

Eve wondered why everything her father said made her want to blush. "We had pheasant for our Christmas dinner, but I made such a pig of myself, there's none left."

Clint glanced at Ted. "She was entitled; she not only cooked it, she plucked and cleaned it first."

"You must have taken Trevor's course in how to get in touch with your feminine side," Ted wisecracked.

Clint was amused; Eve was not.

Her father relished the fresh-caught fish. Clint sat down with him and devoured a whole one himself. Eve was amazed at Clint's hearty appetite. She wouldn't be able to manage another mouthful of food until tomorrow.

"How close did you get with your car?" Clint asked.

"Less than twenty miles. Only took me about an hour. I stopped at the State Troopers' Headquarters and they checked on all the accident reports for this area and the Department of Highways to see what had been cleared out. The plows won't be on this road until tomorrow. There aren't many residents at the lake this time of year, so it's a matter of priorities."

"The first thing I'd better get is a plow blade for the front of my truck," Clint decided.

"Well, I hate to eat and run, but we'd better get started. It'll take us an hour to get to the van and three hours from Ludington to Grand Rapids."

"I have no clothes! My winter coat is at the bottom of the pond, and my wool suit is shrunk beyond recognition."

"Take my jacket; I'm not going anywhere until tomorrow. I have no gasoline anyway."

"I have an idea. We'll leave your jacket at the troopers' office. I'll even give you enough gas to get there in the morning," Ted offered.

A worried frown creased Clint's brow as he handed Eve his coat. "On a snowmobile your legs will freeze!"

"I'll wrap towels around them and I'll take one of the blankets, too," Eve decided.

Ted donned his snowmobile suit and pulled on his boots. "Don't forget my briefcase."

"Your case will fit in the storage under the seat, after I remove the extra gas tank. I'll just fill up, and you can have what's left, Clint." He held out his hand. "I don't know how to thank you for what you did. Everyone thinks Eve can take care of herself, but her old dad knows better."

Alone, she and Clint faced each other. Eve Barlow's sophistication had gone the way of the Alfred Sung suit. She gave him back his blue shirt in exchange for the down jacket. She looked a fright wrapped in the blanket and towels.

Clint reached for his belt. "Why don't you wear my jeans—"

She held up her hand. "Keep your pants on, Action Man." She tried not to let the sound of tears show in her voice.

"It's a bit late for that, Evie."

She burst into laughter. It kept the tears at bay. She wanted him to hold her. *If only things were different,* she thought. "I'll put in your offer first thing in the morning and be in touch as soon as I have something."

He nodded and watched her go out the door. Once she was a safe distance away, she turned to wave. "It was the best Christmas Eve I ever had," she called impulsively.

She watched him cup his hands around his mouth to call back, but the noise of the snowmobile drowned it out.

"Hang on tight—this is going to be a bumpy ride!"

Eve smiled as she put her arms around her dad. The old Bette Davis line dated him. She suddenly realized he must be close to fifty, yet his vigour belied his age. She pressed her cheek against his back. Not only did it shelter her from the cold wind, it made her realize how safe she felt with this man in control. She tried not to think of Clint Kelly. It was no good longing for what could not be. She had lived the fantasy, but now it was time to leave it behind.

Ted was making much better time on the trip back. The sun had disappeared early, as the afternoon advanced. Because the temperature had dropped, the snow was no longer mushy, and had a fine coat of ice on its surface.

In less than an hour they reached the State Troopers' Headquarters. Eve refused to go inside. "It's Christmas, not Halloween," she protested.

"Okay, I'll turn on the heater in the van. You can give me Clint's jacket and put on my snowmobile suit. It'll be too warm to keep it on while I'm driving. I'll call your mom. Are you sure you won't come in and talk to her? These guys probably haven't had a good laugh all Christmas!"

"Just tell her I love her, and ask her to call Trevor for me." Designer clothes were no longer quite as important to Eve, but she'd be damned if she'd let a bunch of macho officers see her in red longjohns!

When she removed Clint's jacket, she experienced a sense of loss—not just the warmth, but a loss of security. And something else, harder to define: an invisible link that connected them. Eve was brought out of her pensive mood when Ted opened the van door and climbed in. "Your mom was so relieved about both of us. Imagine worrying about me!" But Eve could tell he was delighted with his wife's response.

"I promised her I'd drive slowly and told her not to expect us until after nine. She's going to call Trevor and tell him we'll celebrate our Christmas tomorrow."

On the drive home they sang carols and Eve was amazed that her father knew all the words to the parodies of Christmas songs that were currently popular. They were also extremely irreverent, but men get a kick out of being irreverent in these times of political correctness.

· When they finally turned down their street, Susan had all the Christmas lights blazing. "Poor Mom—she's had such a lonely day."

Ted looked up at the lights as he turned off the engine. "She's always been my beacon."

Eve's memory stirred faintly as she remembered them kissing beneath the mistletoe. It was a shining strand, a thread, ephemeral as a dream. "You're still in love, after all these years."

"Passionately," Ted said, watching his beautiful wife fling open the front door and run down the steps to welcome them home.

The first thing Eve did was telephone Trevor. "Hi! I'm so sorry about all this. I guess my mother explained I was snowed in at a country property I was trying to sell."

"Eve, you know there's no need to apologize to me. These things happen. I understand, just as you would have understood when I couldn't take you dancing the other night."

When Eve realized he hadn't shown up either, she suddenly felt a little less guilty. But only a little!

"I knew there was a logical explanation for your absence, and I knew you would be perfectly all right."

But I wasn't all right, Eve thought. *Aren't you even going to ask me about the man I spent the last three days with?*

"Things usually have a way of working themselves out for the best. My mother needed company over the holiday. It's lonely being a widow. We'll celebrate our Christmas tomorrow."

"That'll be lovely, Trevor. I hope we don't get any more snow. Drive carefully from Kalamazoo. I'll see you around noon."

"Good night Eve. I can't wait until you open your present!"

After she hung up, she stood with her hand on the phone.

Surely he was the most understanding man in the whole world. Apparently she wasn't going to get the third degree. Trevor would never display childish jealousy. He was a mature adult.

Susan made them turkey sandwiches and hot chocolate. Eve nibbled on homemade shortbread and Christmas cake soaked in rum while she told her mother about the incredible things that had happened over the last three days. "Can I stay here tonight?"

"As if you need to ask! It'll be fun to have you sleep over," her mother said, delighted to have her baby under her roof again.

"I need a warm bath, and I really need to wash my hair."

"Didn't you have water to bathe?"

"We had water, but it wasn't warm. We had to take cold showers."

"I'll get you a warm robe and some slippers," Susan said, running upstairs. Eve followed her, but she was too tired to run.

When Susan came downstairs, she put her arms around Ted. "Thanks for going all that way and bringing her home."

"You should have seen this Clint Kelly she spent the last three days with. Muscles, shoulders, a real lady-killer. She calls him Action Man. Well, you heard what she said."

"What?" Susan asked.

"They had to take cold showers!"

"Oh, you!" Susan gave him a punch.

Nine

Eve slipped down in the warm water and sighed with pure pleasure. How good the simple things of life feel when you've been deprived of them!

She tried not to analyze the conversation she'd had with Trevor, or her reaction to his attitude. They had been dating steadily for over a year and she had spent a lot of that time asserting her independence, so that they didn't live in each other's pocket. Now, she felt neglected. What a perverse creature she was!

It would be simply awful if the man she was about to become engaged to flew into a jealous rage and demanded she tell him everything. And the truth was, he had lots to be jealous about! Eve blushed, and slid further down in the warm, scented water.

Though she was tired, her body felt good. A bath was a sensual experience when you relaxed. Her thoughts drifted inexorably toward Clint Kelly. Fancifully, she decided a bathroom was the most private place in a house. You always locked the door so that no one could intrude, then you removed your clothes and were free to indulge in your most intimate thoughts.

Eve leaned her head back, closed her eyes, and allowed herself to re-live every moment she'd spent with Kelly. Every look, every word, every smile, every touch, every kiss, every act . . . every climax!

As the water grew cold, thoughts of Trevor intruded. His last words repeated themselves in her mind: *I can't wait until you open your present!* Resolutely, she pushed those words away and climbed from the tub. She'd feel differently tomorrow. A new chapter of her life would begin. She would close the door on her past and open up another to the future. She knew she should count her blessings.

Sunday dawned dull and overcast. The temperature rose, and by the time the Barlows finished breakfast, all the white snow had turned to gray slush.

Still in robe and slippers, Eve opened her briefcase and took out the Offer to Purchase, then she telephoned Judy.

"Hello, Eve? How dare you get yourself into a scrape without me?"

"You don't know the half of it. I'll fill you in on the details someday when you have a few hours to kill."

"How in the world did you manage up there without food, heat, electricity, or telephone? I suppose getting snowed in put an end to any hope of selling the white elephant?"

"Judy, it's not a white elephant. It's a valuable piece of real estate. I'd buy it myself, if I could afford it."

"Come on, Eve, you're a city girl, like me. Watching trees grow can't be your idea of fun."

Judy was in the marketing department at one of Detroit's largest auto makers, and Eve knew she hadn't visited her late parents' property in about two years.

"Judy, I have an offer for you."

"You're kidding! What the hell did you have to do to get it?"

Eve blushed. "Mr. Kelly is offering a hundred and seventy-five thousand. I'll fax it to you in about an hour." A slight pause on the other end of the phone prompted Eve to be scrupulously honest. "Kelly is a stubborn negotiator, but I really believe he'll go to two hundred thousand if you turn down this offer."

"Turn it down? Eve, bite your tongue. I accept the offer. Fax it to me right away so I can sign it before he changes his mind."

"He won't change his mind, Judy. He genuinely loves the place, and the house and property seem to have accepted him. He's a real outdoorsman; scuba dives and all that."

"He sounds like a hunk."

"He is, but he's also a male chauvinist."

Judy sighed. "In my experience you can't have it both ways. If they're hunks, they're chauvinistic; if they accept you as an equal, they're either wimps or they're gay!"

"Fax me a closing date. I have a check here for you. If it's a done deal and the weather cooperates, I could drive to Detroit Tuesday or Wednesday."

"Why don't I meet you halfway and we could have lunch together?"

"Wonderful idea. There's this terrific restaurant I know in Lansing. Mountain Jacks-Okemos on Grand River Avenue; they specialize in seafood or prime rib. I remember that used to be your favorite."

"Still is, to which my hips will grandly attest!"

"Well, this is great. I can't wait to see you. I'll call and let you know which day."

"Okay. Thanks a million, Eve. I appreciate it."

"Hey, it's my job, for which I am well paid."

Eve went into the kitchen where her mother was already working on their Christmas feast. "Mom, will you lend me a pair of slacks? I have to drive to my place to pick up your Christmas presents and put on something glamorous for Trevor."

Ted took out his keys. "Do you want to take the van, or do you just want me to drive you to your car?"

"If you don't mind going out, I'd rather you took me to

my car. Leaving a Mercedes just sitting there is asking for it to be stolen."

Eve faxed Judy the Offer to Purchase before she changed her clothes. Back in her own bedroom, she found herself before the mirror exactly as she had been the last time she was in this room. "Not exactly," she said to her reflection. She no longer needed to ask if she was beautiful or sexy. She knew she was both. Clint Kelly had convinced her of that.

She went to her closet and moved aside a red dress. After the red suit, followed by the red longjohns, she was ready for a change. She looked at the lavender; her favorite color, both because it enhanced her pale hair and because she thought it lucky. However, it wasn't exactly a Christmas color, so she decided on the avocado green silk with matching suede belt and shoes.

Eve unlocked the top drawer of her desk and took out the envelope that held her Christmas gift to her mother and father. Trevor's gift wouldn't be so easy to carry. She got out her luggage carrier and loaded the carton onto it. It wasn't really all that large, just heavy.

Eve heard her fax machine and was surprised at the speed Judy had returned the signed Offer to Purchase. The closing date she suggested was thirty days, or sooner, if it suited the client. Eve knew Clint Kelly would be thrilled. How she would love to hand him the acceptance and watch the grin spread across his face. But that was out of the question. She mustn't see him again, if it was at all possible. They had made a clean break, and that's the way she had to keep it.

She would send all the papers by courier, then his lawyer could collect the check and the signed documents. She glanced at her watch. Kelly couldn't possibly be back yet. This was a good time to call and leave a message. She dialed the number. Her stomach lurched as she heard his deep voice.

"You've got my machine, so talk at it."

"It's Eve Barlow, calling Sunday the twenty-sixth. Your offer has been accepted with a thirty-day closing date, or sooner, if you can arrange the money. I'll send the documents over by courier. Congratulations!"

When she hung up, her hands were shaking and her mouth had gone dry. What the devil was the matter with her? She was behaving like an adolescent with her first crush. She admonished herself sternly to pull herself together. Today would probably be one of the most significant days of her life. It was a special day for Trevor as well, and she had to be very careful not to spoil it in any way. Trevor was a sensitive man who could pick up on her vibrations, so she had to make sure they were happy ones.

Eve threw on her coat, picked up her briefcase, and pulling the luggage carrier behind her, took the apartment elevator to the ground floor. She was relieved that she arrived back at her parents' house before Trevor got there. Her mother warned her, "Don't go in the family room. Your dad's setting up your Christmas present."

Eve was mystified about what it could be.

"That's a beautiful dress, dear."

"Thank you," Eve said, rubbing her hands over her hips. "I love the way it feels."

The doorbell chimed.

"Oh Lord, he's here," Eve murmured. "Don't tell me it's already noon."

Trevor came in bearing gifts. He gave Susan a huge poinsettia and when Ted slipped in from the family room to greet him, Trevor handed him a bottle of imported sake.

"Thanks! I haven't tasted this stuff in years."

Eve smiled at Trevor. He'd put a lot of thought in the bottle he'd selected for her dad. "How's your mother?" she asked, taking his coat.

"Much better. She'll be just fine."

"Shoo," Susan said. "If everyone stays out of the kitchen, I'll have dinner ready in an hour."

Eve and Trevor moved toward the living room and Ted began to follow them.

"Not you, dear," Susan called after him. "I need your help."

Trevor caught Eve's hand and pulled her beneath the mistletoe. He kissed her gently and, after a brief hesitation, she kissed him back. "You look lovely," he told her. "Would you look at this tree—it must have cost a fortune." He sounded as if he didn't quite approve of spending so much money on something that was simply for decoration. When they sat down on the couch, he asked, "How did you make out up north?"

For a moment, Eve stared at him, not knowing exactly what he was asking. She colored slightly, before the penny dropped into the slot. "Oh, I sold it."

"Good for you," he said, patting her knee with his smooth white hand. "You have to forgive your dad. He's from a generation that doesn't realize a woman can do anything a man can do."

But a woman can't do all the things a man can do, Eve protested, silently. She had been prepared to tell him about the frightening pond episode, but suddenly decided against it. If she admitted to fear and helplessness, it would negate her equality, and she would seem diminished in his eyes. At least she suspected she would. It was all very well to claim equality on an intellectual level, she thought, but the reality was that on a physical level, comparing strength and endurance, a man was superior to a woman, or he should be.

Eve changed the subject so that the conversation focused on Trevor. A few months back he had been passed over at the university for Head of Department. It had been a bitter pill, but with Eve's support, he had gotten over the disappointment.

He told her there were rumors flying all over the campus

that the professor who had been promoted over him was proving unsatisfactory. Everyone in the English Department was grumbling over one thing or another.

Eve gave him all her attention and sympathy, but she couldn't help wondering if this was what the rest of her life would be like—politely listening while Trevor catalogued his grievances. *Stop being a bitch!* she told herself. Trevor had been devastated when he was passed over. He was a sensitive man who craved approval and affirmation, and up until now she had been happy to oblige.

Eve was relieved when dinner was ready and they joined her parents for the festive meal. The table was a work of art. Her mother was an accomplished hostess and a gourmet cook. There was turkey with chestnut dressing and giblet gravy, as well as a whole glazed ham patterned with cherries and cloves. The vegetable dishes were culinary delights. Mushrooms with almonds and shallots sat beside cinnamon yams, tender steamed leeks, and balsamic-glazed pearl onions. Baby brussels sprouts sat on a bed of wild rice, and a whole squash had been stuffed with gingered pork.

Susan's homemade pickles included walnuts, olives, and dills, and she had combined cranberries with orange peel for a sauce that was piquant in taste and aroma. Ted opened both red and white wine so they could have their choice. They drank to Steven's health, toasting him across the world.

When the dinner was over, none of them had room for dessert, so they decided to have it later, after they had opened their gifts. They moved into the family room and Eve saw her Christmas present immediately.

"Oh my gosh!" she exclaimed with genuine surprise. "When I mentioned I needed a treadmill to keep in shape, I never expected you would actually buy me one! Thank you both, so much."

Ted showed her the different speeds and how to preset a program with the multi-window electronics. He also demonstrated it, then Eve tried it out and so did Trevor, who seemed as pleased with the useful gift as she was.

Eve opened her purse and handed her mother the envelope. Susan opened it and cried out with delight. "Oh, honey, you shouldn't have. Ted, it's cruise tickets! We fly to Tampa, then sail ten days in the Caribbean. We visit Martinique, Barbados, Antigua, St. Maarten, St. Thomas, and San Juan. I can't believe it!"

"Well, I'm ready for a second honeymoon; when can we leave?" Ted teased.

Eve was filled with so much warmth, her heart overflowed. Her parents usually went to Florida or Arizona for a month in the wintertime, but they'd never been on a cruise.

Susan made Ted dig out the Atlas so they could see the route the cruise ship would take. Trevor presented each of them with an identically wrapped gift and sat back to watch as they were opened. He hadn't really approved of Eve spending so much money on her parents, but what could he say? She earned the money and was free to spend it any way she chose. He had not protested because he avoided confrontations at all costs.

Susan and Ted unwrapped them at the same time. They were monogrammed passport holders. "Thank you so much, Trevor. I guess you knew about the cruise tickets."

Ted handed Trevor the present Susan had picked out for him, with their daughter's advice. Trevor was delighted with the pair of brass book ends, declaring they were exactly what he needed. When he opened Eve's gift, a great lump came into his throat. It was a leather-bound collection of the complete works of Shakespeare. He'd coveted books like this since he was a boy.

Eve watched Trevor's hand caress the volumes with reverence. She preferred Dickens, but Trevor lusted for Shakespeare, and when she saw how he treasured the books, she was glad she had ordered them all those months ago.

The afternoon light was gone from the sky; it looked as if they were in for another snowstorm. Ted turned on all the lights in keeping with the cheery holiday atmosphere. "Let's have that dessert now, Susie," Ted suggested.

Trevor was just as happy to wait a little while longer before he gave Eve her present. A little suspense was good before a dramatic moment. Rather like a play, he thought fancifully. Trevor winked at Eve and whispered, "They say anticipation is the best part."

Don't you believe it. Clint Kelly's words slipped into her mind with amazing facility. Eve forced her memories away from Kelly to focus on her mother's delicious desserts—rum pecan pie, lemon cheesecake, and traditional mince pie.

As Eve forked the last mouthful of lemon cheesecake, she sighed, "I'm surely going to need that treadmill after today."

Trevor helped himself to another piece of mince pie. "These are even better than my mother's."

Ted could not resist trying everything Susan had baked. "The woman is a temptress."

"Well, the way to your heart is certainly through your stomach. Help me load these in the dishwasher. Trevor would probably like to give Eve her gift in private."

Ted's eyes met Eve's. She wanted to cry, *Don't leave me!* Ted looked mutinous, as if he didn't want to leave his daughter with this man, but he rose reluctantly and carried out the plates.

As Eve watched Trevor take a small wrapped gift from his pocket, his movements seemed to distort into slow motion. Eve experienced a moment of sheer panic. She jumped up quickly and babbled, "I'll be right back. I have to go to the powder room. I don't want to spoil this moment for you."

Eve locked the bathroom door and leaned back against it. She had had to get out of the room; she had felt it closing in on her. She was so tense, her stomach muscles were in knots. *Dear Lord in heaven, what am I going to do?*

The answer came back clearly, *Pull yourself together and get back out there. You cannot spoil this man's precious moment for him.* She did not dare look at herself in the mirror. She turned on the tap and let cold water run over her wrists, then she splashed her flushed cheeks until they felt cooler. She had let this thing go too far to draw back now. She straightened her shoulders. She would not allow a brief infatuation ruin her future plans. She took a deep breath and unlocked the bathroom door.

As Trevor handed her the gift, she gave him a tremulous smile. She removed the silver ribbon and wrapping paper with steady hands, but when they held the velvet jeweler's box, they began to tremble. With an iron resolve she pushed away a feeling of dread. She opened the box and stared down at a pair of diamond earrings!

Ten

Eve looked up at Trevor in disbelief, then her gaze dropped to the small velvet box to make sure her imagination wasn't playing a trick on her.

"You look so stunned, Eve. I thought you guessed I was buying you diamonds."

"Diamonds did cross my mind," she admitted in a faraway voice. A small ripple of relief began inside her that spread through her veins. By the time it reached her brain, it was a tidal wave! Trevor was not giving her an engagement ring. This man was not asking her to marry him!

"Trevor, I don't think I can accept these."

He looked a little sheepish. "They are sort of a bribe, or I suppose a more correct word might be *incentive*. I think it's time we started living together, Eve. If we can do that successfully, then I would have no hesitation about getting married down the road."

"Down the road?" she repeated vaguely.

"Perhaps next Christmas. It's time we started thinking about a permanent commitment."

"Next Christmas?" She felt like a parrot.

"It's economically unwise for us to pay rent on two apartments when we could share one. The only thing is, I've been considering living in Kalamazoo, where I work, and where my mother lives. Of course, I understand this will be a big decision for you, and want to give you plenty of time to think about it."

Eve's eyes made direct contact with Trevor's. She took a deep breath. "You're right. This is a big decision. I don't know if I can accept what you're offering me, Trevor, though it's an honor to be asked." She smiled feebly. *At least you believe you're honoring me, you poor deluded man,* she added silently.

Ted Barlow walked in on them. "Sorry to intrude, but there's a weather advisory on TV. We're in for a severe ice storm. Perhaps you'd better get cracking, unless you're going to stay put for the night."

"Oh, no, I have to get home—I have work to do," Eve said quickly. "I'll leave my car, though; Trevor will drive me." She showed her parents the diamond earrings, which they admired thoroughly. At the same time Ted and Susan exchanged glances and raised their eyebrows. Both of them had expected Trevor to present Eve with an engagement ring. Ted was relieved; Susan only wanted what Eve wanted.

They all said their goodbyes and thanked each other again for the Christmas gifts and Susan's marvelous dinner.

"Mom, I want all your recipes. Do you have one for coconut cream pie?"

"You're going to start cooking?" her father asked with a frown. Perhaps these two were going to move in together after all.

"A New Year's resolution," Eve replied.

On the drive to her apartment, Eve was strangely silent. The rain, which was rapidly turning to ice, was coming down pretty heavily and Trevor had to keep his mind on his driving. She knew when they got to her place, he would take it for granted that he could spend the night. Eve knew she had to speak up before he parked and turned off the engine.

She turned to look at him. "Trevor, I don't want you to

spend the night at my place." It was brutally blunt. She softened it a little. "You've given me a lot to think about and I have some decisions to make. I need to be alone."

Trevor's mouth turned sulky, but after a minute he said, "I understand. Take all the time you need."

"Thank you. Good night, Trevor." The kiss she gave him was a generous one. It was probably the last kiss they would ever share.

"I'll call you tomorrow," he said.

"I'm going to the office, so call me tomorrow night."

Once Eve was safely inside her own apartment, she pushed the dead bolt on the door and let the second wave of relief wash over her. She felt free, like a bird escaped from its cage. Perhaps the cage had been safe and sensible, but it had come to her in a flash that she hated safe and sensible!

She threw off her coat and shoes and danced about the room. She had no plans for the future, but she was very sure of one thing: that future did not include Trevor Bennett. She sat down at her desk and began preparing the papers that Clint Kelly would need to sign, about a dozen in all. There would be more later, on closing. She then prepared a list of costs and adjustments regarding paid-up taxes, settlement and transfer charges, and brokerage fees.

Eve then called the courier service and was surprised when they arrived for the pickup within thirty minutes. She gave the young man a generous tip because it was Boxing Day, because the weather was appalling, and because she felt benevolent toward everyone on earth tonight!

As she climbed into bed, she realized it had been an emotional day—emotionally exhausting, then emotionally exhilarating. Her mind flitted about like a butterfly, momentarily touching one thing, then off to another. But always, it came back to Clint Kelly. Thoughts of him clung to her; he was completely unforgettable.

As she drifted off to sleep, she heard a far-off fire siren and she knew she would never hear that sound for the rest of her life without thinking of him.

The following morning, Eve took a cab to the office. The streets were extremely icy, but the sky looked clear. Only a couple of agents showed up and it was quiet enough that she got caught up on all her paperwork. Eve felt restless, so at lunchtime, she took a cab to her parents' place so she could pick up her car.

Her mother insisted she stay for lunch, and her dad turned off the one o'clock news on television so he could join them in the kitchen. "Fire last night," he informed them.

"I heard the siren. What was it?" Eve asked.

"Industrial warehouse across the city."

"Eve, your dad and I were convinced Trevor was going to give you a ring for Christmas."

Eve shook out a napkin and sat down at the counter. "To be honest, so did I. When I opened that velvet box and saw diamond earrings instead of a diamond ring, I couldn't believe my eyes!"

"Were you terribly disappointed, dear?" her mother asked gently.

"No! It sounds awful, but I was relieved. Trevor isn't right for me, and what's more, I'm not right for him either. I feel wretched that it took me this long to realize it."

"I've always known he wasn't right for you," Ted insisted.

Eve gave her dad a curious look. "You never said anything."

"Your mother wouldn't let me!"

Eve gave him a skeptical look. "Right. As if that would stop you."

"It's true. She insisted I trust you to make the right decision."

"Why, thank you . . . both of you. I had no idea you didn't like Trevor."

"Honey, we have nothing against him. He's a fine man, but we want you to have skyrockets!"

Eve looked from one to the other. "You have skyrockets, don't you? It's funny, but I've only realized that lately."

"Did you end it last night?" her mother probed.

"No. It took me by surprise. I was all psyched up to get engaged and resign myself to being a professor's wife—I couldn't think on my feet when he threw me a curve."

"When will you tell him?" Susan asked.

"Tonight. I'll tell him tonight. The last thing in the world I want to do is hurt him, but a quick, clean break is best for everyone."

Her parents didn't pursue the subject any further. Ted suspected her weekend with Clint Kelly had put an end to Trevor Bennett's hopes. But he knew Eve would confide in them in her own good time.

"If you're going home now, why don't I bring over your treadmill and set it up for you?"

Eve almost told him he was too old to be carrying heavy stuff like that. She bit her tongue. He was only fifty, and he was the best judge of his ability. She had to trust him to make his own decisions, as he had trusted her.

As he was adjusting the digital settings on her treadmill, her father talked about the International Fly-in that Oshkosh, Wisconsin, held every summer. Because of his experience with planes, he'd been invited to be a judge of the "home-built" flying machines entered in the week-long event.

As Eve listened to him, she finally understood why her mother was still in love. He took a vital interest in everything and he kept himself in great shape. Eve had always known that her father was a man's man; now she saw that he was also a woman's man.

"Thanks, Dad. I could never have figured it all out on my own." It was only a slight exaggeration; she couldn't have learned how to set it half so quickly.

When she was alone, she began walking on the new treadmill. She decided it was a wonderful invention. It gave the body a workout, while allowing the mind total freedom. She spent the next couple of hours rehearsing what she would say to Trevor when he called. When the phone rang at exactly five o'clock, she said to herself, *God, he's so regimented!*

The moment Trevor spoke, she could hear the vulnerability in his voice. He was expecting her to reject his offer and she was going to fulfill his expectations. Eve felt like a monster. She knew the kindest thing to do was get straight to the heart of the matter. She would not indulge in a cat and mouse game. It was at this point that she became absolutely convinced she was doing the right thing. When she was cast in the role of cat and he was reduced to a mouse, it was all over.

"Trevor, I've thought about us all day and it isn't going to work. We're wrong for each other. You need someone I'll never be. I take the blame for the failure of our relationship. You've been gentle, kind, and understanding from the beginning and none of this is your fault."

"Eve, please don't be so hasty. Give us another chance. I won't pressure you into living together; I'll forget about marriage."

"It's best to make a clean break, Trevor. I don't want to give you pain, but I think we should end it."

There was a long silence, then in a resigned voice, he said the thing he always said: "I understand."

Eve sat down to write him a kind letter. He understood and appreciated the written word. She used a philosophical tone, implying "What will be, will be." She knew he read Omar Khayyam. She told him she had been enriched by their relationship, and that with all her heart she wished him well. Then Eve wrapped up the diamond earrings and called the courier.

It was the same young man she had generously tipped the night before. He returned the package of papers addressed to Clint Kelly.

"I'm sorry, Ms. Barlow, there was no one home at this address. I tried to deliver it last night and again today."

"Hang on a minute—I'll telephone him." Eve dialed Kelly's number and heard his deep voice, but only on the answering machine. "It's Eve Barlow, six o'clock, Monday the twenty-seventh. Would you give me a call as soon as you can?"

She told the courier, "Leave the package and take this one instead." She gave him another generous tip.

Eve made herself dinner, then hesitated to go down to the laundry room in case she missed Kelly's call. She rinsed out a few things in the bathroom sink. She was in such a reflective mood, feeling guilty over Trevor, justifying ending their relationship. Eve desperately needed an escape from her introspection. She felt like running five miles or climbing a mountain, but the weather was so foul, she couldn't even go for a drive.

She almost turned on the television set, then she happened to remember she had bought a Christina Skye novel just before Christmas and hadn't had a chance to read it. Eve curled up on the couch and began to read *Hour of the Rose*. Skye was a superb writer. From the first haunting sentence, Eve was swept away to another time and place.

It was after midnight when she glanced at her watch. She was torn between reading 'til dawn and putting the book down so she could savor it and make it last longer. She decided on the latter; she just might be spending a lot of her evenings home alone for awhile.

When she got to the office the next day, Eve was inundated with people who were looking for new office space. It seemed as if every lease in Grand Rapids expired in January. She tried phoning Kelly a couple of times, and when she was unsuccessful, called Judy to tell her their lunch would have to be postponed.

"Do you think there might be a problem?" Judy asked.

"No, no," Eve assured her. "Mr. Kelly is a fire chief who works shifts. It's just taking a while to get together with his lawyer. It will probably be after New Year's before I have everything for you."

"That would be better for me too, Eve. By the way, I had the phone taken off holiday service and also had the power put back on. I don't want anyone else getting into difficulties up there."

"That was a good idea. I'll put the costs in the adjustments," Eve assured her.

She worked late at the office, then on impulse on the way home, took a detour to Clint Kelly's apartment. There was no answer to her knock. She pulled out a business card, wrote on it, "Call me!" and shoved it under his door.

She waited for his call all evening. When it didn't come, she convinced herself that he had taken such offense over her rejection that he was deliberately avoiding her. *To bloody hell-fire with all men!* Eve picked up *Hour of the Rose* and took it to bed with her.

When dawn arrived, Eve found herself lying awake, reflecting on all that had happened over the holidays. She recalled reading somewhere that more romantic relationships ended at this time of the year than any other. It was like the adage said— if it wasn't rock solid, it wouldn't survive Christmas!

Men seemed to fall into two categories. They were either mothers' boys or macho chauvinists. Where were all the men in between? Where were the men who could be strong and take control when it was necessary, yet show ineffable tenderness or be moved to tears at life's poignant, touching moments?

Eve laughed at herself and threw back the covers. The ideal man was a myth. And if there was such a paragon, he was seeking the ideal woman!

When she opened her closet, she knew she needed to choose something that would lift her spirits. She decided to wear her lucky color. Eve pulled on a pair of lavender slacks and a lambswool sweater to match. They were the antithesis of a power suit, making her look soft and feminine. She even put on her amethyst earrings that were strictly evening wear, deciding she would never be regimented again.

Eve's car seemed to have a mind of its own this morning, heading in the direction of Kelly's apartment building rather than her office. Upstairs, she knocked politely on his door and waited. Perhaps he was sleeping. If he'd worked all night, he could be dead to the world by now. Eve lifted her fists and pounded. Absolute silence met her ears. She should have saved herself the trouble by phoning!

Eve was annoyed. This was no way to conduct business. She was his broker, representing his purchase of a house. He should at least have the common courtesy to touch base with her. She drove to the office, fuming all the way. When Maxwell arrived, she followed him into his office.

"Did you have a scuba lesson last night?"

"No. There was no lesson scheduled for the week between Christmas and New Year's. We pick up again after the holidays. Thinking of joining the class?" he asked casually.

"No," she said sweetly, "I'm thinking of drowning someone."

By noon, her patience snapped. She decided to track Action Man down. Eve was hungry and knew exactly where she was going to eat lunch.

Kelly's Sports Bar and Grill was crowded. She searched the room looking for a six-footer with black hair and dark blue eyes. She ordered a corned beef sandwich and a draft beer. The dill pickle was so good it made her tastebuds stand at attention. It must have been pickled in a barrel.

At one o'clock the crowd thinned out dramatically, and Eve carried her empty mug to the bar. The resemblance was so marked she had no difficulty realizing this was Kelly's father. The retired policeman was heavier, of course, and his handsome face lay in ruins, but he was hard-edged and cocksure; still master of his domain.

"Hello, Mr. Kelly. I'm Eve Barlow and I'm looking for your son, Clint."

"Call me Clancy," he said, giving her an appreciative look that swept from breasts to thighs.

Clancy? I don't believe it. He's more Irish than Paddy's Pig!

"You're not a reporter, are you?" he demanded.

"No. I'm his real estate agent."

Clancy whistled with disbelief. "Well, I'll be damned. He sure knows how to pick 'em!"

"Mr. Kelly—"

"Clancy."

"Clancy. Do you know where I can find your son?"

"Nope."

"You have no idea where he might be reached?"

"Nope."

"It's imperative I get in touch with him. Doesn't he come here to the bar?"

Clancy rubbed his nose thoughtfully, then seemed to come to a decision. He reached beneath the bar and pulled out a newspaper. It was two days old.

Eve's eyes ran down the page, then stared hard at the picture. It portrayed a firefighter carrying a child in his arms. His helmet was decorated by a row of icicles. His face was grim, his eyes stark. Quickly she read the headline, then the article.

Two boys had been playing with matches on the third floor of a furniture warehouse. The ten-year-old had been rescued and taken to a hospital. The nine-year-old had not survived.

"Fire Chief Kelly said the floor collapsed before he could reach the second boy. He performed cardio-pulmonary resuscitation for over an hour, but it was hopeless. Kelly's crew fought the fire for twelve hours in below-zero temperatures."

Eve looked up from the newspaper to find Clancy's eyes on her.

"When something like this happens, we don't see him for a few days. He likes to be alone."

Eve nodded. She looked at the eyes in the picture again, and felt his pain. She handed back the paper. "Thank you," she whispered.

Eve Barlow threw jeans, sweaters, and underclothes into an overnight bag, then grabbed makeup and shampoo. Her instincts had taken over and she had a gut feeling about where she would find Clint Kelly.

On the drive north to the property she made one stop at a store to purchase a present and put it in the trunk with her overnight bag. Eve drove carefully, but as fast as road conditions allowed.

She could not get the picture of Kelly holding the dead child out of her mind. Why in the name of heaven had she thought Clint incapable of tears? His job did not merely deal with danger, it encompassed anguish, fear, and tragedy. It involved the loss of life, as well as property. On a daily basis Clint Kelly was expected to perform heroically, and to deal with death when heroics weren't enough. No wonder he had taken over so completely when her life was in danger. He had been trained to cope with emergencies and disasters. Treating hypothermia was probably second nature to him; he and his team must have experienced it firsthand fighting fires, soaked to the skin, in below-zero temperatures.

Clint was a born leader; a take-charge kind of man who made instant decisions and issued orders, expecting them to be obeyed. The time she spent with him had taught her so much about him, certainly enough to make her fall head-over-heels in love! But she now realized she had barely scratched the surface. There were still volumes to learn, depths to plumb.

Clint saw her Mercedes as it pulled into the long drive. He started running. He reached the car in time to open the door for her.

She watched him run toward her. He was carrying something black in his hand. She smiled when she saw it was a camera.

"Eve!"

"Hello, Clint. I've been trying to get hold of you for days. I didn't know about the fire until I went to your dad's bar."

"He didn't know where I was."

"No, but I did," she said quietly, getting out of the car and standing close, looking up at him. *Thank God the pain has left his eyes. This place is good for him!* She would be good for him, too. She'd start by making him laugh. "Remember that engagement ring I was getting for Christmas? It turned out to be diamond earrings."

He didn't laugh; his eyes burned into hers. "Marry me, Eve!"

It wasn't a question, it was more like a command. His arms went around her. "Evie, if that's what it takes to win you, I'll even quote poetry."

She laughed into his eyes and called his bluff. "Let's hear you."

Clint's dark brows drew together for a minute. Then he said:

> "I'm only a man,
> We'll get along fine,
> Just so long as you remember
> I'm not yours; YOU'RE MINE!"

Eve melted into his arms and lifted her lips for his kiss, knowing that was an effective way to stop his dreadful doggerel.

"I take it your answer is yes?"

"Clint Kelly, it's no such thing! You're going way too fast for me."

"When I see what I want, I walk a direct path to it."

"We have nothing in common. You would turn my life upside down."

"We can work things out. Come inside and we'll negotiate. If we talk, we can find common ground."

"We have so little in common, it would be a disaster."

"You think I can't handle disaster?" He raised one black eyebrow.

"I know you can," she said softly. She knew if he began to touch her, her objections would dissolve along with her bones.

In front of a blazing fire, with Clint Kelly sitting across from her, Eve's resistance began to thaw. He was such a persuasive man—she knew she had to negotiate while she still had her wits about her.

"I want a fifty-fifty partnership. I don't want a marriage where the man is the boss and the woman is the little housewife."

Clint grabbed a piece of paper and began making a contract. "Agreed; fifty-fifty," he promised.

"I intend to work, whether you like it or not. I won't stay home baking coconut cream pies."

"Agreed," he said, scribbling furiously. She was independent, assertive, competitive, and combative, but every once in a while he knew she would lean on him.

"And I don't want to have to break your arms every time I want to drive."

His face was sober, but his eyes danced with amusement. "You missed your calling. You should have been a comedian."

"This isn't meant to be funny—I'm serious! These are definitely not jokes."

"Then why am I laughing?"

"Because you're a sexist swine, of course."

"Evie, I'm so much in love with you, I'll agree to anything."

Eve stopped talking and looked at him. This man was everything she'd ever wanted. It was time to face the truth. She tore the paper into small pieces and threw it into the air. It came down like confetti. "Clint, I wouldn't want you any other way!"

He threw back his head and yowled like a wolf. It was a cry of victory. "Now that we've got business out of the way, can we indulge in a little pleasure?"

She took his hand. "Come with me. I have a present for you." Eve unlocked the trunk and handed him her overnight bag. Then she gave him his present. When Clint opened the brown bag and saw the bottle of whisky, a wicked grin spread across his face.

"I'll let you be the judge of that, Action Man. You're going to have to reel out more hose, or get closer to the fire. Just don't rub me the wrong way!"

"After experiencing Christmas Eve," he said, making a word-play of her name, "I can't wait for New Year's Eve!"

More by Best-selling Author
Fern Michaels

Complete Your Collection Today
Janelle Taylor